Cathy

Hope it's
worth it

Percy

P J Myers was educated at a large Secondary School in West Wales. Having been married for some 40 years, she has a large family, including many grandchildren. The author has travelled extensively.

In the past Peter has been a town councillor and a member of the county darts squad. She has successfully been involved in a number of business enterprises such as a taxi proprietor, running a shop and door to door salesperson.

Petra has been writing for over 30 years, mainly as a self-indulged hobby and providing a number of local newspapers with reports on sporting and entertainment events. This culminated in the writing of Lisa, the first of a three-part trilogy.

LISA

Petra Jamie Myers

L i s a

Chimera

CHIMERA PAPERBACK

© Copyright 2002
Petra Jamie Myers

The right of Petra Jamie Myers to be identified as author of this work has been asserted by him in accordance with the Copyright, Designs and Patents Act 1988

All Rights Reserved

No reproduction, copy or transmission of this publication may be made without written permission.
No paragraph of this publication may be reproduced, copied or transmitted save with the written permission or in accordance with the provisions of the Copyright Act 1956 (as amended).

Any person who does any unauthorised act in relation to this publication may be liable to criminal prosecution and civil claims for damage.

A CIP catalogue record for this title is available from the British Library
ISBN 1 903136 20 2

*Chimera is an imprint of
Pegasus Elliot MacKenzie Publishers Ltd.*
www.pegasuspublishers.com

First Published in 2002

**Chimera
Sheraton House Castle Park
Cambridge England**

Printed & Bound in Great Britain

Chapter 1

On a wet Monday morning, Lisa Knott sat at her kitchen table; coffee cup cradled in both hands, feeling unsatisfied after a weekend which had ended just a few hours ago. Alone, her latest lover, Dean, leaving in the early hours of the morning, looking at his now empty chair, the dirty dishes, his crushed cigarette stub in the ash tray.

Gazing at the rain lashed kitchen window, Thinking, it was in for the day, another miserable lonely day, full of boredom. Why she should feel so despondent after a weekend, full of lust and pleasure, her spirits should be joyous and contented, yet she felt so hollow and empty.

Dean was and had been, for sometime her favourite from all the men she become acquainted with after her divorce almost four years ago. He was tall, handsome, wealthy, somewhat happy-go-lucky in nature, considerate, well mannered, treated her with the utmost respect, took her to the best restaurants, where everybody seemed to know him, nothing but the best for Dean.

He was fine in bed, but only fine. What the hell did fine mean, was he inadequate?

Was his lovemaking insufficient to satisfy her sexual needs? That seemed unlikely she'd been sharing her bed and body with him for some time.

Lisa, thinking back to the first year of the divorce, and the inferences of fine in bed. The early years when she'd felt so bitter and unhappy at living alone. A painful period, with the feeling she was a has been, a failure as a wife, a lover, and above all, a woman, but then slowly the feeling faded, she learned to live again, now she enjoyed the freedom of being single again.

She'd been blessed with good looks and as she'd grown

older they'd stayed with her, through lots of jogging and regular work out's at the Fitness Suite. Her long shapely legs and well developed body had retained the physical and sexual appearance that men so much admired, she looked younger than her forty years, men still gave her admiring looks of lustful desire.

Lisa had decided once her bad patch was over, no divorce was going to finish her life as a woman, and she wasn't going to allow her changed circumstances to stop her having a the feel of a man inside her when ever she desired one.

Lisa for almost two years after the divorce had lived a sad lonely life of celibacy. David's betrayal destroying her sexuality, Lisa lost all trust of men. That had changed the night she'd been persuaded to go out for dinner by an old friend from her college days, for the first time for so long she dressed carefully, she was single now, a free woman.

The evening her courage fortified by least half a dozen large vodkas before leaving, she'd let herself be seduced by a middle aged good looking businessman, seduced not by his charm, but by her own stupidity of becoming hopelessly drunk. Truth was she'd was naked on a bed, head spinning feeling nauseous a man with swollen penis kneeling between her legs before her drink sodden brain registered she was going to be fucked.

Much to her surprise, the sight of his hard stiff cock instead of feeling revulsion rather pleased her, as it slipped inside, her body welcomed the intruder. Lisa remembered little after that, the man driving his flesh deep inside, she'd lain unmoving, lifeless, her orgasm nothing more than a sharp groan, one quick release then it was over. Lisa left the snoring, sleeping man, dressed and came home.

Restless, the memory of that night pushed out of her mind. Lisa left the table, wandered through the house, ridding herself of depressing thoughts, reaching the bedroom looking at the dishevelled bed before standing in front of the large full length mirror.

So, she was over forty, slowly removing the Terry towel dressing gown. Her skin was smooth and fresh looking, the stomach flat no sign of sagging. The breasts firm, standing out with large dark nipples. The body, shapely, gently curved, appearing as to belonged to a much younger woman. Thank God she'd persevered with her fitness regime every day, it had made her thighs, legs, hips and shapely rounded ass look tight, firm, strong, vibrant, willing and ripe.

Heads turned to look when she walked down the street. Men smiled in her direction, in their eyes the lecherous shine of want Lisa loved that look.

After the night she'd tasted a mans flesh for the first time since the divorce, Lisa changed, there came a realisation, she had a life style that was comfortable, a certain amount of wealth, and above all a gorgeous body with looks to match. It was as if that one swollen cock inside her opened her mind to what life and pleasure could become.

She had embraced the feeling that came with it, so much so. Now her life had richness that she'd never thought possible.

Lisa liked her life, as a person, as a woman. Above all to be able to satisfy her sexual needs and desires with who ever she choose, and as often as possible. Men always desired her. It was a freedom in mind and body, men and their strong hot cocks revitalised her over and over again.

Lisa suffered no pangs of conscience after having her pleasure's satisfied.

Her husband David had satisfied her for many years. Until suddenly four years ago her world collapsed. The thought crushed her, turning to the rumpled bedclothes she removed the white semen stained sheets, lying on the bare mattress her eyes closed. She'd put on a pair of black satin sheets, she decided. The soft smooth touch of the satin on her naked body so stimulating when she slept alone.

Her thoughts returned to the kitchen table, why did she feel emptiness from what should have been a satisfying weekend?

Lying there trying to bring her mind and body to salvage something of value. To relive the sensations of Dean's hot penis in her vagina, her mouth on his, her nipples hard against the hairy chest, as he'd come within her.

He'd arrived early Friday afternoon, black overnight bag in his hand, she'd greeted him a kiss, took the bag to the bedroom while he fixed the drinks. Dean's a martini, hers a vodka straight with ice, just the way she liked it.

Taking a long swig, he grinned in obligingly.

"If only my ex-wife had shown me such a welcome, maybe I'd never have divorced her."

Lisa chuckled.

"Then think what I could have missed!"

Putting aside his drink, wrapping his arms around her waist, bent her backwards, her mind charged with lust, their hips grinding together,

"What a lovely woman," he said, in a voice filled with sexual longing. With gripping fingers, Lisa felt the soft flesh on his shoulders. He carried more weight than necessary, not only on the his shoulders, but on his thick chest and soft belly, no amount of playing squash, which he regular played could hide the fact he was becoming fat. Overweight or not, he was a man. She reminded herself, feeling her body responding, not so much to the man, more to her own anticipation of his flesh within her.

The need and desire plain in her husky breathless words as she spoke.

"Come on, lover. Dinner can wait." Taking his hand, leading him to the bedroom, Dean carrying the martini, Lisa, her thighs becoming ever more moist, her clothes uneasy against her skin, all she wanted was to be naked, and Dean naked beside her.

Every time, so beautiful to feel, warm flesh on warm flesh, to experience such wanton desire, a naked man, a hot, hard willing man, wanting and lusting to fulfil her want. It made being divorced a pleasure in it's self.

Lisa had never in all her married years, wanted or needed other men.

David had satisfied her need for sex, she'd been content, she thought with that.

Until the divorce, after that one drunken fuck, she'd become aware of pleasure and sexual possibilities that opened before her, being single again

First into the bedroom, naked in an instant, Lisa lay on the bed, legs apart, watching Dean undress, first the shirt, followed shoes, socks and trousers.

Standing legs apart, still wearing his black briefs, Lisa

always enjoyed a man in briefs, not like David and others who always wore boxer shorts, in briefs she could see the a mans state of erection, and its dimensions, that increased her desire.

Twirling the now empty glass with his fingers.

"I wonder if there's a refill available tonight?" he asked, suggestively.

Submissively she rose, as asked, glass in hand going to the kitchen, returning not only with Dean's martini, a stiff vodka for herself in the other, Dean sitting on the bed, two pillows propping his head up, still wearing his black briefs, sitting beside him Lisa handed him the martini

Lisa sipped her drink. She liked a few drinks before sex, it inflated her urges just enough to make her desire more demanding, Dean drank until he was ready to begin.

She knew all about Dean. Three times divorced, being faithful to one woman wasn't in his nature. He'd marry again, perhaps wishing to keep their affair going, he'd wouldn't be marrying her, Lisa had no intention to wed ever again, her single status and the new found sexual freedom to precious and exciting to give away for just one man.

Lisa was ready now. Dean concentrating on his drink, displaying a lack of interest in her nakedness, finishing her vodka and ice, with a slow deliberate slyness, she gently slid one hand up over his thigh onto the bulge showing through the briefs to stroke it lightly. Shrinking from the touch, he growled, in mock surprise, "Hell, woman, it takes more than a few fingers to get me started." She laughed quietly; he always said something like that when she began to arouse him. Lisa ran her fingers up to the elastic waist-band, hooked the fingers inside, pulled it down holding it, while stroking his shaft several time with her other hand, before slipping it down around his warm testicles, then closing the hand around the shaft of his cock, not hard yet.

She knew the cure for that, a cure she'd learned to enjoy *immensely*.

Letting go of the partially harden flesh. With a sensual slowness, sliding the briefs down over the hips. Dean raised his hips so she could slip them off. She gazed at his limp instrument lying on his thigh, as always her nakedness, the obvious willingness, failed to arouse him.

Licking her lips, Lisa bent her head over his thighs, hovering there, touched the head of his tool once, gently, with the tip of her tongue before opening her lips, immersing the soft flesh into her warm mouth. She relished the taste of male flesh mixed with vodka, choked for a second at the thought she was about to mix a cocktail.

Dean was unmoved, his hips not pushing against her mouth all he did was to groan in luxurious pleasure, but he never moved, he always started slowly.

She took more warm flesh deeper into her mouth, squeezing her lips tight pushing them down to the root of his flaccid tool, then slowly sliding them up and down over and over again. Lisa becoming wet again as she felt the bulbous head, ever so slowly beginning to swell in her mouth.

Looking up Dean sat head propped against the headboard, martini at his lips. As she watched, he placed his free hand on the back of her head.

"You can keep doing that as long as you like," he said, shifting his body slightly pushing her mouth down on him

Lisa, filled with frustration at her inability to make this very reluctant shaft of flesh stiffen, worked her mouth ever faster up and down, down then up.

Dean's cock responded, slowly at first, then with verve, as her ever-moving lips and soft mouth bruised itself on his ever-lengthening flesh.

Holding her own lust in check, her thighs stiff, refusing to allow them to writhe and twist in her anticipation, she had to give him time, to wait for him, deep down she wanted his cock now, not once but again and again.

Lisa lifted her mind away. To the day when for the first time she had taken an erect male member in her mouth. It was after she been divorced, a first she'd felt a sense of guilt, she never given her husband the pleasure of her mouth, he'd never hinted he desired such pleasures, she had therefore assumed he didn't require it. Now she understood only to well every man wanted there manhood caressed by the lips and mouth of a woman. Lisa wondered if David's new love was giving him what she had never. Perhaps that's why she'd lost him to her. Her mouth working feverishly, Lisa recalled her first taste of a man.

It had been her second lover after the drunken fuck. It was the time of her release from the shackles of the darkness of divorce, the time she'd left her prison of loneliness that had pervaded her spirit for so long, crushing her will and mind, the drunk man had unknowingly, with his swollen flesh. Had lit an ember that opened mind and body, to the delicious pleasure and it sent her into a world sexual pleasure she had never experienced before. Now she was free, sex and men fulfilled her desire, her mind, and flesh so utterly, she could never have enough of either.

The man had ordered her, said, in threatening vicious, ugly words.

"Suck me off!" When she refused to do that sort of thing, he'd rammed her head against the wall, grasped her by the shoulders with hard rough hands forcing her down on to her knees.

Teeth clamped tight, she stared at the rampant throbbing thrusting in the direction of her mouth. Enraged at her refusal to admit his flesh into her mouth, he'd picked her up by the throat, threw her naked onto the motel room bed. Straddling her, his legs each side of her head, slapping viciously across the face several times before snarling in a wild voice.

"Go on take it your mouth. Or I'll beat the living shit out you, and make you do it." She yielded helplessly. His swollen engorged shaft choking her, her lips stretched wide he raped her mouth in wild abandon. When he came her stomach churned at the taste. Then his hands stroked her pussy, without pausing, his fingers rubbed her most sensitive spot, her clitoris pulsing in heated stabs, digging hard out of lust, savage in his power over her she shrieked as he slid two stiff fingers inside her. Lisa began to come, twisting hard, driving her thighs upward into his fingers; helpless in the grip of a wild demand for release of her impending climax he propelled her body and mind to the highest plain of orgasm.

Sordid and nasty as it was, not the method to use to learn how to make older men's instruments of pleasure grow hard, Lisa took a man in her mouth at the first opportunity. He never asked her, she just wanted his cock to fill her, he'd seemed reluctant to perform. She'd change his mind very quickly.

As her progress in the art of oral sex developed, her lovemaking reached a longer more satisfying conclusion, Lisa believed it was for her pleasure, not his. Which it was.

For some unknown reason, as she teased a mans organ to full erection, her mind thought of other matters, like now, her mind preoccupied with her first encounter with the hot flesh of a man in her mouth.

Lisa's soft supple lips bore fruits; Dean's tool stiff and erect, vibrant with lustful strength. Lisa rolled on her back; she was in charge now, steering his thighs inside hers. Dean waited. Damn him, annoyingly she thought, he knew by waiting she'd give him more than he'd ever take from her.

Swimming in a sea of desire and need, Lisa took his flesh in her hands guiding it home. She sighed as the smooth delicious throbbing acceptable shaft made its entrance, lying still, savouring a moment of sheer bliss, receiving its full length a pleasure of exquisite fulfilment.

A moment later it was gone, her mouth's subtle caresses had primed Dean's device of flesh a little to much, sensing his ejaculation was ready to explode, she twisted and writhed against him, instantly in a frantic effort to reach hers ahead of him. She wanted to feel her juices mingling with his, in one wild lust sodden release. So adroit, knowing precisely what was needed to bring her to orgasm. Deliberately she fixed her mind and body on the flesh and sensations, the place the pulsating throbbing bulbous head touched then it slipped away, returning harder, faster and faster. The throbbing organ bucked spewing semen. Sobbing, crazed, almost berserk, she was too slow. Damn the son of a bitch, he was going to leave her screaming with unfulfilled desires.

Why, oh why did middle-aged men enjoy a woman's mouth on their flesh, then last a few short minutes in her flesh? If it continued like this much more, she'd need two of them at a time. The possibility of that, she thought, could be more than interesting.

Dean's passion subsiding, Lisa's need for pleasure incomplete, still, felt a tenderness for a man who filled her receptive flesh, pumping his semen into her body.

Lisa jumped at the sound of the doorbell ringing, her mind so alive with unsatisfied desire, the flesh tinkling with want, the ringing bell, an interruption of her thoughts of the weekend past. Now over and ended for another week, a long time to wait before she could feel a man's hard ridged cock shafting her flesh.

Jumping out of the bed, looking quickly at her face in the mirror, she looked as if she'd had a sleepless night. She had, but, for all the wrong reasons, she thought, grabbing her robe, tying it roughly as she headed to answer the door.

Who could be calling on a morning in such heavy rain? Unlocking the door, opening it no more than a crack. A young man, standing, his head on his chest, wearing a pair of faded jeans and a white tee shirt, looking like a drown rat.

She paused, tidied her robe, adjusting the belt, pushing her hair back. She removed the safety chain, opening the door.

"Yes, young man," she inquired. He'd retreated down the steps, standing his back to the door staring at the pouring rain. He turned around, looking relieved.

"Is Tracy here?" he asked, politely.

"Tracy who?" she responded, he looked confused. "You've called at the wrong house, young man, there's no Tracy living here, in fact there is nobody in house but me."

His disappointment plainly showed on his face.

"Oh! I'm sorry lady I must have got the address wrong," he apologised in a sad defeated voice. Lisa studied his face. It seemed strangely familiar, a round handsome looking youth, a strong jaw, tall, with blue eyes. The falling rain failing to flatten his blonde curly hair.

"Don't I know you, young man?" she asked, in a doubtful tone.

"Yes, ma'am, I'm Jay, remember I use to wash your 'car' in the school holidays, before we moved away, I'm looking for Tracy Rogers actually, we use to spend a lot of time together in high school," he explained in a shivering voice.

"I don't know of any Tracy living around here, Jay, but then

I don't really know many youngsters of your age anyway, you'll probably get more information if you asked down town," Lisa helpfully replied. He was so bedraggled and sopping wet, shivering with cold she felt sorry for him.

"Why don't you come in out of the pouring rain for a while, Jay," she hospitably invited him. "I was just about to have some coffee, a cup would warm you nicely, Jay after being out in the pouring rain."

He seemed reluctant to accept her invitation, shyly replying, "I don't really think I should."

"Don't be silly, Jay, you shouldn't be wading about all over the place, in the pouring rain with no coat, you'll catch your death of cold, come in until it eases, whenever that may be," she urged him, with a smile.

"Well I suppose under the circumstances a cup of hot coffee would go down nicely on a morning like this," he grudgingly agreed, turning to look at the deluge pouring down.

Lisa stood to one side, locking the door behind him, where he'd stood a small puddle of rainwater. Lisa led the way quickly to the kitchen, motioned to him to sit down, telling him to help himself to coffee. She stood looking down at his curly wet blonde hair, his two hands wrapped around the cup, warming his fingers he sipped the hot coffee slowly, a strong looking head, matched the jaw, she noticed. His wet locks dripping water on the table annoyed her. With out a word she fetched a warm towel from the airing closet, standing behind him, dropped it over his head, rubbing the wet hair in a gentle paternal fashion. He pushed her hand away.

"I can do that for myself. Thank you," he snarled, glowering with indignation.

"Fine, Jay, no need to get upset, just being motherly. After you've finished your hair perhaps you'd like a shower to warm you up. If you put your wet clothes outside the bathroom door, I'll pop them in the drier for a few minutes. It's up to you," she spoke in an abrupt manner, upset by his sudden angry outburst. Smiling he apologised.

"Thank you, ma'am, I feel so cold my patience is a little tight at the moment." Sitting down opposite, sipping her coffee, she ran her eyes over him. She sensed an air of confidence about him, scrutinising the wet youth. He had an air of natural well being about him, he'd been and done things in his short life that had shaped his attitude. Lisa could see in his eyes a look of a man not a youth, a brown face which didn't match his blonde hair.

A vitality, a strength, a presence of energy, so lacking in Dean and the men she'd been having in the past. This young man wouldn't need a mouth to prompt his manhood to stand ridged. Lisa sat cup in hand, the boy Jay blissfully unaware of the sensuous thoughts. The silence unnoticed, for a brief second she envisaged him naked, all his youthful naked flesh. The growing sexual awareness within him was lusting for experience.

Lisa felt wetness between her thighs, The idea of being invaded over and over again. So different from what she had grown use to inflamed her.

The realisation of Dean's lovemaking, in this frame of mind, was to her most unsatisfying to say the least. She wanted to be fucked, as if she was still teenager, not as an older woman past her prime. 'Dammit,' Lisa thought, 'I've never been shafted enough to even know how deep my sexual needs and desires went'. Her past lovers where middle-aged men, successful and comfortable in their life-styles. She wanted. No! Not wanted. Needed! to discover her limits of pleasure.

Jay finishing his coffee, looked at her smiling, asked,

"How's Mr Knott?" Surprised by the question, interrupting her reflections, she answered, abruptly,

"No idea, we divorced four years ago, he left me for some girl young enough to be his daughter." Lisa saw his facial expression change from gratitude, to expectancy, his eyes gleaming.

"You live alone then, Mrs Knott, that can't be very nice, no man about the place when you need one," the words dripping in innuendo. She'd seen that look many times in the last few years, Oh yes, a divorcee, past forty, no man. To all men another fading woman, an easy laid, fuck her she'd be grateful, then forget her. She was no easy hump for no man, she liked men, but on her terms, never theirs.

"You've a very brown face, Jay, have you been overseas or something, in the navy maybe?" she replied, in a matter of fact tone, changing the subject.

"No, Mrs Knott, I never joined the Navy, I went to Spain when I was about seventeen, got a job in a bar and stayed there for the last two years or so. I only came home to see my dad, he'd had an accident at work, broke both his legs and fractured his skull, just though I look up some old friends while I was here. Waste of time really, they've all seemed to have moved elsewhere."

The smile never left his lips, his hand reached across the table, the fingers gently stroking the back of hers. Lisa, aware of the suggestiveness in the touch, her mental assessment of Jay had been correct. No trembling virgin youth this one. He was making it quite obvious what he wanted *her*. The age difference seemed irrelevant to him. Lisa had a cunt to fill. He was happy to fill it.

He sat, looking at her, his fingers caressing the back of her hand, the heat in the young fingers electric. Lisa sat, her hand under his. Deep down inside her, a feeling of warmth, new to her, making her thighs twitch, the lips of her vagina, for a small minute second seemed to kiss.

Naked under the robe, her nipples hardening, Jay must have noticed, or at least sensed her reaction. She was beginning to respond. Was his masculine young body and flesh also responding? Lisa wanted him to stop, suddenly, unconsciously, a picture of him naked, his smooth skin, the solid muscles, no sagging belly, his cock upright, erect, No sucking or teasing needed of the boy's hot shaft of flesh before it was able to function.

Lisa was disgusted, shocked, by the very idea. Nevertheless her body wasn't, the flesh around her pussy, hot, wet, sticky. Hand trembling she pulled it from under his, clasping her hands together, in her lap beneath the table, he must have understood he'd excited her.

Not looking at him she poured herself more coffee, Afraid he'd understand the hunger that was slowly building deep within in her stomach, afraid that hunger would be transparent in her eyes.

"Do you still want that shower, Jay?" she asked, blurting out the words, as if in self-defence, to cover the turmoil of her sex charged emotions.

"Might as well, as it's on offer, Mrs Knott, you never know, perhaps the rain will ease before we've finished this nice conversation, don't you think?" He wasn't giving up. Lisa surprised by the word we. She, for some reason for her part, didn't want him to prolong his stay.

"Second door on the left, down the hall, put your wet clothes outside the door. I'll collect them and they'll be dry and waiting for you when you've finished," she told him, making it sound more an order than a request. Still looking into her cup, he rose off the chair. Lisa lifting her eyes a fraction, as Jay straightened up, saw first the belt on his jeans, hands on the table, came upright, stood in front of her, He'd a hard on, the crotch of his jeans bulging, straining against the zip. Unashamedly exhibiting to her what was on offer.

Her breath strangled, as if a knife driving into her warm flesh, the hunger and lust joined as one. The opening was there to be fucked, and to fuck. Having this young man make love to her would be so different from all the men in the past. An experience to savour for many years into the future. Feeling the erect hard flesh being driven, with an energy and brute strength, with the passion only possessed by youth, unleashed it would savaged her very being.

The strangled breath escaped in a loud sigh, her lungs unable to contain the imprisoned breath any longer. His reaction was a knowing chuckle, the sigh had revealed too much of her lust.

"I'll take my shower now," the confidence in his voice. He'd made her want, not him, his youth and all that went with having a young virile weapon extracting from her body every orgasm her flesh could expunge Lisa fighting to keep control of herself, told herself, he's so young, her heart pounded with desire. So sure she'd fallen for his naked blatant offering, convinced in his mind he could love her till she could take no more. She heard his footsteps as he left the kitchen table. Forget his youth, Lisa, her body screamed, *Why is youth so different from last night. If you close your eyes it's just another man with a tool, and you want a tool, how many of them in the past have you excepted, and extracted your pleasures from, but this one will be extracting his pleasure from you.*

Jay had left the kitchen, leaving the door open; Lisa looked up, watching him walk, a bounce in his stride, down the hall, disappearing into the bathroom.

Closing her eyes, her hands together, fingertips under her chin as if in prayer. She felt so wet and hot, imagining Jay's body naked, his shaft slipping in and out of her vagina, her hands on his bum cheeks. Pulling him down, on to her naked flesh. She wanted the boy so badly.

If that was to happened, it would be on her terms, not his. And this was his terms not hers. She'd slept with nor sucked any man in the last two years so just to suit their demands. She didn't intend to start now.

This was all Dean's fault, if he'd screwed for her pleasure, not for just his own selfish desires, the randy young cub in the bathroom wouldn't be making her unsatisfied cunt feel so hungry.

Shaking her head, rising from the chair, mopped up the trail of water from the front door to the kitchen, wringing the cloth in the sink, then wiping the wet floor around the chair where had Jay had sat.

The boy's wet clothes now outside the bathroom door on the floor in a heap. Lisa went to collect them. Stooping to gather them in her arms, she glanced to the bathroom door, What did he look like naked, her mind danced.

Opening the door ever so slowly, no more than a crack before getting to her feet. Oh Lord! she gasped, hands flying to her cheeks. Facing her completely nude, was *Jay!* His cock semi-erect, no sagging testicles firm in the ball sac, not hanging limp and lifeless in appearance as she had seen in the past. The penis thick, long, possessing vitality in its smoothness, a shine of glorious fulfilment permeated from the flesh.

Mouth open, breathing, in short sharp gasps. Lisa thought's frantic with desire, she imagined the cock, fully grown, rock hard slicing deeper and deeper into her now aching vagina. Her mouth could almost taste its flavour, its bulbous head swelling between her lips. Her hands left her face, dropping the wet clothes, ripping open the robe. Both hands, one on top of the other, rubbing her pulsating pussy. She was aflame, body twisting, writhing in ecstasy, she ejaculated, the semen squeezing through her clasped fingers, before dripping on to the carpeted floor.

Chapter 2

As the ripples of pleasure slowly subsided, Lisa, legs weak, her mind in a trance for more, noticed the naked young body was gone.

Hidden by the closed door of the shower cubicle, twisting her lips in frustration. She'd come over her fingers, not for the first time, nor would it be the last. Like Dean over the weekend it wasn't enough. In truth she felt an even bigger emptiness within her now.

Cleaning herself with the bottom of her robe bent down, wiping the whitish splatters off the floor. Going back to the kitchen, threw Jay's wet sodden clothes in the drier, switched it on, going to the bedroom, disregarded the soiled robe, dressed, no underwear, a pair of Jeans and thick roll neck sweater. The rumpled bed could wait.

Making more coffee, a quick swig of vodka, no glass, straight from the bottle, sat down, waiting for the drier to finish. She had to deal with the situation now. The youth would give her all the flesh she wanted and more. Lisa knew how deep and overwhelming her desire had become. The orgasm in the hall, instead of relieving it, had lifted her even higher into the need for sexual gratification.

But not with Jay, once he'd had a taste, he'd be hanging around, calling her endlessly. She, feeling the need, would want him again, he'd fill her so completely, her orgasms would be endless, once that happened, he'd use her, then abuse her. Her needs, because of his youth, his unlimited vigour, her physical sexual response to his fucking, would inflate his ego, then she'd never be rid of him.

She would love to have young virile men fucking her, penis's ever ready. Damn and hell him for confusing her life. In just a hour or so he'd put her back into a world of uncertainty, one she thought she'd left behind forever, after that first drunken fuck two years after the divorce. The following two years had been heaven. Lisa knew that every so often, as her sexual appetite developed, her need increased. Jay was a new desire, untried before, and every time a new need became satisfied. So did her gratification become more fulfilling.

David divorcing her had hurt, it wasn't him leaving her, it was him telling her that day in his office, that she, Lisa, after twenty years of marriage had been removed from his affections by a slut of a girl half her age. If only he'd given her a reason for her failure, not enough sex, not exciting to him any more, nothing, just an abrupt and insensitive few words.

"I'm leaving you, Lisa, I'm sorry, I don't want to discuss it, you can have the house, and I'll give you a generous alimony settlement no strings attached."

And that was it, she'd had been so stunned, flabbergasted, struck dumb, she'd ran out of the building. Blinded by her tears, she drove home some how. For months hardly leaving the house, started smoking again, developed a taste for vodka. Exercised for endless hours in front of the television using keep fit videos.

Blaming herself for the marriage failure, plucking up her courage, fortified with half a bottle of vodka, months later she'd phoned David. He understood, asked how she was keeping. Drunk and uncaring she'd demanded to know why he'd divorced her.

"I fell in love with a wonderful young girl!"

"You fell in love, David?" The words knifed into her heart, a twisting hurting pain attacked her mind. "You were a married man, what did you do, fall out of love with me, and find yourself a young bimbo to fuck you," she'd screamed in outraged anger. *"You wouldn't know what love was if it shit in your mouth,"* shrieking she slammed the phone down, She'd never spoken to him or seen him since that day.

Now four years on she had lost nothing, she lived in comfort, smiling to herself. David paid heavy for his new love, more than he'd ever have to pay for whore. She laughed, out loud at the thought. He was paying plenty and she was doing the whoring. Somehow the laughter made her feel better.

Lisa had always believed their sex together had been great, Not now. It had been just ordinary. In the steady married life they'd had, in those circumstances, loving gentle satisfaction seemed right.

Now Lisa knew different, a rampant cock, hot, stiff, being driven up her vagina, feeling a mans semen coating her inner body, as she unleashed her own juices over his pumping flesh. That was sex, with David, it had been a nothing.

Today Lisa was, in her own way, thankful to him. She'd have hated to grow old without finding out what she'd been missing for forty years.

The drier stopped, breaking into her thoughts, get rid of the boy, out of the house, before his penis and youth poisons your senses my girl she told herself forcefully. Collecting the now dry clothes, carrying them on her arm, knocking on the bathroom door, shouted loudly, "Your clothes are dry, there outside the door on the floor," turned and walked back to the kitchen, shutting the kitchen door behind her.

When he rejoined her in the kitchen, hair damp, looking less blonde, Lisa, noticed a long look of disappointment on his face, seeing her dressed, smoking a cigarette, standing by the icebox.

Her thighs trembled slightly as he looked at her, smiling suggestively.

"Any more coffee, Mrs Knott?" he asked her slyly.

"I'm afraid not, Jay, beside it's stopped raining," nodding her head towards the window, the sun shining brightly outside now. "No need to wait any longer for the rain to stop, Jay, besides I've a million things that needs seeing to," her tone telling him his cock was not wanted.

Lisa walked down the hall, opened the front door, gesturing with her hand for him to leave. He stormed passed her, outside he turned, looked into her face, his eyes blazing, his ego deflated.

"Not good enough for you, Mrs Knott. I'll call again, I used to watch you during the summer while I was washing your car, lying on your back on your sun lounger, in your little white bikini with your legs wide open. Sometimes I'd see strands of your pubic hairs sticking out the side of the bikini panty. You gave me my first erection, sometimes I'd jack myself off looking at you. I always told myself one day I'd return and fuck you. That day is coming, Mrs Knott, soon, very soon." Holding his cock in one hand through his jeans, shaking it at her. "You'll feel my cock up you to the hilt, and you'll love it, good day."

Lisa slammed the door in his face, locking it, leaned against it shaking. The threat didn't frighten her, if a sex hungry Jay wanted to fuck her. No problem, when or if it happened it would be on her terms now, not Jay's.

Almost at a run, onto the kitchen, taking the half-empty bottle of vodka off the shelf she drank heavily, gagging as it burned her throat. Her vulva quivering, the thought that Jay, at the age of thirteen or fourteen taking his young developing shaft in his hand, masturbating himself at the sight of her almost naked body. She envisaging him coming, the semen shooting out of his clenched fist, it made her head swim.

Banging her head against a cupboard door. *Stupid! Stupid! Stupid!* she said over and over again. Lisa stood legs apart. Jay a fit looking youth with an instrument capable of satiating her flesh's desires, in her house and she'd shown him the door.

Get a grip of yourself Lisa. Dean wouldn't be back for almost a week, she couldn't wait that long for a man, not now, Jay and his youthful body, his sleek looking shaft, the threat of him forcing her to fuck. Forcing, that's a joke, chuckling softly at the idea. She did all the forcing with her sucking lips, her hot pussy having forced many a man to fuck her again, long after they thought they were finished.

Forget it Lisa, she told herself, going to the bedroom. Taking a new, unwrapped pair of black satin sheets out of the closet, tonight she'd sleep in luxury, the smooth silky satin would caress her naked flesh, her breasts and nipples so susceptible to the cool satin texture, her stomach loved the feel of satin. Throwing off the now dry semen stained sheets, loving remade the bed, finished, picking up the soiled sheets off the floor. I'll wash them now, and it's done with, she decided quickly. Then the doorbell rang.

He'd come back, Jay wouldn't take no for answer, shoving

the sheets in the washing machine. Looking through the lounge window she saw not Jay, instead a coloured youth, wearing thick glasses with round florin face, reminded her of Joe Ninety from the television program 'Thunderbirds'.

Opening the door, he offered his card, saying in a quiet voice, "I've come to service your boiler, ma'am." She looked at him questioningly. Harry, your usual fitter is sick, I'm just filling in for him for a few days, hope you don't mind, it will only take about half an hour, then I'll be gone," so polite and friendly. Lisa nodded.

"Fine with me," pausing to look at the white card in her hand. "Come in, Mr Nathan Karnov, can I get you a cup of coffee?" she offered smiling.

"That would be most welcome, thank you kindly, ma'am, and the name's Nathan, just call me Nathan." She studied him while he spoke, no older than Jay, possibly a little younger, yet well muscled, narrow waist, black hair, quite good-looking, his smile permanently on his lips, a nice boy, and young,

"The boiler's behind the fire in the lounge, you make a start, and I'll bring you the coffee."

"Thank you," he replied with polite shyness. Back in the kitchen she brewed coffee, carrying a cup for Nathan in her hand, he'd taken off his jacket, the white tee shirt underneath. Tight fitting, Lisa as he took the cup from her, noticed how hard his biceps looked, she could she the ridges of muscle on his stomach beneath the tee shirt. This was a fit strong boy, to hell with it. She'd see if he wanted to fuck. The thought of having her first coloured instrument exciting her beyond belief.

It would be her first. She held no thoughts about colour. She just had never been in the situation of being with one that was all.

Don't rush him, this isn't the impetuous Jay, she cautioned herself, She would use subtlety, let him know she was available, with a little gentle titillation, just enough to wet his appetite, a little flesh, a hint, the odd touch, He'd never resist her wiles, too young by half.

Leaving him and going to the bedroom she changed into a tight grey skirt, not too short, just a few inches above the knee.

Panties white, the sort with little more than a covering for her quim, the elastic waistband, a mere thin strip on her hips. A blouse, no bra, just thin enough to make her nipples slightly visible, leaving the top three buttons undone, exhibiting just enough cleavage to encourage him enough to want a second look, finally a pair of high heeled slippers. Looking in the mirror, wetting a finger, rubbed it across her eyebrows, fluffed up her hair, smoothing the skirt down over her shapely hips.

Nathan my boy, you've got no chance, when you leave I'll have sucked you dry. Lisa already feeling her vagina moistening in anticipation returned to lounge. Nathan was on his knees, hand beneath the fire, head just inches off the floor, looking upwards. Lisa stooping down, a few inches away from his head, knee's together buttocks touching her heels.

"Everything all right Nathan, no problems I hope?" she inquired in a quiet of matter fact voice.

His head turned a little towards her. Lisa watched his face, as she ever so slowly parted her knees a few inches. His eyes looking straight at her flimsy covered pussy, the panties so narrow in the crutch, as her knee's parted it had slipped inside the wet lips of her cunt. She could almost feel the heat of his eyes staring up her skirt. He seemed transfixed by the naked flesh, Lisa opened her knee's a little wider, heard him gasp, the whites of his eyes seemed to enlarge. He rolled over on his back his breathing sounding ragged. Lisa stifled a groan, his weapon was already stiffening, so apparently clear in swelling bulge inside his jeans

She had him, one deft touch and he would be hers, ever so slowly, putting her fingers gently on the muscles ridged stomach, stopping for a few seconds. Don't frighten him. Not now, her own advice, so alive in anticipation hard to except. Control yourself, lead him slowly. Fingers, barely touching she moved them down, over the muscled midriff, past the belt, downward, he jumped as her middle finger touched his growing phallus. Lisa widened her knees a little more. She was in ecstasy, her finger on the tool burning hot. Lisa closed her eyes, her hand now stroking the covered lengthening shaft of flesh, a sweating hand touch her inner thigh, then a warm finger slowly traversed up and down her wet sex-lips.

Hunger and desire overcame her, her hand shaped the cock through the jeans, trembling they searched for the zipper, she wanted to feel the naked flesh, to measure the shafts size, it's girth, the length, in her hand.

Stroking it, her breath coming in strangled gasps, Nathan's finger on her cunt lips becoming ever more incessant, her fingers found the zipper, holding her breath, sliding it down.

Gently with the softest of touches slipping her hand inside, the warm flesh came into her hand. Lisa, whispering a low moan, as the warm root sent shivers up her arm. Nathan's finger pushed against the sunken panties. Blinded by lust, her passion touching every nerve for her being.

"Nathan come with me, Now!" her voice, trembling with need, she left him, almost running to the bedroom. She was naked before he came through the door, he still looked shy, his prick didn't, still inside the jeans, zip open.

Her naked body afire for man flesh, she kissed him on the lips, eating his mouth with hers, her tongue an ever moving snake of flesh seeking his, her hand pushed back inside the cloth, fingers caressing the now fully erected cock. His exploring hand found a breast, the nipple hardening, choking with desire, he squeezed it with finger and thumb, so hard, and pain stabbed her breast. Lisa could hear the gasps of their breath, his deep and strong, hers rasping, a sob, echoing into her ears, the lust laden sobs of need, the call of desire.

Lisa needed a cock, her vagina needed cock, she had to be fucked. Stepping away from the still clothed youth.

"Let me see you! Please Now!" she begged.

Slavishly he stripped, standing naked, eyes averted in shyness, before her.

His cock, stood ridged against his stomach, standing straight, it breathed life. No lover in the past ever matched this shaft of flesh, not in size, it made all those older men's weapons appear feeble, yet at the time she had lavish their cocks, as she would this one, with no less desire.

The dark ebony skin tight, the head more pinky, the shaft pulsed blood, the veins swollen, those closer to the surface of the flesh throbbed. The bulbous knob, the orifice opened and closed, shining as if moist. The testicles like Jay's in the bathroom, fitted snugly beneath the stiffened shaft of flesh.

She wanted him in her mouth, this young weapon of love, to have her lips slip over the blood engorged head, the flesh so young, as all things tender, it would be so sweet, the taste beyond desire.

But not yet, she was on the brink of ejaculation, just a touch of the youth's shaft on her lips, she'd come.

So wondrous a sight, his cock, thick, long an instrument of manly erect flesh. A throbbing shaft, her most fevered thought, now ready to slip deep into my avid cunt. Her fingers moved upward to the pinkie bulbous head.

A mindless haste drove the shaft of flesh, with skin now tight and glistening, she saw the beat of pulsating blood in the pumping vein's, in one quick movement, she laid down, Instantly he was over her, thrusting his strong hips forward, the ribbed veined cock pulsing. The clumsy stab missed her open vulva, she moaned as she lifting her legs.

"Take My! Now! Hurry!" The blunt weapon bucked up through her twitching hairy mound. *"Oh, Don't come yet, Not so soon, I know he's coming."*

She shifted her loins frantically, trying to place herself to meet the instrument. Yet again, thrusting blindly, it missed, she had to make him slow down. The idea he'd ejaculate any second over her belly, the thought of the waste. Locking her legs around his hips, his wildly thrusting hips restricted. This third time, driving the breath from her lungs, Nathan's cock drove, hot and throbbing into the damp centre of her lust.

Nothing to savour or enjoy. The penetration to her very quick, so sudden, he was already twisting and rocking in a raging frenzy of fucking.

Lisa gasped, gasped a second time. The flesh inside was a shining weapon, brushing aside everything as it thrust deep again and again, to her deepest vitals.

"Oh, please yes. Oh my God!" She panted, not knowing she spoke. Far beyond her normal usual foreplay, she felt herself abruptly trembling as she went into orgasm, her vagina stimulated by his impetus as he thrust and withdrew.

This violent physical lust had to end. His cock started pumping its pent-up overload of semen, she felt the first hard spurt of come, hotter than her own hottest flesh, a tangible feeling, drawing a moan of pleasure from her closed lips, She thought he'd finished. Nathan was still coming, each pumping spurt, coating her insides more fully than the last. He filled her loins, the slapping of their semen wetted thighs, so beautiful, *so perfect*. A small tear escaped from the corner of her eye.

Short of breath, her lungs aching, when had she last drawn breath into her body, she didn't know. Taking a quick gasp, the oxygen filling her with new energy lifted her to a higher level of sexual fulfilment, the desire for even more. Nathan, finished, had still more of an erection than she'd come to expect from any of her previous lovers. Slowly she continued to writhe after he stopped moving.

Lifting his upper body, a grin on his face.

"Never had been screwed like that before, have you?" he chuckled. "Now you fuck it, *you old slut*, Fuck it!"

Lisa was angry, shocked, this grinning young insolent youth. She could not believe it, this courteous boy, so pleasant in appearance, less than twenty minutes ago, would speak with such arrogance.

She closed her mind, smothering the waves of guilt before they engulfed her. This gloomy wet Monday morning, she had, because of Dean's inadequate lovemaking, the sight of Jay's naked body earlier, his young cock, so vibrant to her mind. She had permitted herself to seduce this young man Nathan. And his large cock still proud, semi-hard in her flesh.

Lisa could not believe she'd done it, and yet despite all her guilt, her shame at sinking so low, she continued to press and move her wet thighs up against a renewing erection.

Her thoughts vanished, Nathan, responding to her writhing, his cock, attacked her wet vagina, with even greater vigour than the time before.

She matched him, pushing her body to meet his, all too soon. As he groaned, she sucked out of his rampant weapon of flesh an even greater flood of come.

They collapsed, lying in a lather of semen and sweat, her lungs gasping for air. Nathan's body in her arms, his sweat drenched hair resting against her neck. She could feel the twitching, the shudders of male body in completion, further amplified as her own flesh, surrendering to a beautiful sensation of contentment. Lisa had never experienced in her life, such sexually satisfaction. *Ever!*

Stroking his wet hair, head resting on her breast, a comfort to him, just the same as the sexual release would become to her in a little while.

Lisa lying with the naked male body beside her, sexually happy, the cock that had given her that bodily satisfaction relaxed against her thigh, so wet and warm.

Her mind was in turmoil. She was old enough to be his mother. And he knew it, to him she was nothing more than an old lady, desperate to be fucked. Lisa smiled to herself at the idea, if he thought that, he was right, she had been desperate. She hadn't been lovemaking, she'd had sex. It had been Cunt and Cock. Cock and Cunt.

Shock by the use of the words, so alien to her mind, the use of such vulgar words rarely spoken in her life. She needed a man like Nathan.

After this morning her life would be forever changed. Dean and the others before, even her ex-husband David, never gave her the feeling of having been fucked so utterly as this sweaty hairdo, coloured youth she had in her arms now. Lisa having tasted the pleasure that erupted inside her vulva. The strength, the vigour only the young possess, the cock's that could bring her to orgasm not once, but two or three times on their first erection. Those young weapons she could take between her lips. Her mouth would love them, as she would.

She made the first step into the world of having young men fuck her. Today Jay wanted to fuck her, she'd refused. Nathan never resisted her advances.

David had divorced her. Why? Because he'd found some slut of girl, young enough to be his daughter to fuck. Had he been shafting that girl while he was married to her? She was a free woman now, no husband, no children, and her need to be filled with a cock from time to time, the same as other females.

Lisa, her mind not fully cleared of the feeling of guilt, came to the conclusion she'd let events take its course. Not just today, everyday.

Nathan stirred, "Have you any idea what you said to me?" she asked tenderly.

Not lifting his head. "Did I say something?" She laughed quietly.

"Say anything, you said a little too much, young man. You called me, Old Slut, said, I'd never been screwed like that before, so fuck it, old slut, fuck it."

Nathan sat up, looked her in the face.

"Did I say that, you sure?" his gaze one of disbelief.

Lisa held back the laugh, the look of shocked surprise on his face so innocent, child-like. "You surely did, young man."

Suddenly his expression became serious.

"Please, ma'am, you can't expect a man to be a gentleman when he's..." Stumbling over his words, then continued, stammering, the words coming in a rush. "He'll say crazy things when..." pausing again. "Don't hold it against me, Mrs Knott, I would never have said that, to you, it was in the heat of..."

She completed the sentence as he hesitated. "*Of fucking.*" Reaching up, taking his cheeks in her cupped hands, she kissed him gently on the lips.

"I'll never hold it against, my lovely Nathan. It shocked me, words so coarse, it hurts to be called an 'old slut'. You sounded so masculine, so contemptuous, as if your tool had an arrogance of its own."

His eyes gleamed, at her words.

"I'm truly sorry," cupping one hand, in a gesture of familiarity over her damp pubic mound.

"I've never had a woman as beautiful as you, Mrs Knott. *Honestly. Never.*"

If he hadn't looked so innocent, almost bashful she'd have giggled. "The name is Lisa, Nathan, and I think under the circumstances which we now find yourselves in, first names would more in keeping with our nakedness."

With some reluctance he spoke her name, eyes downcast,

not to look at her, her name.

"Lisa," was a whispered sound, to her ears.

That was it, she was an older woman, sadly she always would be just that to him. She considered for brief second. To him, why just to Nathan, most of her past lovers had been younger than her, not as young as this well-endowed young man maybe, and yet still younger. Have I any thoughts of having him again? Stop now Lisa, she warned herself severely. "*To him you're just a good fuck, a one off, tomorrow he'll forget you, within a week or so he'll shaft some other woman. This was only a man you used to still the hunger for flesh, to release your semen over a stiff hard cock, you've done that, now leave it be; it will only lead to a hurt. To him your, a wet morning fuck, once he leaves, he'll not be back.*"

Abruptly she got up.

"Move yourself, lover, these sheets are sodden, together we've made them soaking wet," she ordered, chuckling happily.

"You going to help me make the bed again, Nathan?"

Shyly, he rose, standing to watch her strip the damp stained black satin sheets. Pity she thought, having only laid them on the bed less than an hour ago, tossing them on the floor in a heap. "Fetch a clean pair from the closet over there," she said, pointing towards closet.

Bringing them back, watching her, unfold the pink sheets. One off it maybe, Lisa told herself, but he'll not leave until I've had him again. On clean dry sheets, it'll be slower this time, a leisurely slow lovemaking, her vagina twitched in anticipation, her thighs warming at the thought.

Surprised when she flapped out the first sheet, he expertly laid it on the mattress, tucking the ends underneath perfectly.

"Where did you learn to make a bed so neatly, Nathan?" she asked. "Your mother show you?"

He looked at her. His features squeezed, anger in his blue eyes. "My Mother showed me nothing," voice raised, almost shouting, "Ran off with some man when I was twelve years old. Never saw her again. My father never got over her going like that." He was close to tears.

Lisa felt her heart missed a beat. That's why he'd called her an Old Slut. In the frenzy of fucking her, in his mind he'd been invading a woman, about the same age as his departed mother, as he'd reached the pinnacle of orgasm. She. Lisa. Her cunt, he'd been punishing her, his revenge on his absent Mother. Hurting her, insulting her, thrashing her body with all his might, using his cock, her willing wet cunt, in an attempt to purge the person from his mind. The unhappiness inflicted on him. Lisa in his mind, a surrogate. She become the slut in his mind, The woman he'd known as Mother.

The bed making finished. She was close to tears, guilt ridden, as never before. She seduced him, so innocent, vulnerable, and he given her so much pleasure. Her shame so painful, he needed love, affection, not raw sex.

Stepping quickly round the bed, wrapping her arms around the naked youth. Head down, looking at the floor, his arrogance of body, the vibrant youthful vigour had vanished, replace by abject misery, a shell of the man that had filled her body. Her vagina so completely, with a cock, so delicious. It had made her cunt pump come over the rod of flesh so copiously.

Lisa, holding him felt a shiver run up his back.

"Get away from me," he shouted, shoving her away roughly. Shocked, her gesture of pity and comfort rejected, stumbling backwards, the calves of her legs coming in to contact with newly made bed. She fell on her backside, with a thump, on the mattress.

She looked up into the anger twisted features. No longer showing, any interest in her nakedness or his own. He fucked her, now it was. She could see, to him, nothing.

The rejection, to her, devastating, a cruel selfish arrogant trampling of her sexuality. A shadow, briefly, touched her thoughts. Had this crumpled specimen, naked before her eyes, his instrument of love, shrunken now, no majesty or power visible, really made her come so avidly.

Her feeling of guilt drained away, as if Nathan, she knew not why, had a guilt on him. She could face hers, he couldn't. No anger in her against him, no shame in her mind now.

While fitting the sheets. She'd conjured up the fucking, the nutty sweet taste of a warm cock in her mouth, his weapon ridged driving again and again as their orgasms flowed.

Forget it Lisa, she commanded her mind, it's over. Let him leave, closing her eyes, disappointed, acute hunger gone. Nathan hadn't satisfied it. *He killed, it damn him, stone dead.*

Getting off the bed, coldly she said, "Get dressed, Nathan". He nodded obediently, turned her back, getting a clean robe from the closet, wrapping it around her, walking past him as he bent to pick his scattered clothes, and went to the kitchen.

She'd chosen Nathan, it could have been Jay, in truth. She couldn't deny that, she didn't want to.

Lighting a cigarette, before making coffee, had she made a foolish mistake in having the boy. *Maybe. Maybe not, only time would tell, her body's response to him, her still wet inner thighs and sticky vagina, had no regrets.*

What hell, a man once forced her to suck his cock. Examine it Lisa, analyse it, nothing new in having a man, it's just another cock for your pleasure, and you've had few of those over the last two years, treat Nathan in the same manner as Dean, Mark and all the others. You fucked them. They fucked you. Then after awhile, the excuses, the phone calls. 'Sorry Lisa my love I'm away on business for next couple weeks.' or, 'Can't you see for a while the wife's becoming suspicious.'

She'd then search for a new middle-aged cock to replace her departing lover's. That was the problem, to face. She could never, in her mind, think of Nathan or picture him as another middle-aged cock, *impossible.*

Lisa Knott had shared lustful sex with men often enough, no feeling of shame, or guilt. Did knowing Nathan change that, and why should it change her? The only thing new in her life was his age. The strong large thick ebony cock, was the other.

The fact he'd never visit a second time. That's a joke, why should she care if he did or didn't. She never concerned herself before, it never troubled her when a lover, became an ex-lover. Not after David's betrayal, the cold heart manner he cast her aside, after that, a man leaving her bed meant nothing, his cock did.

The reflections on her past, cleared the fog of confusion, replaced with a clarity of purpose. She enjoyed, no, it went deeper than enjoyment, she revelled in expanding her mind and body through having men fuck her, every new kinky sex act she performed. Her sexual horizons opened wider.

The first flesh in her mouth, the first tongue that made her come, the first time, hurtful an experience that it was, when a man had taken her from the rear, in the ass.

Lisa, lighting another cigarette, making her mouth in an, O, blowing a lung full of smoke, head tipped back, in rings at the ceiling. Decision taken. Conviction in her mind, no guilt or shame. She was going to use words, not her tits and pussy. Seduce Nathan once more, only this time she'd trap him into returning for more.

Chapter 3

She collected the soiled black satin sheets from bedroom floor, while waiting for the youth to join her, The heady aroma of their semen on the sheets, the pervading smell of good sex in the bedroom, her nostrils wide, breathing in the heavy scent. The lips of her vagina rubbing together, sending shivers up her insides. The hunger for that boy's cock, *deep in her vitals*, had returned.

Lisa, for a moment thought he'd left the house. The bedroom was empty, in a panic, ran out of bedroom, sheets under the arm, heading for the front door. Relieved as she rushed past the open door of the lounge. Thank heavens, the first thought in her head, seeing Nathan kneeling, screwdriver in hand, finishing the job her white panties had so successfully lured him away from.

Back in the kitchen, sheets shoved quickly in the washing machine, cup of hot coffee poured sitting down she waited.

He shuffled more than walked into the kitchen, eyes averted. Ashamed of his outburst. His whole being emanating guilt. Lisa, the boy's shy now, she realised, use it, and massage his guilt gently. Like you would his stalk with your mouth.

"Sit down, Nathan, have some coffee," speaking in a gentle maternal voice, "Don't let your outburst in the bedroom upset you, it's all right, Nathan my love, I'm not angry with you, I shouldn't have made fun of you like that, not after you'd given me so much." Pausing for a second. Letting him feel less vulnerable. He tangible relaxed. Easy now Lisa, she reminding herself, you've made an opening, small it maybe. She reached a hand across the table, gently smoothing the back of his hand, for an instant he stiffened, then it was gone.

"Do you think that I'd be annoyed with you, Nathan?" she asked coaxingly. Of course he would, she **was** annoyed.

He didn't answer, just a sharp nod of his head. "Look at me, Nathan." She waited. He sat, head down, afraid, his youth a skin of shyness, their age difference, a barrier she had to overcome if she was to succeed.

"If you can't see my face, Nathan, and I can't look at yours, neither of us will be able to forget this morning, just lifted your head my love." She begged gently, becoming a little desperate.

He took her by surprise, one minute curly hair, the next, a pair of glass covered eyes stared at her unblinking, fixed ridged, expressionless.

"There now, that wasn't so difficult, Nathan was it?" smiling sweetly, her tone, gently, lovingly. Standing up, reaching across the table, she cupped his chin in her hands. Lisa kissed him on the lips. So soft, so gentle, a touch of lips on lips, for a second or two.

He stiffened, unresponsive, cold. She sat down again, the touch of his cold lips, an ache to her heart.

"That wasn't very good, Nathan, perhaps if I did it one more time, you'd realise I want us to be friends. I don't want you leaving my house feeling miserable, ashamed, or guilty in any way." Changing the tone of her voice, making it sound she, Lisa felt the guilt, not him.

"I'm sorry for what I did, Mrs Knott," he suddenly said, quickly, having difficulty with the words. "It would never have happened if we'd had our clothes on," his voice rose sharply. "The last time I saw my mother, she was naked, making a bed, watching her, a naked man, and it wasn't my father," the words come faster now, a sob in his voice. "Next day she was gone. *Forever!* When you asked me if my mother showed me how to make a bed," tears trickling down his dark brown cheeks now. "It all came back, the sight of you naked, making the bed, me naked watching, to me, an enactment, of the one scene in my life I never wanted see ever again, you became for a few seconds, my naked mother, me, that big man. I felt I was reliving that day, It hurt me so, so very much, her leaving turned my father into a drunkard, when I was seventeen he hung himself, she'd killed him, in body and mind, it broke his heart. **In That Bedroom!**" Pointing in the direction of her bedroom, eyes wildly, screaming words dripping with venom, "You've been fucked by me, like my mother was fucked by that man, and I watched her become a slut before my own eyes, behind my fathers back."

Lisa was thunderstruck, speechless. Her pity for the crying youth was overwhelming. Her guilt deep, heavy, for what she done, in innocence, Her desire for hard flesh, now flooding her mind, a feeling of shame, immense, overpowering. Hating herself for the first time in years.

She sat, the only sound in still house, the sobbing boy Nathan. Lisa wanted to hold him, soothe away his pain, cloak him in comfort and warmth, and share the anguish of his soul. Salve her troubled conscience. But she didn't know how.

The silence, the steady tick of the clock on the wall, eerie, oppressive, disturbing to her, the unnatural quietness, instinctively she said,

"Have you always worn glasses, Nathan?" The words, so out context, sounded silly. His answer, a quick shake of the head. "Why don't you tell how all this happened to you?" Quickly, while she had his attention, tenuous as it was.

"Would it help if I told you how my divorce in some ways scarred my life, but I healed those scars, Nathan, not with anger, or hate for my ex-husband David, it wasn't easy, it took two long sad painful years. I turned my life around completely, and now, today, I enjoy how I live, and what I do. From the ruins of my marriage, I've built a new life, so different from my old one, so satisfying, so full of the pleasures I'd never tasted, or enjoyed, for feelings unknowing to me. I like my life, I like what I do, and above all, I like myself as a person for the first time."

That's a bit thick Lisa, she chided herself, over the top, yes, yet it was not lies. That's how she saw her life now. A little deceitful, yes. She shivered, for second, a feeling of wickedness in her mind. The deceit, the omission of the fact, that the contentment, pleasure, feeling the ethos of her happiness.

Cock!

"It's not so easy to forget for me, you didn't suffer it as a child, I did." Defensive, the answer, without conviction, he's not sure, Lisa interpreted.

"Have you ever talked to someone about it, Nathan?" Lisa

inquired holding her breath.

"Nobody," a sharp one word reply.

"Not even your father?" she asked, a little slower, waiting.

"*No never*,"

"Nathan, you must tell someone, it's always better to unburden the mind, everybody suffers heartache and pain at sometime in their lives, your not alone in your troubles, if you keep it bottled up inside, the pain eats away for ever, it will consume you, your so young, in front of you a life time, tell someone, let them help you, before it eats your heart and soul." The silence returned, head bowed again, sitting stiffly, as if in deep thought.

"I'll tell *you,* Mrs Knott," he suddenly blurted out, "because for the first time since that day," looking boldly into her face, now he's found conviction, it was in the voice, her thoughts stopped. "In your bedroom, I felt something new, I had sex, without shame, or agony of mind for the first time. And you've explained my troubled thoughts. First time, you took away the sight of my mother's naked body, with yours, please forgive me for putting it this way. You fucked her out of my mind for the first time in my life. You've explained, without realising, something that has haunted me since the day I watched her being fucked and fucking a man."

Explained, explained what, confused as to how he'd arrived at that conclusion. Lisa dismissed it from her mind. She wanted him, and his youthful vigour, naked, possessing her. Let him think what he wanted how he wanted.

She was sure, no not sure, whole heartedly, utterly, utterly positive. Lisa wanted shout with joy, dance round the kitchen, she'd won, his youth would be hers, as if that difference between them, had evaporated, she was going to have. She wanted to shout 'I'm going to have the Fuck to end all Fucks', the cock I need will be mine again today.

Calming her feverishness of mind she said,

"Nathan pour some more coffee for us, and take it to the lounge, it's nicer to sit in comfort while we talk, I won't be a minute." Rising from the chair, smile into his eyes now minus the glasses, his features so different, the chin stronger.

In the bathroom, stripping of the robe, looked at her naked body's reflection in the mirror, utilise the flesh, the black forest of hair, the tits, the legs, everything, make it available to him. He's to young to resist a naked female body, he might try, but the essence of all men, the cock, would not.

Quickly, washing between her legs and armpits, drying, spraying perfume all over, including her bum cheeks, going into the bedroom, searched in a draw in closet, finding, put on a pair of black stay-up stocking, rushing now, back to bathroom, slipped the robe back on, one last look in the mirror as she tied the robe, not to tight, she wanted it to open from time to time, titivate the boy, the hotter she made him, the more virile his weapon of flesh.

In the lounge, as she walk in, noticing bright sunlight shining through the window. Nathan sitting on the white fur covered lounger, a cup in his hand, looked at her, a weak smile on his lips, it widened intentionally, the loose tied robe opened. She made certain the stocking clad legs, and the strip of naked flesh of her upper thigh became exposed, for a brief second, a tiny flash of lust rippled across his eyes.

Sitting next to him, drawing her feet up, then kneeling facing the boy, the robe falling away from her legs. She was loving every move she made, the eye's. Thank God! He left the glasses on the kitchen table, opening her knees a little wider, just perfect, he was gazing at her pubic hair, eyes hot, licking his lips. Lisa heart gave a leap, I've got him now, hook line and sinker.

"Now, Nathan, my love, you tell me all about it, hold my hands, you'll find it a big comfort. I know you haven't asked me, but I want you to understand, whatever you tell me, is between you and me, not one word of our conversation will heard outside this room, *Ever*." Lisa, feeling a stab of self satisfaction, nice touch that, tell me your secret, Lover, after the telling, you'll will still have your secret.

He swallowed hard. She heard his throat flex. A deep, lung filling in take of breath, staring hard in to her eyes, face stiff, he began to talk in a timid voice.

"Don't interrupt me please, once I start telling you, if I stop my courage will fail me. I remember every thought I had that day, every feeling, but I can't explain it as happened that day. I was just twelve years old. I didn't really understand what they where doing, or why, I was just a child, now I'm older, almost twenty. Now I know exactly what they were doing, we did it in your bedroom not so long ago, try and understand, I saw it as a child, I'm telling you as a man. It's a twelve-year-old boy's experience, my experience. Sometimes it will be jumbled together, the re-creation of a child images of that day, in the words by man, a mans description, yet that of a child." A long pause, a very long, long silence.

Unsure, as if collecting his thoughts, in preparation. Lisa waited, don't weaken my lovely boy, echoed in her head, smiling, an encouragement, a tiny wink with her left eye. She leaned forward, brushed his cheek with her lips, the cheek was cold.

"It was the day after my twelfth birthday. Mother had organised a birthday party for me the day before, I had no brothers or sisters, so my parents spoilt me, not all the time, but spoilt nevertheless. I must have eaten too much at the party, because the next day at school at lunchtime I was sick, vomiting three or four times. So a teacher drove me home, dropped me at the gate telling me if I didn't feel well in the morning I needn't go to school. Mother wasn't home, the front door was locked. Thankfully, father always keep a spare key under a big flowerpot next to the front door, so I let myself in. I went upstairs to my room, I wanted to change my tee shirt and jeans, they smelt of vomit. I had just as a put on a clean tee shirt, I heard the front door open, then shut. Mother was home. Aimlessly changing the soiled and smelly jeans, then I heard the front door bell ringing and mother was talking to someone in the hall. Being inquisitive I walked across the landing, in my bare feet, looked over the handrail, below in the hall, my mother with her back against the hall way wall, standing in front of her was Leroy Matts. He wasn't coloured like my parents or me, he was white, a hulk of man, huge shoulders, thick arms, bald shiny head, he was older than my father, in his fifties, he always cut our lawn. I thought he was a nice man, sometimes he'd sit me on his lap and let me drive his big mower, he'd cut the grass three or four times before he wanted paying, then he'd call and mother'd settle whatever was owing. As I turned to go back to my room, mother started to walk past him to the kitchen, I saw him push her roughly back against the wall.

"'Don't rush away, my dear,'" I heard him say. "'You're always rushing away from me'."

"'Oh, Mr Matts you know…'"

"'Yes, I know, you're a happily married young lady,'" he interrupted her, "'I know all about that, but it doesn't stop you from giving old Leroy a little kiss does it now?'"

"I just watched, they didn't know I was in the house, the sun was shining through the glass in the front door, I could see everything below me, kneeling down to watch, I was hidden, so they couldn't see me.

"He put his big hands on mother shoulders, and leaned forward, mother moved her head to one side, then he put a hand behind her neck, pulled her head towards him and pressed his lips over her mouth. I saw her twisting her head trying to prevent him kissing her any more.

"From here on, Lisa, remember this is a child that's watching his mother, what I witnessed will be in the words of man, that day I didn't know the words to describe what they did. I do now.

"By the way he moved his mouth, now I know, he was trying to force his tongue into her mouth, but she wouldn't let him. His other hand went down to the small of her back, and he tried to pull her closer. Mother stiffened, keeping her distance, his hand moved lower. I could see everything. The hand went lower, his palm was over her bottom, then he moved his mouth an inch away from her lips.

"'Come on, honey',", he coaxed her. "'Just a nice little kiss, a proper kiss, honey, no one will ever know will they?'"

Mother stood stiff unmoving. She was going say something. I'll never know what she intended to say. The second her mouth opened to speak, Mr Matts mouth dived back to her lips, mother eyes closed, his tongue was probing through her parted lips and teeth.

"He moved his head from side to side. I was puzzled by that then, but not now. He was giving her mouth a thorough gamming with his tongue. His hand behind her neck slid down to her buttocks, and clutching each cheek of her bum, he pulled her hard against him.

"His strong arms and strength was to much for mother, for a second she resisted, then her body was pulled against his. I watched him press himself hard against her, all the time he was rubbing his belly in a circular movement against her. His lips never leaving her mouth for a second.

"I heard mother give a low moan, then another one, louder. Her arms came up round shoulders, embracing him. It was the first time she'd touched him. I watched as he kept his mouth hard on mother's, now her mouth moved from side to side, I could see her throat flexing, she was tonguing Leroy's mouth, as he tongued hers. Then he eased her body slightly to one side, mother's stomach no longer pressing against Leroy's.

"The front of his body squeezed against her side. His right hand came round from her behind her, to settle, palm downwards, over mother's skirt, covering her belly.

"Slowly the hand turned, the fingers pointing downwards, then the hand moved slowly, a just a little, until the fingers rested in the vee between her legs, then rubbed there for a few seconds. I could tell he was pressing mother hard on that spot. She opened her legs slightly, as if to ease the pressure of the probing fingers. Instantly Leroy's fingers and hand slipped between her legs, his wrist moved, the fingers pushed my mothers' skirt up over her knees, Leroy was shoving fingers into her body, along with her underwear. Mother, closed her legs, the hand almost disappeared."

Lisa's hands hurt, Nathan's finger nails, digging into the soft flesh of her palms. She wasn't thinking, totally focus on the boy, his eyes closed, the story he was telling, sounded disjointed, he seemed to pick certain words, avoid using others, as if he wanted to explain it all in nice way.

This is a tale about sex, that meant cunt, cock, fucking, and all the others adjectives that one use's when coitus is the subject matter.

Kissing him on the lips tenderly. Then she knew not why, said in, soft coaxing voice,

"Nathan, my sweet, your eyes are closed, remember what you witnessed that day, with the eyes and mind of the child you where on that day. Then recite what your memory unveils as a man Nathan, because you are a man. Not a child any more, face it as a man, be strong, in mind and body. Be a man, the man you were when you loved me in the bedroom, a bull of a man. A big man, in body and flesh, with the power to fuck an '*Old Slut*' in way she'd never been fucked before." If words didn't touch him. Motivate, on seconds thoughts, described more closely what she'd intended, he'd take all bloody day.

To her surprise, he squeezed her hands, nodded, resumed telling his story.

"I could tell by his motions he was trying to frig her; faster and faster his arm moved and jerked, I heard mother moaning, no longer fighting him or his probing fingers.

"Now she willing, responding to his lewd caressing, he took his mouth from hers. She panted for breath, her eyes closed, standing there as he masturbated her through her clothing, she was enjoying Leroy fingers.

"He whispered something in her ear. But she began to wriggle even more furiously on his palm.

"Mother's whole body was jerking, a funny expression on her pretty face. Flushed, moaning continuously panting. I watched spellbound, a strange feeling came over me, I was fascinated by sight below me, from my concealment I became hypnotised by the sounds, by my mother's shaking quivering body, Leroy's hand between her legs, and what it was making her do. To me it was a grown up game I'd never watched before, where did it end, who would win, Leroy or mother, what were they going to do, to finish the game, nobody talk about it, why didn't they tell us about this game in school.

"I heard him say. 'When will Nathan be home?' mother didn't answer. He kept whispering, the hand between her legs kept moving, she was shaking her head, shaking it emphatically. He just smiled and kept on muttering. I wished I could hear what he was saying. Straining my ears, a caught one word, it made no sense, a stupid word, I never heard it before, what on earth was a ***Fuck?***

"Suddenly mother opened her eyes and looked Leroy in the face, she seemed angry. She grabbed his wrist, stopping him from rubbing it against her, but failing to push the hand right away from body.

"He released her, immediately dropping on his knees in front of her, clasping his huge arms round her waist, pressing his face against the front of mother's skirt. I could see him kissing her skirt and then meeting her eyes as she looked down at him, he said, '"Go on, raise your skirt for me, you know you want to'."

"He resumed kissing, and licking the material of her skirt. If mother did that, if she raised her skirt, his face would be right in front of her knickers.

"I watched his hands slide down from her buttocks until they where behind her knees. He clasped her around the legs, his fingers wrapped around her knees, then his hands moved upwards, feeling her legs.

"Mother appeared as if she didn't know what to do. Her face looked confused.

"His hands disappeared, he was feeling her legs. I could follow the hands, moving up and down under mother's skirt, abruptly, mother leaned forward, gripped the hem of her skirt and pulled it up quickly.

"Her long legs, sheathed in flesh-coloured stocking were reveal, they, like yours, Lisa, shapely, to me on my knees, as yours are, lovely to look at."

Lisa, startled, to hear her name smiled. Her body had impressed him, hope some other areas of my naked flesh had the same effect, she thought hopefully.

"I could see his fingers now, rubbing and pawing at the naked flesh on mothers' thighs, above the stocking-tops and just below her bright yellow knickers. Why was mother standing there, her skirt held above her waist, what for? Why was Leroy kneeling down in front for her, his face a few inches from her knickers? What was he going to do?

"My mind questions were answered by Leroy. Suddenly he pressed forward, his mouth open, he slobbered wet kisses all over the front of mother knickers, for what reason I couldn't understand.

"I watched his fingers move inwards and upwards on her thighs. Instinctively, I knew what he was going to do. A feeling of anticipation swept over me, I was overcome by tingling funny sort of throb, my chest seemed to tighten. Leroy was going pull my mothers knickers down!

"I'd never seen a woman without knickers. I had no idea what knickers hid. Here, unseen, I didn't know what the feeling I had as I watched. I do now Lisa. It was the thrill of seeing *a cunt for the first time.* I was as eager as Leroy for that sight.

"Mother must have known what he was going to do, but she made no effort to stop Leroy. Standing legs apart, eyes closed, sucking her middle finger, not so much sucking, sliding it slowly in and out of her mouth, the lips shaped in an 'O' sometimes she pushed it in deeper.

"Leroy's fingers curled inside the narrow elastic waistband. I was panting like a dog. A loud hiss of breath from mother. In one quick tug, her knickers slide over her hips.

"Head swimming, eyes wide, I blinked, Leroy's head was pushed tight against mother's lower stomach, covering were the panties had been a second ago, I could see his throat moving, as it had when he'd been kissing her. His tongue was in my mother. She was moaning, head thrown back, pushing her stomach forward into Leroy's face.

"The disappointment I felt, such anti-climax, all I had seen was a black mound of curly hair covering mother lower stomach, Leroy had been so quick, in the blink of an eye, he'd replaced her knickers with his mouth.

"What was he doing, how he could kiss my mother in between her legs, what was kissing, and why? Why did mother seemed enjoy having a tongue inside her, and inside what?

"Without warning, he stood up, leaving mother groaning, I saw him looking into her eyes as he straighten up. His hand had replace his head between her legs, it moved gently in and out. the skirt still held up by mother.

"'You want a nice quick fuck, my dear, don't you?'" he said softly, his hand never stopping.

"Mother nodded.

"'But there isn't time. My boy Nathan will be home from

school soon'."

"'Oh no he won't, not for over an hour at least, my dear'," Leroy replied.

"'I've got some rubber's in my back pocket, it'll be quite safe, I'll use one if you want me to. It won't take long. A pretty woman like you needs plenty of cock, you know. How many men are giving it to you at present?'"

"'Oh, no one, only my husband Gary, of course'," mother retorted, sounding cross at his suggestion.

Leroy laughed, "'No need to get haughty, my dear. Look how easy it was get you worked up. You want a fuck, don't you, you know you do'."

"Mother nodded her head. 'Yes Leroy I do, I have to admit. I really need one now'."

"The hand still moved. That word again, *Fuck*. How did you do it, they knew. My mother and father did it, mother had just said so, but when? *How*? The mention of my father, Gary, something didn't seem right. If mother did it with father, then why did Leroy want her to do whatever it was with him as well?

"Leroy was patting her cheek. She'd let her clothing fall back in placc, the hand wasn't between her legs any more, just an arm around her shoulders, looking into her face.

"'Let me hear you use the right words, my dear. Don't forget I've had my tongue in your cunt, so there's no use in being shy and modest'."

"Another new word. *Cunt*! Leroy had said, 'I've had my tongue in your *Cunt'*, not in mother's mouth. I started shaking, feeling cold, as it dawned on me, hidden inside my mother knickers, all women's knickers and girls' knickers. I knew it what was called. *Now* what it looked like, nothing. A blank.

"Mother was talking again, not looking at Leroy, 'Oh, Leroy, you make me feel so naughty. I would like to be... you know... to be *fucked'.*"

"He smiled, 'Go on say it louder, say it nice and loud, I like to hear pretty women telling me'."

"Leroy was stroking the front of mothers' blouse, were it swelled out from her chest, he left the rest of her body alone now.

"The force, the loudness of voice mother's made me jump, I heard her say, 'I want to you fuck me. Oh, yes, Leroy. I want to be *fucked*, to be *fucked!'* she was shouting at him, emphasising the word, *fuck*.

"'Of course you do, my dear, and so you shall be. Come on, let's go up to the bedroom, and then I'll give you a nice long, satisfying fuck.' He put his arm around my mother's waist and they walked towards the stairs.

"I was rooted to the spot, terrified to move, if mother found me, spying on her, watching her and Leroy. If I moved they'd see me, in terror I watched them start up the stairs. Mother leading, Leroy behind, his hands under her skirt, he was rubbing the cheeks of her bum. I closed my eyes, a few more steps and they'd be on the landing.

"The footsteps stopped, I peeped through the banister spars. Mother had stopped climbing the stairs, she'd turned round. I couldn't see her face. Leroy, his head hidden under mother's skirt. In a flash, on my hands and knees I scrambled across the floor into my room leaving the door ajar, and sat on the floor behind it holding my breath.

"I heard them walking across the landing. Leroy, his voice, sounding hoarse, saying, 'I think my dear, your cunt will really love what I'm going give it, will you give my cock what it needs in return. You must tell me. It will make me fuck you much harder and nicer'."

"'Leroy, you can have all you want, I can't wait to feel it buried deep inside my cunt. Please Leroy, fuck me hard, very hard, I want you to make me come all over your cock, not once, but as many times as you can make it happen'."

"Mother sound strange, her words, her voice, husky, hot sounding. I heard the bedroom being opened, then silence. Lying down on my stomach, my head on the floor, looking around the bottom edge the door.

"Mother's bedroom door, wide open. I could see my parent's bed.

"Mother and Leroy, standing at the foot, locked together, mouth on mouth, as they'd been in hall, only this time. Mother had her mouth over, Leroy's, her throat flexing, rubbing her stomach, rolling it from side to side hard against Leroy's.

"A strange unaccountable sensation stabbed through me, I was sweating, my legs seemed to stiffen. Mother shouldn't be in my father's bedroom with Leroy, what she was doing was bad, she was being bad, yet as if in a trance I didn't want her to stop.

"They'd parted, Leroy his back to me took off his clothes, mother I couldn't see. He was a giant, massive all over, legs thick as tree trunks, arms enormously thick, huge bulging biceps on his arms, and covered in thick black hair, every where, on his back, on his shoulders, on his buttocks, tuffs of curly black hair, he reminded me of a gorilla.

"Sitting on the side of the bed, back still towards me, he said to my hidden mother, a little roughly, 'Come over here, and look at the cock that is going to make you scream when I fuck you'."

"Mother came in to view, naked, walking towards Leroy. My mouth opened wide, I could see all of her. The part where her chest swelled, big breasts with a large black circle at the end of each, jutting out of the black circle, a sharp dark brown teat. Her narrow waist, long shapely legs, and most exciting, to me, a bush of black curly, in a line spreading down her navel in thick line before disappearing between her legs.

"My heart pounding, I stared at her, a warm odd feeling spread from inside my stomach, moving slowly downward, flooding into my groin, I had another feeling in my head, totally different. That day, a hurting pain my heart, I didn't understand. Now I know it as a feeling of jealousy. Yes, Lisa, I was jealous. Jealous of Leroy. I wanted to kiss her, I didn't want him to fuck her, even though I didn't know what a fuck was, or how it was done. I *wanted to fuck my own mother, have you any idea what it's like, to think a thing like that, then later find out exactly, what I had wanted to do it with my mother, that day if I could have, if I'd have know how, if I'd had the instrument to do it? My mother, naked that day in the bedroom was the most desirable, most beautiful thing I'd was ever seen in my life. May I rot in hell for saying this, if she stood here naked in this room. **Now I would fuck my own mother senseless.**"*

Lisa, stunned, flabbergasted and frightened now. She loved

sex, all sex, thrived on mens love organs. But not this. Nathan was talking incest, pervert lust. She felt a tender, loving feeling, after she had a good fucking.

But not this, I started this situation, a bleak thought, but true. I'll help him finish the story and that's it. She decided abruptly.

He'd regained control of his inflamed emotions, the mental effort, the inner struggle, etched on his face.

"My mother reaching the sitting Leroy." Talking faster, somewhat agitated he continued. "She threw her hands on her cheeks, eyes wide, she cried, her voice full of admiration and delight, 'Leroy, what a big... I can't believe it. It's... it's huge, it's *enormous*!'"

"Leroy laughed.

"'Yes it's a beauty. Come and sit here on the bed with me and play with it. There now. Oh, your hands are so soft and warm, stroke it gently. Does your husband, Gary, have a cock like this?'"

"I wanted mother to say yes, my father's was even bigger, even though I couldn't see how big it had to be. I waited, with baited breath, her reply, a defeat for me, a more painful one for my absent father.

"'Oh no Leroy, yours is much bigger, so much thicker, and quite a bit longer as well.'"

"'That's the way Ella, you pull the skin right back.' It was the first time he had used her first name. 'That'll make it grow even bigger. You'd like it to be even longer and thicker wouldn't you, my dear, come on, tell me then, that's a good girl.'"

"'Yes please, Leroy, I've never had a big cock like this before, *ever*, you're so big now. I never thought a man's cock could ever be so massive.'"

"'If like it so much. How about giving it a little kiss? Come on, bend your face over it.'"

"'No Leroy,' mother protested, 'I can't, I can't do that, I've never done that, not even to Gary.'"

"'Of course you can, just push your face down that's it, now open your mouth, wider than that. Ah yes, there now, you have it in your mouth now. Doesn't make you feel nice and randy, Ella, my dear? That's lovely, give it a nice sucking. Oh yes like that, just like that. There, you're enjoying the taste now, aren't you?'

"I was frustrated, annoyed, I want to see, to watch my mother sucking a cock more than anything, I was curious, to say the least, to find out how big Leroy's shaft really was.

"My feelings of annoyance turn to anger. My mother, admitting, to Leroy, my father had a much smaller cock made me angry.

"But it was telling him she never had one in her mouth, let alone suck one. She didn't want to do it with my father. But she'd put this old man's in her mouth, because he asked, he never made her, she had willing obeyed, and from the sounds I could hear, was sucking the old man's cock avidly, sucking it like a lollipop, hungrily.

"'Not so much, my dear. You'll make me come in minute and then you'd have to postpone the pleasure of feeling this giant cock in your belly making you come with your love juice all over it.'"

"I heard a wet, popping sound, Leroy rose, turned round and lay on his back on the bed. His size of his cock was unbelievable.

"I know I'm well blessed Lisa. But Leroy's was out of this world, it must have been ten inches long, and so thick, it was as round as a man's wrist."

"She wanted to interrupt Nathan. His description of Leroy's tool. She imagined. The ten inches of hard flesh. The thickness. It's weight in her hand. How a monstrous implement, such as that would fill her insides. She'd want to come on it for days.

"Mother was kneeling beside the bed facing me, her breast's resting on the duvet, her eye's, riveted on Leroy's cock. She had a funny smile on her lips.

"'I've got a condom here if you want me to wear it?' Leroy said. 'But I'd rather have it in the raw, you'll feel my cock inside you much nicer with out one, wouldn't you?'"

"'I always make my husband, Gary, wear one, always,' mother replied, her eye's appeared puffed, still staring at Leroy's rod.

"Standing up, facing me, she stretched out on the bed, lying on her back beside Leroy, his huge frame hiding her from me.

"I wanted see more, slowly standing up behind the door, before peeping my eyes around the side. I could see both of them, the naked bodies, the cock, all my mother's naked body, everything. Lying on her back one hand smoothing Leroy's shaft. Her dark brown hand. Her colour much darker than mine, almost black.

"Her ebony dark hand rubbing up and down on the white flesh was fascinating to watch, the contrast excited me, shivering, I sensed a hardness come into my crutch.

"'Leroy give it to me *Raw*.' Again, she was giving, a gift, a present to him of something she wouldn't give my father, **WHY?**

"'Give it to me *hard, rough,* let me feel every inch of your great solid monster weapon Leroy. **NOW!**' she panted, in a tortured, strangled high-pitched voice. Leroy lifted himself up, straddled my mother. She opened her legs wide, very wide. Involuntary I groaned, a whisper of sound escaped my lips. I could see it. My mother's cunt, before my eyes. Exposed.

"The pink lips, a thin line separating them, it look like a closed mouth, That was it, it was there Leroy's tongue had been. That was why mother had moaned and groaned in hall. Leroy's tongue had been in a different mouth.

"He was kneeling between her legs now, the head of his cock touching the lips of the cunt.

"'I want to chew your teats while you guide me in, come on Ella my dear, open the door of your cunt there's a good girl and let my big cock fill your belly for you.'"

"Mother's hands slide down over her stomach, slender fingers parted the two pink lips, as she pulled them open I saw inside, her flesh, not pink, red, light red and wet looking. The big bulbous head of Leroy's cock slid between her hands, and slowly disappeared from sight, he lowered his head on mother's teats. He was pulling the ends with his teeth, then swallowing part of the teat in his mouth before sucking it, like a baby feeding on its bottle.

"My gaze moved back to my mother's cunt the white shaft of flesh now half way inside my mother. Her head rolled from side to side moaning as she wrapped her arms around Leroy's neck, his buttock's moved as he pushed down on mother. Then he'd pull back, his cock shining wet.

"Every now and again, he stiffened his buttocks, and thrust his hips hard down towards mothers. Every time he did it, her mouth flew open, her eye's rolled and she'd let loose a small scream.

"'Tell me, my dear, are you pleased you decided to let *Old Leroy fuck you*? Is it better than being fucked by Gary? Come on, tell me I'd like to know? Tell me loudly, Ella dear, then you can have all of it, deep inside your nice hot soft pussy.'"

"He stopped moving, looking down at my mother, waiting for an answer, mother moved her arms, put them inside his, slide them down his hairy back on to his bum cheeks, opening her fingers, she dug them into the soft white flesh.

"'Oh yes, Leroy. Thank you for helping me to want you to fuck me. But you've only started to fuck me. Gary has never fucked me like this. Oh, please Leroy, don't make me talk any more, your cock is making me so horny. If you fuck me *now!* Make me come, slam it in hard. Make your monster hurt me, let me coat him with my hot semen, and then I'll ***FUCK YOU!***'"

"This is was how to fuck. A woman and a man naked in bed, the man shoved his cock between the woman's legs into her body through her cunt. Then they held on to each to each other bucking up and down.

"The way mother was groaning, and talking. Leroy the same, it must be very enjoyable, I thought.

"Leroy's shoved his hands under mother's back, he pushed them upwards, his arms disappeared, until his hands were on her shoulders, fingers gripping tight.

"'So you want old Leroy to give you a hard hurting fuck, my dear? You want me to make you come, do you? It's a long time since I've any one as young and pretty as you, my dear, and you've such a sweet tight pussy. I'm going to fuck you so hard you'll lose your mind.'"

"As he finished, he drove down on my mother hard, his shaft slid in to her, deeper than before, his fingers biting into my mother shoulders. He did again and again, faster and faster, harder and harder, every time he slammed into to mother, less and less of his cock could I see, he was sweating profusely, it dripped off his face, ran down his back.

"All the while mother, legs open even wider, moaning, twisting her body upwards, mouth wide, mewling like a wildcat, the cock now almost buried up to the hilt, only a small length of white flesh to be seen.

"Leroy stopped, withdrew his rod until only the bulbous tip was in mother's body. Taking a deep breath, stiffening his buttocks. I saw his back muscles knotting, he dug his fingers into her shoulders then Leroy thrust his body down, viciously hard, onto mother. His massive instrument slide in to her, their bellies slammed together with a loud, vibrating slap, his cock was gone, his ball-bag crushed against mother bum.

"She screamed, a long wailing ear-splitting sound, like a wounded wild animal, the sound so unreal. Her lips curled back, her teeth gritted. I could hear them grinding together.

"Leroy was hurting her, I wanted to shout, 'Leave her alone, you're hurting my mother', but no sound left my lips, my mouth dry, I watched.

"She was shaking uncontrollably, tears ran down her face, eyes closed, mother, in a hoarse husky voice, whispered wildly. 'Leroy, Oh please, again. Please Leroy, do it again, *HARDER!*'"

"He thrust over and over again. Mother unceasingly writhing, moaning, squealing underneath him. Then she began moving, slowly at first, then faster, lifting her body, arching her hips to meet Leroy's plunging root. Her body began arching higher. I could see a gap between her buttocks and the bed, she started pulling him down on her, her hands on his bum, fingers dug deep in his white flesh, dragging Leroy into her.

"She was muttering into Leroy ear. So softly I couldn't hear what she whispered.

"Leroy shook his head, he appeared as if he wouldn't agree with what she was whispering. Then I heard him say.

"'You want old Leroys cock more than once, do you, my dear? Well now if I it give to you the way you want it. Will you give to me the way I want it. Ella my dear?' he asked slyly."

"'Oh yes Leroy, anything,' mother laughingly agreed. He reached down with his shovel like hands, grabbed mothers ankles, lifted her legs, force them wide apart, pushed them backwards until mother laid with only her head on the bed, her legs bent so far back her knee's rested beside her ears.

"Leroy leaned forward, body arched like a bow, his cock hard resting inside mother.

"'Now Ella my dear, I will fuck you again, and after I've made you come. I just might fuck you in your lovely round soft ass.'"

"He thrust himself in to mother faster and faster, the full length of his cock going in and out of mother furiously.

"She was inciting him to punish her body, begging him, pleading for more, talking continuously.

"'Oh yes Leroy, again please Leroy harder, aggh, yes, oh! oh yes! Fuck me Leroy. Aw, aw, don't stop! Hurt me! Oh God yes, yes, yes again, Leroy, please, Leroy.'"

"She was not my mother, not now. I didn't see or recognise her. The bucking and gyrating twisting naked coloured woman, underneath a bull like old man white man, incoherent in mind and body.

"Louder, almost shouting in desperation, her garbled words, beseeching Leroy, never stopped.

"'Hurt me Leroy, hurt me, aggh, aggh, oh, oh, oh, yes, like that again, more, more, now, make me, awww, awww, uh, uh, aw, oh, oh, harder, give me your cock, Leroy, faster, faster, hurt me, oh please Leroy.'"

"Her face was twisted like a gargoyle, screaming now.

"'I'm coming Leroy, help me, hurt me, fuck me harder, fuck. Meeee aggh, awww, lovely, yes, yes, Oh! Oh! Oh! Ram it in my cunt, Leroy, agggh, agggh, aw. Make ME COME! I'll do anything you want, anything, I promise, Leroy. If you make me come now! I'm coming I'm, Oh God! Ohhh, Leroy, fuck me, fuck, yes, Leroy like that. NOW, LEROY, I'M COMINGGGG, YES MY LEROY, AGGGGHH, AGGGGHHH, OW, OW, AW, AW, OH! OH! AGGGGHHH. THANK YOU, LEROY, I MEANT IT YOU CAN FUCK ME ANY WAY YOU WANT TO, LEROOOOOOY!'

"Mother collapsed trembling, her legs flopped back on the bed, she lay there quivering, gasping for breath. Leroy lifted himself off her body, his cock wasn't so big looking, it was slimy

58

wet, white coated, I saw flecks of blood mixed in the whiteness.

"As I watched their thrashing bodies, white on black, their movements, the sound of mother's pleading, the wild exclamations, the screams. Leroy's rutting driving cock. The whole scene affected my body and mind, it was like I was in a trance. I became filled with a strange, weird feeling, my groin throbbed, without realising my hand was inside my jeans, I began to rub my little cock, it grew bigger the more mother shrieked and moaned. I rubbed it with my fingers faster and faster, my legs went weak, a funny shaking kind of feeling came into my belly, the rubbing changed to a lovely warm feeling in my cock, it grew stronger and stronger, just at it reached bursting point, mother stopped moaning and twitching.

"Oh, Lisa, I've try to blank out that day ever since, pretend it never happened, make myself believe it was a bad dream. It only works for a while, then the confusion in the mind returns. and always when I make love. Today, with you, Lisa, that was third time, the two others, I felt nothing for, I treated them badly, after, much worse than I did you."

Lisa, heard every word in silence, enraptured by his graphic oration. his description of his mother, her words, her movements, her body. Leroy's massive shaft. She had come, not big climax, just a tiny release, as Nathan, head thrown back, repeated his mother's, screaming, begging, cries at the height of orgasm. She shivered, not with cold, with jealous envy, with a desire, a lusting hunger to be fucked as Ella had been fucked beyond reason. In to mindless raging passion, on a man's erected shaft of flesh.

Control your body, she bullied her mind. Fight your instincts, you're ripe, hot, randy and ready. Forgetting the pleasure's of the flesh.

She thought, no it wasn't a thought that entered her mind, an inspiration, yes it was an inspired realisation.

Nathan, dare she be right. No never, he couldn't want to, or did he, if she was right, should she tell him, what if he didn't understand?

"What if told you?" he interrupted her tumbling indecision. "Mother kept her promise, she mounted Leroy, when she'd finished, with her mouth, made him hard again, I watched mother willingly allow him to do exactly what he intimated he might do her. He fucked from behind, in her ass. She was as eager for it, as Leroy." He released her hands, what a relief, he'd squeezed so hard, for so long, she had pins and needles in her fingers.

Lisa had a problem, two in fact, Nathan, which thought she could handle. The other more complex. She wanted his virility, his flesh. But not his mental hang-up. Yet she felt they shared one common feeling. *Jealousy.* She was jealous of his mother, she felt jealous, because it wasn't her flesh that received the monstrous instrument. Nathan's jealousy he'd planted in his own mind. He wanted to be the man. He wanted his mother to love him, to offer the love to him, she had showered on the man Leroy.

"I think you've told me enough, Nathan," she decided abruptly. "You know what bothers you." Tell him – *now* – straight to the point, if he didn't like it, so be it.

"Your problem is not what you witnessed, it is not what your mother did, or your father hanging himself." The boy, looking at her, a shocked expression on his face.

"You can't live with the sight of your mother in the arms of that man, you wanted it to be you, and her loving every minute he was fucking her, you know why, Nathan? Don't shake your head at me boy!" Stopping for a few seconds, Lisa, telling herself, with grim determination, dominate him, your older, treat him like an erring child. Taking her own sound advice, with a blunt forth righteousness she never thought she possessed, told him very firmly, *"Because you wanted to be that man, but you couldn't, you never could be, she was your mother, you've known that ever since that day, your problem with women is in your own mind. You imagine you're fucking your mother, but they don't talk and act like she did that day do they, Oh no! Nothing like her at all are they, and when you've finished, you remember it all. Don't you? Your ashamed of yourself, yet you're raging inside because you can't fuck like that man, Leroy, the women don't scream do they Nathan. They don't beg you for more cock. And you can not live with the idea that he made your mother beg him, and what screws you up even more, worst of all is, your mother, the one person you've loved more than any one, or anything else in this world, allowed an old man fuck her out of her mind, and she, and this is the crunch, Nathan,* **SHE LOVED HIM FOR DOING IT!** *That's what you can't except, isn't it, Nathan?"*

She'd been brutal, honest. The boy's mouth gaped wide, eyes blazing, his face, contorted half anger half in anguish. Lisa, she was frightened now, she saw the violence in his face, he was going to hit her, now!

Shrinking back, closing her eyes, stiff, tensing herself, anticipating the punch to come.

Nothing happened, nothing. Lisa tentatively cringing, opened her eyes slowly. The boy, sat head down, chin on his chest, crying.

Lisa, ashamed of her words now, ashamed of herself, this is what happens. Oh yes, when, in her desire for cock, instead of kindness and a little subtle use of body and mind. Just because some totally unknown woman, if the boy's story was true, and she had no reason to doubt it, had received a huge cock. Something she desired to feel inside her, her jealous thoughts, her need for such a cock. Lisa had, she knew, with malice, a great deal of it, had taken her spite out on the now crying boy.

Wrapping her arms around him, cuddling him into her chest, crooning. softly, her head on his, said, "I'm so sorry, Nathan." Lisa, close to tears herself, mind in agony wanting so badly to help him, "Be strong now, hold me tight, Nathan." she encouraged him tenderly as his arms closed around her waist. His bare hands came in contact with her naked hips. The robe was open, it must have happened when she moved forward to cuddle him. He stiffened as the fingers touched her skin, then relaxed, his fingers resting on her warm flesh then moved gently down over her hip, down her upper thigh, then back up, slowly, up, up, stopping as it closed over her breast.

Nathan, felt his anger subsiding, the lovely soft smooth skin touching his fingertips soothing away his rage, this was a beautiful lovely shaped woman his fingers were caressing. The silkiness of her flesh excited him like no other woman ever had, he felt a stirring in the groin, his phallus was gently extending. Lisa felt a tremor in the youths spine, held her breath, not wanting to disrupt his thoughts. Think nothing, do nothing, let him find himself.

Lisa, unmoving, felt his hands roaming over her skin, the hands pushed the robe off her shoulders, she gently slackened her arms grip on his neck. She felt cool air on her now naked breasts. A hand enclosed a nipple, caressed gently, then squeeze the breast. The lips, sweet soft lips, closed hard on the swelling nipple.

Nathan heard the sharp intake of breath as he closed his teeth on the hardening nipple, his cock quivered. God he wanted this woman, her words, her body, had almost erased his desires and thoughts of his mother from his flesh and mind. Replaced by a hunger, a powerful need to fuck her again.

His other hand roughly untied the robe, touched the warm skin below the navel down it went through her pubic hair, over the mount of the pelvis, one finger caressed the moist pucker of her sex-lips, pausing of a brief instant before he slipped it deep inside her pussy.

Nathan's heart beat thumping in his ears, his flesh ever lengthening, this naked woman, a stranger wanted him to be fuck her, wanted him as a man and lover.

This time he can seduce me, a little bit like Leroy had his mother. It would add something to both their pleasures. She hopefully concluded, decided hastily, this time she wouldn't help him, Nathan's finger inside the warm flesh sending fingers of desire into his mind.

"Move your legs, Lisa, my dear, I want to give more, come on now there's a good girl," he asked quietly. Sitting upright, back against the lounger, legs outstretched she smiled at him. The smile mimics the smile he seen on his mother's face that afternoon, and she reacted to the instructions just like his mother. "Open your legs, My dear," he coaxed softy, holding his breath. Instantly she complied, he inserted a second finger, rubbing her clitoris with his thumb at the same time.

Lisa writhed with pleasure. Her mind instinctive grasping, at this moment in time, to him, she was mother. He was Leroy. Oh well, if a little play-acting will incite him greater heights of passion, why not, she unhesitating decided.

Nathan bent his head, kissed the warm full mouth, her hungry tongue slipping into his mouth, he probed her wet pussy. Lisa moved on the fingers, thrusting her hips to meet the fingers on the way in, the intruding digits of flesh moved slowly, easy, nicely enjoyable.

Nathan lift his lips away from her mouth, grinned into her face.

"You want my tongue, don't you, Lisa, you have to tell me, I like it when a woman asks me using dirty words," he softly insinuated.

She found it so difficult not to orgasm, her eyes caught sight of the huge swollen bulge in his jeans. *No, No, Not yet!* Beg him, just like his mother did Leroy, trembling, her vagina ever wetter, she panted in a hoarse voice, she wanted to feed his incestuous lusts, inflame his minds desire's.

"Oh yes please, Nathan, give me your tongue, all of it, my cunt is burning for you, make me come, Nathan. Please! I will *come on your tongue* if you want me to."

That should do the trick, Lisa knew, after she lead him to the bedroom, and then she'd get all loving she desired.

Chapter 4

His mouth inches from her flesh so close she felt his panted breath warming her thighs. Nathan slipped his hands under her buttocks, digging his opened fingers into the soft rounded orbs of flesh. He touched her softly with his tongue where his fingers had rested earlier, used his hands to raised her buttocks, lifting her pussy up to his lips, he smelt the aroma of her body, tasted her sweetness before invading her flesh.

The wet tongue so delicious on the lips of her pussy, its entry sheer bliss to her vagina, with grim resolution she dampened her lust for orgasm. She had shared her flesh and desire with many lovers since her divorce, without exception, all middle-aged. Never with a youth so young, she could not believe she was actually making love with teenager, cradle snatching, would this new experience change her needs. Was he just another lover? Another cock, somehow she didn't think it was that simple.

Nathan watched her face as he tongued her flesh, saw an occasional blink of her eyes when ever he increased the rhythmic thrust of the tongue, she was some woman, hotter than hell, sex hungry enough to satisfy every desire or fantasy a man might have.

Lisa shivered; he wasn't just another lover, not with a shaft like he'd been blessed with, an instrument she'd want over and over again. She realised her sexual needs. One good taste of young hard erect flesh thrusting with a vigour into her vagina, a sensation never enjoyed before, never again would a middle-aged cock satisfy her.

Then, unexplainable, a ghost from the past, it made her heart weep. The memory of Eric James Cheats, flooded her thoughts. Eric. The boy who touched her heart like no other. She had loved him. Not even David the man she'd married, had she felt such love. Never like Eric.

The agony, the tears, the anguish and pain. When, because of her lack of conviction, faith in herself. And him. She inflicted a mortal wound into her heart and soul. Now the licking tongue, the lips caressing her warm cunt. Was like her feelings for Eric. One of deep love. The only difference to Lisa. Eric was the love of her heart. The young man, head bobbing between her sticky wet demanding thighs. She felt the same love for him, but the feeling of love came from her cunt.

Lisa, somehow had to overcome the terrible hurtful feelings running through her mind, she lost Eric then suffered. Lost David and suffered. Have Nathan fuck her and suffer again? Not on your life Lisa, she reprimanded her own thoughts. If you have the boy inside you, enjoy it. To hell with the result. Then find yourself another toy-boy to fuck, whenever the need arises.

"Nathan I'm coming," she said trying to talk calmly. Her hands on his black hair, smoothing it back over his head.

He looked into her bright shining blue eyes. For some unexplainable reason he didn't want to make love as if he was Leroy. I think she'll give me much as Nathan. She's a warm hearted woman, who knows what she wants. And to fuck with Leroy and my mother. This is one naked lady who will get fucked by me and I'll share that pleasure with no man.

"Would you like to finish what you've started in bed?" Her words cutting off his thoughts. She sounded anxiously, her mouth softening nervously.

His reply, with lips sliding up over her stomach. "Listen, Mrs Knott, I've never had a…" speaking low, faltering, searching for courage.

"As old as you, you're older than my…"

"Mother Lisa," as he paused, finished it for him.

"You don't have to apologise, or explain, just you forget past and be yourself." a vexed edge to her tone.

"I offered it, so you took what was offered. Right? Come on, boy, do you want me again?" bullying him now. "Because I want you, Nathan, more than you will ever know!"

He became alive at her words, his mouth on hers, hands

touching, caressing her everywhere, thighs, nipples, back, her bum cheeks, revel in her flinching when he touched then ran a finger between her bum cheeks pushing against the entrance to her ass.

He pulled her to her feet. Lisa stroked his bulging crutch, robe at her feet, naked, his arm around her waist, the other hand rubbing her vagina he walked her towards the bedroom. Thank God for that. No more Mother, no more Leroy. Lisa, her vagina tinkling with anticipation, with need for the big long thick black ebony cock she was aggravating inside the cloth.

Once they reached the bed, Lisa, lay down, legs apart, waiting, licking her lips. No shyness now. Oh no. The tee shirt, pulled over his head, tossed on the floor. Breathing, in quick gasps, fingers on his belt, undone, the zip down. "Come, Nathan", she begged feverishly, "Please hurry. Oh yes, now, now. Let me see," her mind in a fever.

His flesh hidden as he bent forward removing the last of his clothes, he stood, looking down at her. The cock, beautifully hard, an erect column of flesh, it's shining head pulsating, before her eyes. Lisa arms wide, an invitation, offering up everything, he wanted.

Tenderness in waves swept through Lisa, heart and soul, as he laid down beside her cradling her in arms. She groaned in ecstasy as his cock, came to rest on her naked thigh, burning hot, a living weapon of flesh.

His arms encircled her, she rested her head on his hard muscled chest, lay there listening to the beat of his quickening heart. She had such a feeling of power, a wondrous overwhelming sensation, she had overcome his deeply rooted sexual phobias. Now all his young desire and lust would run free.

Nathan's hand moved down her back, under the orbs of buttocks. His voice trembling, huskily he cried.

"Give me your mouth. Oh, God, Lisa, suck me, Give me head."

Not understanding at first, then, slithering down to his hips. Lisa gentle dragged her fingernails down the stalk, she was captivated by the eager response, such a magnificent young implement, so vibrant in flesh, so hungry.

Tickling the glands, before, with forefinger and thumb, ringed, grip taut, she slide it down the thick root, down slowly to the black pubic hair, where it erupted from. The hips rose to meet her fingers, a drop of liquid glistened in the tiny aperture. Moving her head closer, she glorified over his cock seeking her lips. It would taste, like nectar, so sweet, so fresh. Her tongue, a flicker, quick, like a snake, extracting the bead of juice, he shivered luxuriously.

"You're incredible, Lisa, better than anyone." Nathan groaned hoarsely, she had no need to speak, her answer was to his manhood. Wrapping her tongue tip around the groove beneath the bulbous head, as her mouth enclosed the cock, absorbing it, greedily, as she sucked the cock it throbbed against her lips. It's taste, a salty nutty flavour, shivering with the sensual transmission of the pulsating muscle hard flesh between her lips.

Nathan's hands were on her head, his urging unnecessary, his throbbing hard flesh was hers now, he ached for her to swallow it, to consume, every pumping throbbing inch. She closed her lips, tight, sucking feverishly, breathing through her nose, for as long as she could hold it. Deep, retreating, slowly upward, back up the shaft, mindful that this young cock, being so frenzied ministrated he would come and it was to soon, much, much too soon.

Nathan, with the driving demand of masculine need, turned her, bodily. His rod stayed in her mouth. Lisa was overjoyed, she wanted – no needed – to feel and taste his come. Her sensuous desires rose, his mouth found her clitoris, he was going to... shaking, her vagina afire, give her what she had wanted in the lounge. A gift, her reward, as he began fucking against her face, groaning through her closed lips, admitting a low humming sound, his come would be hers, trapped inside her closed lips.

Lisa spread her loins, offering, opening herself to him, offering willing more than she ever offered to any man. Mouth coated into wetness, his lips gaping wide, then closed in a bite of loving sharpness, on to her tender soft flesh. Gripped in mutual rapture of passion and pleasure, in unison they began fucking hard into each others willing mouths.

She let him feel the sharp edge of her teeth, a gentle yet

cruel pressure, sinking into the hard flesh, he in return, nibbling her most sensitive part, clitoris quivering. She was in orgasm, he had the ability to interpret, her state, translating her bodies needs into ecstasy. Riding her moving loins, Nathan pushed, with vigour into her open mouth. Mouth bruised, yet with tenderness, she would not surrender his cock, not now, the throbbing flesh, a pulse then the expansion of his shaft, now the ejaculation was imminent. When the come flooded her mouth, a taste not unlike salty sticky seawater, she gave in to a moan of insatiable lustful craving.

The cock was softening, her vagina had no feelings of warm lips. Suddenly, overjoyed, his lips kissed her bruised mouth, as his cock, half-erect, stabbed at the entrance of her love tube. His youth, his eagerness to fuck, the exuberance of the young. Lisa felt a moment of pleasure, his immaturity, his rawness, her loving arms and cunt, would exploit his inexperience. Reaching a hand between their bodies, to guide Nathan's cock to her opening, where he desired to be. The part inert tool, bending in useless thrusts against her flesh.

Clasping both hips, pressing his body, with both hands down on hers. Lisa, controlling her urges, whispered lovingly in his ear, "Be slow, Nathan, my love, take your time, nothing matters now, only our pleasure."

She started to move under him, at her pace, her hands, fingers spread wide on the rippling muscles of his buttocks, slowly coaxing him to slow down, and lengthening his stroke.

Her rhythm transmitted to Nathan, rolling her thighs into his, settled under him. It was deliciously satisfying to be fuck so sensually she could feel the softened flesh pushing, withdrawing, then pushing again, just inside the folds of the tender lips of her wet pussy. The movement building a hot feeling of fire, ever increasing in her already inflamed clitoris.

She could be. No, not could be, would be content forever with this feeling.

Then, a minute pulse, for a mere split second, inside her, followed by one more, something beyond her wildest dreams, his cock, growing in size, hardening, beginning with each stroke it slipped deeper, penetrating inch by inch deeper.

Abruptly, Nathan, lifted up on to his elbows, looking into her face, and Lisa, by instinct, knew, as if their joined flesh welded both bodies as one, a telepathic understanding of thought, he wanted her to lie unmoving, impassive, as he fucked her.

He wanted to dominate her, enslave to his youth, she, an older woman, must submit to him. Lisa, opened her thighs wider, his pace his rhythm now, slow and long, all the way out, all the way in. deep in. A constant rhythmic thrust, tirelessly, he fucked her. The beat of his stomach against hers, the cock seeming ever harder, ever deep, the fountain of inexhaustible youthful strength. Nathan could ride her for hours.

He smiled sweetly down at her, beads of sweat on his forehead; she knew he was, once more, relishing, gloating, the in knowledge, of what he could do to the Old Slut.

Lisa was concentrating on steady thrust and drive, drawing the feel of his flesh, the sensations in her now pulsing vitals, her vagina's spreading quivers, taking them down deep, storing it as her being stiffened for a new orgasm.

Nathan increased his stroke.

"What about it, Old Slut?" gasping for breath, he asked. "Ever had a cock like this one, **ever?**"

"No Nathan," as breathless as he was, gasping, "Oh, my God, no, *Never!*"

"You like being fucked, don't you?" he whispered hoarsely, "How do you like your fucking now?" Noticing his sweat dripping on to her breasts. "You love it. How many mens cock have you had, *Old Slut?*"

"Just one! Yours, only yours," she gasped.

"Don't you lie to me. You've had dozens of cocks in your old cunt. You lying *Old Slut,* admit it, I'm right, aren't I?"

"Yes!" she replied, "But never one like yours. Oh, God, not as good, never like yours."

She had to reply in words, as her body was answering his, she was his, possessed, now he owned her. Why he needed to degraded her, debase her, was it something born out of his thoughts for his mother, making her pay him, his mother's penance.

The name, *Old Slut,* to him, was her acknowledgement of

his youthful, male, dominating supremacy. Now it matter little, all she wanted was to be fucked, now and forever, over and over again by Nathan, once it finished, then it was over, not for today, every day over. This day, *Now…* was all she might ever have, of loving his rod of flesh.

Nathan went on and on, time lost all meaning, his ever moving flesh inside her rampant, sliding deep, he wanted to make her tremble continuously, he wanted to hear her moaning, feel her voice demand and beg for more, as his muscle hard body relentlessly fucking her willing body.

Lisa, flesh sexually alive like never before, entwined herself in the sweatiness of warm flesh, wallowing in wet slapping sounds before his body became glued to hers.

Nathan, with all the power of his immortal youth, reached a new height in his lust to fuck her glorious body. He'd changed, no longer insulting her, heightening his intensity. Unaware of her as a person with a mind, body or soul, he was using her, in his feverish need to reach an orgasm, she was an object, a female recipient for his ejaculation.

No longer, Lisa, Mrs Knott, *"Old Slut",* she was just woman, a pussy, a cunt, a woman with a beautiful, hot, warm, love channel.

He had regrets, no guilt, she accepted it, to have a man abandon himself utterly, to the flesh, her flesh.

Lisa loved him for that surrender, she was to him only a cunt, to her he was only a Cock. How many men, had any of her lovers, including David, Eric, Mark, or Dean, achieved such a level of forgetfulness as a man, separating himself from all reason.

Consumed, immersed, her body totally enwrapped in the act of achieving orgasm, not individually, together, a collective expunging of sexual body liquids. To Lisa, the ultimate overpowering satisfaction of every fuck.

Nathan groaned, quietly, in his throat, a strange almost strangled cry for help. He beginning to weaken, he had, after all, come twice earlier, and then again in her mouth, copiously, each time, his youthful body knew its limits, He didn't.

The urgency of his flesh, no less ridged, he drove harder,

the stroke shortened. Again his shaft of pleasure, a burning arrow of fire in her vagina, it felt as if he'd reached the peak ejaculation. Lisa anticipating the flood of semen. She shuddered, the realisation, a twist of cramp, inside her.

His face, contorted, twisted, ugly looking, he was on the point of failure.

Lisa sensed a stab of understanding that Nathan in spite of everything needed her to give him more of herself, than he could give her. She cleaved to him, to nurse, to caress from his throbbing weapon his imprisoned semen, cupping a hand on his neck, the other on the base of his spine just above his thrashing buttocks, driving her body upwards, crying out in glorious agony, as his pelvic bone crash into hers. Lost, as never before in passion, she loved him with her entire body. How she reached such a degree of consummation of her body and his, she knew not. Maybe? it was the thought, that his failure would have been hers, or vice-versa. His naked desire to ejaculate had been born in of her flesh, a woman's flesh.

Her insides gripped his instrument, holding in the swollen glands of his cock for a brief second, arching her buttocks, lifting her pussy milking his penis. A small pulsation began, sliding ever faster into her now, the root swelled, Nathan, moaning as he came, not in a wild urgent gush, as before, an almost leisurely flood of warm molten come coating her vagina.

Lisa hadn't come with him. Being able, for those short minutes, for the first time, to overcoming his youthful male domination, when he needed her more than any woman before, the sensation of being, not an older woman, an equal in flesh as gratifying as a climax.

"Oh, God, I thought I'd never come," he croaked, gasping for breath.

"What did you do to me?"

Lisa was satisfied, warmed by his words. Then he moved, his hardness subsiding, the softening flesh being withdrawn, she placed a hand on his chest, rushing her words said," Wait a minute *Please*! Wait."

Nathan, with effort, stalled his cock withdrawal, softening but *there*. She tightened the muscles of her vagina around his receding shaft, pulling in her stomach muscles, gently she masturbated the flaccid flesh inside her. He lay on her unmoving, his lips on her neck, dry against her wet sweat covered skin.

Lisa, from experience, had learned over the last few years, when the fire need to be rekindled in middle-aged men, how to use and flex her pussy on a shrinking cock.

Nathan, bless him, she thought, as he slowly harden under her ministrations, slipping both hands over the cheeks of his bum, before pulling gently him into her, synchronising her slippery wet cunt masturbation of his rod, with her movements of his buttocks. The cock re-erected slowly, deliciously it swelled, ever growing deeper and deeper.

Lisa, moaning, bit his shoulder, her mouth tasting his salty sweat. She changed her body movements, still milking his flesh, sliding her vagina along the bar of flesh, her orgasm building. A knotted twist in her vitals began screaming for release.

Lisa, her brief moment of supremacy, so uplifting, evaporated. She wanted this young flesh, warming her insides, so badly again. **Now!**

"Fuck me, Nathan. Fuck me, Oh, please, Nathan," she cried out, her frustration intensifying Nathan, his arms around her waist, rolled over on to his back, his cock never leaving her loving clasp. "I don't have the strength, Lisa, not after last time," his words, spoke not as an apology, angrily, as if annoyed.

That she, Lisa, an old woman, could still need him to fuck her again.

She had, in her urgency for orgasm, damned herself. This wasn't a male of her age. Nathan, the youth in her vagina. She had bruised his most sensitive emotion, his *ego*!

Already she sensed, it wasn't a feeling, it was a rejection of her body's affection, his warmth and ardour, perceptively cooling, his shaft hardness subtly, tangibly softening.

Lisa rolled her hips, panic sweeping through her, if she didn't achieve ejaculation, to surrender her come, over this hard cock. The thought, to her, terrifying. Soothe his ego, massage it, rebuilt it in Nathan, make him believe he is still the superior being. What was she demanding, a release, her words.

Her every movement on his body, her cunt sliding on his

root, everything she did. He, Nathan, had elicited every act she committed, with his large cock. Her need for him, his body, the fucking he had bestowed on her. Bestowed, not given.

Lisa, still wanking his weapon with her cunt. She liked the word bestowed, made it appear, the shaft, his shaft he had given her a gift, a man's gift, to her, an older woman.

"Nathan, my sweet boy, don't be angry with me," her mouth whispering the words huskily in his ear, "I can't help myself, you're so strong, so virile, so masculine, your big cock drives my flesh wild," pushing down on his rod, emphasising her words.

"I have to receive more of your flesh, it's not me, Nathan, it's you with your beautiful, thick, long hard cock, it's making me and my body want to please you."

Lisa, moved her legs, till, no longer her body on the youth's, hands on his chest, she knelt on her knees, looking down into his face. One leg at a time, manoeuvring herself until with soles of her feet firmly planted on the mattress, she squatted over his hard cock.

She wanted him speak, just a word, just one small word. He just looked at her, dumbly. She couldn't hold her orgasm back much longer; the semen had become an ever swelling knot of agony inside of her.

Lisa, control of her need weakening, it wasn't just weakening. She realised it was evaporating completely.

Slowly, pushed one hand down on the muscled hard chest, lifting her thighs, reaching behind her with her free hand she grasped the swollen weapon, wrapping her fingers around the base, lifting her thighs a touch more, placing the pulsing head against the lips of her pussy. She slid her vagina down the hard of flesh, the walls of her wet love tunnel pushing the outer skin on his cock down the shaft, held it for a split second, her cunt filled with flesh, her mind ablaze for release, she whispered, filling her voice, with all the love and tenderness she could muster, beseechingly she cried, *for you my beautiful young lover. Nathan, I give my love my body, my cunt, to you and your magnificent... massive...* **COCK!** As the last letter, dying on her lips, drawing in a deep breath. Lisa drove her thighs viciously, hard, fast up and down the ridged *cock.* Swallowing completely into her cunt, it bit deep, her bum cheeks smashing into his testicles, their covering of pubic hair, digging into her already sore labia lips, the weapon of flesh, a burning blade, slashing, parting all flesh before it, stopping, it seemed to hit an invisible wall in her depths, for an instant, bend, then cut through the wall, hurting, burning, a hot scorching stab at the core of her very being.

The ambrosial lusciousness, of her cunt so utterly filled, a cunt pulsating with a mixture, of pain, pleasure, carnal sensuality, it had never been touched with before. She lost her mind, all thoughts, wiped away... nothing in her mind except cock, coming and *fucking*.

Mindless, Lisa, mouth wide open, eyes closed. She shivered in her lust for flesh, riding the massive invader faster, the cock burned with the friction of her stroke, her cunt touching his balls, then the bulbous head was at the entrance of her vagina, in an instant, she buried the exposed weapon down to it's source. She wanted to come, her mouth opening, a guttural groaning sound omitted from deep in her throat.

Nathan hands where over her hips gripping her buttocks, assisting and increasing the speed of her moving loins. Where he found the strength from he had no idea, this sweating woman writhing above him, her pussy swallowing his swollen rampant cock, her driving sensual plunging thighs had unleashed sensations within his mind so strong he pushed her down savagely, his hips ramming upwards, impaling her vagina onto his throbbing column of flesh. Lisa, the knot inside seeming to engulf his raging, driving shaft. She heard sounds, not words, indecipherable, garbled, groaning, moaning, she was coming. She felt her body swell, puff up. Nathan, held her, his cock, barely touching her fluttering, slimy, wet opening, tantalising, his hands, still on her bum cheeks, the fingers seeking the orifice of her ass. She could not wait, not now. Nathan, could, oh yes, the youth had recovered, renewed his vigour, with her bodies prompting. She never failed in resurrecting a man's cock for one final, wild orgasm. Lisa, filled with pride, gave herself to her body's lust laden needs.

"Nathan give me your cock..." *Now! Make me come, no*

one ever made me come the way you can, my love, no one!

The words galvanised him, simultaneously his thighs drove into her, he pulled her downward on his cock, as his shaft, slammed into her willing grasping cunt. He felt possessed, in the grip of an overpowering physical urge to make the heaving sweating woman scream, his finger penetrated her rectum, screaming, her semen, like a tidal wave, of hot burning liquid, flowed in waves, over his embedded hurting cock. Lisa, her body twitching, convulsed in a depraved intoxicated pleasure of ejaculation, so intense. She thought she had lost her mind, shouting and screaming at the heaving body beneath her.

"DON'T STOP, MY BOY. THATS IT FUCK ME, OH, YES... OH GOD ALMIGHTY! WHAT A COCK! AGAIN, NATHAN, HARDER, AW, AW, OH, MMM, THAT'S IT LOVER, HURT ME, BURY YOUR COCK DEEPER, AGAIN, DEEPER, AW! OH, AWO, AW, MORE, OH, OH, OH, OUCH! YES! OH YES! MORE, NATHAN, OW, OH, OH, OH, AGAIN LIKE THAT, OH, PLEASE JUST LIKE... COME WITH ME, UH, UH, AW, AW! NATHAN FUCK ME! FUCK MEEEEEE! OH YES I CAN FEEL YOU. YOU'RE COMING! OH MY DEAR LORD! YOU'RE SO BIG! FILL ME – FILL MY CUNT WITH YOUR COME! YES! NOW! YOUR FILLING MEEEE! OH YES! OH YES MY BABY! ONCE MORE DRIVE YOUR BEAUTIFUL WEAPON. LET ME FEEL IT ALL, DRAW THE LAST DROP OF JUICE FROM MY BODY! OH YES NATHAN FINGER MY ASS! OH LOVER, NOW DO IT! NOW! AWWWWW, UHHHH, AWWWWW, EEECAAH, AH, AH, OHH, OH, OH, UMMMM, AWWWWWWW."

Lisa, clawing at the chest below, drawing blood, demented with lust and blinding passion. She had never sunk into such depths of degradation in pursuit of pleasure. Never before. And she, for the first time, a fleeting seed of thought coming to mind, but not the last, she had bared her soul, on the massive cock. Her words, her body, her flesh had ignited Nathan, inflamed him, raised him and his cock, to an even greater height of male sexual power.

She was having the most magnificent, body twisting, pleasurable, longest, most copious, *ejaculation of her entire life.*

The last spurt of semen from Nathan coating her vagina walls. Lisa, deep inside, felt a tiny globule of semen, as if trapped, left behind to weak in its birth to slip over the pinnacle of her passion.

Lisa, desirous of absolute satisfaction, weak, sore, gasping for oxygen. She lifted her cunt up the wet sticky shaft of flesh. Nathan lay still, eyes closed, chest heaving.

Reaching the tip, drawing a deep breath, closing her eyes, tight. She drove her vagina down the rod of flesh. The tiny remains of her semen, swept over the precipice, washing over the cock. Then a blackness swept over her.

Lisa, opening her eyes, groaned, disorientated, faint. She was lying on her back. Nathan, one arm around her neck, the other across her stomach, his now flaccid, wet, slimy cock, resting against her hip.

"You all right, Lisa?" he asked, smugly. She turned to look into his face. "You're some woman, you really are something else," he said fondly, "I never thought I'd be able to finish that last one."

Lisa, the lethargy of such a sweet satisfying completion, in mind and flesh, "No need to talk about it Nathan my sweet, not after it's over," she replied. "Don't talk about it, my love, just leave it be."

He slid his hand across her belly, resting on her wet sweaty stomach, his voice suddenly rough. "Now you listen, Old Slut!"

Lifting her head, looking him directly into his eyes, "Yes, you have something to say?"

He averted his eyes, turning away. "Oh, it's nothing."

She reached over, stroking his cheek, tenderly, "Oh you sweet boy, Nathan. You thought I was too old, passed my prime, didn't you? When I showed you my pussy in those tiny white panties. You'd just wanted a nice, quick fuck, and I'd be grateful, and you'd get to hell out of my house. You really believed an 'Old Slut' like me wouldn't be much of fuck. Didn't you, my love?"

His embarrassment obvious, Nathan stammered an apology. "I'm sorry, really I am, I never meant to... to..." desperately he searched for the right words.

"You mustn't hold it against me, I couldn't help myself, you made me lose my senses, I said the words instinctively."

"I don't," she said tenderly, "I liked it, to tell you the truth. *I loved it*," smiling, a chuckle in her voice. "I've heard it said, lovers in height of passion, achieve a greater affection for each other, because of their lust and out bursts of words."

"I'm not so sure," he replied with sullen expression on his face. "I don't know much about that sort of talk," his tone, sullen, like his face.

Lisa touched by the honest confession, her mind as satisfied as her body. A feeling of regret came over her. He would leave, never to return. Made more, her unease as he put his feet on the floor. "Won't you stay a little longer, my love," she hopefully inquired.

"Sorry, ma'am, got to earn a dollar and I'm way behind schedule," grinning, a mischievous twinkle in his eye, "My Old Slut, had me working on a more enjoyable service and it took a lot longer than I ever expected." laughing as he finished talking.

Picking up his pants, started to dress. Lisa opening her legs. He had said 'My' now she was a possession of his, like a car, a dog, his alone, a personal property. She wanted it to be just that.

Standing, looking down at her naked shape, eyes drinking in the flesh he invaded, loved, fucked. He wanted more, more time to absorb the heat she had generated within his flesh. More of the pleasure his cock had enjoyed within her sweet grasping cunt. He knew he return.

She wanted. *Him* so desperately again. Tomorrow, every day. A lump in her throat, doubt in her mind, his story in the lounge, his twisted emotions, she had to know the truth.

"Nathan, what you said in the lounge, did you mean all that about your mother and the part when you said you wanted to fuck her senseless."

She stiffened, tensing her mind and body, anticipating an angry outburst of rage.

He looked at the floor; voice almost a whisper sounding, bashful, ashamed, shy. "Yes, when I was kneeling, between your thighs, my tongue in your flesh, you became her. But when with your body, you started to… to fuck me, asking, no telling me how to love you, I wanted you. So badly, but not as my mother, you made feel powerful, so much of a man." His shoulders seem to tremble. She wondered. Was he crying?

This youth so strong in his manhood, so sensitive in nature? A wave of motherly tenderness touched her. She wanted to hold him, ease his pain and her own.

Abruptly, his eyes, features locked in hard look of anguish. Stared in her face. He appeared locked in combat with his mind, lips moving, mouthing soundless word. Tears in his eyes held back by sheer will power. A torrent of words flew out of what sounded, like his tortured soul. "*I fucked you as a woman, not my mother. As an Old Slut. As… As Mrs Knott. I'm no longer afraid of my mother's scars or the memory of watching her being fucked, you have erased it from my mind while you fucked me.*"

Unable to stop herself. Lisa held up her open arms up to him. He fell on her, clasping him to her breasts, shivering, she recalled a memory, a feeling from the past, a graphic sensation, of Eric. The night he broke her heart. He was forever lost.

Nathan, his agony today. Hers all those years ago. Kissing his wet hair, gently smoothing his back. "Come on now, my sweet Nathan, be the man you are," coaxing him with lovingly spoken words. "You should be proud, of yourself, not grieving, you where a child, when it happened, now your a man." Lisa had the proof of his masculinity, it had fucked her into *Oblivion*. "Let it go, Nathan, with me, you did not need your mother, I don't think you ever did, all you need is yourself. The man. My lover."

Nathan lifted his head, smiled, kissed her. A gentle, lovers kiss. It's genuine tenderness she tasted, more that felt.

"I must go, Lisa," he said hurriedly. "I've loved ever minute with you, honestly". Lisa spirits soared not because of what he said. More than just his words.

The sincerity in the voice, so distinct, so full of conviction. "I've spent a long time just servicing one boiler, your neighbours will".

"Wonder what you've been doing? she continued, for him, "Let them wonder, she said, rashly. "Your not the first man they've seen come and go. They don't seem to care. If they do, it's my problem, not yours."

"But, Lisa…"

"A young man", she replied mockingly. "A boy as young as you? He looked confused, so swift, her dismissal of his fears. He left her arms, starting to dress again. Lisa shivered, his warm flesh gone.

He would leave her now. Would he come back again? Had she given him the taste of her flesh and sexuality, a scent of her need for him?

Offered enough of her body's willingness to him and his huge young organ. Lisa wanted him, again to have satisfaction. For her overwhelming attraction for his huge sexual device. And the pleasure only he could inflict on her flesh with his vigorous young shaft.

Dressed, walking to the door, he was going. "Nathan, will you…?" Lisa stopped speaking. Torn between her desire for him and the fear, by asking him she would become open to be used by him on his terms, not hers.

Lisa's desire for the flesh. His flesh. The empty vacuum left in her vagina, where his cock, not so long ago, had filled so completely, so massively. The emptiness, the still pulsing tiny nerves in her cunt, a reminder. Stronger, to her than sane reason, She blurted out, "Will you call to see me again, Nathan?" He turned agonisingly slowly to Lisa, her insides knotted, heart beating faster. Hanging in suspense, trembling, she waited.

Nathan gazed at the naked body reclining on the twisted dishevelled bed. Call again, wild horses couldn't stop returning, his cock still throbbed from the pleasure's he'd extracted from her flesh.

"Would you really want me to?" suspiciously, warily, he replied. Kept her guessing, next time she'll be so hungry for it she'll give me everything.

Persuade him, Lisa unequivocally decided, you've gone this far. Offer him, a hint, a lightly concealed suggestion of a promise – next time if he did not call, insinuate what he could be losing.

Lifting up, propping herself, resting on her elbow's, opening her legs wider, smiling, filling her eye's with all the naked desire she could muster, said in a warm husky voice, laden with innuendo, "If you call again, my lovely sweet Nathan *you can have all you see, you can take everything! All of me, any way you want, as often as you desire and it will be different for you. I will refuse you nothing! I will give you it all willingly."*

The boy's face opened like a flower, eyes twinkling, smiling with undisguisable pleasure, "All of you Lisa. Anyway I want you, anything I ask for will be *mine, willingly*! He looked her, disbelief written all over his face.

She gone too far, overreacted, to her own advice. Too late now. She'd hooked him and his cock. She wanted to do that very thing from the very beginning, her foolhardy headlong hunger for his young body, had, she thought, hooked her to him. Nathan could, wriggle off her hook, wouldn't return. If he did call again. Her promise, imbedded her on his hook, so deep. She would never break free, until he was ready to release her.

Nathan, his gaze changing from disbelief with the realisation in his mind. Of what pleasure her sexually offered largess held for him. The naked open legs, the shapely tanned body, her flesh, *All His*. The envisaged enactment of satisfying his every sexual desire and fantasy made his cock pulse.

Lisa watching his reactions, standing looking down at her, she could have sworn. The cock, hidden in the crutch of his pants moved.

"Mrs Knott, Lisa, what you suggest. If I call again... I will expect." he never finished what he intended to say. He turned and walked out of the bedroom.

Lisa was devastated, her spirit, just small crumbs of desolation and pain, head falling forward resting on her chest, defeated, rejected, hurt, close to tears.

Then a hand touched bare shoulder. "You'll see me again, Lisa, Old Slut, one night I'll give you a call". Nathan, chuckling, glasses on, tool box in his hand. Smiling down at her, kissed her on the lips. He walked away, turned in the bedroom doorway gazing lovingly her at naked body, shaking his head. "Next time. I'll be the one who makes you want to fuck. I'll make love to you, Lisa like no man ever did before," he said chuckling, his face registering his intent. Her aspirations and desire's now restored.

"Don't get up, Mrs Knott, I can see my self out, Goodbye you lovely lady, see you soon," still laughing happily, he left her, a few seconds later the front door slammed shut. He was gone, she felt an aching for her loss, of his youth, his sexual flame, his strength, his muscled hard firm body.

Chapter 5

The minute the door closed, Lisa was alone, her plaintive mood changed with startling results, to one of buoyant exhilaration. The extraordinary, striking, the taste, the flavour of this morning's adventure into the world of sexual satisfaction with a young mans cock. Renewed in her mind. Lisa, laughter on her lips at the memory of the boy, as he had, with youthful savagery plundered her ever-willing flesh.

It was the opening to a new avenue of sex, unparalleled in her life in her participation of sexual promiscuity. Not even the time, when the realisation that she had the freedom to have any man. Even in those months of frenzied lust laden orgasms, which she had dealt with in her mind, her lovers, men of affluence, professional types, cultured, from her own level in life, sharing a time in life, from her generation.

Nathan had been her first from, to her, an alien era. The only item in life that connect them, that of male and female, and the natural act of sex.

Together naked in the bedroom, they where Woman and Man. The era, the generation, eradicated from mind in the height of passion, by Cock and Cunt.

She was surprised by the words in her head, as Nathan, alien to her, her own outburst of expletives in the heat of coming on the massive shaft inside her, another dimension of her experience with the flesh, far from disgusting her, it had heightened in her, an even deeper erotic sensation, so profound. Lisa wished she had the courage to employ the garbled phrases of her lust before today. The *Words*. So blunt and crude, yet so true of her feelings at that moment. Before today in her upbringing, the words dirty, nasty, foul, sinful, words, forbidden to be expressed by a lady.

Now, they were words for her to shout, scream, while in the grip of ejaculation, her release became magnified by the crude, dirty phrases of sex.

Enraptured with her thoughts in the knowledge. She, and her desire for flesh, its very ethos, had been exposed, so graphically, by his hard rampant *COCK USED, ENJOYED, COATED IN SEMEN, HER SEMEN,* To Lisa, the ultimate gratification a woman could ever achieve.

Lisa, the revelation of why her need for flesh, men, and sex over the previous two years had been clearly defined in her mind. All her thoughts, reservations and conscience, with regard to sex evaporated, expunged from her mind today, forever.

She would satisfy her sexual needs, her desires. Not justifying her actions in her mind first. Oh no, not any more. Have the man, the naked body. *The Cock, The Orgasm's First! Justification After!*

Floating on a cloud of euphoria, mind freed of all inhibition's. Lisa left her place on the bed. Rushed to the full-length mirror, stood looking at her naked body. Hands on her shapely hips, pushing her belly forward, drawing in a deep breath, squaring her shoulders, to tighten and expand her large firm breast's, nipples protruding stiff and proud, her gazed evaluating her body. He *loved* my body, even if he did name me 'Old Slut', she told herself. It may be an old body to him, yet he couldn't stop himself from touching, feeling, tasting, and fucking it.

Her body had induced, his oh so beautiful cock! To rise shining and hard, hungry, striking his muscle hard belly with a thud, so swollen and rigid she could still see the rolled back flesh as it gathered under the bulbous dark pinky coloured knob.

In her mouth, still, the flavour of his sweet manly taste, his orgasm in her mouth, hers in his, a foretaste of more, always more, *for her*.

His flesh, its manly scent, the aroma of his sweat, young and fresh new to her nostrils, excited her senses, incredibly inflaming her vagina to a heat never felt before.

She had seduced Nathan, with her flesh, his young virile shaft, his body, she made her own for a short time, if he did not return, God forbid, the thought, an agony. She would, find another youth, use her body, ensnare him into her bed by any means possible, even Jay, if he called again.

The idea of looking for a boy. The wicked little wiles, the mode of dress she would employ, a little subtle show of a little of her naked flesh, a hint willingness of an older woman so hot, desperate to be fucked.

Lisa, in an the grip of own sensuousness, uncertain if it was her thoughts of Nathan, or her ideas for the seduction of young men, pressed both hands on her round soft contoured hips, before sliding them down between her thighs. Her crutch still moist from her earlier fucking and her present sexually consideration for the future. She had rekindled her senses, her sexuality reborn her hands, touching her flesh. Lisa, shivered, it felt like she was in deep orgasm and gripped both hands tight over her now wet crutch.

To stop her rising craving, going to the kitchen, lit a cigarette then returned to the bedroom. Blowing smoke in the air crossing her arms across her stomach, the lighted cigarette between her fingers, elbow cradled on other hand.

Gazing at her naked body. She was looking at a different person, same body but with altered attitude to men, sex, with totally new horizon, clear of all doubts about the rights and wrongs of her sexual satisfaction.

Winking at her reflection, she told herself, with a smile; if you're going to fuck young boys and have them fuck you in return. Shaking her head, at her image. *No if* about it, after today, no more middle-aged men, ever again!

You'd better get a few extra packets of cigarettes, young boys like to smoke, and some new skimpy clothes, short and tight and sexiest smallest panties you can find, no young hot blooded boy can stop his cock erecting at the sight of a woman panties. Even if they were covering an old cunt. Cheerfully making a mental note for future reference.

A lovely thought, young boys, she ruefully decided. Nathan said he'd call again. It wasn't a promise. Lisa, high spirits shrivelled. She was just a new glamorous experience, so exciting when you're young, she cautioned herself. Maybe she was just rainy morning fuck to him. Don't dwell on it, my girl, her own stern advice, just you treat it as a nice change, something different to what you've become accustom to having.

She stubbed her cigarette out in an ashtray, went and stood looking down at the rumpled bed, a deep sigh in her throat. The damp semen stained sheets. She could smell the pungent aroma of Nathan, his sweat, his semen, an odour of good sex. The scent of him coveted instantly, to flesh, ardour, and above all *Cock!* Not just any *Cock*, "***Nathan's!***"

Wrapping her arms around her naked body, cuddling herself, in her mind flashed an image. *A Boy laying on the bed, naked, cock proud, waiting and wanting to shaft her again.*

The vision in her mind faded. She, conscious of the fact the vision was fantasy. Her personal overwhelming desire for the youth. Sitting on side of the bed looking at the dishevelled semen stained sheets, her hand tracing the contours of the drying semen, his mingled with hers, out loud said, "Come back soon".

"I need you Nathan."

Standing up, stripped the bed, rolling the sheets in a ball in her arms, before smothering her face in the sex soiled cloth. "Don't make me wait to long, my sweet, if you do your place will be filled by another, not only in my bed but in my pussy as well, she said to herself, words muffled, head still buried in the sheets. Lisa had no illusions as to where it all would end. The *Boy* had opened her mind, her flesh, with his youthful strength, his stamina, together with his hard, long shaft of flesh. How potent his speed of recovery, the ability to come how many times? Four? Five? In the space of a few hours.

She trembled at concept, if he'd stayed all day, better still, all night, with a little encouragement, how *many*. The answer, she had no idea. But she knew where her answer lay. And how to get it. *Screwing* with *young men.* If he achieved a dozen? The concept of such abundance had made her cast aside, her scruples, her conscience, and yes, possibly her self respect. Eventually sinking down to, using Nathan's description, too benign **An Old Slut.** Being fucked in every way imaginable, by any one, young, old, fat, ugly.

Lisa, blankets in arms, would, with open arms, welcome

such pleasures. *Why*? It was the concept of a man or boy ejaculated his come in her body a dozen times. The ecstasy, the feelings that only a stiff hard cock could produce in her cunt and body, her lust filled perception, of *TWELVE BEAUTIFUL BODY TWISTING, MIND BENDING ORGASMS, OVER A COCK, ANY COCK.* She knew what to expect in the end, pain. "Fine. Okay", she told herself, bluntly. "You led yourself in to it. For a long time, to long, you've needed youthful young flesh without realising your need, now your hidden desire have been exposed, you'll pay the price for satisfying your flesh, and in time Lisa my girl, you will start to hurt.

Lisa didn't what to hurt, not after Eric, then David. Her will and determination had been drained, by their betrayal of her love, her spirit weakened by the pain. The thought of the mental anguish in mind and heart, too much to suffer a third time. Her presumption of the future. Of a lonely miserable life full of dark tortured heartbreak.

Lisa remember Eric, the divorce, after that she'd sworn that never again would she endure suffer such pain, ever again. The day, much same as any other day, at breakfast, David casually remarked, looking at her over the early morning newspaper, "Are you going any where near the office day? if you are can you call in about lunch time? "Sure, fine, I'll do a little shopping while I'm in town." David put the paper down, rose, taking his jacket off the back of the chair.

"You taking me out to lunch?"

"No. Just something we need to talk over."

She could find nothing in her mind, to explain the serious expression on his face. "Do I have to come to the office? It can't be that important, why we can't discuss it now?" He looked at his watch, hurriedly slipping into his jacket, for some reason, appeared flustered.

"Not time now, About lunch time. Don't be late."

"Lunch time then," she replied mystified. "If you feel it's that important."

Lisa spent a few hours casual shopping. She was a married woman, no family. She had never been troubled, or David, as many other couples were over the fact they had no children. Her life was comfortable, she had her own money, an inheritance left to her by her parents, a substantial one, very substantial. David's salary was enormous, befitting his position as the president of one of the largest bank in country. He was an inexperienced lawyer, just out of college when she married him.

It had always been a source of pride to her, to be married to a lawyer with the brains to become a banker.

She was treated by sales staff at her favourite stores with a respect reserved only for the more affluent customers, and those that always settled their accounts on time.

As a special treat, just for herself, she bought a white short tight fitting dress. The salesgirl, somewhat enviously, congratulating her fine figure, thanked her saying so, lightly adding, a few pounds off my bum, would make it even better.

Some small purchases of a few necessities, a pleasant half hour in the coffee shop, before driving to the office. Oblivious to the horror, and agonising hurt, the heartbreak that a waited her.

Lisa, her mind more on what to get for dinner that evening. She would ask David, he possessed an exceptional perception for good food, always had. She was still day dreaming, as she read the gold plaque outside his office door. Mr David Knott, President. The letters always gave her a feeling of security, her place in life, her affluent lifestyle secured, protected by the gold letters. Lisa, her pride in David, his achievement from lawyer to this even loftier elevation in society, and the prestige of being the wife of a bank President inflated her feeling of well-being.

He was, what is called, a pillar of society, and she basked in the shadow of his elevation, her shield against all life's ills and woes.

Opening the door, without knocking, no plain decor. Oh no, not David, thick carpets, wood panelling, expensive paintings hang on the walls.

To Lisa, the office, a testament to David's success it was more than a look of just wealth. A luxurious opulence, the undeniable proof of the success of his ambition, and the accumulation of large private wealth.

"Go right in he's waiting for you, Mrs Knott", his receptionist said, in an over-friendly tone.

With a nod of thanks she walked straight in. David, sitting his chair facing the window, she could only see the back of his head. The tinges of grey hair more pronounced in bright sun lit office. The office as the receptionist, expensive drapes, dark wood panelling, leather furniture, a concealed drinks cabinet.

Lisa had a feeling of unease, like she was a client seeking a loan. What was so important? That it concerned David so much it couldn't be discussed at home.

David turned his chair to face her, smiling. Nervously she thought, pointed to her to take a seat.

Sitting down, said in a bright tone, "Well, David, I must admit, you rarely ask me to call at your office. What's this problem all about?"

He appeared a little nervous, apprehensive. The one thing he never showed, no matter the circumstances was any hint of uncertainty, always smooth, confident, utterly professional, but not that day.

David stood up, sorted some papers lying on the desktop. "I have spent a long time agonising over this, Lisa and how to tell you and I think this is the best place for me to…" he paused, looked at her, glancing round the office. As if, in here, his personal fortress, the place of his power, his control over the bank, gave him a strength he did not possess in their own home.

A shaft of undefined fear, swept through her heart. "Tell me what, David?"

He looked at her, a soft bland look on his face, "I want a divorce."

"A DIVORCE?" stunned, unable to say only the word, instinctively. "Why, David, why would you want a *DIVORCE*?"

In a somewhat graceful yet bashful voice he replied. "To be perfectly honest with, Lisa I have fallen in love." He seemed as shocked to say the word love, as she was to hear it.

Lisa, was thunderstruck, a shaft of pain stabbed her soul, so devastated, her reactions, a twisting tangling ball of hurt. Not once, *NOT EVER*, in her marriage had the idea of *DIVORCE*, entered her mind.

David had appeared happy and contented with her and his career, with everything they did together.

And then came the anger, the blinding rage. She, Lisa, who loved the man standing in front of her. Half her life spent working to make him happy, sharing his frustrations in their early married life, loving him, holding him naked in her arms when. On times he lost faith in himself, giving him the tenderness of her heart, and body, to make him strong, to repair his ambition with her willing flesh.

Now, rejected, cast aside like a worn out pair of old shoes after twenty years of giving him all her love and affection used up. Replaced by another woman. Tears streaming down her face, she shouted at him stupidly.

"You can can't just fall in love, you're a married man, married to me."

"I'm sorry, Lisa, it just happened," he'd recovered his poise, sounding superior, experienced, worldly knowledgeable. "That's the way it is, it happens from time to time, I'm just a sorry that it happened with us, Lisa, but it has, my lawyer will be in touch with you, and you'd better find one to handle your side of it."

It was David the lawyer now. Courtroom logic, do something bad, tell the jury how sorry you are. Then sum up, the sorrow, show penance, then justify the act, THAT'S THE WAY IT IS, as though it solved all the worlds problems.

She was choking, no longer caring about life, not now, "You're a bloody fool, David Knott, and I'm a bigger one," screaming her anger in to his smug looking face, the venom in her voice startling her. "You go to the slut you've found, and I hope you live a life of hell, You've killed me, David, and it will be a long lingering death. ***YOU MISERABLE EXCUSE FOR A MAN!*** You didn't have guts to tell me this a home, no not you, I had come to your palace, that is hurting cruel, and to demean me even more, you made me visit you to tell me you… you… you… ***You Lousy Bastard!***"

Lisa ran out of the office, blinded by her tears, her heart felt it was tearing, shredding into small slivers of nothing.

Lisa ran blinking out on to the street, ignoring the lunch time traffic, ran across the road, never hearing the screeching brakes, the shouts of rage, the foul mouthed insults shouted in her direction, in the dash to her car.

Fumbling in her purse for the keys, finding them, in her panic to get away from the scene of her nightmare, dropped them on the sidewalk. Squatting on her haunches, her hand sweeping across the ground seeking the fallen keys, oblivious to everything around, except the blinding tears and the pain in her heart.

She was ripped back to reality by a strange voice saying. "Well ma-am if you have inside your panties anything that's as nice as what I can see, then I think it should be fucked."

She look up through her streaming tears, standing in front of her, a middle-aged distinguished man looking smiling down at her. In her frantic search for the keys her skirt had ridden high up her thighs, with her knees wide apart, looking at herself, in that position, her crutch was fully exposed. Her pussy saved from the hot eyes at staring her by small covering of white satin in the crutch of her panties. Getting to her feet, unlocking the door she glared at the man. Using a word she never spoken, at home, or in public, shouted into his face in outraged anger. ***"FUCK OFF!"***

Oddly pleased, at his shocked expression as the crude expletive assaulted his ears. She drove home. Somehow she must have driven by instinct, obeying the traffic lights, staying in the right lane, even negotiating the two box junctions in the city centre, without causing other drivers any inconvenience. She remembered nothing about the drive home.

Her mind full of the realisation, the stark reality, in her heart, as in David's office, she was now alone in life, when she reached home it would be an empty house. Its lifeblood, the memories, a love shared, ripped out of premises. As her life had been destroyed in that office, as her life now was, with a destructive abruptness, empty of a man.

Driving in to the garage, she took her shopping, and the bag containing the new white dress, stabbed the button to close the garage door, before letting herself in.

She looked blankly around the hall, in the kitchen, a sense of emptiness overcame her, an alien feeling, as alien as her new man empty life.

She went to the bedroom, why; she didn't know, perhaps to find solace, a balm for her tortured soul. None was forth coming. The thought of David, his expensive black pin striped suits, golfing outfits, and neatly folded white shirts in his closet, blotted out everything.

She was crying again, her tears seem to burn a furrow in her cheeks, her make-up a mess. *WHY?* The word rebounded over and over again in her head.

Lisa sat on the bed, staring vacantly into space. *WHY! WHY! WHY!* If she could understand *WHY*! He had no reason. She'd never been a nagger, unfaithful never, ill tempered or demanding, kept the house spotless, their sex life always satisfying. She would have liked a little more flesh from time to time, a few more orgasms. But if he was contented, for her, that was everything. But that, as in all things, David's wants came first. Sitting on the bed, like a bolt of lighting, a thought, more than a thought. A revelation, *SEX!* A mans weakness, his Achilles heel.

That must be it. The reason. Her crying ceased. For the first time since David had brutally lanced her heart from his. Her mind changed from anger to confused hurtful pain. Her blind lashing out at David with outraged indignant words, her departure, the overwhelming desire to get away from the nightmare he'd thrust upon her. She never thought to ask who the woman was. The one who had taken her place in his life.

Her anger swelled into a feeling of resolve. David you... you... *Bastard!* after wasting half my life, you're not walking out on me. Lisa Knott, that damn easy, she told herself, defiantly.

Picking up the bedside phone, she dialled the bank. Wiping her tears away with the corner of the duvet as she waited.

"Could I speak to Mr David Knott please?" Choking on the name, as she replied to some receptionist's request.

"I'm afraid Mr Knott has left the office for the rest of the day, madam. Can I take a message madam?"

Already her life changing, instantly. She'd become Madam. No longer Mrs Knott, well at the bank any way.

"No, you damn well can't take a message," a savage indignation in her voice. "You just put me through to my husband's office NOW, thank you". A muttered apology in reply, a click. Then silence.

Beside herself in frustrated rage. She rang the bank again,

this time David's personal number.

The receptionist who told her earlier to go straight in to the office answered. Her anger at fever pitch, her tone stringent, she said angrily, "Perhaps you'd be good enough to tell me, the name of the woman that my husband is *FUCKING*, because he sure as hell hasn't got the guts to tell me himself."

"I'm sorry, Mrs Knott," sounding as if she was taken aback by the demand for information put in such brutal terms. "I have been instructed not to talk to you under any circumstances, and I don't need to tell you what will happen to me and my job if I do. I didn't like the way Mr Knott treated you, and I certainly do not like the way he has been deceiving you. I know how it feels Mrs Knott, my husband ran off with a younger woman and it hurts. Her name is Sarah, she is twenty years old, and works in accounts. If I you ask me, your husband is old enough to be her father, that is all I can tell, Mrs Knott, goodbye and I hope you find someone else. I never have." then the phone went dead.

Lisa stared at the instrument in her hand. Thunderstruck, another woman yes, but a young girl half his age. She gave him up then. Left him. Locking into the mind and heart the fact David was gone. *Forever.*

Lisa tried to visualise David in bed with a twenty-year-old girl. That image she could not picture it in her mind.

Their marital sexual had always been good and satisfying, though, as she'd thought earlier, the last few years not as often as she would have liked. Never more than a weekly occurrence, sometimes not even that. In her own private thoughts she'd never complained believing, wrongly, she knew now. It was sufficient for David needs, if not hers.

Lisa, not even when her desire for flesh became an ache, did she consider another man? No more than it had entered her mind that David would want or even look for sexual gratification with a younger woman.

She descended into an even blacker mood of depression. Another bleak thought crept into her mind. She was a failure as a woman. Her husband had abandoned her because she had not satisfied his sexual needs.

Don't blame yourself Lisa, she admonished herself. He

could have told you of his disappointment, he didn't have to look elsewhere to fuck, he wanted to.

Lisa, at least, taking comfort from the fact, as meagre as it was. A mere crumb of knowledge. She had a *reason!*

The cause of the Divorce. Not being young enough any more to satisfy his sexual desires. That was it, of course. David simply wanted to have a younger, warmer, firmer body. He was pathetic really, she thought, he's not the young, hard strong man he was when he married her, not any more.

As if it would help, she tried again to picture David, naked, with his young girl Sarah. His life style, the ever increasing number of formal dinners, had begun to have its effect on his slowly ageing body. His stomach no longer flat, he'd become quite portly, his face much fuller, the cheeks fatter, smoother. No longer able to make love as he had in the past. She remembered how the rounded belly felt on hers. His hard masculine shaft, no longer touched her deeply an more, not unless she helped him, often a remarkable effort for both of them, before he could a achieved a full, deep penetration.

That she accepted, partly, was her fault, it was a fact. Her life had become too comfortable, contented, too routine, easy. She never exercised, gave no thought to what she ate, at her age dieting would have made a difference.

Sarah, young Sarah, *she'd accepted* David's soft rotund middle-aged body. Found it, enjoyable, obviously she had too, why else would she want it permanently. Leaving Lisa with nothing.

Her mental anguish intensified, transmitting from the mind to her body, so unexpected, defenceless. Her agony became a physical reaction.

She climbed into the empty bed, her flesh ice cold to her touch, shivering, she huddled under the covers.

Lisa wanted to cry, sobbed her heart out, yet no tear slipped from her eyes. Not wanting to live the life of misery that faced her. Not wanting to except the truth. That this was the tragic ending of her happiness. A disaster that was not happening, Yet it was. *It is*.

Lisa lay. How long, Time was motionless, a long thread of nothing, as if some greater harm would befall her, a physical threat to her already savaged soul, she remained in a coiled foetal position her knees against her breasts, arms wrapped tight about her ankles.

Ultimately there became a change, so fine, so subtle, her body's reactions deceived her mind without her realising what was happening.

Her flesh became afire, burning hot. Throwing off the bedcovers she got up and stripped naked, dropping her clothes in a scattered heap at her feet. Laid down again, her body in a feverish shivering sweat covered only by the top sheet.

Her thoughts of the last few hours tore across her mind, with all the fury of an out of control tornado, David lying naked in the arms of a young woman she knew only as Sarah. His deceit. Her betrayal. His love and flesh, lavished on someone else.

Inexplicable in her misery, everything became linked together, her misery, her hate for both of them, the picture of them entangled naked, sweating, moaning, and her deep rooted urge for revenge, her body claimed itself, in a need far greater than anything she had ever experienced, a feeling beyond *LUST!*

Thighs writhing, she surrender to her body to the gnawing hunger to be held tight, locked in the arms of a man, naked, his flesh on hers, so sweet, the thought of being fucked, by a man, any man, his great rock hard shaft driving into her womanly depths. The image, a small victory for her, made all the sweeter because the man she imagined, wasn't her husband David.

But it wasn't a man. *It would never be a man AGAIN, EVER*!

In a desperate sexual longing. Lisa hands closed on her mound. Overcome with revulsion, in self-disgust, she snatch them away.

She rarely touched herself in that fashion, almost *never*, not even in her youth. But this day was different, a hell on earth to live through. A hand wilfully, with stealth, crept down her stomach, finding the sensitive clitoral flesh. The house deathly silent, she lay still, fingers caressing her clitoris. Eyes closed tight, she did not want to know what her fingers were doing. Only the feelings they where producing. Ever so slowly, against her will, she began a circular, twirling motion, its sensation had an addictive effect to her flesh. A creeping warming flame ignited within her body. Progressively, little by little, her fingers became faster, her legs straightened until they squeezed the fingers tight to her loins.

The profound realisation. *This is all I'll ever have from this day forth, forever*, she warned herself, a stark reality of a black sadness overcame her.

The conception unleash a frenzied lust laden craving, opening her legs wide, she thrust her thighs feverishly against the hand. Not just two fingers, all of them her hand dripping wet from the heated clammy moisture released by her seething heated female tissues. The ejaculation wanted release, to escape. But she had never *ever* come in this way before.

Weeping now, in frustration, Lisa at a loss, with a feeling of bitterness, for herself and the world in general, sat up, legs open, knees wide apart, bent outwards, feet turn inward, the soles almost touching, she manipulated her vital organ mercilessly, fingers buried inside, her palm locked on her pulsating vagina. Sobbing pitifully, shoulders racked by her sobs, utterly helpless she tore through a panting moaning, isolated lonely climax, her hips pounding against the imprisoning palm, making a slapping sound of wetness and unfettered discharge.

It subsided, slowly, eventually Lisa lay, unmoving, Still the hand gripped her now wet, sticky hairy mound as the tears streamed unnoticed down her faced. Sniffling unlady like, she turned her face into the pillow.

She never knew exactly when sleep inter-mixed with her pain and sorrow. A full day, twenty four hours later, she emerged from her sleep, in to her new world, prepared by courtesy of Mr D. Knott, for the his *former ex-wife* Lisa.

Chapter 6

Lisa would have slept on if hadn't been for the for the incessant *breep breep breep,* of the bedside phone intruding into her sleep drugged mind.

Lisa turned over and sat up, staring in dumb amazement at the ringing phone, shaking sleep from her mind. Picking up the phone sat staring blankly at far wall. "Hello, Lisa, this is David, I've been phoning all day, in fact I became somewhat concern when I couldn't get a reply; You all right?"

All right be damn, coming awake instantly, no she was not all right, quite the reverse but she had no intention of saying so. "What do you want, David? You made your position quite clear yesterday, and I have nothing say to you except *Goodbye*." she abruptly replied, to numb to say any more.

"Look, Lisa, I know it must have come as a bit of a shock," he was talking fast as if to prevent her interrupting his flow of words. Lisa felt weak, she wanted to rage at the voice in her ear but like a whipped dog all she could do was listen. "If you hadn't run out of the office. I would have explained it to you and why it happened, I fell in love with someone else, that's all."

"That's all, David? she shouted in the mouthpiece, unwilling to except it was so simple. David certainly thought it was. And that was a lie.

"You fell in love with a bimbo, David, a young girl, young enough to be your daughter. You have not found a new love, you damned fool, you're in love with her body and it makes you feel you're a big man. It inflates your ego, just you wait a few years and you put on a few more pounds and you can't fuck her twice a night, not even twice a week. In fact you're not capable enough to fuck me more than once a week now, and what a shame, what a stupid blind egotistical man you are, David. I would have given you all the loving you ever wanted and needed, yet after twenty years you couldn't see it." She was crying again, not because of David or the divorce, it was the thought of never giving a man, or a man giving her, the sort of fucking she now so dearly wanted to have experienced.

"I know how upset you must be Lisa and I'm sorry that I've hurt you in such a cruel manner." He never finished what he intended to say. Lisa lost her temper completely. Arrogant swine, she thought, he knew how upset she was. No you bloody do not Mr David Knott, but you soon will.

"Your a damn liar, David, and don't try using your lawyer tricks with me, if you know how upset and hurt I feel you'd never have left me. And if you really did know, don't spin a yarn about falling in love with someone else because you never loved me in the first place, you love yourself. I was just a woman who you felt contented with, till something better came along, I only wish you'd have discovered her twenty years go. You file for damned divorce, and get it over with. Now goodbye, David, I wish you all the bad luck in the world and when the day comes and you find out your new love is being fucked by another man, then you talk to me about hurt. Now you fuck off forever," she shrieked, slamming the phone down.

Lisa sat for a long time, indifferent to everything, devastated, so lost, her emotions confused, twisted, sitting stiffly, hands folded in her lap. The remains of sleep still heavy in her, a dead lifeless feeling. Her whole life felt as dead and lifeless as the sleep.

She made herself get up and go to the kitchen, ran the cold tap, watching the water drain down the plug hole. Love and water go together, partners. She thought, it flows, turn it off it stops, the sink empties, it's gone. Love comes like water, it flows between a man and woman, one day the flow stops, the love vanishes, draining away, and like water in wash basin, is gone and life as the basin. Is empty.

Cupping her hands together she bathed her eyes with the cold water, she'd gone to the kitchen, not wanted to she her face in the bathroom mirror. After a few minutes bathing the stinging contact of the cold water in her eyes' stopped.

Venturing into the hall, she looked into the mirror hanging on the wall. Her face looked swollen, eyes red rimmed, puffed from her weeping.

Lisa looking at the reflection in the mirror, realised with some degree of shock, she was naked.

She didn't want to see her naked flesh, the plumpness of the thighs and the pitted look of her flanks, nor the flesh on her stomach sagging, flabby, the breasts no longer firm, sagging downward, ugly. Lisa fought back the tears, held them back by will power alone. I'm not going to cry every time a thought enters my head, if you don't like it fight it, do something constructive to combat your dislike, she told herself.

Lisa, deep down comprehended, it wasn't her neglected body that caused the anguish. It was the knowledge that very few men, *IF ANY!* Would be interested in her. She had nothing to offer physically or sexually.

The manifestation in her mind of spending the rest of her life, without having a orgasm on a hard erect cock, to feel a man, deep inside her.

The pleasure of flesh, the erotic desires of a man coming, her bodys fevered wetness as her semen mingled with his. No, Mr David Knott you will not haunt me for ever, now and again maybe, but I will overcome the pain and hurt. And when I'm strong enough in mind and body, then I'll have my revenge.

Lisa, resolve swelling inside her heart and mind, coming together, a feeling of resolute determination within growing ever stronger, for the first time since she'd heard the word, *DIVORCE,* came a seed of hope. She, Lisa would survive this hell.

Her revenge, to give every man she took to her bed, everything she'd wanted to give David, she'd offer it all to them, when they fucked her and she'd fucked them over and over again in return. To her, their cocks would steal David's treasure, his body, her love, and **HIS CUNT.**

Lisa her vulnerability still badly bruised yet buttressed by her new found inner resolution, going to the bedroom. Threw on a robe, she couldn't face the demands of dressing and returned to the kitchen.

The strangeness of the house closed in, she was alone, her

home, a place of silence, the fabric of the building, a vacuum of loneliness from now on.

Making coffee, Lisa looked at the clock, perplexed and bewildered for a few minutes. She had slept for whole day, twenty-four hours and yet she still felt a melancholy fatigue. The coffee-pot bubbling distracted her thoughts for a few seconds; pouring a cup. She needed a cigarette; desperately. A vice she had given up a few years ago, not by choice.

She stopped smoking because of David's everlasting complaining. Called it a filthy habit, occasionally she'd sneak outside onto the patio, so he wouldn't know she still had a cigarette.

She unearthed a crumpled packet at the back of the cutlery draw. She remembered how she'd hidden it that day, full of determined resolve to quit. Hungrily, she opened it, six cigarettes. Stale and dry now, nevertheless, she placed one in her lips; needed. A light rummaging in the draw again she found her lighter. Thumbed the spark wheel, Nothing. She tried again, frantic to feel the nicotine laden smoke in her lungs. The lighter, unused for so long flamed feebly, then went out. She flicked harder, felt the rough wheel dig hard into the ball of her thumb, briefly it flared into life and puffing hard. Greedily, inhaling deeply, the sudden rush of smoke into her lungs was exhilarating, heady. Head spinning, eyes swimming she resisted the urge to cough, exhaled, took a longer deep slow puff. First thing she'd do in the morning, get half a dozen cartons of Phillip Morris cigarettes. One more small piece of her life with David. Eradicated.

Standing, the open drawer, forgotten, smoking with relish. Lisa, the smoke in her body, so gently soothing to her mind. That first cigarette. In time became a treasured memory. It coincided with the last time she spoke to David. He never turned up in court for the divorce hearing, sent some young lawyer in his place. Used some legal term. A no fault divorce, it didn't require his presence. No fault that was a bloody joke, he'd been *fucking another woman while married to me!*

She was in tears when the judge said solemnly. "It seems quite straight forward, your husband has given you a generous alimony settlement, the house, and a new expensive Mercedes car." It was over, down and dusted in ten short minutes.

She never saw him again, never spoke, nor did she want to.

Sitting at the table, coffee in one hand, a second cigarette in the other. Lisa, the idea, from now on, she would be eating alone, no husband to cook for. No one to talk with.

How did you cook for one person, having prepared and cooked countless meals, smelling the food cooking? Lisa would be alone at the table. Perhaps she could use her changed circumstances. She could diet now eat salads, fruit, lose the loose flesh off her thighs and stomach. Exercise, get fit, go jogging, maybe in time join a fitness club, or a gym.

Lisa, staring at the clock on the wall, experienced a tangible feeling of a new growing strength within her. Filling her mind with feeling of salvation. She would discipline her mind and body. From this moment on. To rejuvenate her whole being, *mind and body,* until one day. ***She would feel a man again, his body, his COCK, his semen inside her Cunt!***

It was more than an idea. Not a thought, To Lisa, a manifestation in the mind, the dawning of her rebirth as woman.

So armoured with resolve. The terrible disaster of her life shattered into a million pieces yesterday. Lisa committed her every thought to achieve her new ambition in life. Little knowing, it would succeed, far beyond her wildest dreams.

Thinking about food and dieting. She felt a stab of hunger. She had eaten nothing since breakfast yesterday morning. It was now early evening, the day after. Rifling through the cupboards, finding little that she fancied settled for a few slices of wholemeal bread and a solitary tomato from the icebox. Not much of a meal, she thought, looking at the paltry meagre food in front of her. No time like the present, to begin the process of constructing a new life, with a body to match, she told herself. Gripped with an iron-will of determination she ate, with relish.

Until that evening in which she sat at her lonely table eating her bread and solitary tomato. Lisa Knott had only once been involved, emotionally, with another man other than David.

It was in high school, she hadn't been short of friends, was popular, in fact well like. Lisa was never short of a date for

Saturday night, a cheerleader for the basketball team, she worked in the school library.

Yet, cool, quiet, remote, looked upon somewhat in awe by girls and boys alike, she been untouched by the agonies of sexual turmoil's the rest of her school friends had experienced.

That mould had been shattered, only once. When she began dating a senior, she was sixteen years old, he was nearly three years older.

Eric James Cheats, one of the schools misfits, a wild boy, with a gang of followers, a raunchy bunch of youths, with motorbikes or old noisy cars, who hung out at a dingy pool-room on the other side of town.

They took no part in any school activities, never participated in sporting events, Except for Eric, he liked boxing, the word had it he only boxed because he enjoyed punching boys senseless, the football coach, hated everyone of them. They arrived at social functions, noisy and raucous, filled with bravado and drink. Hanging about outside, baiting the boys, making obscene gestures and suggestions to the girls.

They came mostly from the other side of town, the sons of the mill workers, and factory hands, living in rows of shabby, dirty houses. Full of contempt for the students from a good family. Such as Lisa, whose father was a senior partner of real estate company.

Eric was for some reason the leader of the group, possibly because he was the eldest, he had twice been arrest for fighting, and once for speeding.

Lisa, in her remote aloof manner, didn't realise who it was, the day as she closed the door of her locker. Standing in front of her, a dark skinned, handsome youth, tall, broad shoulder, a mop of black curly hair, with blue smiling eyes.

"You know the shiny Harley Davidson bike in the parking lot with The Beast written on both sides of the fuel tank in black letters?" he asked, aggressively.

"I'm sorry I don't," Lisa told him, amused by his effrontery to even speak to her. "Any reason why I should?"

"Yes, you should," he growled. "Because when school turns out you'd better be sitting on it waiting for me."

Then abruptly, he pushed past her, mingling with the other students. Lisa continued towards her next lesson. When she reach the classroom door, opening it, looked back down the corridor. He stood in the rapidly emptying passageway staring after her. Catching her eye, he smiled, nodded his head in the direction of the parking, then winked.

"Who is that?" she asked a passing schoolmate. The boy looked.

"Eric James Cheats." He pulled a face. "Don't bother with him, he's a damned hooligan, you're not interested in that lout, are you? He's not your sort, believe you me, Lisa."

For the rest of the school day, she gave no thought to the crude invitation. She changed her mind about the word invitation. Instead, it was a strange challenge. Yet, as she walked through the parking lot to the pickup point where her mother always waited for her. Lisa paused for a few minutes, searching for the described machine. Seeing it gleaming in the sunlight, the words The Beast, for some reason, held an odd attraction for her. She had never been on a date with anyone, who owned such a machine; her dates usually turn up, driving their fathers Buicks or Cadillacs, carefully.

She went across to her mothers car, leaned through the open passenger side window. "Mother, I'm going to the library for an hour or two, I've some books to itemise. I'll be home before six-thirty, is that all right?"

"You could have called me, Lisa and saved me the trouble of driving down town," her mother grumbled.

"Sorry, Mother, but I wasn't told about it until just before the class finished, I didn't have time to phone."

"And how will you get home? I'm not going to be hanging about waiting, Lisa."

"It's all right someone will give me a lift."

"All right. But make sure your home in time for dinner, or your father will get very upset, so don't you be late."

Putting her arms through the open window, she dropped her schoolbooks on the empty passenger seat. Lisa stood and watched her mother drive away till the car became part of the flowing traffic.

She didn't give a thought to what she was about to do. She didn't want to. Walking back to the fast clearing parking lot. Her quiet remote mind calm, in spite of the somewhat odd and different situation she was placing herself in. Leaned against the seat of The Beast, the leather cover warmed by the sun, burning her buttocks, through the thin summer dress.

She waited for quite a while. And began to think had she made a fool of herself. Eric suddenly appeared, leaving the school building, followed by the rest of his bunch of cronies. Halfway down the steps, he stopped, looking at her leaning against The Beast. He turned spoke to his friends in a conspiritual fashion. Glancing in her direction from time to time, the group split up, leaving Eric. No male banter or suggestive comments, they just stared at her curiously as they walked passed.

Eric came across to her. Handed her a big black helmet. "Put this on," he ordered her gruffly. She obliged without comment. He sat on the bike, pushed it off its stand, started it up, the roar was ear splitting. "Get on," he said, as if she had ridden on the bike many times before.

Lisa climbed on. Eric revved the engine, blue smoke spewing from the exhaust. With a squeal of tyres the bike shoot out of the parking lot.

She was almost thrown from her seat behind him by the sudden unexpected surge of power, it lifted the front wheel off the ground, as it hit the road, to retain her balance, threw her arms around Eric's waist and hung on for dear life. Her chin resting on his broad shoulder.

Lisa was terrified, her eyes closed tight as he weaved in and out of the traffic, as they passed each vehicle, she heard a whoosh of air. Her loose fitting summer dress was blowing behind her, she could feel cold air on her bare thighs. Passing a large truck, the driver blew his horn continuously. She opened her eyes for the first time, stared up at the driver. He was pushing his tongue in and out between his lips. Looking down. She could see her dress was around her waist. The lorry driver could see her naked legs, the only thing hiding her nudity, from the waist down. Her white panties.

For the next half hour. A hell of a lot of drivers saw more of her than any man had seen before. She was too frightened to do anything about her nakedness. Lisa heard the throbbing engine change to a quieter tone. Her grip on his waist slackened. He had taken her far beyond the outskirts of the town. They where in hills over looking the river. The bike came to a halt in the shade of a huge spruce tree. The air still and muggy. Lisa her body shaking let go of his waist. He kicked the stand down stepping off the heated machine.

She felt too badly shaken to move. "Take that helmet off, before your head melts."

Placing her quivering hands on each side removed it. Shaking her head to release her tangled hair. Eric was standing looking at her naked legs.

Lisa made no move to cover herself. Why she did not know. But she felt a strange thrill, caused by the hot look that came into his blue eyes.

Eric dropped his helmet, stared hard in to her face. Lisa smiled, matching his gaze with out flinching. He stepped towards her, one arm when around her waist. She shivered as his bare hand came into contact with her bare back. The other was behind her neck, pulling her head forward.

The kiss was that of a man, strong and as warming as she had anticipated. She had been kissed before by boys, but boys where not men. Eric was a man. His kiss had all the rough sophistication of an adult. No boy would think of attacking her lips as directly as Eric was doing. No youth would dare to caress her lips so sensuously with a tongue.

Something tangible moved Lisa, a warm glow deep inside ignited. She lifted one leg over the seat, put both arms around Eric's neck. Pulled him to her. She felt his jeans rub against her still naked thighs, returning his kiss with all the fiery passion as she received it. Locked together, mouthing greedily, she felt her lips warming, hungrily she open her mouth, his tongue, avidly seeking hers. She was wanting him, wanting it all, everything. A warm hand caressed her thigh, before moving slowly forward, she felt it seeking to slip between her legs, she opened them, arching herself against the searching hand. A gentle moan, in her throat, as the touching fingers departed. Her mouth opened wider, the flesh of his hand returned, her panties wet to the touch. She groaned again as one finger traced the divide between the lips of her secret opening, a place where no other hand had ever touched.

His touch electrified her flesh. The finger, a beautiful breathtaking sliver of raw heat, her heart pounding, lungs panting she felt waves of intense passion echoing through her unrestrained desire for more. The erotic manifestation within making her flesh smoulder.

In unison, there lips parted, the kiss broken, they gazed into each other's shining eyes. Lisa trembling with a passion newly awakened in her body for the first time.

"Holy shit, girl!" Eric said, softly.

Lisa smiled at the burst of disbelief in his voice. His discovery of the willingness of her flesh to be aroused by his touch surprised her as much as it did him.

She pulled him to her again, his fingers probed her inner thighs, a finger gently pushed the wet crutch of panties between the lips of the entrance to her inner body, as the sensual sensation engulfed her flesh.

This is moment that it's going to happen, her mind untroubled by the thought, in spite of her body's sensation. *But with him, Eric James Cheats, of all people.*

Eric, his head on her shoulder now, voice husky, soft, said, "I always thought there was more to you than meets eye. I've watched you walk about the school like butter wouldn't melt in your mouth, a right little snob, and yet you always had a warmth in you. I kinda sensed you had a fire in you and it centred between your legs, waiting for good old Eric to ignite it into flames!"

"You're wrong," she told him, truthfully. "It's not like that at all, Eric."

"Don't give me that crap," he snorted. "You wanted it, badly girl, you couldn't wait for me to touch you up, could you?"

"No," she replied. She put her hands on his head, lifted it off her shoulder, her fingers rubbing his neck, its thick muscles sensually exciting her, as she pulled his face towards hers. "Kiss me again, Girl. Long and hard." And she mashed her lips on his, mouth open, taking his lips inside hers.

Lisa, felt his hand on her panties, fingers curled around the crutch, a sharp burning sensation on her hips, in an instant they were around her knees.

She was trembling with unexplainable need, his fingers inside her, straining in their renewed embrace, kissing rapturously. Her naked flesh thrusting into his naked hot fingers. With the fingers inside her, caressing, probing, poking, deeper, blindly. Lisa could feel her thighs hardening, the scent of her own sweating body odour in her nostrils. Her teeth bit into his upper lip, tasted blood as the movement of his voracious fingers sent her body into a voluptuous erotic writhing orgasm that ripped through her body, she felt a thick hot molten liquid coat the probing fingers, her mind and flesh contorted into blissful release. Never had she been able to achieve a release when she did it to herself. This was her first climax.

Trembling with waves of passion, they parted once more. A lethargy of languid satisfaction swept over Lisa's flesh.

To be aroused and brought to an orgasm by a man's fingers was a new world of exquisite sensation.

Eric removed his leather jacket, laid it on the ground. "You enjoy that didn't you, Lisa? Now it's my turn, take you panties off and lie down on my jacket and then I'll fuck you properly".

"No, Eric, I can't," she told him.

He stared, thunderstruck. "What do you mean, *YOU CAN'T?*

"I've never have, Eric, never," she explained.

The confession made him angry, "Don't give me that crap! The way you let me finger you, you loved it."

"It's not crap, Eric. It's the truth. I've never been with anyone before. And I can't."

His eyes narrowed. He didn't believe her. Angrily he grabbed her, threw her on the ground. Lisa did not protest, he ripped her panties off completely. He kissed her, a long kiss, the hand was back between her legs. Embracing him, welcoming the fingers and his hot hungry demanding lips. Lisa surrendered to sensation of lustful pleasure of imminent orgasm. Abruptly, with savage fury, Eric rolled on top of her and fought to spread her legs, to open her thighs.

The impending assault was the most exciting sensation so far. Lisa still burned with the desire to. As her classmates put it. *'To go all the way!'* Yet still deep inside her mind she resisted that small step of capitulation, holding her back as she teetered on a knife-edge of surrender. She felt a power in her resistance, the knowledge that she was able, with her femininity to lift Eric, a man, to such heights of reckless passion and need.

His assault became more aggressive, savage in its extremity, too determined. Lisa, with some effort sat up, disentangling herself from the grip of his rampant sexual need.

"I'm not staying here if your going to behave like that, Eric, if that is how your going to treat me then you can take me home. *Now!*" she said in a prissy frosty tone.

"I can't believe this!" Eric replied, his face twisted, through clenched teeth, snarled. "No girl that goes as far as you do, can tell me she don't want to be screwed."

Smiling, touching his cheek. "Oh, your so sweet, Eric," she said tenderly. "Please, don't be angry and mean about it."

Still breathing heavy, panting, he lay beside her, legs straight. "Don't be bloody mean." he cried wildly. "Have you any idea what your hot lips, and little tight wet pussy has done to me." His hand on his fly as he shouted, with a sharp swish the zip opened, his huge shaft erect, leaped into view.

"Put your hand on it," he crooned softly. "Touch it. *Please.* Lisa. *Touch it!*"

Lisa, eyes wide, stared. She'd never seen a male organ before, much less one stiff with an erection. So unbelievably huge in it's size, too thick, too swollen, to perform the act she knew it was meant to perform. To envisage that thing in her body, completely devoured inside her flesh, was impossible. It would tear, rip, hurt, make her bleed.

"Put you hand on it," he begged. "Just touch me, Lisa, that all I ask. Let me feel your warm fingers on it. I've got come to get off before I die."

Captivated, She leaned forward for a closer look. It jerked in spasms, the reddish-purple head had a life of its own, seeming to swell and pulsate, spasmodically. Lisa *Imagined* how it would feel, pulsating like that inside her body, in the place of where the fingers had been earlier. There was no way, in her mind that it could fit in there, she told herself, furiously.

Eric, eyes closed, lay back, "Touch it, Sweet Lisa baby, I'll keep my eyes shut. I swear, I won't look, I promise," his words, ragged, as if in sexual agony.

The convincing promise of applying her hand unobserved, to shaft of flesh, charged Lisa with a boldness. Tentatively, her hand touched it, a fingertip brush of the swollen gland. His fiery hot flesh seeming to burn at her caress; Lisa searching to feel the pulse of his manly needs clasped it in her hand. The throbbing sex organ jumped in her fingers, it shuddered with life, a living organ of man's desire. It was alive. Lisa chuckled, at the pleasure of knowing how much life it possessed.

Eric turned towards her, blindly he put his hand between her legs, seeking the opening of her body. "Yes," he whispered. ***"Now we fuck!"***

His weight and the throbbing shaft bearing down on her. Damn, she wanted to taste the pleasure of feeling the hot pulsating rod vibrating *inside her*. She was eager and frightened at the same time; her mind spinning, senses swimming, now she was fighting herself more ferociously than she was Eric.

He poked her between the legs, the entrance dangerously close to the swollen shaft. It pushed at the wet lips of her vagina. Only an instinctive grab saved her, her hand closed over the object, so tantalising near. She closed her hand into a fist around the shaft, rubbing it, slowly, then faster.

Eric, a moan escaping through his gritted teeth, as if protesting, while his hips irregularly in the throes of paroxysm spasms thrust his weapon through her pumping fingers.

He suddenly, for an instant, the shaft of solid flesh in her hand swelled, knotted.

His ejaculation, so violent and sudden took Lisa by surprise. She felt it coat her naked stomach, before spewing up over her dress bunched around her waist, then spurting the dregs of the wet sticky feeling juice over her pubic hair.

Lisa was startled and shocked; disturbed by the discovery,

that a man convulsed in such a mindless fashion to reach completion. A feeling of tenderness, and enormous achievement overcame her, this time she had been triumphant, she had won.

Eric lay on his back looking up at the sky, breathing heavy. She continued to stroking his fading erection, gently, in her sticky hand until his body cease to tremble.

Opening his eyes, he sat up. Looking at the staining on her pubic hair, little white coloured globules, scattered, glistening in the sunlight. "Jesus, your really something else," he said sullenly. "Next thing you'll tell me you're still intact."

"Intact?" she replied. "*I am*, if you mean what I think you mean?

He glowered at her. "You know what I mean as well as I do," angry now. "You're trying to tell me, that after coming all over my fingers, willingly, then wanking me until I shot my load all over you, that your still a virgin," an incredulous frown of suspicion on his face, head shaking in disbelief.

"I have never been touched, nor have I ever touched anyone, until today, Eric."

Her words seem to quell his doubts. But his tone remained insistent. "Is that the truth, Lisa?"

Wrapping her arms around his neck, her head on his shoulder. "It's the truth, Eric."

His arms enclosed her, squeezing her tight to him. Holding each other, in silence. They relaxed in peaceful contentment in mind and of the flesh. Eric broke the idyllic mood, when he said, "Next time, Lisa. Promise me, next time. You'll let me love you, won't you?"

She moved away from him, looked into his bright blue eyes. "I don't know, Eric." Her voice was gentle, filled with tenderness for him, and the memory of her desire. Yet unshakeably resolute. "Perhaps. But I'm not sure. Be patient with me, Eric, then maybe one day you'll make me a virgin no more.

This was her great love affair, the first. When the school became aware of it, it became the most talked subject of the year, a scandal. Lisa, immune to all criticism and warning from her friends concerning the outcome of having an affair with a low life such as Eric, disturbed her little.

It bothered her, knowing Eric could never pick her up for a date from her home, nor would there ever be, the long tender farewell kiss at the front door before he said goodnight.

His bad reputation, his often crude, rough language and aggressive nature, coupled with the overwhelming will to take her virginity, even that did not prevent her being enthral by him – even his attempts at kindly soft clumsy tenderness had a fascination for her.

Through it all Eric, no matter how much he tried, or attempted. And there were many such confrontations. He never achieved his ultimate objective, in his constant endeavour to sever the hidden rampart to her inner flesh with his erect pulsating manhood.

It was Lisa, with her virginal and sexual innocence that controlled the affair. Within the parochial narrow boundaries of the relationship, which she set. She set the pace, and the level of their lovemaking. Every time, as she had, since that first day she willingly, eagerly yielded her body and vagina in to his hands. She opened her mind to the pleasures of male flesh. Her hands and fingers exploring with a vociferous vivacity that equalled his.

Manipulating the small nipples on his hairless chest gently, coaxing them to come erect, stroking his balls, weighing them in her hot hands, applying her fingers to his huge blood gorged shaft of flesh, stroking it, caressing it lovingly, teasing it, watching it jerk and throb, in it's lustful desire, to possess, and be possessed.

Eric commenced always full of optimism, *today,* this *time* he would succeed. He held the aged-old belief, a myth that any girl, once she'd touched a man's most potent possession, his *Cock,* the struggle for her submission had been won. Blindly he believed, in spite of bring shown, frequently. That it was a misplaced assumption on his part. To his ego, the idea, that this one girl named Lisa, could show an express such avid greed for him and his shaft, lusting for orgasm continuously without yielding the citadel.

Lisa, with her desire for sexual pleasure and her manipulative fingers reduced Eric to a pitiful, sad, human being.

He no longer made demands to receive, what he considered to be his male rights, he begged her for the ultimate surrender, the total consummation of her flesh with his – and always-helplessly – submitting to her clever fingers for release.

Never, despite the burning craving to step over the line into the world of complete sexual satisfaction, the territory of herself. A minute grain inside her mind prevented her, Lisa could not, would not, surrender her cherry.

Not even when, after a great deal of loving persuasion, he escorted her to a social function at school. Dressed for the first time in a suit, she had to admit, with his handsome face and sparkling blue eyes. To Lisa the best looking student in the building. It wasn't a success, quite the opposite, Eric endured, insults and ridicule all evening. So determined to behave in the manner that she had expected of him, he suffered in silence.

It was later that night, lying in bed. The realisation, a deep feeling of tenderness overcame her, like suffocating blanket of warmth. She loved Eric, not just for his hands, because of the man he was.

A few days later. High in the hills, her private domain she shared with Eric. Leaving him sitting on the warm ground looking down at the river in the distance. Lisa, behind his back. Stripped naked, something she had never done with him before, yes, many times he'd undone her clothing, removed her skirt and blouse, her underwear always. Yet never had she until that day stripped herself completely nude.

Today was different, the feeling of affection she had for Eric, had changed to heartfelt love.

Boldly standing in front of him, his eyes charged with desire at the sight of her naked flesh. Mouth open he reached for her.

Lisa, smiling, looked into his blue eyes. She didn't want to tell him. His reward for the suffering she had inflicted on him. Lisa wanted to convey her gift, without words.

Gently he pulled her to him, tenderly he laid her beside him, leaned his face over hers. In a voice she had never heard before, words impregnated with desire, love and wanton need, he cried, "My God, your so beautiful. *I love you more than you'll ever know.*" The words raped all thoughts of resistance from her soul.

She kissed him liked never before, pouring every ounce of her being in to her lips. Her virtue, remaining intact, virginal, meant nothing to her now. It was her sweet Eric's, to take, plunder, ravage, destroy forever. She quivered in anticipation of the pleasures it would herald.

Eric hand's ran all over her naked flesh, on her breasts, stroking her nipples, then down her shape, squeezing the hips, caressing the thighs, running a finger up her now moist vagina. His lips left hers, moved down her face slowly over the chin, then the neck. She gasped, the warm wet lips enclosed a nipple, *sucking* hard, as a two fingers manipulated the other one, pinching it before squeezing the erected teat. The tongue moved downward. She felt every wet touch, as it tortuously, gently travelled over her now tingling flesh. Stopping for a few seconds at her navel.

Lisa groaned out loud, when the hot slippery tip, ran round the tiny indentation in her belly, before slipping inside the small aperture in her flesh, to lick the hidden knotted piece of now harden gristle that had been her lifeline before birth.

Lisa's flesh was on fire, her thighs had become sopping wet, the tongue still moving down, lips now kissing her mound of black curly pubic hair.

She leaped in shocked surprise, ridged for an instant, as the wet tip of the tongue probed her most sensitive flesh, her *clitoris*. It moved agonising slow down between her legs. She kept her eyes closed, tight, afraid to look at what she was allowing Eric to do to her body. Mingled with the thought with her eyes open, in some way, the delicious feelings coursing through her flesh would change. The tongue traced the line that separated her now twitching vagina lips.

Eric, she could feel it in his still stroking hands, tense, as if somehow, unsure of her motive's. He had to suffer many painful sexual disappointments in the past.

She had repulsed him, so often, when he'd believed she would surrender. Now in his moment of triumph, no confidence to go beyond a certain height of sexual pleasure. She had shattered it with her unflinching will to remain a virgin.

Running her hands through his sweaty curly hair, opening

her legs a little wider. Composing all the tenderness she was feeling for him. Now, in a husky cooing voice, softly said, "Don't stop now my wonderful; lover, I'll not refuse you today, I love you Eric, now you love me, as you've always desired to, since the first day we meet."

Lisa sensed in her hands, the stiffness in his body, evaporating, the tongue became moister.

The warm wet tongue tip against her virgin flesh, unsoiled, unbroken, and now available, presented by Lisa, his reward, her most precious possession, a piece of her body and life, once given, never to give a second time. She had never wanted to say. I *lost my virginity,* no, never! She always had desired to *give it.*

Her body seemed to have a will of it's own. Surely not, he'd never go that far, the tongues insistence increased. He was going to… she felt the tongue pressing. He was. "*Oh… My… God,*" her mind screamed.

Lisa left the world of right and wrong. Transported by carnal desire, she panted, "Let me touch you, please, Eric. I need to feel the your *Cock in my hand before you… you FUCK ME!*"

Lisa, hands searching in mad desperation for the shaft of flesh, grasped it, groaning as it's heat filled her hands, so massively long, so thick, throbbing, leaping in her fingers, squeezing in hard, felt the blood thundering though the swollen veins, rubbing it furiously, its awesome power, its living heartbeat, joining hers.

She was going to climax, it swelled inside her, an ever growing gathering of passion building up within.

Opening her legs, so wide, her hips hurt, moaning, her fingers pumping the seemingly ever expanding column of flesh viciously.

She bent her legs towards her planted her feet solidly on the warm ground, lifting her buttock off the floor. Eric's avid mouth left her wet thighs, her vagina flexed at the loss. She wanted scream. *No*, not yet, please, her desire to feel the sensations of a man's tongue within her flesh so powerful, interrupted when the warm mouth was replace by his fingers. Lisa's frenzied flesh erupted, three fingers slipped easily deep in to her vagina, filling her flesh with wild tremors of passion as she rotated her loins savagely, the fingers roaming within, touching, stabbing, caressing very tissue and nerve of her pussy.

God damn it, she swore bad temperedly. If I had know that day I would wait another twenty five years for my first orgasm on a man's tongue, that day would have change my life for ever, dragging hard on the half smoked cigarette. The recollection swept her mind back to hillside and Eric.

Lisa felt her orgasm spurt, a flood of warm liquid ripped through her flesh, coating the driving exploring fingers.

The rampaging animal like carnal lust within, unleash words from her mouth, the like, she'd never heard or spoken before, in a manner and language total alien to her lips and mind. Uncontrollable.

Lisa screamed, writhing in sexual agony. *Yes, Eric, touch me, oh yes please, let me feel, ah, ah, uh, umm, umm, go on lover, fuck me with your hand, god that's, ar, ar, awwww, my cunt's afire for your massive, long, long cock Eric, I can't wait for you to fuck me, now!*

She felt the hand leave her body, opening her eyes, Eric towered over her. Sweat running down his face, dripping, on her hardened erected nipples, his edges of his mouth coated with whitish looking saliva.

Lisa, hand still pulling his rod, looked down. The purple-red head swollen.

Eric's weight came down on her sweat stained flesh; his shaft rammed in to her, so frantic to take her fortress, it missed its mark. She moaned as the rampant weapon, drove over her clitoris and parted the wet pubic hair, again he attempted to reach his goal, pushing harder, again he failed. Lisa, as hungry for Eric, as he was for her, slipped a hand between his body and hers, taking hold of the shaft, rubbing gently, guided it to the doorway of her body.

She cried out in pain, as the bloated crown of the shaft pushed marginally into her body, it felt as if her flesh was tearing.

Eric went stiff, his face contorted in a picture of ugly twisted pain, eyes rolling. He screamed into her face. *"You Bitch, you dirty lying, prick teasing little slut"*. Lisa shrank, frightened by the twisted look of hate in his eyes. And the venom in the words.

Her hand was wet. Tears filled her eyes. Pain struck her heart, an agonising feeling horror swept over her. He had ejaculated, on the point of entering her with his flesh.

Lisa, collapsed, mentally and physically. Eric shoved her arms away as she attempted to hold him. Left her lying, legs apart, naked. The naked body, and her. To him an abomination, a loathsome creature.

She curled up in ball, as if in the foetal position, she could return to the womb that had given her life. To start again. The life she now lived in ruins.

Numb she rose to her feet, dressed, Stood beside the machine of gleaming metal, waiting for Eric.

When he walked over to the bike, not looking at her, eyes averted, staring at the ground. Tentatively, she gently put her hand on his arm. Roughly he knock aside.

Tears running down her cheeks, she haltingly said. "I'm so sorry, truly I am, Eric, it just happened this time."

"Oh Yeah, I suppose, it always just happened, like it just happened every time you made me finger fuck you," his words filled with anger. Yet she could feel his hurt.

"I love you, Eric, and I treated you badly I realise that now, But when you said you loved me more than I'd ever know, it broke my heart to think every time I spurned you how much I must have hurt you. But now I understood why you had never forced me to submit, and you could have, we both know that, yet you didn't," sobbing bitterly, she forced herself. To bare her soul, unconditionally. "Eric, today I was yours utterly, I would have endured the pain, the agony, we both realise what that huge length of flesh you so proudly possess would inflict upon my virgin body, because of the love I feel for you and to make amends for not showing it you, or giving you the respect and affection you so richly deserve, in this place today you where the man", she paused, not sure how to put her final, confession. Looking him straight in face, said bluntly, with clear conviction, "The first man I ever... I ever wanted to *Fuck me* and you still are that man."

Overjoyed, as his eyes softened at her outburst. His reply had lost the hard edge of his hatred, and anger.

"I don't know, Lisa, I'll have to think about it, you'll never know how much you hurt me, nor the misery and agony you've put me through, I no longer know my own mind, the need inside for you, is killing me body and soul, if I could only understand you but I don't, now get on the bloody bike." Back in town, as she dismounted handing him her helmet. Eric push up his visor, features hidden except for the sad looking eyes, said, "See you tomorrow, maybe..." then shot away, the bike leaping forward, roaring.

Lisa stood, watching the silver machine till it disappeared out of sight, she was disconsolate beyond belief, her mind a confused jumbled vortex of black misery.

In a state of mental shock, unconscious of her surrounding, mind a black nothingness.

She lay in bed sobbing, the walk home, a mystery.

Eric paid her little attention after that fateful afternoon in the hills, he spent most of his times with his erstwhile cronies, spoke to her, not unkindly, yet cold, distant. She came to terms, if that was the right word, with her misery and pain.

Lisa's hurtful emotions caused her the most heartache. She couldn't decide, in her head, which part to except losing Eric, or the loss of his dextrous fingers.

The affair came to a disastrous end for Lisa. Out of the blue Eric asked her to go with him to a concert. To see some rock band she'd never heard of.

Lisa, using what had become a constant deception in the past, lied to her mother, again, told her she was going over to a friend's for the evening and meet Eric at the dingy pool room where he hung out with his cohorts. It was, so he told her, to make sure she understood exactly what being at the concert entailed.

Never being a couple to spend their time together, as others did, at the drive in movies, or the bowling alley, they headed out of town, directly to the hills overlooking the river.

Eric parked in the usual place, on the edge of the cliff, so they could watch the sun going down, casting shimmering coloured shadows on the water in the distance. He was somewhat subdued, almost nervous. Must be remembering the painful failure of the previous visit, she concluded.

Lisa, as she had so many times in the past, with practised ease put her arms around his neck. Her inner thighs moist, or to use Eric's terminology, her sweet little cunt was becoming feverishly hot and wet in anticipation of his stroking probing fingers toying within her vagina. A pleasure she had desperately missed over the last few weeks. Hungrily she pulled his head towards her for the first long, lust constructing kiss for some time.

Surprisingly, Eric resisted. Body stiff, preventing contact, shaking his head, he unzipped his jeans. "Don't start that shit," he told brusquely, for the first time since their affair began she smelt alcohol on his breath.

"You know what you want, don't you? Now take the damn thing out and toss me off."

Lisa, chuckled at the new dimension of pleasure, reach inside, ran her fingers alone the shaft, freeing from the confines of the jeans. His *cock,* she had promised herself, to help heal his wounded pride, she would use his crude words, words never spoken in her shelter cosy life, she practised them, rehearsed them her head, privately, secretively, to get her mouth to utter the bad forbidden terms he used.

The *cock,* hot in her hand, strangely whitish in the brightening moonlight. Deliberately, slowly, she teased the skin down over the head, skinning it, overjoyed, as it erected, quivering upwards, becoming fully hard with her expert fondling. Eric stood unmoving, the only part of him un-yielding, his shaft.

"Kiss me, Eric," she said, ever so softly. "Eat my mouth with your lips while I do it to you, touch my pussy as I stroke your beautiful, gorgeous cock."

"Just get on with it, and jack me off," he said roughly.

Lisa's hand paused, looked at his face, "Is that all you want?"

"That's all I'm ever gonna get from you ain't it?"

"No it is not, Eric", hurt indignation in her voice, "You want more, you can have more, if my fingers no longer provide the satisfaction you need, than be a man and take it, if fucking me means so much to you, quit complaining and ***Do it, Now!"***

Her tone, the words, a challenge to his masculinity. He stepped away from her, staring, depriving her hand of his cock.

"Fuck you? Like you led me on last time, let me kiss your cunt, fill my hand with your come. Oh yes you'd like that won't you, make me believe in my mind and cock that you cared enough for me at last, to chain ourselves together, body and soul, as only a man and woman can, naked as one flesh, then you jack me off at the moment I experienced more love than I believed possible for ***You!"*** he shouted, into her face, tiny spots of spit from his lips striking her cheeks.

There it was, the core of both their hang-ups. Eric with his wounded male ego, raging in her face, the rage directed towards her was an outburst of his own frustrated sexual desires.

While she, with her fear of what agony his rampart shaft would inflict on her flesh.

"Do whatever your hot fingers want, I don't care anymore, have your own way. Just cut out all the other shit and get it over with. I'm tired of your stupid games."

Lisa knew as a cold icy finger touch her soul. She had won many sexual skirmish in the past, small but important in defence of her virtue and virginity in the past. But this was the final confrontation, the battle for complete sexual supremacy. For her cherry and his manly pride, to have dominance of both their carnal desire's.

And she had lost, been vanquished, defeated. If she surrendered her flesh to him, now, from this moment on it would be on Eric's terms. Or never at all. Indecisive. She wavered, for a moment. She had never desired Eric with such depth of feeling as she did now, in his aggressive renewed manly forcefulness. Stronger than ever before.

She wanted his flesh, to feel him against her will, and better judgement, the weight of his naked body, on hers.

To be opened helplessly, impaled on his cock, feel it drive hot and nakedly alive, deep in to her pussy.

Wasn't this in both, their hearts and minds? Didn't they both, deep down in their physco's want the same thing?

If only Eric had exerted his masculine power, to rip away the female fear, the stop sign he could never pass. Lisa craved to give in. As she had once before. But that was on her terms. And yet he deserved a second chance, he'd earned his place in her heart. In spite of his crude, rough ways, he'd shown patience, on times, in the understanding of her fear that surprised her on occasions, even on times loving her gently, with a tenderness sweetness.

Lisa's only concession, to think in his manner and to talk dirty, she loved Eric deeply. She craved, and desired him passionately. No other man or boy had entered her mind, her heart, her very soul, or her sexual desire's, her wants, as Eric had consumed hers.

All this, in a clear instant clarity of thought with deep feeling she analysed. Yet her stretching hand still went out to his hard stiff cock, her fingers closed over the warm flesh, softly, she sadly said, "All right All right, Eric. I'll toss you off."

It took seemingly, ages.

Eric standing, his back to the silent motor-bike, casting a long shadow, legs apart, hands on hips, unmoving, his stiff cock in her wildly moving hand, no orgasm filling his cold hard body. Using every movement, every sinew in her pounding fingers, all the little clever tricks and squeezes she'd ever learned. In desperation to finish, she place her other hand, cupping his balls in the palm, momentarily leaving his ridged shaft, her other hand, wetting it by rubbing it against her moist cunt

She was breathing heavy, panting from her exertions, her hand became a flying fist, Eric responded slowly, her fingers aching, her hand a blur of white, he groaned, grunted, groaned a second time, then his come spurted white looking in the pale yellow moonlight, raining down on her clenched fist.

Eric stood frozen. Her hurting, sore, damp fingers, painful and stiff, still gently stroked the failing hardness of the cock. Removing her hand, deliberately. Lisa, instinctively understood, her hand was no long good enough to satisfy Eric needs.

Resigned to her fate. Lisa started to put her helmet over her head. She wanted Eric, She loved him, but this was not the time to tell him. He would never believe that now she wanted him so badly, her breath became strangled in her own throat. Not to fuck her. *So, She* could *fuck him*.

"Hang on a minute," he said nervously.

Removing her helmet, "Now what?" she inquired.

"I won't be taking you to the concert on Saturday night," he said, eyes down-cast, sounding like it was painful for him to say, "I'm taking Rina Hepworth."

"Who the hell is Rina Hepworth?" she asked slowly. "I never knew you where dating someone else Eric."

His voice full of male bravado, yet sad sounding and unhappy. "I wasn't, not until last Friday night."

"Fine, Eric," heartbroken she replied.

"I got inside her panties on our first date," bragging now, his male ego asserting itself. "Not with this," waving his hand at her, "With this," grabbing his crutch to emphasis his point, "Not once, but twice, I shot my load deep inside her warm pussy."

"And why do you think it took you so long to jack me off? She gave me head last night, all the way, took my come in her mouth. How do like those apples, Lisa baby?"

He was mocking her, to make her feel jealous, and she was. "All right, Eric. All bloody right, if she's what you want, then you go spend your time with her and let me be," the words spat out through her clenched teeth

"She isn't a teaser, like you, you're a right P.I.T.

"P.I.T.?" she muttered, stupefied.

"Of course, you'd don't know what it men's do you, oh no. Not sweet innocent virgin Lisa, a prick teaser, your a Prick-Innocent-Tease. I should have realised that a long time ago, I suppose I'm not the first one, nor the last man you'll leave with a rock hard cramp in his cock."

"I don't understand you," she said numbly.

"No maybe you don't, but you don't care, do you. Because you always come your juice. Yeah, you make sure you get yours, don't you?"

"I love you, Eric. I really do." she said forlornly, yet bravely.

His voice softened, quietly he said, "I know you do, Lisa. Like I'll never love another."

He turned, put his helmet on, twisted the ignition key, climbed on the ticking machine, waited for her to sit on the buddy seat, and took off.

All the way back to town, Lisa, arms around his waist, head cuddled into his broad back, sobbed her heart out.

He stopped behind a parked lorry, two blocks from her house, at the bottom of the hill. She dismounted, took the helmet off, handed it to him

Caring little how her eyes puffed from crying looked. He flipped up his helmet's visor, slipped the offered helmet over his wrist, smiled at her weakly, said in a stammer, "Bye, lovely sweet Lisa, see you around." Slammed down the visor, and roared away in a cloud of smoke, leaving her standing, alone, on the kerb, blinded by her tears.

The memory of Eric's visor closing so suddenly failing to hide the tears oozing out of his eye's lived with her ever since.

Moving slowly in the moonlight, in a trance, pushing her aching body, and bleeding heart, she climbed the hill towards the house. Her heart in time healed, the scars forever had *REMAINED*.

Chapter 7

Lisa was in the grip of enlightened happiness.

She had not felt so blissfully aware of life since she was in junior school; at sixteen she had met the boy named Eric. He had opened the door to new universe of passionate love, and sexual lust, it had ended, an uncompleted sexual relationship, but she learned a lot about love. Even more about sex.

Her body, now fused with the same feelings, of desire, and passion, more vibrant, deeper, totally alive, more than it had been for over twenty years.

Every morning she awakened, convinced. *Today*, Nathan would ring her front door bell, strong and ready, sexually vibrant, as he had been before, it made her feel so good, and stupidly silly at the same time.

The sound of a car engine, any car engine in her secluded affluent street she heard stop, had her rushing expectantly to the front door. The ringing of the telephone spread shivering waves of expectancy through her body, once she pick up the receiver, she could only speak in panting gasps.

Her nights were troubled, waking up, once or twice every night, sometimes more, searching with clawing hands for the naked flesh of a man. Nathan's preferably.

Desperate. Deprived of satisfaction, she'd lie on her stomach smoking a cigarette. A pillow clasped between her thighs, something to rub her moist pussy against. She had to have something tangible to feel against her gentle quivering vagina.

At times, Lisa attempted to persuade herself out of her stupid affliction. Realistically, she reminded herself, Nathan had only hinted he'd return. The possibility of making love again, never stated clearly. Yet her body, eager flesh and ever damp thighs, refused to except he would not call.

When the feeling, agonising in the extreme, for a hard, big rampant cock, reached its pinnacle. She remained light hearted, a glow in her flesh, a sweet feeling of her spirit afloat with happiness.

Nothing could shake her body's faith, if Nathan delay his visit to long, even that idea, only lowered her sexual excitement for a short while.

She would find another young man with a ready cock, and the stamina to leave her weak. Why one, why not *Two*, at the same time?

That thought, and what a thought it was, after tasting the wonder's, the everlasting pleasurable carnal lust with a youth half her age. Lisa, in her newly discovered world of avid pussy filled fucking. A new dimension of sex, where she had orgasm after orgasm. So gratifying to her flesh, unknowingly at the time. Yet she knew it now. She had become addicted to young cock. That addiction to the mind, flesh and vagina, and to her was as potent as... *Heroin*.

Even when the stark realisation of the dangers involved arose in her mind. Lisa knew the dangers of addiction and all the ramifications, the manifestations it brought to the human body and mind, how addiction, be it alcohol, drugs, gambling. It disassembled the mind, the flesh, the very being of all things human, slowly corrupting, in the most insidious gentle fashion. Charging the mind with visions and images, indecipherable only to the addicted mind. Irrevocably ending as in life, with *Death*.

She had, everybody had, through the constant never-ending media exposure, in the newspapers, on television, in magazines. The danger's of addiction.

Lisa disregarded all her minds warnings, ignored them utterly. The consequences of surrendering her mind, her flesh, her very soul. Into the waiting arms of the ravenous beast of sexuality, the mighty demon of all human degradation.

She had no thoughts, no feel of fear, her mind empty of revulsion, no illusions about the depths of decadence her mind and flesh would inexplicable sink to.

Lisa embraced her demon. Excepting it in to her soul, with all the passion that she would lavish on an ejaculating, heaving cock. She married her demon, with her flesh. "Till death did they part". The minute Nathan's big shaft penetrated her vagina all the way in to the hilt. Her personal demon. Her partner from Hell. The beast growing within.

Flesh, naked Men cocks! Fucking orgasm's, an ever full Cunt! Legions of huge rampant shafts filling her continuously, never-ending exploding hot come coating her deep inside!

Lisa, it came as no surprise to her. Once she allowed her mind to be seduced, willingly, her sexual boundaries vanished. There wasn't any. Replace by a magnificent aura of freedom, sexual in its intensity, devouring every sexual inhibition she had ever possessed, wiping her memory clean.

She felt so alive, so confident, so complete. Reborn into a new world, her new world. A dimension of life far more exciting, more vibrant. Yet it contained, no conscience, no right or wrong, no barrier of any description, no laws or rules, no punishment. The only requirement of her, in this wild new universe. Her absolute fulfilment of her sexual desire's.

To allow her beast, no matter how degrading, to wallowing unabandonly no matter how depraved, in any sexual perversion, any act of debauched vileness, completely.

Lisa embraced her demon, wrapped her mind around it, inserted its very being it to her brain. She drew into her body, with a greater love and desire than she ever lavishly administered to an erect cock.

As the days past, her impatience, her need blossomed Over and over, in rapacious detail, she pictured their love-making.

Lisa, far from having any doubts or misgiving regarding the dramatic, and in some ways violent disintegration of her lifetimes experiences and the taboos she been taught, together with her own prejudices regarding sex.

Having the psychology of her life erased. It didn't effect her newfound happiness. Lisa overjoyed, ecstatic, in the enlightenment of her new life into pleasurable avid promiscuity. Her wonderful feeling of wellbeing expanded, then magnified to even a greater height her ecstatic euphoria.

As the days past, the impatience, her need blossomed. Over and over, in rapacious detail, she *pictured* lovemaking. Nathan appeared more than often than other image is, but vision's of other naked faceless men also leaped into focus, including the erected shaft, of one Leroy Matts and the rebuffed young Jay.

Her mind had never been so vividly illuminated, evoking graphic images of sex. She envisaged how Nathan's cock stood stiff, hard, a quivering column flesh against muscle ridged belly flash across her mind. Her vagina shivered as the lean strong lines of his body, the contours of his chest, the flat hard belly sloping down to his curly black pubic hair, it made her cunt trembled, the memory of the heat, the driven power, unleashed by the massive cock, the thundering breathtaking vitality, as he'd fucked her. The tip of her tongue slithered across her lips, as once more the taste of his semen in her throat returned to her mouth, as she'd extracted his come, made all the sweeter remembering her love juice had been coating his tongue, at the same time.

The revisit in her imagination, made her unbearably wet and horny, almost impossible to endure. But with stubborn determination, she spurned self-satisfaction, the solace she'd receive, too limited.

The act of self-masturbation, alone and in private, a waste of precious semen, better saved to anoint his weapon of love.

If he didn't call soon, very soon, someone else would deprive him of the sexual bounty that was rightfully his.

The phone calls that week, constant to such an extent, it drove her frantic. Each time Lisa pick up the phone, trembling, always the voice on the other end would be His.

The phone had lost it importance to her as the years of solitary living past, until Nathan, now once more it became vital to her.

Many calls were wrong numbers that week, other just meaningless time wasting chat. Those she cut short. Lisa didn't want to be chatting endlessly, the priority was *Him*.

The first call, on the third day of waiting, was from Dean, who Lisa, had alrcady removed from her mind, no more middle-aged lovers for me she decided. He made the usual noises, how was she, the weekend had been wonderful. For you it was, not for me, she recalled, as he talked on and on.

Lisa had no more need for Dean or his muted lovemaking. She cut in on his conversation abruptly, "I'm sorry, Dean, I'm afraid the coming week-end is impossible, I'll have to give you a rain-check this time, something's come up and I'll be away for a few days. Give me a ring some time next week and we then we can sort something out. Sorry to rush you like this but I'm expecting an important phone call and I need to keep the line free. Bye, don't forget to call," and hung up.

What a pack of lies, she rebuked herself. No time like the present to start leaving the old world behind. Twenty minutes later, the phone rang again, with Nathan and sex so strong in her mind, she believed it was him, this time. Instead it was Dean; again, graciously suggesting he'd take her out to dinner, but couldn't promise to stay the night. Lisa disinterested, absentmindedly thought. Fine, you buy me dinner, a few drinks, drive me home, and by way of a small thank you for my generosity, You can put your sweet mouth around my cock, and when it's big and hard, I'll place where I want put it, then fuck you. Once I've come in your lovely active pussy, if you want it again, I'll lay back and you can help myself,

Her sexual practices and techniques she shared with every middle-aged lover, as well as Dean, left her cold now she wanted no more. The only men in her mind now, were big, strong, virile, and about all, young, able to fuck and fuck and fuck again, able to recuperate quickly, with the aid from her lips, mouth and insatiable vagina. Rising to fuck her again.

It was unnatural, to have to *make* a man screw her, to extract her satisfaction, from a *Man.* The very concept degraded the whole essence of man's dominate superiority, to meaningless charade, which they concealed with a thing they call ego.

So conceited, so arrogant, when they reach middle-age, they never know the contempt women have for their puny efforts after they fuck.

"Not tonight, I'm afraid, Dean," she said, and hung up.

Next morning she regretted hanging up on Dean. Not her instant brush off.

The lack of diplomacy. He rang twice before lunch again in the evening and left two messages on the answering machine

He rang first thing the following morning. She could tell by his tone he had realised she had lost interest in their affair. He dangled a number of suggestions to encourage her to reconsider, until at last he offered to take her to the Bahamas for a weekend. At his expense, off course

"You'll enjoy the soft sandy beaches, the nightlife has to be experienced to believe, we can go scuba diving, you'll have a marvellous time, and the food is great," he sounded confident she would, say yes.

Lisa actually wasn't really listening, just wondering why he had never asked her before. Probably because he been taking other women instead. Dean's voice faded, he was waiting for answer. It held no interest to her whatsoever, she was at a loss what to say.

"Well?" he asked impatiently, "What do think, doesn't that sound great?"

"It sounds wonderful, Dean," she said slowly. "But not this time. It's really sweet of you to offer Dean, my love. Thank you."

"A week in the Bahamas, and you refuse," his voice raised, filled with astonished shock.

Lisa was becoming tired of being pressured by a man who didn't like being refused.

"Dean, I'm afraid I have to tell you. I don't intend to see you again. It's finished." her words, brutal in there honesty.

Silence... "Found a new man have you?" his voice, strangely subdued.

"It doesn't bother me if you have another lover. I don't see what difference that should make your woman enough for any two men, providing one of them is me. I'm quite happy to share your beautiful body with someone else, Lisa, my love."

She chuckled, quietly, "I don't think that's what I had in mind, Dean, share it I might, but for my satisfaction not yours, except it, Dean. It was nice while it lasted." If he didn't get the message now. He never will, she thought.

His voice remote, resigned, "Oh well. Take care of yourself I'll miss you, Lisa. Give me a call sometime."

"One day maybe, Dean," she replied. But the phone was already dead.

Lisa replaced the receiver. There had been so many calls since Nathan had arrived that wet Monday morning, and this was the fifth day of her longing for him. So many calls, she agonised as to whether he had phoned while she was speaking to another caller.

She felt a little angry at the thought. If the calls had been of some importance it would have been understandable. Just bored friends wanting to chat, most of the conversations useless natter, scandalising and complaining about, kids, husbands, and life in general. If that wasn't enough, for some unexplainable reason, as if by some strange coincidence.

Invitations from many of the men she had dated in the past, to take her out to dinner, or to the theatre, one offered to take her to a ball game. One by one, with no preamble, told them. She was sorry, it had been lovely while it lasted, but not to call again, she had no wish to enjoy their company further. At least, in some respects she had been honest to her spurned ex-lovers. She did not want see them again. She didn't care; she simply could no longer stomach middle-aged men, with their tired cocks and their unsatisfying lovemaking. Not after being fucked senseless by Nathan.

The most offensive fault to her mind, all of them, after making love. Expected to have their egos massaged. To be grateful to them for satisfying her, for giving her such a wonderfully fucking. When actually the boot was on the other foot. Lisa gave them a good fucking, it had to be. She using hands, mouth, body, and pussy, that had inspired them all, lifted them to a height of sexual excitement they had forgotten twenty years ago.

Lisa had left that life behind, burned her bridges, old lovers removed, gone forever. It was young men, *now*, with never-ending stamina, enormous vitality, and above all a shaft of flesh as insatiable as her needs.

Lisa, in fear of missing Nathan's call, or possible visit, hadn't left the house. All week she waited.

On Saturday, when she had to make a quick drive to the supermarket. Hurriedly, buying only some essentials, plus a few cartons of cigarettes, two bottles of Valdivor vodka, a six-pack of Bud for Nathan when he visited. She drove home, ignoring two red lights. The blast of the horns and insulting screams from other drivers unheard.

Lisa put the Bud in the icebox. He would call. She had a deep, deep feeling, a total conviction in her mind. He would have to call, soon, very s*oon.*

Last night had been hell, her palms, still sore from gripping the mattress to prevent her fingers ravishing her sweating moist pussy into climax. And one ejaculation would never have satisfied her. *Never!*

Slamming the door Lisa made some coffee decided, to help take her mind off Nathan, she'd rub sun block all over, put on her skimpy white bikini, the one that tied on the hips and behind her neck, fix herself a few vodkas and sun bathe out on the patio.

Lisa loved to lie in the sun, the lounger soft and soothing to the skin. She felt good, lying on her belly, the strings on the hips undone, nothing touching her exposed flesh, only the sun's hot rays.

Later, when the flesh on her back reached the point of burning. Turned over, arranged, the pantie part of the bikini, skilfully, so it covered only her vagina, leaving her pubic hair exposed, the top she removed, liberally smearing her nipples with sun-block. Vodka in one hand, cigarette in the other. At peace with herself.

Lisa, never sunbathed any other way, all the years she'd been married, this was her way. As a child, when she became a teenager, after she married David. The most ridiculous sight she had ever seen. A woman with a beautiful brown suntanned body, with lily white flesh skin, showing where her bikini had been. It looked hideous to Lisa, the brown, made the white flesh whiter. Many a lover remarked how much more lovelier she looked than other women did with her all over tan.

The day had begun to cool before Lisa finally rose off the sun lounger. Swaying as she walked through open patio doors. You've had a few too many vodkas my girl, she chided herself, and why not, if no Nathan to fill my belly, it's better than nothing to ease the need.

She ran a cold bath, lying soaking her hot body, the cooling water relaxing her as she slowly smoked yet another cigarette.

She was drunk, and she knew it, vodka, a vice that had sneaked up her in the dark lonely, barren months after the divorce. Later as her awakening pleasure for sex increased. No that is not true, she re-approved herself. It wasn't sex, be honest it with yourself, it wasn't the sex you fell in love with. It was naked flesh of ***Cock!***

A few glasses of vodka, in those early days, made her less inhibited, more alive, more avid and horny.

It had become part of life. Just as being fucked had effected her mind, now it was vodka, men, and fucking. She enjoyed all three, with the same passion.

Tomorrow, if he did not call or visit, she would, on Monday morning, would seek-out a youth to satisfy the burning need. Extinguish the soaring fire inside. If he failed. Then she would find another. Any youth. Class, colour, or creed, messenger boy, mechanic, short order cook, rich or poor, black, white, Mexican, Puerto Rican, it was immaterial. All she required, was a male instrument, a vibrant long length of a male flesh for her and the demon

Maybe it was the alcohol, confusing her mind, she didn't know. Since electing to embroil herself totally in pursuit of sexual pleasure, it was not only her sensual senses altered. The mind, her way of thinking, how she expressed her thoughts, had become different. When, as she was doing now, thinking in her mind, no longer illuminating her thoughts.

She was using the word cock, that was it, no flowering adjectives, such as, rampant, throbbing, pulsating. Lisa, mused, was it her desperation, the ever moist flesh between her thighs, stopping her from inflaming them further.

Lisa lay back, head resting against the gold taps, closed her eyes wriggled down in the bath, immersing herself until only her head remained above the cooling water.

Somewhere, a distant ringing sound, penetrated in to her head, getting louder, incessant.

Lisa opened her eyes, the bathroom, cloaked in late evening semi-darkness, water cold, her flesh feeling wrinkled, shivering. Alarmed, frightened, jumped out of the bath. She had fallen asleep. Through the fog of sleep and fright, the front door bell was ringing. One thought exploded in her mind. *NATHAN.*

In a blind panic. Lisa grabbed a towel, running fast, switching on the lights, flying through the house, reached the door gasping for breath. It was only a hand towel, it barely covered her breasts, just long enough to hide her wet pubic hair.

Her back was naked. Uncaring, unlocking the door, fingers nails scraping the paintwork, threw open the door. Her vagina physically twitched, its lip's puckered.

Standing, looking into her eyes, smiling, *Nathan*. Speechless. Lisa, the cold body that had left the bath a few seconds before, now burning with out of control lust.

"I fell asleep in the bath," she said confessed sheepishly, "Come in, Nathan, you go into the lounge, there's a good boy, there's some Bud in the ice-box if you want one, or make yourself coffee," she was talking so fast, breathless, pausing for a second before continuing, "while I go and make myself presentable."

Before he could utter a word. Lisa shut the door, turned, heading for the bathroom.

"Mrs Knott, what I can see now, is lovely enough me," he said, to her naked back, sounding excited as she walked away.

Lisa, was afire, she was in the bathroom, dried, sprayed deodorant all over, brushed her pubic hair, applied make-up, hurried to the bedroom, rolled back the covers, shoved her feet into a pair of high heeled mules, grabbed a very short lime green robe, it was no longer than the hand towel, it had no buttons, or belt, just a hook and eye fastener at the waist.

Her head was swimming, her pussy already wet. She had waited so long for this youth, with his massive black cock. The lust and passion within her raging like a wild beast.

When she stepped into the lounge, he was standing, back against the drinks bar in the corner.

Lisa ached to know if he was hard, did his cock want her cunt. **Now**!

Nathan looked at her, his hot eyes drinking in the shapely naked brown legs and thighs and almost naked breasts.

She stepped quickly to him. Without knowing she meant to

do it. Lisa sank to her knees in front of him, both hands reaching for his loins, her fingers caressing the front of his black trousers. *Yes,* if she did possess the sexual attraction, the power to make such a huge shaft of flesh come alive with passion. Then she had the right, to view that power in all its rampant glory. Her quick excited fingers yanked down the zipper. The erect hard young organ fell into her hot waiting hands. Lisa had to, was compelled, to taste it, so large, so beautiful, so ready waiting.

Lisa, with an involuntary groan, took it into her mouth. Slowly, her lips pursed tightly, she slide her mouth down over the blood gorged head, down until she could go no farther, sucked hard, just once, before removing her fingers. The cock, jutting out from its source, unsupported, her mouth open wide, she could feel it's weight pushing down on her lower lip. Gently, using her neck muscles, lips clamped tight she move her head backwards, drawing her lips up along the column flesh, as the lips spread, to slip over the swollen head, her tongue caressed the groove on the underside.

Nathan, moaning, hands running through her hair, before reaching her neck, pressing her head back down on his shaft. "My God, your some woman, Lisa, unbelievable, out of this world," he panted.

She removed her lips, smiled up at him. "Your here, Nathan, now love me to death, fuck me, like an 'Old Slut'. Make me and my body happy.

He began moving his hips. "You're my 'My Old Slut', he said lovingly. "My beautiful hot 'Old *fucking* Slut'."

His cock, moving, touching her face, pressed to her cheeks, searching for her mouth. Lisa rolled her head, recapturing it, sucking hard as he gently moved his hips, fucking her mouth, never thrusting hard, careful not to drive to deep.

Lisa was in ecstasy, both hands between her legs, fingers inside her vagina, probing deep, her thumbs tormenting her clitoris, the fingers slipping in and out of her cunt, unison with the swollen cock in her mouth. "Please, don't make me come," he begged, "I don't want to, not yet."

Lisa didn't want him to come. Yet, she did, Oh God, didn't she need an orgasm. Interpreting his urgency, she slowed down.

She didn't want him to come in her mouth, not yet. She wanted that experience later, when she could spent a long time, teasing him to release, after he filled her cunt three or four times. She loved the fresh young tasting flavour of his shaft, the ever pulsing heat on her lips. She stopped sucking, only holding her lips tightly around the mouthful of throbbing head, as he fucked her lips gently, out and in, in and out.

Lisa could hear his harsh breathing in the still room. She wanted his body, his nakedness, with a blindness her hands left her pussy, unbuckling his belt, slid his trousers down so her hands could feel and massaged the round soft muscled flesh of his buttocks, her palms smoothing the gently flexing orbs, drew him closer to the edge. So near, his thrust quickened, he was on the point of ejaculation. So close, afraid he would lose control. Lisa rising, ripped off the short robe.

"Now, lover. Get in me," she croaked, panting. "Hurry, Nathan. All of it. Get it in. *NOW!*"

He put hands on her hips. lifted her, spun her round. The cold edge of the drinks cabinet pressing into cheeks of her bum. He crouched, placed the head of his hot cock against the moist vagina lips, thrusting upwards. Lisa tried to ingest the impact. Despite her effort, she tottered.

Nathan engulfed with a lust he'd never felt before drove his weapon of flesh, butting it into her vulva, it sliced upwards, over her swollen erect clitoris, ploughing a furrow through her damp pubic hair. She moaned softly, Nathan lifted her, effortlessly, placing her buttocks on the edge of the top, her thighs over his hips, and thrust in deep. Knees bent, he started to fuck with sharp, hard, upward thrusts, his massively hard cock, her vagina on his root, a soft wet tunnel of heat.

Her vaginal muscles had been paralysed by his first brutally savage entrance, responding now, frenziedly, quivering on the enormous male shaft as if withdrew, squeezing her inner muscles against the hardened flesh as it viciously thrust upward, deep into her vitals. For two long minutes, three, their fucking silent, fast, hard driving, the only sound in the still room, heavy grunted strangled breathing, and a solid wet slapping sound of their moist crotch's slamming hard together.

Lisa, ankles crossed, legs locked behind the driving hips, arms behind her back, hands gripping the back edge of the top, sitting half upright, her breasts, jerking, seeming to spread all over her chest every time their thighs smashed together, watching the long driving black cock, appear, then disappear again, almost instantly, back deep in to her vampid vagina.

In a mutual-passionate greed to hurt, to bruise and savour each other's sex organs their burning flesh fed their lust into a greater frenzy.

Nathan, abruptly stopped, Standing stiff, looking hard into the face of the woman, welded to him, wet flesh knitted to wet flesh, held together by his deep-rooted cock in the depth's of her smouldering pussy. "Not here, Lisa. In the bed," he cried, in an outraged angry voice.

They looked snarlingly, manifesting their personal desire's, eye's engaged like mortal enemies, yet locked together, naked.

Lisa, on the very pinnacle of sexual desire, aching for just one more vicious hard thrust to push her over the edge, into orgasm. Nathan, lip grim set, a feeling of cruel pleasure in his mind. He wanted her desperately, he wanted her lying down, he wanted to hear her wild moaning cries of passion as his slashing weapon tormented her vulva into climax.

"Nathan. Here, fuck me here. *NOW!*" Pitifully, she implored him.

His face twisted, eyes afire, he glowered down at her, his face a mixture of rage, and hate. "All right, you '*OLD SLUT*'. You want it here, do *You!* Then I will fuck you, *Here!*"

She moved her thighs, waiting, breathlessly. Lisa felt the slow withdrawal of his shaft of flesh, then his loins slammed into hers, making her moan. "Oh, Nathan!" she cried wildly, arching her back, turning her knees outward, her groin stretched the limit, spreading her vagina wider, offering up her frenzied pulsing flesh. To his manhood. He started slowly, his cock full out, paused, cock full in. A deliberately slow push, until the shaft almost out of sight, then a final savage thrust, hard, burying the shaft deep, each thrust sliding her body backwards.

Nathan grasped her hips, held her body, pinning her buttocks fixed to one spot, holding her trapped, unable to move an inch backwards. No relief from his brutal plunging weapon possible, he left her one option, to writhe, groan, and take it.

Lisa, exalted in taking it, for a week her body, mind, pussy, in turmoil. Her need festering, growing strong every time the phone rang, Now she was being fucked with a merciless ruthless savagery. For the first time ever, In all its pleasurable brutality, as the first spurt of his ejaculation, a tiny fist of a blow against her cervix, a minute amount. Lisa wanted more, much more delightful agony to be injected into her body, by his vibrant infuriating shaft.

Nathan, with enormous will-power, he could feel his heart thundering, committing his very being, to prolong the waves of rippling sensations the squirming thighs, and ever moving pussy administered feverishly to his thrusting cock. Then the floodgates opened. He surrendered to his inner most desire, with a groan deep in his throat, shivering in pleasure his orgasm jetted deep in to the receptive cunt.

Lisa sensed the release, with sharp twist of her thighs, sobbing in ecstasy. Still he fucked harder and faster than seemed possible. Lisa's climax coated his plunging root. Head throw back, eyes closed tight, mouth open wide, whimpering incessantly, writhing as her semen united with Nathan's.

The lips of her vagina, her hips, spasming with satisfaction. It was not over. Nathan, still coupled to her thighs, his cock part hard, part limp maintain a slow rhythm in side her slippery wet vagina.

Nathan, grudgingly excepted, as he slowly slipped his flesh in and out of the wet canal. That Lisa, was an amazing woman, she fucked with everything, body, flesh, cunt, ferociously. Her appetite for his cock was so voracious it was unbelievable. And as he studied her heaving flesh, her eyes appeared swollen, not with pain, with hungry avid lust to be shafted again. He became aware of a perverse excitement, a desire to fuck her, in as many ways he knew how.

"All right now Lisa, you had it your way with me, *'Old Slut'*. Now I want my own way with *You*," he said, in pointed yet quiet voice.

Lisa detected a note of a disguised reason. It was the

emphasis he'd placed on the words, *'Old Slut'* and *'You'*. He'd avert his eyes as he spoke, chin on his chest, watching his shaft slipping in and out of her, hiding his face.

She was suspicious of his motives. What exactly did he mean by have his own way? Looking down, she noticed the clarity of their come on his ebony cock, it was coated in a whitish oily sticky looking film. It excited her, distracted her mind. An obtuse thought crossed her mind. A nonsensical idea. Yet, maybe not so strange after all, she told herself, on reflection.

Lisa had no intention, what so ever, in refusing the naked youth, still gently pushing his half limp cock in and out her pussy.

Lisa realised her disadvantages, the day he left her. Her age, past forty now. She knew it would become essential in insure young men, such as Nathan, after had they used her body, would call, over and over again.

Because she needed them as often as possible. Before time and the advancing years, stole her good looks. Her shapely body became, shapeless.

Her, odd thought returned, it had never cleared her mind. It lay in her head, tormenting, an itch she had to scratch. The flesh inside her, increasing by the second the urge to be fucked again. She removed all Nathan's words except, except three. 'Old Slut' and 'You'. It became crystal clear, transparent. He wanted, his own way. He want to fuck her, use her, to fulfil his every secret, hidden lust, release all his longings, any perverted acts of sexual satisfaction, he keep locked in his mind.

And the best woman to find, an older one, lonely, sexual deprived, willing to be become a slave to a big rampant man's organ, before time destroy her ageing flesh. And never having the one thing in all her life, she most craved. Total sexual satisfaction, total body and mind contentment.

Nathan said it, obliquely. "Now I want my own way. You 'Old Slut'."

Lisa, far from being disgusted by the implications of the words. Or being disturbed in way, at the thought of what dark secret perversions he intended to subject her body to.

Unknowingly he was. She trembled as her mind opened. Not having his own way. Her beast, the demon in her body, would be having His.

Letting go of the edge of the top, arms around his neck she kissed him, a long lingering passion building kiss, her lungs draining of oxygen before their lips parted.

Panting, breathless, "What ever you desire, my Sweet Nathan, you take." she said, tenderly, one hand now on his cock, her two fingers and thumb gently masturbating his sticky warm shaft.

He gazed into her eyes. "You realise what you just said, Lisa?" he quizzed her, sounding unconvinced. She wriggled forward as he spoke. The cheeks of her bum felt numb. "Do you?"

"Or did you ask me, because you thought I would refuse?" she asked him gently. He smiled, his eye's sparkled, his delight coupled with his anticipation showing as the lips widened slightly, his palms gently smoothing her soft buttocks.

"You might regret it come the morning, Lisa," he warned her. His mouth closed over hers, stifling her reply. She jumped as a finger, if felt rather thick, slid between her bum cheeks and press gently, tantalisingly, on the bud of her rectum. He bent his knees, his free arm encircled her legs behind knees, effortlessly lifting her off the floor. Lisa arms around his neck, as he carried towards the bedroom. Her warm lips never leaving his. The finger, playing all time with the pucker of her ass.

The bedroom, warm, bright and cosy, the bed soft as Nathan tenderly laid her down on her back. Lisa, head resting on a pillow, scrutinised the muscular ebony body as it joined her on the white covered bed. The cock, only part hard, still bigger than any implement that had been in her bed. This dark one, only partial erect, thicker, had an aura of power, a virility.

Lisa felt her vagina moistening wetly again. The magnificent organ vanished as Nathan stretched out beside her kissing her softly. His hands pushed her legs apart. The mouth departed from hers, the tongue gliding over her flesh, sucking her nipples, down her stomach, over the black curly pubic hair. Shuddered violently when teeth, his teeth, bit the tender flesh of her clitoris. Her vulva flexed. Nathan's hands caressed her warm flesh, she felt them running down her thighs to her knees. The tongue licking the warm lips of her pussy continuously, moaning with want, as the hands roughly pulled her thighs wide apart. His hot breath warming her inner thighs making her sex-lips flicker deliciously.

Nathan tasted the juices covering the tip of his tongue, savouring the flavour's of love, wanting more. He turned, placing a knee each side of Lisa's head, brushing the head of his tool against the soft wet lips, panted in a triumphant strangled voice, "Lisa, *suck me*, Old Slut, Suck me. **Good!"**

Putting two extra pillows beneath her head. Lisa opened her mouth, slid her lips over the waiting cock, up the rod, lips slowly mobile, shivered with pleasure as her lips touched the matted hair around the balls hanging before her eyes in their wrinkled black pouch.

Lisa, for the first time, had taken Nathan's cock inside her mouth completely. Not fully erect. Yet, it was still more flesh in her mouth than she'd ever taken before.

Sucking hard on the rod of flesh, until she felt it gradually thickening, extending gently. She gagged, locked her neck muscle's, stopping sucking the succulent hard flesh, placed both her hands behind her neck, locking the fingers together. Holding her head up hard, the slow growing implement pushed it's self deeper into her throat

She felt a languid lazy feeling flood over her. Her mouth expanded wider, opening of it owns accord, as the column enlarged

Lisa, stiffened as Nathan, slide his warm wet tongue, down the valley between her buttocks. Quivering as the tip moved over the sphincter of her rectum. His tongue moved all the way down to the end of cleft. On the return journey. It stopped, the tip gently flicking at the now wet sphincter, making it twitch, his tongue touching it in a flowering, tantalising, movement. In her anus, a tiny flickering minute tickle. An intense warming pleasurable sensation.

In Lisa, the desire, for more. As the tongue, moved up over the tight bridge of skin separating his pussy, from her ass, then it slipped back into her pussy, the growing shaft in mouth choking her now.

Lisa's nostrils flared wide, she retched. Yet she refused to withdraw her wide gaping mouth, irresistibly its girth forced her to remove her lips, once more the hard erected weapon, brutally solid, alive, throbbed inches above the eye's, ready to shaft her *Again,* she became alive sexually, physically stronger in body and mind. Senses inflamed by the busy snake like athletic tongue, in a position totally new. She wanted to feel him inside her vagina anew.

Lisa, alive with intense sexually passion. When, for the first time, experiencing the sensations of a wet tongue penetrating her ass.

Her lips kissed the small stud like aperture on the peak of his cock, the tip of her tongue pushed into the tiny indentation. Mimicking the motions of the tongue inside her, she explored the orifice stubbornly with a determined vigour, to drag the youths body to the height of sexual passion, to make his flesh burn for orgasm, igniting within him an over-powering need to fuck her. She thought, for few short seconds. It had worked. The discernible acceleration of movement in his efforts. Instead of galvanising, Nathan. It stimulated her craving to come.

Nathan holding the imprisoned contorted body. His now massively enlarged shaft having it's crown insidiously caressed. The totally new sensations erupting within him mingling with the waves of passion originating from the pussy ravishing his lips so intoxicatingly. His preconceived perception of the woman beneath changed dramatically.

Middle aged she maybe, yet somehow he felt ashamed of himself, he'd asserted his male dominance by calling her an *'Old Slut'.* He arrived with dark thoughts of degrading her further, to use her, to make her perform the same acts he'd witnessed watching his mother. He cursed himself angrily. *'You dumb bastard'* willingly without coercion, she is giving you all the sexual loving affection she possesses. The awareness of his misjudgement, his feeling of deep guilt, conscience-stricken, he lavished his mouth on her flesh.

Her boiling semen, trapped inside her vitals, walled in, held back, waiting to anoint its rescuer. The swollen, rampant, hard driven, hurting, *Cock*.

Lisa, her need for release, reaching demonic proportion. Removed the flesh from her mouth. Shouted wildly, in a voice alien to her ears.

"MAKE ME COME, NATHAN. ANYWAY YOU WANT TO. JUST LET ME COME!"

Her scream, infested his masculinity, he pulled her legs apart to their limit, his buttocks over her face, strained tight, quivering. His fingers gripped the lips of her sopping wet pussy prising them apart, his stiffened tongue sliding easily through the warm, soft, tender flesh.

The change of tempo. The subtle change, the aggressive assault on her flesh, a more demanding, hungry caressing technique. With a startling effect on her ensnared ejaculation arrived.

Lisa's, hands sliding down between their slippery sweating bodies, squeezed a burning breast in each hand, before gripping the nipples, compressing them so hard, a shaft of stabbing pain rippled through her swollen teats. Her love passage filled with a tongue. Now fluently soliciting, amplifying her need for gratification to an even greater elevation, nipples afire, moaning, head twisting from side to side, teeth biting into the flesh of her lower lip. She was lost to the excitement of her carnal lusts. With an explicitness, so lucid, so defined, her orgasm flooded, in gently waves of blissful agony, over the argot implanted in her ravenous pussy, saturating his mouth, and her cunt.

Lisa, in the grip of ejaculation, its beauty, to her flesh, came not from her feelings in her mind. It was coming from the youth's vibrant loving of her inner flesh. All to soon, the last small globules of warm wetness ceased to flow. It was over, the muscles in her thighs, the hard curved spine, were quivering from satisfaction and fatigue. It was not over.

Nathan, released her legs, as she, welcomed the relief to her aching joints, slide his enormously swollen cock, half-way into her vagina, slipped his arms under her waist, turned her on top.

He grinned up at her mischievously saying. "Now I've made you come Lisa. *You* can fuck *Me.*"

Lisa, lay inert, exhausted for a few moments. Knowing she had to comply with the demand. This was the moment of truth for her. Her Waterloo. Failure to obey was inconceivable, if she didn't fuck him now, fuck him to completion. He might be gone forever.

She forced her hips to move. Lisa had fucked from above before, never with David, occasionally with later lovers. She didn't find it particularly to her liking, too difficult to keep the cock seated, more often than not, or not embedded deep enough inside for her liking, too tiring.

But this was Nathan and he was something very, very special to her. Nathan tilted his thighs, hard, upwards, felt the fervour of the warmth in her flesh on his instrument. Marvelling at way she managed to transmit her desires, from her lovely flesh, to his.

He wanted to make amends, to appease his conscience, put it right, gripping her gently curved hips with both hands he ached his spine, penetrating her vagina fully.

Lisa never been perforated so deep, deeper than any cock had done before, when she had assumed the paramount position in the past. The sensation, intensely exquisite propelled her into the passionate grip of sexual energy, her hips moving in a rhythm faster than she ever believed possible.

Nathan thrusting his young cock up into her, it was so demanding, so physically virile, driving up her so deeply, as her downward plunging pussy consumed the shaft, all the way down to the root.

Lisa had never reached orgasm in this position before, well not a satisfactory one, but this youth's cock, and vibrant body, was making her begin to come. Not a with vicious body twitching rush, a slow trickling sensation of pleasure, as her semen oozed over the cock as she rode it with her plunging slippery cunt. Not one orgasm, a sequence of tiny fist clenched convulsions within her, expanding in to an abandoned immoral ecstasy.

Nathan lying beneath her, looked up smiling, enjoying goading her into even greater energetic exertions, thrusting effortlessly his shaft of ridged flesh into her rapid descending slippery wet pussy. Lisa, head swirling, dizzy, her lungs afire for oxygen. Feeling her age, to old for this, crossed her mind.

Yet she couldn't stop, if the shaft inside her, was to return again another day, she had to make it ejaculate, make him believe that in her arms, in her cunt, she would willing provide him with the best fucking he would ever receive. Nathan, body stiff, ridged, withheld his orgasm. The smile gone, face strained. "Roll over, I want to be on top," he panted, in desperation.

"No," Lisa replied. "*NO!*" Determined to make him come in the position he demanded she redoubled her efforts. He attempted to twist her over. "Oh no you don't, lover", she gasped, as she resisted his half hearted struggle to dislodge her. "You wanted me to fuck you, my sweet Nathan. And fuck you *I WILL*."

Nathan felt his release, a somewhat weakly, strained, incomplete climax. She was exhausted, flopped over on his strong muscular body, stretched out, her chest heaving with the effort to inhale enough breath to stop her lungs collapsing. After a few minutes, sensing he remained stiff, tense, unsatisfied, lifting her head pounding head she looked into his eyes.

Half open, dull, anguished in appearance, begging he cried. "Help me, Lisa, suck it out," pleading with her in desperation to help him to completion. "Oh God, baby, *Suck It!*"

Sliding down his body, she viewed for a moment. His still stiff erect cock, a few thin threads of come dripping out of the tiny eye. She tasted the semen, a tremor of pleasure shook her mind, as the salty earth like flavour pervaded her avid lips, when she went down on it. Her mouth full of swollen glands, breathing through her flared nostrils, she slide her mouth ever faster up and down the shaft of beating flesh. Its pulsating rhythm changed, she sense the throb of ejaculation. He twisted, trying to pull away, but she wouldn't allow him to escape. Not now, *Never*. Swallowing his cock's nectar as it flowed. And oh how she loved it. Loved it utterly.

Nathan reached down, with strong yet tender hands he pulled her up, laying her head on his heaving muscled chest. She smelt the masculine odour of his sweating flesh. She breathed in deeply, inhaling the aroma of his warm young body. "Nathan" she said, with tender emotion. "My beautiful young lover, Nathan."

She shifted her body, He thought she was going to move from him. Relieved when he realised she was only getting more comfortable, her head fitting more cosy on his chest.

"Lisa, please don't get angry with me," he said slowly. "I wasn't going to call on you again. I thought it wasn't right to fuck someone of your age the way I did." his voice stalled for a moment. Then he continued, slowly. "Tonight I intended to make you, force you if necessary, to do all the things my mother did." He though for a moment he was going cry. "Lisa forgive me, you deserve better than that, you're not an 'OLD Slut'. You are a lovely tender loving lady, I'm am ashamed of myself, it really hurts me to think what I've said and thought, about a lady as lovely as you who has given me the finest fucking I've ever had."

She lay silent. His heartbeat quickened, it's tempo clear in her ear, she felt a stab of tenderness, he was so sweet. "Don't fret my boy," she chided him. "After you left, that day, the only thing I could think about was you and your massive cock, and what you both did to me, you mean more to me than an a few mischosen words."

She felt his trembling. He sounded as if in pain. "It's all right Nathan, don't upset yourself, forget about what you said, it's the way you love me sexually that matters to me, not what you say, your so desirable to my flesh I would forgive you, every insult, every sexual act you desire of me." Or mine, she reminded herself.

He lifted her head in his hands "Any sexual desire?" he inquired slyly, staring in to her face intently.

Lisa, realised he was not convinced, the look showed he wanted be, his mind need further explanation. Reaching a hand down to his crotch, searching his groin for the flesh all her dreams were made of, securing it within her fingers clutch, massaging the now soft object gently. "You can give me this, Nathan," pulsing her fingers more strongly to emphasis her point. "As often as you like, while your with me, not only in the bed, anywhere in the house, when ever the fancy takes you, just fuck me good, long, and above all hard." speaking slowly, emphasising her words with the movements of the fingers. Deliberate stretching the loose skin up over the head, then slowly back down to the base.

"Are you telling me I can fuck you on the kitchen table, in the shower, bent over a chair from behind?" he asked, in a tone loaded with scepticism.

"Yes!" her instant, bold reply.

"But why, and why me?" "Dammit woman do you realise what you're offering?"

"Yes, Nathan, every word." her daring shameless response. "And why you, Nathan? Because you're the first man to fuck me that has given me absolute sexual satisfaction."

"Oh no, Lisa, it can't be that simple," he said, unblinking, a dubious suspicious look in his eyes.

It was not that simple. Far from it. And Lisa knew it, he was not going to believe her just by being told he was best lover ever in her life, he was too young, too immature.

She wriggled on his chest, till her lips touched his. The kiss distracted his thoughts, disrupting his mind. He waited for her to explain.

How to convince. Tell the truth, or lie. Lying was the best way, she decided, deceit, and their affair would then be on her terms. The truth of the matter, his *Cock*.

Once he had left, in a few days time she wanted the man-flesh again. The boy's cock could be replace by another. And that cock by another. She didn't feel love for Nathan, well not the love of the heart. Love for his body certainly.

Lisa had feelings for him, but not of love. Of gratitude, *Yes*. For unleashing her latent, dormant dark forbidden sexual appetites, for instilling her mind and body with an ever amplifying deliciously exciting desire for sex and. *Man-Flesh*.

Coupled to his youthful vibrance, virility, the stamina of his shaft, his sexual strength to bring her to orgasm time after time. Oh yes, she felt grateful, very, very grateful.

Nathan's heart skipped a beat. He understood her cravings, if he returned to her arms again. It would be on his terms. He would call at his convenience, if she wouldn't allow him to use her, as he desired. He could probably find some other woman who would. They aren't that difficult find. A twenty dollar bill would get him plenty of willing bodies, man or woman in Lower Town.

Lisa, with twinge of conscience, deceitfulness, lying, a ruse rarely applied in her life. Smiling sweetly, she said, "Your right, my Nathan, it's not that simple," her lips, caressing his warm wet neck now. The flesh in her fingers beginning to imperceptibly thicken. "I was afraid you would never visit me again, Nathan and I wanted so desperately to see you again. And now after loving me so beautifully, so wildly sexual tonight, I want you to come back to me again and again." Lisa surprised. Her words carried a ring of truth. It was the truth, and she astutely appreciated it. "When I told you could take whatever you wanted, I thought it might encourage you visit me more often," she whispered, huskily in his ear.

The warm flesh on his neck tensed, his root left her fingers. Nathan sat up, his eyes travelled along her brown flesh, from nipples to feet, then back slowly until her face drew level with his own. "You're telling me, Lisa I can love you unconditionally, to my hearts content, because you want be to come back another day? Offering yourself, like a carrot to a donkey? From my experience, you're the beautiful, lovely carrot. I'm the donkey, and donkeys rarely get to have the carrot that their offered," he said with a cunning slyness.

Lisa discerned his note of cunning. Careful, this youth is a bright boy, she warned herself. He had turned the tables on her. And how. He had become aware, perceived her longing, the craving for his body. Now he was telling her, craftily, he'd cotton on to her ruse. The offered unconditional submission of her body to him, he'd realised was just a ploy to incite him to return.

They lay together, in muted silence. "I'm sorry." Lisa said softly. "I didn't mean it to sound like that." "Honestly." Another lie.

He laughed, a stony hard sound. "Lisa I never did mean to call here again," he said slowly. "After the way you called the tune that first fuck. I thought it wasn't all that good for you." His voice pausing hesitated. "I felt inadequate, not capable, and you lead me by the hand because I didn't know way.

"I never meant it to be like that, Nathan," she replied gently. "I'm sorry my love."

"Oh your sorry are you?" his tone mocking, belligerent, quarrelsome. "You just had to show Nathan, teach him, how to fuck a real woman."

They lay quiet, the only sound in the softly lit bedroom, the ticking of the bedside clock, for Lisa had no answer.

His voice rough said, "After a few days I got to thinking perhaps I ought call again and show you, just once."

Lisa pulled him to her, joyously laughing. "You showed me tonight, Nathan. More than once now show me again as often as you wish. *Please"*.

Laughing together. "I just might hold you to that, Lisa." He sighed with pleasure. "Because your really something lovely, *something else*."

"Tell why I'm so different, Nathan," Lisa urged him, gaily.

Nathan shifted, rolled over on his hip, kissed her tenderly on the forehead before looking deeply into her eyes. "When I told you I called to apologise. I was lying. I would have said sorry. But real reason I call was to *Fuck You*," he said, soberly. "You give everything when you fuck, utterly. Your not ashamed to let me know how deep and hunger you are for me to fuck you. And when I'm deep inside. You're an ever moving body of burning female flesh. I feel consumed by your lust your sexually alive pussy enslaves me, all I want to do is to shaft you.

"Endlessly fuck y*ou,* to look at you, with your cool, remote, aloof in an appearance, like butter wouldn't melt in your mouth. A lady no youth could ever hope to touch."

"It only takes one man to unlock a womans passion. The right man, Nathan," Lisa said deliberately, thinking: it's never been the right man for me, not until this young man, sadly she recalled. How long would he stay the right one?

Reaching down her right hand, she ran it down over his flaccid shaft, cupped his wrinkled scrotum in her palm, It felt warm and hard against her hand. "A man like you," she continued quickly. "With a weapon to match his strength," squeezing his balls gently. "You don't hold back, either do you, Nathan? When your fingers and tongue made love to me, your hunger became as ravenous as mine"

"Didn't it?"

Nathan kept looking into her eyes, nodding his head. To damn right, lady. You want it all. I'll give you it all. His cock stirred gently in his loins, and you are going to get it all again Lady.

His smiling features containing a lustful expression inflamed her aspiration for Nathan, a selfish craving, to satisfy her needs. Enjoy what you have now Lisa, she consoled herself, let him fuck you as he chooses, the future can take care of it's self.

Lisa dismissed all thoughts of losing Nathan, brushed them away. She would have her cravings satisfied tonight. And worry about tomorrow when it arrived.

Her hand smoothing his shaft, she said, in a warm submissive soft sensual voice. "I glad you called, whatever the reason. I waited all week, as each day past I became more afraid I'd never see you again. Now you're here with me. Nathan, my sweet lover. I want you. *All of you,*" the flesh in her hand growing warmer.

His voice stayed sober, "And the offer of y*our* sexual offering."

"The offer?" Lisa, bewildered, caught unawares, a moment's panic remembered. "I wasn't an offer, my love, for you refuse or except. It was a present, for you to keep. A gift to remind you of me."

Nathan, his face, before her eyes, changed from one of sober suspicion, instantly, to ecstatic joy. "Oh, Lady, I don't understand why someone like you would want a boy like me in your bed?" His emotions seemed overcome him. His lips covered hers. His shaft became erect, in. seconds, feverishly he parted her loins, before she collected her wits, the rampant cock was driving into her pussy again with a new urgency.

Lisa, breathless, shuddering, his mouth glued to hers, the violence of his thrusts, pushing her up the bed with every stroke until she could move no further. Her head jammed hard against the head board, moaning in her throat, the huge cock knifing through her vagina with brutal ferocity instigating sensations of pleasurable pain within he pussy goading her body. She was in orgasm. *Not yet!* Oh God! Not this quick, her mind screamed. It was useless. The weapon inside her extract his payment, the due's all women have pay to a man's rampant shaft of flesh, his bounty for giving a woman gratifying pleasure. Anointing him with their semen.

Lisa, her mind, controlled the impulse to climax, however, the response of her vagina she couldn't, involuntarily, her loins arched up to meet his downward thrust, warming to the deep stroke, her vagina tightened on his cock, digging her fingers in to his hips to hold herself ridged. She heard him catch his breath, a sharp gasp: the stroke quickened. Her hips arched up again.

"Oh God, do I love fucking you, Lisa," he whispered hoarsely.

Her arms went up round his neck, embraced his head, pressing his mouth into her breasts. "I know you do, my sweet Nathan."

His mouth, pressed into the tender breast, he began sucking as though it was her nipple, sending long slow rippling thrills over her flesh.

He wasn't calling her Old Slut now, just Lisa, and occasionally Lady. Perhaps he did regret using such terms. Her musing became interrupted.

A slow spontaneous, unforced orgasm was beginning. She didn't strive for it, but let it come naturally, freely. It origin started far down inside, in some highly erotic indefinable place, fusing ever so slowly, dreamily, centring on the neck of her womb. Although her body, now passive under the steady thrusting cock, she twitched and trembled uncontrollably while orgasm engulfed her body.

Nathan's mouth moved to her ear. "Was that a good one, Lisa? A real good *One*?"

"Beautiful," she sighed, as if it was their secret.

"Is that the way? Lady. Tell me? Was it really t*hat good for You*?"

He whispered in her ear, his breath as warm as his words. He paused before stammering, in a shy timid voice. "I'm sorry I was so angry and mean earlier tonight. And for what I called you."

"It's all right Nathan", she said gently. "Forget it. Everything's fine now. Just you fuck me, that's all. Keep on fucking Lisa, as you are now."

Nathan moved his mouth on to her lips. Kissing her mouth with a slow languorously, warm erotic loving passionate touch. It was so different, so tender, so sensual. He sensed a new fluttering orgasm, warmer, sweeter, so deep, flow into her flesh.

Lisa, acutely aware, his body, his flesh, his mind, anticipating her release, as if listening for the throbbing waves of orgasm as they coursed through her flesh, before flooding out of her cervix over his cock.

"Did you enjoy that one, Lisa? Was it good?" he asked again. Overjoyed when she whispered softly in his ear.

"Beautiful, Nathan. Beautiful. Keep on doing it to me. I don't want you to stop."

He fucked her tirelessly, for so long, Lisa, thought he would never stop.

Nathan, never seem to need to an orgasm; his stroke unchanging, rhythmically his hard slippery wet shaft sliding in and out of her ever receptive pussy. Not once had he quickened into an exerting striving.

Lisa, nevertheless, climaxed continuously, floating on waves of flesh quivering orgasms, the like she never dreamed possible, passively allowing the swells and ebbs to flow.

Eventually Nathan stopped, his cock poised, warm, deep in her cunt. One hand slide down between their sweat oiled thighs, a finger slipped between her buttocks, then rubbed the sticky feeling doorway to her rectum, the finger tip, with very quick fluttering movements enticed the door to unlock, the tube excepting the intruder *willingly.*

"Lisa," he said softly, "Have you ever?" then hesitated, less bold, the question, hanging, unanswerable.

"What, my sweet?" Lisa asked, enquiring. "Have I ever *what*?"

Boldly, his tone daring. "Have you ever been," the bravado evaporating, he stammered timidly. "Had it… you know… in the… from the back?"

"You're not making much sense, lover. Don't be shy, say what you mean".

As finger pushed farther into her rear, in sudden a rush of words, he cried, "Have you ever had a man take you from behind, in *There."* wriggling the finger as he spoke, emphasising what he meant.

Lisa, surprisingly, she thought, excepting the question, calmly replied. "Yes, Nathan, but I never like very much, too painful."

The easy calm manner of her answer appeared to strengthen his voice, more confidently he said, shyly. "I've never had a woman like that, never, not in there, *ever.* His voice went lower. "Can I give it to you, in *There?"*

She was puzzled. "Are you suggesting what I think you are Nathan?" Lisa held herself still waiting.

"Will you let me, you know what I mean… in the back, do it in *There?"*

She understood what he wanted. *Now*, she didn't want to say yes. Yet she did not want to refuse. His cock in her vagina, the finger in her behind, simultaneously exciting flesh, distracting her thoughts.

"I don't know, Nathan," she said doubtfully. "I've told you. I didn't like very much. You're so enormously huge, Nathan. I'm afraid it would hurt me."

"Can I? Will you, let me do it there, *Please!"* He began begging, in hopeful pleading voice.

"I won't hurt you. I'll do it slowly. I'll be ever so careful. I will, I promise, Lisa." His words, and tone, so eager to reassure her. Too eager.

"If I start to hurt, tell me and I'll stop. I promise". He imploringly appealed. "I've never done, like that, you know, I just want try it in *There*, and you did say I could have *anything*. I wanted. Didn't you my lovely, Lisa," he said craftily with a sly grin on his face.

She lay quiet, held him in her arms, wondering what sort of opinion he had of her. Was it of a desirable woman, a good fuck, a nice lady to make love with. Or nothing more than lonely middle-aged woman, so desperate for a cock she'd do anything?

Was she, to him, just an *Old Slut*.

Lisa was a lifetime ahead of him in sexual experience. He was. So young. So greedily hungry. So virile. So eager. And above all… *So Big*.

This well built, powerful black youth in her arms. He was begging her for a manner of love-making; she had experienced little of in her life.

But there's a first time for everything, isn't there Lisa Knott, she reminded herself. The fingers that you brought you to that first orgasm. The first cock that made you come. The first time you tasted a mans cock in your mouth. The time your pussy felt it's first tongue. The first time you straddled a man and rode his cock as he watched, she recalled.

Each and every time a new faucet of sex appeared, she'd had, in her mind, misgiving about performing such acts. Yet after her flesh had yielded up its pleasures for the first time. So her sexual appetite expanded.

Lisa, her earlier offer in mind. Her lust for Nathan's vibrant body. The need for cock, wanting him to return, as she lay silent, she knew she would not refuse.

She gazed into his eyes, smiled, kissed him tenderly on the forehead, ran her fingers down his spine.

"Wait a minute, my sweet". Lisa got up, careful going to the dressing table, finding by touch a tube of skin cream. The dimly lit bedroom, with it's darkened corners, and eerie shadows, seeming to excite her mind. Her flesh's heightened anticipation of the wickedly lewd immoral act she was about to commit, made her shiver.

She got back in to bed, lifted the black shaft in one hand, ran her lips down the rod several times, before squirting a generous amount of cream over the it, oiling his cock thoroughly.

"What on earth is that for?"

"It'll help make it less painful – easier."

She turned over onto her belly, slipped two pillows under the curve of her loins. "Now put some on me," she directed him.

Nathan smeared cream his fingers, exploring her buttocks, found the location, touched the site. She eased her buttocks upwards, opening the sphincter for him, as his greased finger slid through the taut muscled aperture.

"Oh yes, it feels so different," he said, his excitement increasing, his heart quickening, breath coming in quick gasps. He was trembling like an excited schoolboy. He evoked the thought, the desires he'd felt as he watched her naked buttocks swaying when she left him in the hall. He could not believe he was going have her this way. Where he'd found the courage, to ask in the first place, he still didn't know.

Breathe slowly, relax, she told herself. Just be calm. I'll be smoother, better. "More, Nathan my love," she said. "Put a lot more."

He squeezed a liberal amount on his fingers, as she'd requested. He caressed her anus with the full width of his fingers for a few moments before one finger slide inside, it probed gently, a second finger joined the first. His scrotum warmed tangible as he watched.

Lisa was surprised, amazed. She had expected to feel discomfort and hurting pain. But no, all she experiencing was a trembling new sensation of pleasure.

"Is it all right now?" he asked, panting with impatience.

She wriggled her buttocks invitingly, saying. "Yes, lover," and involuntarily biting the mattress, her two hands gripping the sheet in her hands tightly.

Nathan trembling in his eagerness as he mounted her buttocks, his cock rammed its swollen rounded head at the entrance, with his first reckless feverish jab against her rectum. To wild, to quick, it touched the entrance, skidded up between the heavily oiled cleft of the two rounded orbs. His breathing was harsh, explosive as he drove a second time. He could not wait, the lust and desire to participate in a new sexual adventure.

"Take your time! she gasped. "You promised, *NATHAN!*" As she spoke, the sphincter opened; the swollen globed head cleaved through, a stab of hurtful pain shot through her rectum. Then it was gone. Replaced by a strange sensation of tantalising desire.

She felt little pain, the discomfort only fed the new pleasure. Her sphincter muscle offered no resistance, Its tautness, evaporated, it softened, as if it welcomed the cock.

Nathan, shaking with a violent desire to ravish her flesh in this, his new virgin area of pleasure, He forgot his promise. He didn't linger for her body to except his flesh. He thrust his shaft in tempestuous rage in to her flinching body, groaning with shivering pleasure as his shaft, perceptively sank deeper and deeper with each mindless thrust.

Lisa's earlier fear of pain had not materialised, what pain she felt mingled with the new pleasures taking root somewhere deep in her flesh.

Lisa was sweating, a cold wetness on her flesh. Desperately seeking an answer for the complex emotions in her mind. A youth was ploughing her in the ass. A place few men had been before. Yet instead of being in the grip of excruciating pain, her only feeling was a new sexual enjoyment.

In the darker recess's of her mind. This was a forbidden act, a perversion, an unnatural coupling of man and woman. And still she was depriving a pleasure from being fucked in this immoral corrupt manner of greater intensity than she ever believed possible.

Lisa forced her mind away from the turmoil in her head, focusing instead on young Nathan, so violently hungry in his desire to ravage flesh, in a place where his cock had never reigned supreme before. So young, so alive, so wonderfully good in her flesh, so beautifully large inside her, so **Real** his stamina, it satisfied her every desire, her every need. *Utterly*, a yieldingness filled her mind. An overpowering desire to give herself to the youths craving to fuck her in the *Ass*.

Lisa felt her body relax, it spread so quickly through her body, it's tenseness melted as it capitulated to his hard thrusting weapon.

Nathan felt the anal ring loosen, softened. He growled then snarled in glorious sexual triumph. She had surrender her body to him completely, granting him total insertion of his tool, Nathan's low animal like cries of deep satisfaction, reached her ears, as his testicles and pubic hair squashed into her soft buttocks. The hands left her hips, he stretched out, draping his torso over her back, his hands palm down each of her shoulders supporting his body. Nathan, riding her ass, as she bucked back against him, fucked her with an ever greater jubilant violence. His breathing, ragged, hoarse, warming her between the shoulder blades as the piston like thrusts of his cock slide viciously in and out of her now responsive, active rectum.

Lisa, alive sexually as never before. Snarled, through clenched teeth, heard the low moan of satisfaction from Nathans as his tool achieved complete incision into her anal channel. He was afire with deep hard lust, reaching an arm under her hip, grasped her cunt in his hand. Two finger inside the slit, he used his thumb to masturbate her clitoris as viciously as he was fucking her in the ass.

Lisa felt the first trembles of orgasm, she was starting to come. Nathan, his sweat dripping off his face on to her back, seeming to anticipate her rising climax. His cock sliding even faster in and out, the friction in her rectum, so heated, his cock, a burning rod of flesh. Head thrown back, moaning in a raptured sexual fervour never experienced before, she climaxed. An orgasm. So abrupt. Unimaginable savage, so strangely sexually different from any orgasm she had ever experienced.

Her release had been a headlong, swift abrupt discharge. Excruciatingly painful, yet beautifully gratifying to both mind and body. Where it originated from, in her vagina, or in her rectum, or some deep niche within her never awaken before, she didn't know.

Nathan jerked spasmodically, firing the final spurts of the most copious vibrant ejaculation he had ever vomited into her flesh.

Lisa knew then. She would not, she could not, wait very long before she was fucked again in the *ASS*.

Nathan withdrew, collapsing beside her, lying on his belly, shaking but contented and happy. "You sure you don't like having in the ass, Lisa?" he asked, breathlessly. "You never screamed with pain, you took all of my cock, my balls buried themselves in the cheeks of your butt, and you don't like it?" he gasped, his voice very suspicious.

She stroked his sweat wet curly hair. Nathan inched closer, put an arm over her, stroking her buttocks gently. "I told you earlier, my love, it only takes the right man, didn't I?" Well you were that man." she replied, fondly. "Was it all you imagined it would be, Nathan? Was it good?" she was questioning him now.

"Good, Oh Boy. It was better than good, Lady, Good is not the word for it. Out of this world. *Unbelievable. Terrific!*" He stopped, his tone changing. "Did I hurt you? Was it as good for you as it was for me?"

"No, Nathan you didn't hurt me, well just a little when you entered, that's all, after that, you fucked my ass and me beautifully." she spoke tenderly, smoothing his head.

"You sure?" his voice more insistent. "Was it really good, for you?"

"It was good," she agreed, "You made me come, you lovely boy. Didn't you feel me having an orgasm?"

"I think so, but I wasn't sure, I never knew a woman could come while being fucked in the ass." In a joyful, almost childlike manner, he hugged her. "I'm so happy it was as good for you, too, Lisa. Because the next time I call I'm going to give it to you like that *Again!*"

"Thank you, lover Lisa will look forward to being ravished again, in the *ASS*. Now you go and clean up, that's a good Nathan," she suggested lovingly.

Lisa lay unmoving in the dimly lit bedroom, absorbing gentle fingers of pleasure trembling through her body. She felt content, relaxed, satisfied, happy to have been, bodily corrupted, sexual used, deliciously used. Her conscience untroubled.

She had been sodomised. Beautifully. She had become a sodomite. A woman guilty of sodomy. For some weird reason she like the sound of the word. So what if I am? she pondered. It maybe wrong, so is adultery, but neither act is against the law, not like murder, robbery, and rape, besides if I want a man in that way, the only one to suffer is me.

Not only had it evoked for her a new enjoyable, different expression of sexual gratification, it transported her flesh into a font pleasure she never realised existed. She chuckled gleefully, at the notion of a good-looking inexperienced youth suddenly discovering he had to use the back entrance. Now Lisa wanted more, more young willing youths, like Nathan, soon, very soon. Her beast had led her into a new world of pleasure. It would lead her other new pleasures, more new exciting sexual discoveries for her flesh, which she willingly would embrace.

Nathan, bless his immature sexual mind. He had given her everything she envisaged while she'd waited for his return. He would call again. Definitely, one day.

No more waiting for a cock, she decisively assured herself, absolutely not. Once he left, if she wanted a man, in his absence, she would have one, possibly two.

Sweet Nathan, she thought drowsily. My strong handsome massively endowed black lover. You know what pleasure you will find in my arms.

Lisa was half asleep, she felt him curve his strong young body into her back when returned, his flaccid shaft resting against her buttocks, one hand cupping a breast she drifted in to gentle sweet sleep.

Nathan lay the warm soft female flesh against his own. Marvelled. In awe, of the woman in his arms. Her hunger, her insatiable rapacious desire to be fucked. The constant free flowing movement of her pussy on his flesh. A tremor of pleasure tickled his spine as he recalled her avidness, her supple yet violent writhing when he was in her ass. He had a feeling within the mind he thought he'd never feel again. It was conscious sensation of affection, for her, for her giving. It wasn't just the sex, orgasms, the pleasure. It was something more, much more. Nathan, his chest seemed to flood with pride. He had never felt so much as man, as he did when he was fucking the now sleeping woman beside him.

Chapter 8

Lisa came awake slowly, eyes shut, one hand searching for the mans body that had felt so comforting against her flesh as she'd fallen asleep.

The exploring fingers found nothing. Only the rumpled sheet with patches of sticky dampness. She was alone in the bed. Opening her eyes, blinking, from the sudden brightness filling the room. Nathan had opened the drapes, and the windows. That's very considerate of him, she mused sleepily.

Lisa stretched, a slow languid movement. Evaluating her body's physical reaction after having her flesh so violently ravaged. He been so strong, so hard, so prolific, and so… so satisfying.

Surprised, thrilled, to discover, except for a little stiffness in her hips, a few sore areas on her breasts. Teeth marks actually. And a slight feeling of gentle heat around her pussy and Ass. Which was to be expected, she abstractly recalled.

"Nathan, you taking a shower?" she called loudly, as she got up. The reply. The echoing sound of her voice.

Feeling anger, intermixed with a growing resentment she checked every room. The lounge still had the evidence of their first wild abandoned fuck. Her green short robe lay in crumpled heap where she had cast it aside. Empty Bud bottle on the drinks cabinet. His clothes, no where in sight.

In the kitchen, an empty coffee cup on the table, propped against it. A note scribbled on the back of envelope.

Lisa snatched it up. Read it slowly.

"Dear lovely, Lisa, sorry to leave without saying goodbye. I tried to wake you two times, all you did was roll over and went on sleeping. It was getting late, I'm sorry I just had to go. Thank you for being the woman that you are. The most beautiful, fuckable lady I shall ever have the pleasure of making love to. Be happy, be patient. I will call to love you again." Lisa smiled as she read the word. Again, he had written it in capital letters, then under-lined the word.

Beneath the signature, a PS it appeared to her as if he'd had a sudden after thought.

"Next time, Lady, no more calling you 'Old Slut' again EVER." Written in the same style as he had again. "And you can fuck me, using your wonderful gorgeous Ass. All my love till the next time. NATHAN.

Her anger drained away as she folded the note. Oh yes, Nathan I will be patient. Visit in your own sweet time. I'll be waiting for you lover. While you keep me waiting, when my hunger for man-flesh becomes a thirsting need. The furrow you ploughed boy will cultivated by other tools.

Lisa glanced at the message again. His word late. Time had played no part, from the minute she had opened the front door, time for her had stood still. Glancing at the digital clock on the wall above the icebox, perplexed to see it showed, in red figures 4-47.

Her mind confused, disorientated. How long had their wanton lust lasted? One hour, two, three. She had no idea. How long had she slept? Lighting a cigarette, considered, for a few moments. Shaking her head.

Why care about time, all that mattered was I have been fucked long and hard. A hard massive shaft had extracted my semen so deliciously, from two different zones. One area of pleasure rarely unexplored. Yet it was as intensely enjoyable and satisfying to my flesh being fucked in rectum as it was in my pussy. You spent almost a week, in a fever, wanting, waiting for his cock. Lisa, reaching for the coffee, calling to mind her impatience during that time. Now you've had what you desired, a strong handsome youth, a massive cock, and a fucking you'll never forget. Lisa, prompting herself agreed, with an added thought. He is not the only youth with the means to feed my beast.

Tossing the note on the table. Dispensing with it. She went and showered. Changed the sex soiled sheets on the bed, holding them to her face from time to time, inhaling the odours of sweat, the scent of the semen, so abundantly expunged from their flesh, the oily smell of the hand cream. Her thighs damping, the heady mixture in her nostrils rekindling the memories, of her uncontrollable depraved lascivious pleasures. The bed remade, clean white sheets, the jumbled heap of bedclothes, re-laid, tidy, pristine. The lounge put back into an orderly precise state. A cup of coffee, then a long warm bath before going back to bed.

Lisa, lying on her back in the sunlit bedroom, legs apart. Relaxed, contented in body and mind. Shivered, she could still feel the presence of the cock, a tangible tantalising physical reminder of where his instrument had lodged in her body.

A hand unconsciously, slipped between her loins, a finger slowly traced the lips of her damp vagina, slide downward between her buttocks, titillating the pucker of her rectum, it opened easily as the finger slipped inside.

She felt a trembling within her flesh, her other hand, fingers tinkling massaged her swelling clitoris, a second finger, sliding tantalising slow inserted itself in her now slippery wet pussy.

Snarling, she tore the pleasure giving fingers out of her body. Damn you Lisa. She angrily admonished herself. If you need an orgasm so desperately, self gratification tonight will be replaced in the morning with an even greater hunger.

To prevent the hands returning to her twitching thighs she clasped them in to a fist and locked them tight behind her neck. Tomorrow, early, I'll go in to town, have a good work-out in the gym, buy the skimpy underwear I promised myself earlier in the week.

Not only would it be skimpy, they would be the most tiny lurid, sluttish looking underwear she could find. Plus seek another youth to satisfy her flesh's pleasure. And satisfy the new hungry craving growing within her.

Next morning driving down the freeway, the sun already giving notice of another hot humid day. A Celine Dion disc blaring. Lisa felt so alive, vibrant. Today was the beginning of a new life. The rebirth of living.

A free spirit, an adventurer. And God did she feel good. No hang-ups, no worries, no conscience. Live for the moment, drink it in, wallow in whatever the day would bring.

Driving faster than normal, overtaking other vehicles, so times four and five at time, the warm draught blowing her hair, the sudden whoosh of air filling the open topped Mercedes as it surged past the slower driver's increased the euphoria in her soul.

Lisa knew, today. She looked beautiful. Felt beautiful. It wasn't just a feminine egotistical belief. A deep conviction in her mind she never held, or felt before about herself, told her how perfect her body and how good she looked.

Waving her hand in the air, as she hurtled passed massive trucks. A response to the driver's constantly blaring bullhorns. Slowing as the traffic thickened.

She dressed thoughtfully, after breakfast. Standing in front of the full-length mirror in the bedroom, No bra, just a short tight fitting, low cut armless white halter, nipples clearly visible. A pair of snug fitting slinky, shiny green panties, with just enough cloth of cover her pussy, the narrow waistband sitting high over her hips, covered by a wickedly short black skirt which barely hid her shapely buttocks. A pair of white Lurex stay-up stockings sheathed her brown straight legs, on her feet high heeled sling back open toe shoes, around her neck an inch wide white jewelled choker.

Lisa laughed out loud, recalling her reflection in the mirror. She'd looked so sexy, her fingers had tingled. If I meet you today lady I'd want to fuck you, I mean it, she'd said, chuckling to her image on the glass.

The heavy early morning traffic, noisy, slowmoving. Her new reconstituted frame of mind to life so excitingly active. She drove through two red lights with a devil may care attitude. Entering the almost empty gym car park so fast the car left the ground as it hit the speed restricting hump at the entrance, the thud of the tyres as it landed. Giving her sharp stab of pleasure when her almost bare bum cheeks bounced several times on the warm leather driving seat, before come to a screeching halt in front of the white painted building.

Lisa, once inside, standing at the reception desk signing in.

"Good morning, Mrs Knott, we don't often see you this early in the morning," said the young petite pretty looking girl behind the polished counter in a friendly voice.

"I thought it better to get a good work-out before the heat of the day becomes to overbearing," she replied, as she put the pen down.

The look of envy on the girls face. Tinged with the almost sexual gleam in the eyes of the pretty blonde hair girl facing her. It gave Lisa a warm glow of personal satisfaction.

She study the blonde haired girl as she turned reaching for a locker key, her nice shapely legs, the gentle round soft looking buttocks, the smooth curve of the hips, a narrow waist, straight back and blonde hair curled in ringlets touching her squared shoulders.

Lisa, looking intently at the body, enhanced by the short spotless skirt, and tight blouse, as she placed the key in Lisa's hand, she observed the young girls breasts, small, perfectly shaped, no sag, jutting out in the blouse. If she isn't wearing a bra, Lisa pondered, her tits must be a sight to behold.

"You look lovely, today, Mrs Knott." Lisa detected something more than friendly conversation in her tone. "Thank Miss, that's really sweet of you, a compliment from someone as lovely looking as you young lady to woman of my age, is a pleasure in itself," she replied, smiling fondly into the girls blue eye's.

The soft cool small hand holding the key resting on her palm disturbed Lisa, not personally, sexually. The thought of sex with another woman had always been in her mind a disgusting dirty act. Until now. The vision of this lovely young girl, smiling demurely into her eyes at this moment, naked, writhing as she tongued her. Lisa could almost feel the pleasure she'd derive from massaging her nipples into hardness.

Lisa leaned forward intentionally. Knowing her low cut top would expose most of her naked breasts, she watched her the blue eyes gaze change. She was warmed by the girls eyes widening, slightly. Her pretty face flushed for an instant. The fingers resting in her palm trembling ever so gently.

Lisa felt her quim moistening. Had Nathan, during his violent ravishing of her vagina and ass ignited another facet of erotic pleasure? Or was it just her beast within?

"Would you like to join me for lunch, young lady? I think you and I have something in common which we would both enjoy," she suggested with an implied intimacy.

"I'd like that very much, Mrs Knott, then perhaps we could examine our interests. If you know what I mean, more freely." The young girl replied, in a husky breathless voice.

Lisa hearing the sound of footsteps in the foyer behind her. Swiftly reached out a hand, cupped it around the girl's neck, pulled the unresisting girl's face into hers, kissed her full on the mouth before walking away towards the fitness room.

"Mrs Knott I take lunch break at twelve-thirty, perhaps we could explore our interests in greater depth, to both are satisfaction?" The words, Lisa realised, as other voices behind her requested locker keys.

An open invitation, if she choose to except it. To make love with a *Woman*. To fuck with a *Female,* and a lovely young girl at that, even younger than Nathan. The concept, conjured up a new extended vista of pleasure.

Lisa, the thought that her body could attract and inflame one so young, inflated her being with greedy lustful craving

In the empty locker room, changing in to a black leotard. How do women make love to each other? Beyond the obvious. Fingers and Mouth.

What you don't know now Lisa, she told herself. The young girl in the foyer will be only to willing to teach you.

You want her, for a reason. Your pussy is itching, your flesh is trembling, *IMAGINING* what pleasure her naked nubile body holds for you.

Slamming the metal locker door shut. Chuckling, tossing her head back. Invitation excepted young lady, she decided.

For the next hour or so, Lisa worked out steadily on a treadmill. The only other occupant in the large, well-lit room filled with it's numerous shining chrome exercise and weight lifting apparatus. The walls covered with large shiny, spotlessly clean mirrors. An overweight middle-aged man who seemed intent on injuring himself, lifting dumbbells of a weight far in excess of his capabilities.

Slowly the suite filled, she studied the new arrivals closely in the mirrors. Just average specimens, all men, nothing about any of them excited her.

Lisa rested from time to time, glancing at the big clock above the door constantly. Time seemed to pass so slowly. Her impatience growing. The need and desire within her increasing, her pussy becoming ever more wet and agitated.

The clock showed nearly ten minutes to twelve. She had become so horny, she shivered occasionally, as ripples of pleasure, short sharp stabs of delightful tremors of impending orgasm crawled ever so gently, softly through her stomach.

Lisa couldn't control her sexual need. It was become so strong. To hell with it, she decided with feverish impetuousness. Switching off the machine, heading for the double doors. Once in the locker room, naked, she would masturbate herself, fingers in cunt and rectum, into a hip grinding ejaculation.

Almost running she made for the big doors. Arms out stretched, ready to shove them open. Just feet away, they opened towards her.

Lisa came to a stumbling halt. In front of her, were two huge young men. One coloured, with a shaven head. One white, sun-tanned, with dark black hair, with matching eyes. Both over six foot, massively broad heavy muscled chests, biceps like corded watermelons, ridged muscled stomachs, their thighs like tree-trunks. Both wearing tight fitting white cycling shorts, the crutches bulging.

Lisa was transfixed, rooted to the spot, her eyes swimming, a low moan sounded in her throat. Oh My God, she cried, silently. Opening her eyes. If I could have both of these young men, simultaneously, *fucking me now*.

The illusion in her mind, of the beauty of their naked bodies, the power and strength they possessed, all being used in her flesh as their cocks shafted her into endlessly orgasms. Her desire for the exquisite sensations they would elicit from her pussy.

Lisa carnal lust rampaging through her flesh, making her legs feel so weak. I'm going to fall down, she imagined, her legs turning to jelly. As she forced herself to walk between them through the doors.

"You all right ma'am?" the coloured one asked. Lisa, mouth suddenly dry, ran the tip of her tongue along her half-parted lips.

"I'm fine, I just spend a little to much time on the tread mill that's all," she croaked, hoarsely.

"You look a little shaky, Ma'am," he said sounding concerned, putting a muscular arm around her back, his hand on her hip. "Let me and Gregg help you to the locker room."

As they gentle propelled her, uncomplaining, down the grey tiled passageway. She caught the quick nod of the one called Gregg, then a sly wink, his buddy's eyes blinked, he looked down at her, stared back at Gregg, an odd smile on his lips.

Ignoring her protests, Gregg open the locker room door. Together, they guided her in to the room. "Which locker is yours, ma'am?" inquiringly, he asked.

"Third row on the left, number seven, Gregg," she replied calmly. She didn't require any assistance, but the feel of the big strong hands on her hips. The sensuous nature of the muscle harden arms on her back intensified her sexual yearning.

Reaching the locker. "What's your name, Ma'am?' We'd like to know whom we've helped. Our good deed for day you might say," he asked inquisitively.

"Mrs Knott, Lisa, Mrs Lisa Knott, and could I enquire what are the names of the two young big strong handsome gentlemen holding me up, in the women's empty locker room," smiling invitingly at them each in turn as she replied.

"Just call me Gregg, Lisa, my buddy beside you is Wayne, but I call him Egg, because of his bald head," he replied laughingly.

"Well, Gregg, you and Wayne can let go of me now, I'm fine now, thank you," she told them firmly.

Releasing her Wayne stepped forward Gregg shuffled behind her.

"You've have a wonderful figure, Lisa." Wayne's eyes hot looking, travelling slowly up and down her body. Gregg pushed his massive chest in to her back. Lisa, flesh trembling, the fire in Wayne's eyes. His intentions alive in his face. *Yes! Oh Yes!* she prayed silently, her inner thighs instantly wet. Relaxing, her heart beating faster, lungs shrinking, breathing strangled gasps of oxygen, arms hanging loose at her sides. Wayne's shovel like hands gently cupped her face.

Lisa closed her eyes, as his thick warm soft lips closed over her mouth, behind her Gregg hands gently moved up her bare back. His loins easing gently in to buttocks. She moaned in her throat when his hardening shaft inside his shorts pushed into the soft cheeks of her bum.

Lisa returned the pressure being applied to her mouth. Wayne's tongue tracing the join in her lips, Gregg's fingers slid under the narrow shoulder straps of the leotard pulling them down over her shoulders. She felt an exquisite erotic jab of pain as the sweat laden garment stuck on her nipples, paused there for a moment, the nipples hardened as the wet cloth released it grip.

Lisa opened her lips, her tongue probed, searching for the intruding warm flesh, she reached up, wrapping her arms around Wayne's neck. Four hands pulled, rolling down leotard over her hips to her knees. She voluntarily lifted her foot, kicking the wet cloth across the floor, two hands cupped her breasts, another two massaged her buttocks, Gregg's body moved away. She felt a coldness touch her back. An imprint of where his hot flesh had been.

Wayne's hand slipped down her stomach, fingers parting her pubic hair before the big hand cupped her wet sticky vagina. She spread her legs, wide, granting his long fingers unopposed access into her flesh, three fingers gently insinuated themselves into her offered wet channel.

Instantaneously Gregg's hands gripped her hips pulled her back against his body, minus shorts now, his erect stiff cock mashing against her spine.

Lisa was afire, flesh burning like never before. Wayne, without removing his lips. She sensed, sandwiched between their huge frames, had somehow removed his shorts.

His tongue became more insistent, the fingers left her pussy. Four big strong hands gripped her hips, lifting her bodily off the floor, She felt Wayne bend down, his lips moved down over her chin, before they started kissing her throat, Gregg's knees prised her legs even wider apart, his hands left her hips, touched her groin briefly then stretch the lips of her vagina wide apart.

Lisa, moaning, a small animal like sound. She knew what was coming. Her body, her flesh avidly, ravenous hungry to receive the drug she become addicted to **Young, Hard, Erect, Man-Flesh**.

Quivering in anticipation, on the brink to orgasm. She cried out wildly. Not in pain. A cry of verbalised sexual pleasure, as Wayne savagely drove the entire length of his erected shaft into the very quick of her pussy.

Lisa quivering, the cock's violent invasion of her cunt, coupled with the hot flesh rubbing between cleft of her buttocks, creating sensations of strange new pleasurable desire's. Her orgasm flooded out of her cervix over the thrusting cock.

Writhing in an agony of lust. Reaching behind with her right hand, grasping the warm hard weapon pushing into her soft buttocks she wanked it furiously. Wayne's had both hands on her bum cheeks, prising them apart. The violence of this thrust fading.

Lisa, content to feel the thrill of his cock, slowly sliding all the way in, all the way out, held there, for a moment, the swollen testicles pushed tightly against the lips of her vagina, before slipping it back until only the pulsing hot head remained.

Greggs hands, once more, palm gently caressing her mount, fingers pinching her clitoris between thumb and forefinger.

God this is overwhelmingly good. Lisa thought, flesh enlivened, goading into submission by passion of the two young men. If I could get screwed this fashion more often I won't need Nathan any more.

Her thoughts interrupted as Gregg pushed one wet finger into her rectum, it seem to, through the thin warm skeletal layer flesh separating her two pleasure giving canals to stroke the flesh of the slow thrusting cock in her vagina. She was coming again, without warning, pushing herself down on the cock moving inside her pussy she ejaculated a second time, so intensely exquisite the pleasure, she began to move her pussy down the shaft as it slid upwards, squeezing her inner vagina muscles tight around the rod on its downward journey.

Wayne's mouth was sucking her rock hard swollen nipples. Gregg's hot flesh left her rubbing fingers, pushing against her rectum. The taut muscles around the orifice relaxed, the sphincter muscle offered no resistance. The enlarged swollen head of his rod, slide, with the tiniest twinge of pain into her ass.

It was more than Lisa could bear. She was being shafted by two cocks at the same time, being fucked, twice, at once. She was losing her mind. It wasn't, she didn't want to be fucked in this manner.

Quite the contrary. I love to be screwed for hours. I want to be screwed for hours, but not like this. Not in a locker room. The sex in itself most enjoyable. Lisa agreed with her flesh. But she felt greatly disappointed by her own physical performance. I want them naked. To have them in my mouth and in my ass. I want to fuck them, have them underneath me, making them moan as I use my pussy to dredged the every last drop of semen from their loins. Lisa was angry at herself, her own desire's unfulfilled.

"Fuck me quickly, boys, my husband is picking me up to take me to lunch. I'll never explain if he finds me naked with two young men fucking me front and back in an empty locker room," she lied pleading, making it sound as if she was becoming frantic with worry, yet willing to be fucked.

A few seconds later she regretted her impetuous outburst. Gregg had come in a few short thrusts, digging his finger into her hips, groaning wildly, as his half insert flesh spurt his warm climax in her ass.

Wayne rammed his cock deep in her cunt several times, then like his buddy, behind her, he filled her pussy with his warm love juices.

Lisa, bitterly disappointed, in mind and body, The need in her flesh, seemingly even more greedy for cock, than it was when she entered the room.

"Do you guys live here?" she hopefully, expectantly inquired.

"I'm afraid not, Lisa." Wayne replied, looking at her with a hungry gaze standing naked in front of them.

Lisa, felt a tiny climax ooze out of her cervix. A minute release. At the sight of their softening flesh. Neither as big as Nathan massive endowment, but thicker, heavier looking. Stifling a moan, as her mind envisaged what it would feel like.

The flavour of their semen, in her mouth, ***Together***.

What new sensations would her beast reveal to her flesh, if both the cocks in front of her had an orgasm the same time as she did, embedded in her flesh.

"That's a pity, boys, I would had loved to have you naked, with both pricks in my mouth together, I wonder how good it would have felt to have your tongues in me, as I sucked your cocks into orgasm." Her bitter disappointment obvious in her tone.

"Sorry but where only here to compete in a weight-lifting tournament tomorrow, Lisa, we'll be heading home in the evening." Wayne replied, regret sounding in every word, as he was picking up his shorts.

"If you're so hot and horny, Lisa, you come to room 179 at the Hilton Hotel on 34th Street, after we've had a good work out. Then Gregg and I will willingly provide you with everything you desire, and more." Staring intently at her he suggested, his face filled with desire.

Lisa smiling, her belly inside trembling, recklessly she decided. An offer I can't refuse.

"Would five o'clock suit you, guys?" she gasped in a hurried reply. Gregg wrapped his large strong fingers around his shaft, rubbing it between the fingers slowly, masturbating the soft organ.

"You just call when ever you like, Lisa. I can't wait to feel your sweet lips kissing this," he said, shaking his slowly shrinking root in her direction.

Chapter 9

Lisa leaned heavily against the grey metal locker door. The cold metal cooling down her sweating, naked back. She was alone – the two young studs had left. Why had she allowed two complete strangers, two young giant muscle-bound specimens of manhood to use her? Well, it had enjoyable, up to a point, she admitted. Was she becoming what Nathan had called her the first time he'd fucked her? 'An Old Slut'.

Well she thought, 'Old Slut' I maybe. One thing I know, an indisputable fact. I have become almost totally addicted to man-flesh, she warned herself, glancing at her gold Citizen watch. The face showed twelve twenty.

Lisa hurriedly showered. I'm not totally hooked on cock yet. She thought, drying hastily. Perhaps lunch with petite lovely teenager in the foyer would open new avenues of pleasure. If it did, then it might make her sexual desires for young men more controllable.

Shona was standing waiting outside the foyer door. Smiling sweetly as Lisa joined her.

"I thought you'd forgotten for minute or two, Mrs Knott," she gushed in an over affectionate voice.

"I'm sorry, young lady, I spent a little longer in the shower than I should have," she apologised politely.

"I'm Shona, Mrs Knott, Shona Raul, I think this will be one lunch break I won't forget for a long time," she insinuatingly replied, holding open the glass door.

"Well, Shona, lets you and I find out just how memorable we can make it, shall we? Mrs Knott sounds somewhat formal don't you think, Shona. My first name is Lisa, I think first names are much more intimate, don't you, Shona?"

"Indeed I do, Lisa, it's much more intimate and I'm hoping

that the intimacy between us will be expressed in more ways than just words," she whispered suggestively, as the door closed behind them.

Walking to the car, Shona dressed now in shiny light blue hipster pants. They were so figure hugging, moulding her shapely body like a skin. Lisa wondered how she managed to get into them. As the diminutive girl walked, her perfectly rounded buttocks quivered with every step. Lisa had an overwhelming desire to stroke them. She trembled slightly.

Shona wasn't wearing panties, it was impossible to hide their shape, wearing pants that tight. Her white top, short, loose fitting, leaving her flat stomach exposed, flesh bare showing a few inches below her breasts, the top pushed out, so horizontally it held the bottom of the garment away from her naked belly.

Looking intently she could clearly see the nipples protruding. Lisa felt her sex lips moisten at the realisation. Shona was naked underneath – she glanced quickly around the now almost full car park. All the vehicles appeared empty. Wetting her drying lips with the tip of her tongue, gently she placed her right hand on the rounded orbs of blue covered flesh.

"You not wearing underwear are you, Shona?" she enquired, her palm caressing the soft smooth cheeks.

"I didn't want to, Lisa, my sex lips couldn't bare the touch after I saw your breasts. And you'd kissed me. I'd never felt so hot and excited for any one as I do for you, Lisa." she confessed, her need and desperation obvious in her voice.

A car behind them started. The sudden roar of the engine revving preventing further conversation.

Lisa threw her kit bag on the back seat of the car. The leather seat, burning the back of her bare thighs as she sat down. You left the canopy up. She reprimanded herself in annoyance. You damned fool.

Wriggling her backside in the seat to ease the heat on her flesh. A cool soft small hand touched the top of her stocking covered thigh ever so gently.

"You have a beautiful body, Lisa," Shona said, seductively. The fingers caressing the strip of bare thigh between the stocking top and pantie before sliding ever so tenderly, tantalisingly slow under the skimpy panties.

Lisa shivered, opened her thighs, as one tiny finger explored her mound then ever so softly fondled her clitoris. Shona's touch was electrifying, so gently persuasive, hypnotic to flesh and pussy.

"You've never made love with a woman before have you, Lisa?" she asked knowingly. She closed her eyes, laid her head back and shook her head.

The finger slipped inside her vagina. Shona's thumb worried the nub of the swelling clitoris.

"Shona can give you pleasures you'll never find in man, Lisa, if you want me to?" her voice lovingly soothing, coaxing.

"I want it, Shona, believe you me. You're making my pussy tremble already. I want to see you naked, Shona, so badly, I'd pay just to a feast my eyes on your nude flesh." Her voice hot, beseeching.

"Oh no, Lisa, you don't have to pay me for something I want to give for free," she replied panting with desire. "Kiss me, Lisa, squeeze my nipples *Hard, very Hard!* Please, Lisa," she brazenly instructed.

Forcing herself back to reality. Lisa so close to orgasm, gasped hurriedly, "Not here, Shona. Not like this. Not in a car."

The young girl's face showed a distinct look of disappointment. "You're right, Lisa, this isn't the place, besides I've only an hour for lunch," she resignedly agreed. Lisa felt the probing soft fingers leave her pussy. It stroked the moist lips of her vagina, rubbed her swollen clitoris briefly, the sensation made her gasp softly, before the hand slipped out of her panties.

"We'll have lunch, Shona, while we are eating, we can get to know one other. I don't want a quick sordid fumble. Not with a delicious pretty girl like you. I want your naked next to me, and not for a brief half hour."

She reached across, caressing the girl's mound through her blue pants, her fingers tingling when Shona pushed her crutch upward into her hand. Lisa kissing the soft pliant warm lips before driving out of the car park.

Driving through the heavy lunch time traffic. Lisa glancing from time to time at the silent girl sitting beside her. Damn shame. She thought. All that beautiful young flesh. *Available, Willing* and she had to wait to discover the pleasure's it would bring.

You can't have everything, she chided herself. Save the girl for another day. There's two young stallions, with lovely big thick cocks waiting for you, she reminded herself.

"Shona, what if I picked you up from Gym on Saturday evening, we could have a meal, a few drinks, perhaps you know a club, or bar where we won't be bothered by men, if you know what I mean. Then you could come home with me and stay the night," she suggested provocatively, waiting for the lights to change to go.

"Oh that would be brilliant, Lisa, I'll take you to the Lim Club. My Auntie Rena takes me there sometimes. I'm not old enough to go on my own. I'll give her call. Auntie's a member, she'll fix it for us," she gushed, in an excited girlish voice.

Pressing the accelerator as the lights changed to go. Lisa felt fingers on her upper thigh. Shona's head moved close to her ear, her voice, hot, lust laden with desire, whispered. "Saturday night, Lisa, when we are in bed naked. I am going love you, make you come over and over again before I ***Fuck You***."

Lisa almost rammed the car in front. Shocked, distracted, by the words. She stared mouth open in to the smiling pretty face looking up at her.

"You don't know how a woman fucks another woman do you, Lisa? she asked, in measured, experience voice. Lisa, having no comprehension what so ever as to how women performed such an act, oddly, found the idea wildly, deliciously tantalising. Then the soft tiny hand cupped her wet cunt over her panties.

She shook her head and mumbled in low voice. "No, Shona, I honestly have not." The shock of the explicitly expressed crude statement left her speechless. The palm sliding up and down over her vagina making it almost impossible to steer the car. The hand moved ever faster. The traffic was so dense now. The heat of the midday sun. The noise of the vehicles around her making her head spin. With just her toes touching the pedals, Lisa spread her knees wide. The small hand pulled her panties down over her hips. Two soft damp fingers slipped easily inside her pussy.

Oblivious to everything and groaning loudly, Lisa felt her orgasm flow over the burrowing fingers.

Shivering, her loins see-sawing back and fore on the fingers, driving by instinct.

Pulling into the parking lot, behind her favourite restaurant. She always had lunch here when in town. And this one served the best chicken salad she'd ever tasted.

Lisa's thighs were sopping wet. She could feel the wetness of her come trickling down beneath her buttocks wetting the leather covered driving seat.

"I think you had better remove your fingers now, Shona, you little minx. God knows how many drivers saw you masturbating my pussy. I think the thought of being seen, in public, driving a car with my quim in full view as I was coming over your clever little fingers made the experience out of this world," she gasped, her tremble's subsiding.

Shona laughing, replied happily. "You just wait until my lips and tongue start tantalising your pussy, Lisa. Then you will really discover how clever little Shona can become with a beautiful body like yours."

"Saturday night, young lady, I might surprise you. Now let's eat. I'm starving," she said, winking at her as they left the car. This time Lisa remembered to close the top down.

Inside, thankful to see most of the tables unoccupied, they took a table in the farthest corner. Telling the girl to order whatever she fancied, Lisa went to the ladies room. Locking the door, she removed her soaking wet panties and threw them in waste bin. She then washed her thighs. Drying herself, she thought about Wayne and Gregg.

The fingers had heightened her desire for man-flesh. Oh yes, she thought, as she dried her vagina. Two young men to satisfy my desire's. The fingers in the car. A nice, warming interlude.

Shona was tucking into a large steak with all the trimmings when she rejoined her.

"Can you eat all that steak, Shona?" she enquired, sitting opposite her.

"You bet your life I can, Lisa, the one thing the good Lord

blessed we with was to be able to eat like the proverbial horse and never put on an ounce," she replied, filling her mouth with a fork laden with red meat.

"Good afternoon, Mrs Knott, how nice to see you again, your usual salad and black coffee? We haven't had the pleasure of your company for some time, everything alright," the tall red haired waitress asked, somewhat over familiarly.

"I'm fine, never felt better thank you, and yes, my usual please, and a bottle of sweet white wine, with black coffee to follow," her courteous, abrupt reply.

Lisa glanced round the near empty dining room. Lowering her head, whispering quietly said, "Shona, you lovely child, you made me come so much I had to throw my panties in the waste bin they were so wet. Damn I like you, Shona, your so sweet and uninhibited, your like a breath of fresh air. I can not believe I drove through town in broad daylight with my panties down around my knees being masturbated into orgasm. And then calmly sitting down to lunch with nothing under my short skirt but my bare pussy, Shona what have you done to me?"

"Made you and your pussy feel happy. Perhaps? Lisa, I only wish you had done the same to my moist sex lips as I did to yours, my pants are sticking to my pussy like glue." she laughingly explained.

"Tell me about yourself, Shona. How old are you, have you any brothers or sisters, where do you live. Tell me how a lovely young girl with a beautiful shaped body like yours, desires to make love to a woman old enough to be your mother. Don't you like men? Have you ever had an erect cock make you come? How on earth did you ever learn to use your fingers like you do?"

The waitress returning with the salad interrupted her questions.

"I'm seventeen, Lisa. I have one brother, his four years older than me. He's in college in New York. I live with my parents over in High Hill. My Auntie Rena made love to me when I was fifteen. My mother's brother, Uncle Roy, divorced Auntie when I was fourteen. Surely you must have heard of a company called Judd Chemicals. Uncle Roy owns that company. He left Auntie for a girl half his age. Bloody idiot. It cost him millions. Auntie took him for every dollar she could get. Now she owns a huge mansion over in Thurston. You know Thurston, Lisa, where all the money people live. Auntie calls it 'The Nook' where all the gangsters who never got caught hide. She has a very low opinion of the wealthy since her divorce. Last month she told me if I was a good girl, when I became twenty-one she'd invest enough money for me to live on for the rest of my life."

Lisa eating her salad listened intently. The wine much to her taste, sweet, and smooth, refilling the young girl's glass each time it became empty.

"Lisa I hope you don't think badly of Auntie making love to me. She never forced me. I wanted her to do it. And I enjoyed every minute of it.

"She went through hell after the divorce, became so unhappy, drinking all the time. I use to stay with her at weekends and on school holidays to try and stop her. After about year she suddenly changed. Listen now, Lisa, I'm not to sure whether I should be telling you all this," she paused, looking hard into Lisa's face, the doubt and her mistrust obvious.

"Have no fear on that score, Shona, your Auntie's suffered the same agonies I have, and I think after what you've been telling me, she likes sex, a lot of sex. Can't get fucked often enough." Chuckling at the expression on the face in front of her.

"Your Auntie and I found the same answer to our problem's Shona. Men, naked men to screw and hump our pussies until we discovered how to live again."

"If I tell you, Lisa, promise me, swear, you'll never say one word to another person. I feel I can trust you now, Lisa," she acquiesced smiling, taking a big sip of wine looking into Lisa eyes.

"I know what your Aunt suffered, Shona. My husband David, did the same thing to me, after eighteen years of marriage he divorced me for a young girl. Shona I found my salvation from the misery and loneliness. Your secret's safe with me. Saturday night I will tell you how I changed my life. I'd like to meet your Auntie Rena one day."

The meal was finished and the bottle of wine was empty. Lisa reached across the table, stroked the girls soft cheek with the back of her fingers, tenderly.

"Now how about spending the rest of your lunch hour shopping. I want to buy the most sluttish underwear imaginable. I've been promising myself for nearly a week I'd buy some."

Driving back into town, her curiosity got the better of her.

"Shona, tell me how Auntie came to make love to you," she asked inquisitively.

"It was about a year after Uncle Roy divorced her, Lisa. My Aunt hired a chauffeur, who turned out to be a marvellous handy man, he could fix everything so Auntie hired him full time. Chet isn't anything special to look at. He's short, about five foot two, powerfully build, black curly hair, doesn't talk much, has nice blue eyes, and a lovely smile. One summer night I woke up and went downstairs to get a cold coke from the icebox. I was about fifteen at the time. As I passed Auntie's bedroom I heard her moaning. I thought she was sick, so I opened her bedroom gently. Auntie lay naked on her bed, her legs bent so far back, it looked as if her knees were touching her ears. Chet was on top of her, his cock buried in her pussy to the hilt. I stood transfixed, Auntie saw me. She winked over Chet's hairy shoulder at me. Oh yes, I forgot to mention it, Lisa. Chet's the hairiest man you'll every see, he's covered in thick black curly hair, look's like a gorilla. Auntie smiled at me, and calmly said, as if being found in bed with a man was quite normal.

"It's all right Shona honey, go back to bed there's a good girl. Chet show my sweet niece what's making me moan so much'.

"I know I said Chet was nothing special to look at, Lisa. But his weapon is. I'm telling you, Lisa if you ever see Chet's erect cock you'll want it. I know I did. Not only is it long, the thickness of it is unbelievable. Now he is devoted to Auntie Rena, he'll do anything she asks. *Anything!*"

Lisa changed gear, and felt her sex lips moistening again. *Visualising a cock, bigger than Nathan's!*

"I went back to my bedroom, Lisa, I tossed and turned. My pussy was hot and wet. I kept seeing Chet's huge cock. I trembled continuously, imagining what it would feel inside me. I couldn't stop myself from masturbating. I bent my legs back in the way I'd seen Auntie. Both my hands were between my thighs, frigging my pussy viciously. I was moaning, my eyes were shut tight. Then Auntie's voice softly filled my mind.

"My Poor little sweet, Shona. Has the sight of Chet's big cock excited you that badly? Would you like your Auntie Rena to help you relieve the pain in your flesh.'

"Needless to say, Lisa. I said. 'Yes'. It was so delicious when she made me come with her tongue. I shivered and moaned so loud. She teased my cunt into orgasm twice more with her fingers. Lisa I never thought my body could give me so much pleasure. I lost my mind. Before I realised what I was doing my mouth was on Auntie's quim. I'll tell you more on Saturday, Lisa. If I don't stop talking about it I'll wet myself," she gasped, panting hard, her voice husky.

Lisa wanted to hold her, Shona sound like she was close to orgasm.

"Oh God, Lisa. I have to come, talking about Auntie and Chet's cock together with you coming over my fingers is more than I take." Her desperation for release was so graphic in her tortured face.

Lisa pulled into a parking lot, handing a ten-dollar bill to the attendant and telling him to keep the change, she drove into the first available space she came to.

"Get your pants off, Shona. *Now!*" she shouted, bringing the car to a halt, tyres screeching.

She switched off the engine, and turned towards Shona. Shaking her head in disbelief, she saw that the tiny girl was naked, her hipster pants and top thrown on the back seat. Lisa blinked, staring incredulously, she had no pubic hair. The lips of her glistening wet pussy were bare. 'Holy shit!' Lisa thought, her cunt looks like a baby's. The sight was so visually perverse, so strange in appearance, sexually inflaming. She kissed her on the mouth, covering the girls lips completely her tongue sliding between the soft lips. One hand cupped the naked pussy. The gear change stick dug into her ribs.

Shona was moaning uncontrollable, rotating her vagina against Lisa's cupped hand. Removing her hand, she reached over the writhing girl, searching for the handle which tipped the seat backwards, finding the plastic sheathed metal rod she push the handle downwards.

The seat fell back instantly. Lisa looked at the petite naked girl lying spread-eagled. Her legs were as wide apart as the space in the car would allow. She wanted to touch every inch of the naked flesh before her eyes. Suck the brown nipples, eat her hairless pussy. But her own desire for orgasm had become inflamed at sight of the naked, offered cunt. She tore her top off. Shoved her short skirt over her hips, hitting her forehead on the steering wheel as she hurriedly bent forward to slip it over her shoes. Lisa cried out in pain when her wet pussy banged into the knob on the gear lever as she clambered over it, straddling the moaning Shona, laid her naked flesh down on the hot moving body beneath her. The girl's mouth closed over one breast, she winced as the teeth grazed the swollen nipple. Her cunt pressed into the girl's naked pussy. Shona rubbed her clitoris against Lisa's, making them both moan, She lifted her legs, putting her heels on the dash board, hands gripping Lisa head. She was afire like never before. Auntie had never driven her flesh to such heights of passion. The fire within, overwhelming her reason she cried out in unbridled lust.

"Eat me, Lisa."

Lisa kissed the flesh beneath her, moving her body down. Kneeling on the floor, the hard metal digging into her knees. Slipping two hands under Shona's buttocks, lifting her tiny body up to her face.

Wetting her lips with the tip of her tongue, she studied the sight just a few inches from her. The pink lips glistening wet, the line of soft flesh, the cleft between the sex lips. She felt a tiny climax erupt deep inside her vitals. Her beast had awakened. What you see Lisa, is the source of all pleasure, she wistfully reminded herself. It's the entrance to the citadel of your pleasure and the naked girl's moaning above you. Love this lovely willing young girl's hot cunt as you would have your own. Opening her mouth wide, she covered the naked pussy, pushing her tongue inside.

Shona cried out, thrusting her hips hard against her face.

"Yes, Lisa," she shouted wildly, in a hoarse demanding tone. "Like that, push your tongue in and out as fast as you can, suck my clitoris." Her tiny fingers touched Lisa's cheeks briefly before gently pulling back the lips of her vagina, thrusting her hips into her face. Shona bucked like a fish out of water, her fingers wrapped themselves in Lisa's hair.

"I'm coming, Lisa, Oh God this is beautiful, don't stop, Lisa." She went ridged for a few seconds, she could hear the girls heels beating a tattoo on the dashboard. "Drink my come, Lisa," she moaned softly, her orgasm flowing effortlessly, writhing in sexual pleasure as her come varnished the divinely probing digit of flesh.

Lisa tasted a woman's semen for the first time. It was different to a man's. Less salty, thicker, almost creamy, and she enjoyed the flavour.

First Nathan. Now Shona. After this; she'd need to find more female pussys to sample.

Ten minutes later, the attendant's shocked, wide-eyed face stared at the sight of Shona's still naked breasts as the Mercedes shot past the toll booth. Shona shrieking with laughter.

As Lisa joined the heavy traffic.

"Never in my wildest dreams did I imagined the first woman other than Auntie to eat my pussy would make me come in the front seat of a red Mercedes. Oh, Lisa it was fantastic," she gasped, wiping away the tears on her cheeks from laughing with the back of her hand.

Lisa offered no comment. Concentrating on her driving. She became so sexually aroused. Her thighs twitched. Her vagina physically convulsed in spasms. It had been a wonderful release. But now she needed a mans flesh in her.

"I'm afraid we will have to wait until Saturday before I can return the compliment, Lisa, I've an aerobics class at two o'clock, and I'm late back from lunch as it is," she apologised, in a tone full of regret.

"Saturday it will have to be then, Shona. I'll you drop you back at the Gym. I'm as sorry as you are my sweet. My pussy will just have to be patient for a few days. If it can that is, Shona," she replied smiling.

Lisa watched the girl's gently swaying blue clad buttocks as she walked between the cars before disappeared through the entrance door of the Gym. Remembering the long mouth-caressing kiss Shona given her as she left the car. Thank God for Ebony and Ivory. If they can't satisfy this burning need for *orgasms!* She let the thought die.

For the next few hours she went down town and bought the lingerie she had promised herself, underwear so bright and flimsy. Panties so tiny. To wear them she had to shave off some of her black pubic hair.

In one store, regardless of the cost, she purchased a small yellow short backless satin dress with a low cut neckline. The material so thin and soft wearing anything underneath would be impossible.

"You must have a very understanding husband, madam, if he is willing to let wear a dress like this," the assistant said, whilst wrapping it, the sarcasm in her voice quite plain.

"And why, may I ask, do you think I'm married, young lady?" Lisa angrily asked the grinning girl. "When you have finished wrapping that dress, you can kindly wrap a red on as well, just make sure it is two sizes smaller than the yellow one, if you don't mind," she said haughtily.

She didn't feel quite so haughty when the girl, after wrapping the dress's separately said. "That will be sixteen hundred dollars plus tax, madam, will you be paying by cash or credit card?"

"Credit card, I don't carry that sort of cash in my purse," she told the girl, abruptly, putting her American Express card in the out-stretched hand.

Leaving, she felt a dislike for the girl and her sarcastic attitude. I'll not be visiting that store again, she decided

Window shopping, just to waste time, Lisa wandered around the huge shopping mall on the three floors, a pink bikini caught her eye. The panty bottom was nothing more than a tiny diamond of pink satin, the waist band, a thin pink string, it had no back to it, instead a thin thong of satin.

The top was two small cups of satin. No strings. They looked just big enough to cover her nipples. Lisa visualised how it would look wearing it.

Lying on the patio in the sun. Her pussy dampened at the

thought. It cost her three hundred and twenty dollars. Money well spent, she told herself, justifying her extravagance.

She glanced at her watch. Still two hours to fill before she could have the pleasure of Ebony and Ivory's hard erect flesh. Her pulse quickened contemplating the orgasm's she would release. Shivering slightly as she felt her vagina palpitate into to wetness.

Chapter 10

Lisa awoke with the bright hot sun shining in her face. Annoyed with herself. Close the drapes before you get into bed next time you lazy bitch, chastising her forgetfulness.

She had been in a mood with herself for last two days. After returning to the Gym. Shona had been with an aerobic class so she left the tiny red dress with a receptionist, with the instruction to tell Shona to phone her.

She had waited, in the foyer of the Hilton for over three hours. Calling room 179 from a pay phone constantly. Her naked pussy becoming ever more moist. The anticipation of the naked man-flesh so agonising real. It became almost too powerful to control.

She left, it must have been around 6.30. Her body and mind aching with need... ***The Bastard's***... The dirty lying shits. They'd used her. That she could cope with. Not being fucked by their two tremulous cocks simultaneously she could not.

That night, without showering. She drank a pint of vodka. Against her better judgement. Swallowed two Temazepam sleeping tablets. Without them, she would never keep her fingers from violating her vagina ***CONTINUOUSLY***.

The next day Lisa didn't remember. She didn't want to. Her need for orgasm stifled by drowsiness and a blinding headache.

Well my girl, she thought, stretching, feeling much her old self. So much for that escapade.

Lisa startled by the harsh tone of the front door bell ringing. Glancing to the bedside clock sat up blinking. Never, her first thought, 5.30. the damn clock had to be wrong.

She leaped up, pulled on a pair of jeans, hastily slipped the nearest top she could lay her hands on over her head and quickly dashed for the front door.

It's Nathan, her primary thought. Or maybe Shona. I don't care which one.

Lisa unlocked the door, flung open. "Hello again, Mrs Knott, how are you today. I hope you don't mind me calling but I think I owe you an apology."

Lisa caught off guard, for a moment just stared, then stammered quickly. "Ah yes, thank you, Jay. I was expecting someone else," she replied, running her fingers through her uncombed hair to cover her embarrassment.

"I'm awfully sorry, Mrs Knott. I should have phoned instead of bothering you," he smiling apologised.

"Oh it's all right, Jay. Now that you're here maybe you'd like to share a pot of coffee with me. Providing you behave yourself that is. I could do with little company right now," she said lightly.

Lisa, for an instant, noticed his blue eyes widen. "You sure you want me in your house, Mrs Knott. I made a right arse of myself last time you invited in. I said a few things that was rather crude, and insulting," he countered turning away.

"Oh come on in, Jay," Lisa said, as if he was still the young boy she remembered.

He smiled, nodded his head, and obediently followed her to the kitchen.

"Sit down, Jay, coffee wouldn't take a minute. By the way how is your father, you did say last time he had an accident". she inquired, conversationally.

"He's on the mend, it's going to take a while before he's fit again, other than that he's okay," he replied, sounding pleased at her concern for his father health.

Drinking her coffee in small sips, regarding him. This wasn't the Jay she'd known as a boy. Lisa read an air of assurance about him. A confidence she noticed the last time he'd sat at her kitchen table. In this deeper scrutiny, his blondness, the deep brown tanned face, something of an exotic sensualness.

"How come you went to Spain?" she asked inquisitively.

"It just happened", he said in a matter of fact tone. "There wasn't enough money to sent me to college, so I just answered a job advertisement for overseas employment."

"I think that's marvellous!" Lisa exclaimed. "You must have had enjoyed yourself. All those young girls."

"It was damned hard work," Jay admitted. "Hot, sweaty, and bloody difficult until I learn the language."

"There isn't many boys of your age, Jay who get the chance like that."

"Yeah, I suppose your right. But I still miss being at home," he said modestly.

"Everything seems to have changed so much in three years I've been away," he went on wistfully.

She watched him closely. "I suppose it have," she said thoughtfully.

"Everything changes as we grow older, Jay." Pausing to find her meaning. "Your not the innocent youth you were when you left the States. You've have had the experience of a foreign exotic country. Some wonderful escapades no doubt. I bet you've had more than a fair share of the pleasures that came your way if you know what I mean," she laughingly suggested.

His eyes gleamed. He smiled at her, somewhat coyly, head tilted to one side. "Oh yeah, I sure had plenty of that, Mrs Knott I must admit," he ventured slowly. "Yet in all honesty. Never once have I felt so aroused as I did when I used to watch you sun-bathing in that small white bikini when I was young boy." His face exhibiting his thoughts as he spoke.

"Don't get angry, Mrs Knott please. I say as a compliment. You used to look so lovely. I couldn't help myself. I still can't when the memory crosses my mind." The apologising words, tinted with a pleasure and a hint of regret.

Lisa absorbed his conversation. The look in his eyes. His upper body had stiffened as he talked. The coffee had cleansed the sleep from her mind. Instinctively she knew. He wanted her.

His smiling apology at the front door. A ruse, a deception. He had not called to say sorry. Hell No! He arrived with the intent. To find out if it was possible to ***Fuck Her!***

Unheeding the long silence, her face flushed with softening lips, she considered. Jay in place of Nathan. Lisa wasn't as sure of herself with Jay. He had a hardness with him. A confidence in his make-up she found disturbing.

Lisa sat gazing at Jay. He fidgeted in his chair, as if unconsciously aware of the consideration she was giving to her thoughts. With a hasty gulp, he finished his coffee. Lisa adroitly refilled his cup anticipating his move to leave.

"No need to rush off, Jay, why don't you stay a while and keep me company? We could talk about old times," she said casually. "I think you and I have a few little secret thoughts from the past we might want exchange." She gazed straight into his eyes, "I'd like to find out how my white bikini effected you so badly," she said softly, reaching across the table to stroke his forearm.

"Well, I don't know?" embarrassment by the offer, "Yeah, okay, I'll stop a while," he added hastily, with slight shrug of his shoulders.

He sat stiff under her touch. The silky texture of the blonde body hair under her fingertips, the warm heat of his young brown tanned flesh, with a slight tremble she acknowledge inside her a sweet slow spreading warmth. She was acutely aware she was naked beneath her jeans and top. Surely Jay could sense the swelling nipples, had he become aware his deception had been successful.

Lisa began talking at random, fully aware of her fingertips continuing to caress the forearm. "Remember you told me the last time you sat at this table, Jay. You used to, what were the words you used? Ah yes jack off while you watched me sunbathe. Have ever you done that with other women?" she questioned him gently.

"Hell no, *Never*! Mrs Knott. I've seen more women in bikinis than you'd believe possible, in Spain you see thousands of them every day." He responded, his eyes set, fixed on hers.

The statement electrified her mind, her naked loins were hotly wet. The reservation she harboured about have this youth fucking her evaporated. She could not believe the deep-flesh movements twisting languidly inside her pussy.

She was consumed, mentally, physically, and sexually. The conception that she was past forty years old with a body that still had the sexual power to enslave this youth's mind like no other womans. It wasn't pride in her flesh. This was more than pride. It was power. The sexual explicated desire for her body that he lusted for. A lust he could never extinguish, until he satisfied that desire for her flesh with his... *Cock.*

"Did you find the girl you where looking for, Jay." Casually increasing the pressure of her fingers on his brown skin, changing the subject

He didn't move away from her touch. "No I never, she'd married a mechanic and moved to somewhere in Utah. Her mother told me she hadn't heard from her for about two years." He breathed deeply. "I guess I should have realised would she have found someone else. I just had to find out for myself."

Before she had time to forestall him. Jay rose up from the chair. The crotch of his grey chino pants level with her eyes across the table. She couldn't fail to see the apparent spectre of the unmistakable bulging shape of his erection through the thin material. It was an urgent hard-on; it visibly pushed against the confines of the restraining zip.

She didn't know how she knew, but she did. He wore nothing underneath. She squeezed her thighs together hard. The vision of his throbbing manhood springing free. The strong sun darkened body in front of her eyes, the vibrant youthful weapon exposed to her gaze. The young flesh covered muscles of his body with the loins sun tanned brown as was his face and arms.

Lisa for a brief moment thought he intend to render himself naked. Instead, he sat down as abruptly as he'd stood up. She knew he was aware she had seen the hard-on her caressing fingers had elicited from his eager flesh.

With trembling voice he blurted out, "Have you still got that white bikini?" His face was flaming. The words stopped. Flustered he began once more. "If only I could see you wearing it *again*." He bowed his head.

Lisa, in spite of the rising heat within, and the increasing moistness between her legs. Instinctively sensed a falseness. Jay's words, his stammered phases, a charade.

She was mentally shaken. The change in Jay. From a confident young man who appeared to possess a hardness within his character, blushing wildly, stammering like a shy girl. It made her feel uneasy.

Yet, the hot liquid like heat in her vagina intensified despite her uneasy thoughts. Did she Really want this boy sexually? A deep hard thought grew in her mind. *"Vodka and sleeping pills for company tonight to dampen the desire for orgasm. Or... Jay.* The first thought was horrifying. Not of Jay. It was nightmarish pain and suffering in the flesh for orgasm.

She knew the cure for that problem. **'*Getting... Fucked'*.**

She dreaded the implications of her first thought, ashamed of her weakness. Yet, the flesh inside was shaking, her naked inner thighs wet and heated. Her hands trembled slightly, surely he would notice her condition.

The possibilities of her second concept. Another night without relief for her tortured mind and body. It terrified her mentally, bodily, and sexually.

To conceal her shaking hands, she clasped them tightly together. "I should never have told you how much your body effected me." Jay's tone sullen with self-perfidy.

Lisa laughed at his confession. A low, nervous laugh. "Never feel ashamed of revealing your real feelings, Jay," she told him gently.

His head still bowed. "Maybe your right. But I've always found people use your feeling against you if you tell them your real thoughts."

"Not everybody, Jay," she motherly explained.

He just snorted, rubbishing her statement. Her hands stopped trembling. Thankfully.

"Jay you have no idea how much a woman of my age enjoys being told by a handsome young man such as you. He still feels a certain desire for her body."

The information improved Jay's composure. "That is nice to know," he said generously. He looked up, mouth firm.

"You always were... to me". Speaking with effort, forcing the words, as if against his own will. "Of all the girls and woman I've ever meet, the one that excites me most is you. And you always will be," he said with conviction.

"You've changed, Jay. More grown up now, with a maturity you never possessed when you used to wash the car," Lisa observed warmly.

"I may have changed, Mrs Knott," he said, speaking with dogged sincerity relaxing visible. "But my thoughts about you are just as powerful today as they were then." He gazed earnestly in to her face, leaning unconsciously across the table.

Lisa could detect a shine in his eyes. She had an awareness. He's got a new hard-on, she realised in a flutter of sensual excitement. And this time he has no desire to hide it.

"Stop saying Mrs Knott, Jay, call me Lisa!" she exclaimed. "I think we can be more familiar with each other under the circumstances. Don't you think?" she suggested lightly.

"Okay, Lisa," he demurred. "Look! I called to apologise for my behaviour... *All right!*" suddenly he appeared angry, aggressive. "And now I've done it I don't want to offend you a second time, Lisa. But I this is the only way I know to clear my mind of the thoughts I have about you."

The tone of his words, disturbing. The youthful sexual intensity in his eyes, frightened her.

"They have been within me for years, tormenting me. So I'll tell you the straight honest truth. No Bullshit. Then I'll leave". He took her hands in his, gripping them tight. His face set firm. "I will be completely honest, Lisa, I'm sorry if it sounds crude and dirty," she smiled weakly, concerned, motioning, nodding her head in consent.

"The greatest desire I have ever had, after watching you as young boy. *Was... to... Fuck You.* I wanted you when I called last week. I want you, *Now*. I'll want you tomorrow. I'm sorry, Mrs Knott. Forgive me I don't know why. I had sexual fantasies about you ever since I was child. Now I can't rid myself of the those thoughts."

Her breath felt it was locked inside her lungs. He had opened the door. *Wide*. The portal first unlocked by Nathan. She lusted to have him, excepted, acknowledged it now, cutting through her vagina like a shining bright sword. Making love with this youth sitting opposite would be divine. To feel the raw strength, the vibrant passion only the young possess in her body. The uncaged lust would ravish her like...

The imprisoned breath in her lungs released itself in a rush, its escape. A long deep sigh. They gazed into each other's lust laden eyes. She had revealed herself to him. He didn't make a move. Her lusts his. His hers.

Don't wait for it to happen, she commanded herself. Make it happen, didn't I make happen with Nathan, Shona, and how many times before that.

She knew with Jay it would be different. He was going live out the sexual fantasies of childhood. His hunger for her flesh would be insatiable.

She leaned forward, brushed her lips against his cheek.

"Would you like to see me in my white bikini again, Jay," she whispered coaxingly. "Just to refresh your memory, let you feel that old need, before you fulfil all your childhood dreams and *Fuck Me, Jay!*"

Eye to eye, their gaze locked, face to face. The outside world had no place within; here in the heady secret world of lust. Jay's features altered, cheeks flushed.

Shy, Lisa told herself, almost motherly. His youth still overawed by an older woman. His childlike discomfort made her heart ache.

She only needed to make the invitation. His years of pent-up desire and lust for her would carry both of them onward. By design, she stood up. Jay rising before her. Moving around the table, she put her arms around his neck. Gazed in to his eyes, saying softly. "Kiss me, Jay," relishing the embrace of his strong arms about her waist crushing her against him, so fiercely, so powerful, she could barely breathe.

Her head tilted back for the kiss, his mouth searched for her mouth. His warm soft lips covered hers. His kiss wasn't enough, not now, she need more. Opening her lips to taste the tongue demanding entry into her mouth, with her right hand she reached blindly seeking his waiting flesh. Her fingers trembling as she felt its heat through the thin cloth, measured it hungrily for length and thickness.

Lisa, for a brief instant, felt disappointment. Jay wasn't endowed with the length of shaft Nathan had been. Feverishly her fingers closed around the instrument in her stroking fingers. She moaned, her fingers enclosed its girth. Her already moist loins became even more moist, felt the throbbing as it convulsed under her touch, in ecstasy at the discovery of thick hard roundness of the flesh in her hand surpassed Nathan's.

Her breath like fire in her lungs, as she stroked, his young body trembled continuously against her own.

Burying her head on his shoulder, she gasped in a shaky voice. "Jay do you really want me to wear the white bikini *Now*?"

"Oh God, yes, more than ever *Now!"* he cried, in child like begging voice.

Lisa, flesh still in her moving hand, "Give me a minute to find it, Jay and when I'm ready I'll call you," she whispered seductively in his ear.

"Don't take too long, Lisa," he pleaded hoarsely.

Lisa was in the bathroom naked, her jeans and top in a heap in the corner. Hurriedly she bathed her wet thighs, brushed her hair, applied a little make-up, sprayed herself liberally with a sweet smelling deodorant, including her pubic hair and pussy, then hurried to the bedroom.

Finding the white bikini. Be honest Lisa, she chided herself. You knew were it was, it didn't need finding. Standing in front of the full-length mirror tying the waist strings above her hips. So strong her hunger to feel and experience his young cock exploiting the yearning in her pussy.

Her whole flesh completely consumed with need. Every disappointment, all the pain full agonies of the last few days forgotten. Obliterated by her ever increasing hunger for orgasm.

Something was not quite right. The bikini fitted perfectly, she racked her brain, she remembered Jay, saying he seen some strands of pubic hair. She checked in the mirror. More than enough black strings of hair showing for him to feast his eyes on. Oh Yeah, sunblock, her memory recalled. He had always seen her body coated with sunblock. She went to the dressing table, knocking over several bottles in her urgency. No sunblock. In desperation she grabbed the bottle of body oil she kept to massage in to her legs muscles after jogging. She applied the oily cream, somewhat wastefully, to every inch of her naked flesh.

Placing the pillows three high, she climbed on the bed, lying on her back, legs spread wide, called out. "Jay, you sweet boy.

Mrs Knott is ready for you to spy body on her again." Hoping her well chosen words would ignite his lust even higher, his manhood even more.

Lisa felt her thighs dampen at the thought. She closed her eyes, shivering gently in anticipation, *Cock she wanted. Cock.* not his manhood. Not to fuck my pussy, she told herself with reckless abandon. In my *Cunt.* He's going to fuck it with his *Cock*!

The words, the language, so alien to her mind and thoughts, shocked her.

She'd used the same dirty forbidden words and thoughts with Nathan, never counting crude dirty sex word's as part of her vocabulary before that. Now with another youth. Strong and vibrant.

Those once foul expressions now excited her. It fitted their exotic youthfulness, the effortless stamina, their young flesh in the deepest depths of her mind, as in her body, her avid flesh, touching where no man had ever been.

To hell with it. She decided fiercely, rotating her naked slippery oily buttocks against the silky bedspread. I hope I come a dozen times. No I don't, she scalded herself. *I Want* to come a dozen times.

His strong muscular fingers squeezing her nipples made her wince, she heard the low chuckle of his delight in his throat at her discomfort as he ripped the skimpy covering off her breasts. " Lovely to see you almost naked at last. Keep still Lisa, or I'll whip your ass," he said gleefully, his hands encompassing her now swollen breasts.

Lisa's fear, the threat of physical violence, in her mind the pain inflicted on her naked flesh if Jay did lash her body terrified her. She closed her mind, refusing to believe he really meant what his threats suggested.

Should she resist? Fight. Scream. She briefly struggled against the leather belt he'd used to bind her hands to the bed frame. The fingers on her breast bit deeper. Raw pain coursed through her chest. You're naked, your hands trussed up, the strength of the youth and the need to satisfy a dark secret sexual desire from his childhood. Resistance is useless, she told her crazed mind.

Then, so unexpected. She stiffened as his mouth gently touched her dry lips. "Your skin feels smooth, just like soft satin," he said gently, suddenly his voice devoid of anger.

Lisa's dread of imminent imagined abuse declined. His voice betrayed his intention. It made his threats sound, superficial, shallow.

She studied him closely. The blonde curly hair, the blue eyes, the mouth, his broad shoulders, narrowish waist, the shape of heavy muscled thighs clearly distinguishable through the light material of the Chino pants.

The fingers no longer hurt her fleshy breasts. His touch had become a gently methodical sexual caress. Instinctively, praying she interpreted the caress. Had she decipher the tone of voice correctly? Timidly, warily she said. "You won't beat me will you, Jay?"

"I just might."

"Why, Jay? Why hit me? You've no reason to." Keep it going Lisa, she will herself, forcibly. "I'm naked. Tied helpless to the bed. I haven't the strength to fight you, you'd to big, to young and strong," she pleaded, desperately.

She took full advantage, seeing the look of indecision in his eyes. If I get this wrong... alarm bells ringing in her mind. She blurted out. "You told me ever since you were a child you had strange hot desires, Jay. You didn't want to beat me in those fantasies years ago did you?". His eyes seem to glaze, as if to refresh his memory.

Lisa threw caution to the wind. Anything to prevent a beating. If I get it wrong, she shuddered inside, the consequences would be a hurtful agony. Squashing the conception. Taking a deep breath, with all the tenderness of tone she possessed said gently. "It's the desires for the pleasures from the past still unfulfilled, Jay you need to satisfy. Not the anger you feel towards me because you blame me for afflicting your mind and body for so long."

Jay's eyes had closed ever so slowly as she spoke. His facial expression altered dramatically, from an anger flush. To one of dream like smiling child.

Lisa felt her fear evaporating. Submit yourself to his secret childhood fantasies. Whatever they may be. I'd sooner except some sexual indignity's of the flesh, than I would having it beaten black and blue, she consoled herself.

"Come on, Jay," coaxing him gently. "Think how you used to feel, what you did while you watched me sun-bathing on the patio. How your flesh felt looking at my near naked body through the garage window." Watching his face intently.

Jay's mouth opened in a wide smile. Displaying two rows of perfect white teeth. His right hand left her flesh, went to the bulge of his pants and began smoothing it with up and down motion with the palm of his hand. The finger tips of the left hand travelling down her oily coated stomach. Touched the strands of exposed pubic hair, briefly, moved down over the thigh tracing the leg down the ankle before making the return journey back up the other to her breast.

Jesus, she looks even more beautiful now. He could not believe how easy it had been. Thank God for that, relieved to know he won't have to force her. Deep down he didn't have the guts to hurt her, and he knew it. But I sure as hell can have some fun before I screw her. The threats would make her ever so obedient. For him.

She realised, the moving fingers making her flesh tingle. With a soft relaxing within her body and mind. Now the fear of being flogged diminished, thankfully. Jay just might... introduce her to a new exciting sexual experience.

"Look at this, Mrs Knott." she turned her head. He had unzipped his pants. His hard manhood held in his sun tanned fingers. The sight of the white column of flesh with it's enlarged swollen dark red head. A trace of moisture in the tiny aperture in the crown. The engorged blood vessels on the shaft visible. Nathan's had length. Jay's had thickness.

Lisa loins dampened. The sight of young man-flesh being slowly masturbated before her eyes overcame her. She wanted it, needed to taste it, savour its girth. Feel the cheeks of her face being forced wide as it slipped between her soft warm lips into her waiting mouth.

Jay lowered his head, kissing one nipple then the other, his hand cupped her mount. She spread her legs wider. A finger traced the thin line where her sex-lips touched gently, making her moan. I wish to hell he'd rip off the bottom half of the bikini as he had the top, she complained to herself, silently.

Jay sucked a breast into his mouth, masticating it roughly. His cock was ridged. Ceaselessly he stroked her cloth covered pussy. I don't know what turned her into a sex hungry bitch, whatever it was. I sure am going to exploit this opportunity to the hilt, he decided, relishing the thought's of the sexual freedoms, the moaning woman on the bed might succumb to. Instantly replacing his finger with his wet tongue. One gentle touch. A small kiss, so quick, so deliciously sexual. The shiver of her pleasure made his eyes close.

"Watch me, Mrs Knott. This what Jay used to do in the garage," he panted. Lisa watched. Captivated by the flicking wrist moment as the ever moving fingers masturbated the thick shaft of flesh. As the speed of the fingers increased, so the wrist twisted and the stroke lengthened. He looked so out of place, she thought. It looked strangely perverse.

Standing fully clothed, with the bright sunlight shining through the windows making his blonde appear almost white.

Nevertheless, surprisingly, Lisa, witnessing for the first time a man masturbating himself was the most sexually exciting act she had ever seen.

His hips jerked, groaning he threw his head back. He was in the throes of ejaculation. Oh no. Lisa cringed. Her vagina pulsated. As she E*nvisaged* the warm semen coating her vulva.

"Oh my God. *Yes Now*! Mrs Knott. *Now*! hand moving at a speed she never believed possible. As the second strangled shout, *Now*! reached its peak.

"This time, Mrs Knott your going to see exactly what I use to do in the garage. *Everything*," he heard himself groan, his thighs tightened, shivering he climaxed.

Lisa, mesmerised, the aperture in the swollen plinth of flesh opened, spewing long whitish strings of semen over her naked breasts. "Now you know what I did in the garage don't you, Mrs Knott? he gasped hoarsely. She couldn't answer.

Her panoramic view, as his shaft exploded out of the

feverish moving tunnel of his fingers, disgorging the gossamer cobweb-like threads of come. Her body of it's own volition. From some unknown recess deep within her flesh. As the warm semen splashed on her cream shining breasts. She endured the most pleasurable climax she had achieved.

It wasn't a body writhing, flesh quivering orgasm. Just a tiny minute stab of exquisite ecstasy. Her hot skin, for an instant seemed to burn. A microscopic measure. So fiery in it's content it seemed to scalded her inner flesh, trickled ever so gently in to her womb.

The pleasure became further magnified, heightened. As she squeezed her thighs together, in her desire to hold, prolong the enjoyment within her vagina. You've achieved an orgasm, so beautifully erotic Lisa. Her mind so overwhelmed by lust, informed her, she realised, she had come without. Her body, her flesh receiving any male physical or sexual exploitation.

Jay studied his slowly shrinking root, small lava like strands of semen dripping from the tip. So close to her flesh. so tantalising near. He wanted her, desperately. Not yet, subduing his inflamed desire. She'll be an even better fuck, if she's starved and tantalised first.

Lisa looked into his face. "You enjoyed watching me, didn't you, Mrs Knott?" he inquired, sounding pleased yet sarcastic. "It's shame you never watched me when I was a young boy. Now look at the mess on my cock. It's all your fault you know, so I think you should clean it off. Don't you?"

Lisa still troubled by his implied threats of violence. Smiled weakly, then nodded her head. Had Jay, the cheeky smiling, blonde hair child who had washed the car years ago. Matured into a youth with a cultivated pleasure for sexual gratification through inflicting pain. She could not believe he become a sadist. Beside, he only implied that she may be beaten. And then only if she resisted.

The horrific sceptre of pain dimmed. Resist... resist what. Refuse, spurn a young man. Turn her back on being made to submit to lusts and desires of his thick vibrant... *Cock... Never...!*

The fear in the mind diminishing, focusing her eyes on still clothed Jay. Hands that had encompassed his tool, now dextrously unbuttoning his white shirt.

Lisa, more at ease with her situation, digested his every move. Her heart beat quickened, as he pulled it over his head. The light blonde hair surrounding the small dark nipples on his chest fascinated her, the heavy shoulders, the deep sun tanned flesh, his powerful biceps. Her eyes followed his hands down over the hard brown stomach. Felt her pulse rate sharpen while he unclipped the waist of the Chino pants. He didn't bend, just left them drop to the floor. Kicked them off, followed by his black casual shoes.

Jay stood legs apart. 'Jesus' he's got massive upper thighs muscles. Lisa noticed. Hands on hips, staring down at her. The soft tool hanging limply down between the parted legs. The lank looking testicles dangling, loosely covered with thin blonde hair. She felt her crotch dampen. He looked so youthfully powerful, felt the bed sag as he knelt over her. His knees few inches from her face. If her hands had been free. She would have grabbed his slack rod.

"Now be nice to Jay, Mrs Knott," he commanded her, gruffly, placing the tip of his sticky member against the soft wet lips. "Clean it Mrs Knott, Jay always wanted to feel your red lips on his cock before he it put in. Now do it nicely for me," he ordered her quietly. Putting a hand behind her neck lifting her head.

Needing no encouragement sliding her lips over the soft head. She tasted the remains of the salty nutty like semen, the oily cream his hand had absorbed off her flesh, slipping her pursed lips down the warm shaft of flesh. Only stopping when the lips touched the testicles and soft matted pubic hair.

If only I could hold it in my hands. Feel the weight of his balls in the palms. Take his soft buttocks. One in each hand, pull the man-flesh into my mouth. The very idea inflamed her craving for sexual pleasure.

Lisa applied her passion excited mind to her own desires. Slowly, her lips, tracing the length before running the tip of her tongue around the hollow behind the now swelling head. Lisa ran her lips down the underside of the growing thickening shaft.

Opening her mouth wide swallowing as much of the testicles her mouth would except sucked them greedily.

The distraction, the threat of having her flesh slashed and bruised had not diminished her eagerness, or longing for young cock. Ah, youth, she thought in sadness and delight. The rod of flesh, she was caressed avidly with her lips lengthening and growing ever thicker.

Jay, fingers spread wide gripped the back of her head. Holding it hard, he heard her gulp in quick gasp of oxygen, sigh. Gazing on his weapon's extending... swelling... flesh between her lips he pushed it into depth of her throat.

Lisa gagged. He is trying to choke me. Panicking. Her head immovable clamped in a vice like grip. Her eyes watered dragging in breath through her flared nostrils. "It's all right, Mrs Knott. Jay will not choke you." he dreamily whispered. The choking sensation stopped. The obstacle of flesh strangling her breath moved away. Only to return, slowly, rhythmically it slid in and out. His breathing quickened. Her mouth being forced open wider and wider by the now fully erected shaft of warm flesh.

There was now in Lisa a wonderful glow within. A stirring in her vagina. Her beast. The demon that overwhelmed her reason. This is the way it is, she told herself. That's what makes you so alive, it's what you live for *Cock. Naked Young Men*. Accept your beast; accept its pleasure's. One goes with the other.

Relaxing totally, clearing her mind, obliterating everything She spread her hot wet thighs wider. Consumed by the pleasure of being fucked in the... ***Mouth...***

Lisa sucked, used her tongue, when she possible could. She wanted to taste his semen. To glory in having her mouth filled with the nectar only a youth could deliver. The middle-aged men from past never able of the matching the abundance of creamy fluid of the young.

The large throbbing head gave a jerk. His was going to orgasm. She closed her eyes. Heart pounding. Shivering in anticipation of pleasure to ensue.

Lisa suddenly cringed. The flesh was torn from her mouth, her lips made a sharp plopping sound as they closed.

She made herself open her eyes. Look up. He watched her

face, eager to see fully her physical reaction. She let him see and feel all that he desired, running ran the tip of her tongue along the wet pink lips, exhaling with a soft sigh: flexing her thighs, arching them delicate upward. Jay, delirious happy, her senses conveying her bodies total submission. Surrendering her desires, her flesh, to the power of his... *Cock* released even more warm wetness.

"Jay has always loved Mrs Knott and her gorgeous body," he whispered in a devoted child like voice.

She made herself look at his hard cock. It thumped invitingly against his brown belly. The blood engorged veins visible, pumping; making the thick pinkish tool looked gnarled in appearance. Oh Lord, what sensations will it elicit and inflict within my hot quim. Her flesh burned, the nipples swelled as the overwhelming lust filled her mind.

"Would Mrs Knott like little Jay to show her much he loves her?" It sounded like a child pleading. "You wouldn't tell Mr Knott if I show you will you? He'll get angry and tell my father what I did. Please, Mrs Knott be nice to Jay, tell me you will... *Please...*

Something perversely fearful within Lisa did not want to respond to the request. Nevertheless, she did. Without pausing to examine her obscure, cryptic reluctance. "Will Jay untie my hands if I say yes?" she gently suggested. "Oh no, Mrs Knott, Jay wants to show you how much he loves you first." he said in an aggrieved tone. Lisa realised, his refusal was final. The belt around her wrists now digging into her skin. Her arms aching mercilessly.

Go with the flow, girl. Play his game. The sooner you agree. The sooner it will be over. Use your wits Lisa. Think! she ordered herself forcibly.

He's tied me to the bed to inflict, to make me suffer, because he blames me for his sexual agony as a child. I told him, advised would be a better word came to mind. What was it she had said earlier, searching her memory frantically. The boy now stroking his manhood slowly, standing beside the bed, waiting with an expectant look on his face distracting her thoughts.

Satisfy your desires from the past. Oh My God. Lisa's mind recoiled in horror. Jay the youth with his erect prick in his hand had become Jay, the child of years past.

Chapter 11

He keeps referring to me as he did as schoolboy calling me Mrs Knott. And he is continuously saying Jay in a child like voice. One time he'd referred to himself as, Little Jay. Lisa's furtive quick analysis made sense. Other elements of his behaviour, the words he chose. Never stating. I want. Nor I am going to. Or I will. Always it was Jay wants, Jay loves. Jay the youth had become the surrogate of Jay the schoolboy. She had unknowingly rekindled his childhood desires. All his sexual fantasies for her body had become reborn.

Take your lead from the boy, she instructed herself. Treat him as a child. Talk as if he was a child. He may be under the mental illusion he is a child. But the thick weapon he has in his hands is a man's. A grown mans *Cock*.

Remarkable how the sudden thought, and sight of naked man-flesh always makes a difficult decision on my behalf, she noted. "Come then, my sweet little Jay. Show Mrs Knott how much you love her. There's a, good boy," she crooned softly.

Jay face creased with gleeful surprise. Then frowned. "You really sure you want me to do that, Mrs Knott."

Such childish wariness; her spirits sank. With an effort, she kept her tone light, her voice softly persuasive. "Of course I do, Jay. I've often wonder what it would be like to have a handsome young boy like you touching me."

He regarded her suspiciously. "Why do you want Jay to do it?"

"I want to feel you touching me, Jay, your so young and fresh, It's something all us older married women crave for is having a young boy making love to us." Lisa's voice revealed sudden a girlish shyness at having to say it in so many words. "It's something we both need, you lovely boy, Jay."

Her body tensed. Lisa waited for his reaction. There had to be some response. He appeared to relax. His brown face showing a deep flush he leaned forward bent his head and began kissing the tiny piece of material covering her pussy. His lips, so gently, she felt only a slight touch. Then a wet tongue moved slowly up the enclosed hot wet sex lips, depressing the flesh inside it's flimsy covering.

Lisa experienced relief while the tongue licked. The moment was gone. She had risked something there. Perhaps a severe beating.

"Would you like to take off my bikini panties, Jay? she asked, hopefully, moving her thighs as encouragement, before raising her head to watch.

"Oh yes please, Mrs Knott, Jay would like that," he panted. She winced, in his eagerness his finger nails scratching the flesh on her hips, feverishly clawing at the knotted strings.

He untied the one on the left. The other proved more difficult. "Bite it Jay," she ordered sharply. Submissively, his white teeth bit hard into the chord, the blonde head shaking. He reminded her of dog worrying a bone. The chord parted, clamping it between his teeth, with one vicious tug it ripped clear of her body.

Lisa's heart missed a beat. Jay, face contorted into a look of child like wonderment. Then changed into one of undisguisable lust when his eyes digested the sight of her now naked pussy. His features altering ignited her vagina. She needed an orgasm. Wanted so desperately to feel a hard erect cock being *Thrust Deep* into her body. To release her from the agony of want she endured for almost three days.

"Would my sweet Jay like to do it to Mrs Knott?" she said, attempting to make her sexual request sound like a child's.

"Do what, Mrs Knott?" he replied, rather shyly, as if confused, looking blankly into her face.

Do it, I can't bloody wait. Fighting his desire he looked down at the naked woman. At least, I'm come once, she must be going crazy for a fuck. Besides, this game is almost as good as a fuck. Jay decided.

I can't stand much more of this stupid charade, Lisa

complained to herself. She wanted a fuck. Her flesh wanted to taste the new young vibrant flesh. ***Her Cunt Wanted A Cock Now!***

"You'll have explain to Jay what you mean, Mrs Knott. He doesn't know what. *Do It* means. Or how it's done," he rather slyly confessed.

"It's very simple Jay," she'd had enough play acting. If he whips me. So be it. "*Fuck me* Jay. Do you want to *Fuck* me? Or are you just going to stand there playing with yourself," her blunt crude outburst seemed to embarrass him.

It made him blush, his cheeks reddened sharply. His eyes downcast, looking at the floor he answered. "I want to, Mrs Knott... but I'm only a boy and a little boy's *Prick* is to small to do. *It* with a grown up lady," he stammered, whispering almost inaudibly.

"Ah, but your different to most young boys, Jay, you've been blessed with a cock as thick and long as a grown mans," she paused, waited for his reaction. He just shrugged his shoulders. Well perhaps a few glib lies will convince him, help sort out his jumbled thoughts. Lisa decided. "It's longer and heavier than Mr Knott's instrument, Jay. I've never had one as large as you got," she coaxed him in a soft serene voice.

"You're not just saying that so you can make fun of Jay. Are you, Mrs Knott?" he replied, still looking and sounding unconvinced. His left hand on the erect weapon starting masturbating his flesh again. In the right he held the bikini bottom. Lisa watched him put it to his lips, lick the cloth several times before rubbing it all over his face. His blue eyes closed to tiny slits, and he shivered, visibly.

Lisa stared, eyes wide, hypnotised by the hand rotating, rubbing the dark nipples on the brown chest with the wet looking bikini bottom. Down it travelled over the flat stomach. Through the shiny blonde pubic hair, up along the column of hard flesh. The wet material stopping when it covered the swollen peak.

Oh you liked that Lisa, maybe I can drag the process out a bit longer yet. Jay felt a tremor of lust in his spine. I think I'll wrap my cock in it then give her a taste. It would, he decided, be rather exciting.

She watched, spellbound, as Jay wrapped it around the enlarged orb. He held his manhood at its source. The hand concealing his testicles, while the other twisted the loose waist ties around the cloth over and over again. Relinquishing his hold on the root, tying several small bows to the ends of the chords.

Lisa had never seen a more confusing picture. Only the large head and about two inches of flesh was covered. The other two thirds or so stood appearing strangely white. You can't decide if looks erotic or plain idiotic, can you; she quizzed herself.

The bed sagging cut off her thoughts. "Open your legs wide, Mrs Knott, now Little Jay will do it. I'll do my best, honest I will, Mrs Knott," he shouted, in a wild excited shaking voice.

Opening her legs. Lisa don't you waste your mind on why, or what. You concentrate on getting him to fuck your wet pussy into orgasm, forcefully ordering herself.

Jay knelt between her thighs. His buttocks resting on his heels. His thick hard shaft pointing straight at her wet sex-lips. The discomfort in her shoulders and wrists forgotten as he shuffled forward. Stopping when she felt his hard bony knee caps pushing into the soft flesh of her bum cheeks. The cloth encased head pushed, indenting her vagina entrance made her flesh shake. Jay hands gripped her slippery oiled hips, so hard, the fingers digging into her flesh made her wince, lifting her hips on to his thighs, then wriggling his thighs under her buttocks. Tiny spasms of pleasure ran through her buttocks when the hard muscles of his upper loins slide along her slippery flesh.

Craning her neck for a better view. Lisa sighed softly. One small thrust and the cock would be hers. "Now, you sweet young boy. *Now!* Shove it into Mrs Knott. Please, Jay. Be a good boy for me. I want to feel you *Inside Me Now!* she pleaded in desperation.

Her words seem to galvanise Jay. Whether it was his lust, or her sexually oral demand for flesh. Which ever. It mattered little to her.

Groaning in ecstatic delight, Jay's hooded flesh jabbed against the moistly wet lips shrouding the entrance of her vagina, split them apart savagely as the organ married itself to her avid receptive flesh.

Lisa, disappointed because the invading flesh wasn't naked. Yet grateful to feel her hot love tube being expanded, panting with desire watching the covered rod disappearing slowly in to her pussy. Bit her lower lip when she felt the knotted string scratch then graze the tender soft hot flesh as it entered her inner sanctum. Her most secret place.

It was not enough flesh. She needed more. Much more. All she could take. All he had to give.

She slackened the inner muscles of her vagina. Arched her thighs, forced her legs open to the limit. Offering her pussy, assisting his instrument's full penetration of her cunt.

Lisa shivered as the head pushed its passage up her vulva. It stopped, abruptly. Jay's hard shaft withdrew slowly. The hands on her hips pulled her body forward, her slippery buttocks slide up his thighs, the cock made the return journey in to her vagina.

Uneasiness rolled in her stomach. Jay's face, firmly set in concentration gave her no clue to his intentions. She tried to pull herself forward, digging her heels hard in to the mattress for purchase attempting to slide her buttocks up his thighs. "I want to come in your bikini, Mrs Knott. Jay always came in his hand when he saw you in the white bikini," He sighed, in far away dream like voice.

Lisa, lust for orgasm had become a hungry need. No longer able to hold her head up to watch, with neck muscles aching, let her head fall back on the pillows. "Jay, will you please by a good boy. Mrs Knott can not take much more of this." Lisa begging him, twisting her hips wildly. "If you love me, sweet boy, end my suffering please."

She waited with disheartening patience, the repressed climax within made her stomach ache.

Jay closed his eyes, lips clamped to together hard. His breathing quickened, she noticed his nostrils widen, the fingers on hips ground into her greased flesh and he began sliding her body up and down his shaft.

Lisa felt her vagina dilate, the knotted chords chafed the soft sensitive flesh. Yet he never moved. Stiff as a statue, Jay propelled her irritated pussy ever quicker back and fore.

Despite herself, friction was friction, she yielded to the new unsatisfying procedure. She could feel the swollen head pushing through aperture of her vagina. Then ventured inward only to end of the covering around his rod, before withdrawing. It was unpleasant, dissatisfyingly devoid of pleasure.

Jay slowly opened his eyes, peering down at the woman's voluptuous seductively shaped oily body, noted the arched hips, felt the willing receptiveness of her pussy, the reciprocal thrust of her thighs, the avidness of the vagina muscles attempting to drag his shaft deeper.

What an arsehole you are. If anybody has got shit for brains you top the charts, raging at his stupidity, slowing the woman's sliding movement. You've threatened her, lashed her to the bed. Arsed about, playing silly buggers. For what; you dumb prick. She's so hot and horny, begging for it, she's dying to be fucked.

Lisa for her part. So aroused yet unsettled. This wasn't coitus, she told her unsettled mind. Sex it maybe. It's perverse. A corruption of... *Fucking*... He isn't shafting me. It's some weird act, a fixation from his childhood. My pussy has become the hand he wrapped around his prick in the garage as a boy. The devious swine is masturbating, using my vagina for a *Fist*. Flustration turning to smouldering anger, to hell with this idiotic charade, enough is enough, with reckless bravado, resolving to put an end to it. *Fuck or Flog me.* It was over.

She'd sampled and enjoyed the many whims and vagaries of men's sexual desire's over the last couple of years. Her flesh nor body was deriving nothing from this.

"Jay will you please quit horsing around and take that stupid piece of cloth off you prick an act like a man, and untie me. If you want to play games, fine, just piss off and go find someone else." Her aggressive tone, coupled with the bluntly dismissively spoken words fracturing the silence of the sun-lit room seemed to stun him.

Jay mouth sagging, gazed down. For an instant angry. Lisa caught the flicker in the blue eyes.

"Well now, Lisa," he said, smiling broadly. What be came of Mrs Knott? she wondered. "I'm glad you said that. I was getting right pissed off with all that play acting myself," he admitted laughing. "Nothing worse, than a man kidding around with a hard on when there's a lovely naked willing lady, hot and horny, waiting to be fucked," Leaning back on his heels, weapon now in his hand, feverishly struggling to untie the knots.

Lisa gave him a gentle smile, "Nothing worse than being tied to a bed naked watching a handsome young man with a nice big thick hard cock ready to fuck, just horsing around." Mockingly mimicking him, as he leaned forward releasing her aching wrists.

"Look upon it as a stupid joke. My stupid childish joke. Okay, Lisa," he confessed, grinning boyishly, rising from the bed to stand looking down at her.

"Take a good look, Lady," he said, in a lewd salacious tone, taking his instrument in hand with confidence. She watched him peeled back the uncircumcised foreskin to the limit, revealing the swollen purple red-blue glands. "This all yours," he chuckled excitedly. His hand aiming the shaft at her pudendum. "And you are going get it… *All!*

Lisa was delighted. "All right, Mrs Knott." Jay's voice deepened. "And I warn you; you are going to have to take *all*. and more than ***Once***."

She grinned at him. "That's the sort of threat I've been waiting for, Jay," she replied invitingly. "You might be the one who has to give it *all*. But I will be the one who decides how many times you do… *Once*." They both laughed at each other's fondly delivered threats. As he joined her on the bed.

Lisa shifted down on his thighs. One leg over his heavy upper thigh, rubbing her oily coated pubic hair on his hot flesh. His cock again had gone lax; the laughter had diminished it. She rubbed some of the cream off her stomach with her hand, reaching down began massaging it into his blonde pubic hair, stroking subtly around his sexual implement

"Hey now, Lady, do you give massages as well as sex?" He inquired comically, wriggling his loins.

"Whatever the man wants," Lisa laughed gaily. Wrapping an oily hand round his cock. "I only charge middle-aged men, and those who don't measure up. If you know what I mean, Jay?" she chuckled in playful voice.

"Do you want some, young Man?"

"Do I have to pay for it?"

"Oh dear, I forgot to mention. I give it free to strong handsome young men who are under twenty one, providing they have the necessary instrument dimensions." Provocatively caressing the flesh in her hand while she spoke.

Jay propped himself up on his elbows. Closed one eye, twisted his head to one side. Looked at her quizzingly. "You lying to me, Lady?" he asked quickly.

"About the massage and charging. I sure as hell am, boy". she confessed. "The part regarding young men, and dimensions, is the truth." Lisa admitted gleefully. "Care for a demonstration, Big Boy."

She was already stroking. The heat of the cock stiffening in her hand making her aware of the wetness lubricating her pussy, responding to the sudden turn from the inflicted sensuousness to outright greedy lust.

She shifted her loins, sat astride his heavy thighs, watching with hot eyes at the reaction of his organ to the manipulation of her slippery oily fingers. Tightening her grip as the hand engulfed the swollen bulbous head, peeling the loose skin down to the base of the stalk. The pink young cock sprouted, twisted contorted veins filling with blood. Feeling the flesh, the throb, of Jay's rising desire. Lisa calmed her stroke.

"Jesus, Lady, where did you learn to excite a cock? From your husband?" Jay whispered, the questions ending in a drawn out moan.

"He didn't show much interest in sex. The damn fool. I discovered the pleasure of men, and fucking about two years after we divorced. I went out to dinner with an old friend from my college days. Got drunk. Woke up in a hotel bedroom being fucked good and hard by total stranger. After that happened, all I wanted was to enjoy pleasure with men. And you're a man, a very young one with a nice thick shaft." Lisa said, provocatively.

The slow rhythm of her hand matched the tempo of her words as her mind recalled past sexual encounters.

Jay gazed up in to her face. "You lying to me again, Lady? You, Mrs Prim and Proper Knott. You always gave me the impression that sex was something you could do with out. And now you're talking like a whore."

Lisa was delighted. "Would I lie about a thing like that. With an erect cock in my hand? I'm telling you, Jay, it has been a wonderful experience. I've had big cocks, thin long cocks, a black cock, middle aged men's cocks, English cocks and Mexican cocks, and one time I had two at the same time. Some were small, other cocks were big, some curved up, others had bends to the right and some to the left. You have no idea how much men's sex organ's differ. It's incredibly. I really love a circumcised cock. It's a pity your isn't circumcised, Jay. I just love cock, any cock. I'm only sorry that it took me so long to find out what pleasure's I had been missing. But all those cocks, loved my pussy, and hand; oh brother did they love *Them.*"

"Lady, you've got to be lying. I can't believe what I'm hearing," Jay said, with a look of incredulity and shock written on his disbelieving face.

His shaft was hard; as she talked, her fist had begun sliding more swiftly on the rod. Placing her other hand at the origin of the erection, she circled the root tightly with forefinger and thumb.

"It's the truth, Jay. But I have changed from the person you knew when you used to wash the car. So much so, all my lovers always come back for more". Lisa boasted. "And you'll come back, Jay. Want to know why they want more?"

He didn't ask. Now, with her other hand, she was massaging his balls, tickling them with teasing fingernails. His hips began to thrust against the stroke. She felt a stronger pulse in the swollen sinews of his sexual instrument.

"I have a little secret," Lisa said in a soft sexy voice. "I give men pleasure of a kind most woman don't. And because I have never had a teenage cock before." She glibly lied. "I'll show you my little secret. If you asked, nicely, Jay."

"Show me your secret. Please, Lady," he gasped, hoarsely.

In one quick movement, Lisa raised herself, positioning her hips over his. Her hand holding the erected flesh in position, she fitted her pussy over it, slowing lowering her vagina down, taking the cock fully and *Deep* she gently seated her buttocks down fully, Jay, moaned, gasping, was in orgasm, ejaculating. So overjoyed with herself, she laugh. Not loud, just deep chuckle from her throat. Lisa rode his bucking hips, sitting upright, her buttocks pressed hard into his loins, as the thick pegged-in cock reamed her vagina she rocked back and fore, synchronising her movements to writhing hips beneath her as her cunt soaked up his come.

She felt his hands begin to caress her nipples and low sigh of pleasure escaped from deep in her throat. She bent into him, offering him her breasts to suck. He took the swollen teats, sucking each in turn, his eyes closed, his face a picture of desire.

Lisa was not even close to orgasm. She did not need to a climax now. Why she didn't understand. It was enough to take, to feel his copious ejaculation pumping into her inner tender flesh. Jay, at completion, lay arched ridged, letting her pussy milk his cock of the last dregs of semen. His eyes shut tight. She sensed his mind sharing the same pleasure as did his flesh.

Jay descended down out of the tumultuous orgasm, she stayed firmly implanted on his slow softening shaft. Wriggling her thighs, squirming until she'd position his softening crown against her swollen aggravated clitoris, quivering he soaked up the delicious ripples of sensation of a shrinking erection. Was she for real? He didn't know. Everything, her every touch, movement, her moaning, the gyration of her thighs on his flesh. The indescribable pleasure he absorbed from her inner flesh. How the hell a woman of her age could fuck like this. The answer whatever it was, he realised, far beyond his knowledge or experience.

She moved faster and harder. His implement juddered, jerked, quivered in to swift growing hardness again. He gripped her hips, digging fingers deep in to her burning flesh. He cried out hoarsely, lifting his body, arching his hips savagely up to meet the pussy massaging his cock into climax.

She felt his hot spurt of semen, the force of it coating her insides, her flesh crumbled and dissolve into vortex of passion as she varnished the cock with her orgasming juices

Only when the cock became utterly flaccid and limp did Lisa lay herself down, her nipples resting softly against his.

Jay held her in his strong brown arms. "You didn't really have all those men? Did you, Lady? His tone was dubious.

Lisa chuckled; he truly disbelieved her boasts. "I most certainly did, Jay," she replied." No point in lying, she decided. Stretching the truth just a little maybe. She placed her fingers against his cheek tenderly. "I developed a love for men, so complete. I just have to have their hard flesh. I have so much desire for cock in my mind, Jay, that feeling is as strong in my flesh. Stronger, it's an avid greed for fucking. And young men like you I crave for. I thought the idea of your Lady fucking all those men." She giggled mischievously. "It turned you on, didn't it? Made you all hot and horny. Got me excited, too."

He hugged her. "Lady, you sure have changed, " he muttered sceptically. "You've become an unbelievable fuck."

She wanted him to say something more. Something affectionate. He didn't... so she let it drop.

Content to lie in his arms, her head cradled on his broad warm chest, Lisa's feeling of languid drowsiness of satisfaction, holding the pleasure of sexual completion gripped to her flesh and mind.

"Jay, did you really mean to beat me?" she whispered, her voice destroying the feeling of mutual contentment. "And why have started calling me Lady?"

"The answer to your the first question, Lady is no. I had no desire to hit you what so ever. I called you Lady, because ever since I was a boy you always looked so lovely, so prim, yet friendly. You had such a calm serene appearance I always thought of you as a Lady. Calling you by your first name doesn't seem right to me. And I refuse to refer you as Mrs Knott. I came to your house to fuck you. I tied you up because I was afraid you wouldn't allow me to have sex with you.

"Naked, spread-eagled on your bed. I was going to screw you. I was going to satisfy a craving I've carried in my mind for almost seven years.

"Yet some thing inside me, a strange deep feeling I couldn't understand. Call it conscience. Perhaps it was the memory of the childhood crush I had for you. I honestly don't know. But the thought of making love to you. A woman older than my own mother, and calling you Mrs Knott. You lying naked. Wanting me, willingly. Your beauty, your lovely shaped body, your soft shining flesh, being offered to me unconditionally made me feel ashamed. I felt I had degraded you, in doing so. I degraded myself and I am a lesser man because of it. I carried a longing for you, deep in my mind. I held that desire, in my heart, I never wanted to degrade you, Lisa. My desire, I always felt it was a lust of beauty.

"I know how terrified you became after I tied to the bed and threatened to flog you, Lady. I saw the raw fear in your pretty blue eyes. I'm sorry, Lady, you didn't deserve to be humiliated in that way." He spoke in a tone so sorrowful plaintive, virtually childlike.

Lisa listened. Had she misjudged Jay feelings? Her soul had leaped when he had said his desire for her flesh was a lust of beauty.

"Jay, you have just said some of the nicest words I've ever heard a man utter," she thoughtfully replied. She wasn't lying. When is the last time a naked man held the thought you where a Lady. Not one. She ruefully reminded herself. No man ever considered any woman a Lady. Not after she had sucked his cock, then allowed him to jerked himself off and come over all over her breasts. Then sit astride his thighs and milk his cock dry of semen.

What subtle shift had taken place in his feeling for her to change the terminology of his heart, and mind.

She looked up at him. He lifted his head. Smiled sheepishly, "I guess you think I'm some kind of idiot now?" he said, turning his head to one side to hide his obvious embarrassment.

"I don't believe that a naked young man. Old enough to be my son, who feels that lusting after my flesh is an act of beauty can be called an idiot, Jay," she murmured softly. "I wonder what it feels like, for an older woman to be sweetly kissed by a randy young man who wrongly believes he's an idiot," Lisa hinted smiling suggestively.

He lifted her, hands under her armpits. Sliding her slippery body over the muscled chest. Held her suspended inches above his face. Gazed, his features displaying tenderness. Closing one eye, his mouth shaped in a saucy grin, he winked. Stretching his neck upward, lowered her down. Kissed her forehead, raised her again. She sensed the gaze he applied as he ogled the breasts hanging before his eyes. Followed by a stare, a tiny flash of lust in the hot eyes as he drank in the sight of oily wet pubic hair now plastered to her flesh.

A brief second past. A sharp intake of breath. Their lips meet. Jay's tongue probed. Strong arms wrapped around her back, clasped her body to his. Lisa nipples pushed hard into sweating chest, sending shivers of pleasure in her breasts. She encircled the blonde covered head in her arms. Opening her lips. Offering her tongue.

You are cradle snatching again, as they called it. Lisa told herself. And then; *Isn't it fantastic!* She had to quell her desire to laugh. The agile tongue, the soft moving lips ignited an immediate ache of desire. His cock, so impossibly resilient in it's youth, swelling once more as it lay trapped against her stomach. Lungs drained, starved of oxygen, gasping for breath their lips parted.

She smiled fondly into the flushed face, slipping a hand between their wet greasy stomach's, enclosing the shaft of slowly lengthening flesh in her palm. Isn't it incredible how a young mans cock can return so swiftly to it's full capability! Of the men she had known as lovers over past few years, only Nathan had been capable of sustaining constant multiple orgasms. Now I have another youth. Jay, like Nathan, a wonderful mixture of boy and man. Lisa reflected.

Their youth compels them to be dominant, yet they submit to domination. Maybe because am a *Much* older woman, more experienced in the act of love making, Young men feel they can exercise all their sexual manly desires. And I appreciate their charms. I'm grateful, very grateful.

I allow them. Give them licence to fuck me in a manner that a youth could never achieve with some young girl. I'm beginning to understand the thoughts and desires of both man and boy, she concluded astutely.

And now this, with Jay? This devouring hunger for young man flesh?

Even now, she experienced a savage deep stab of carnal desire to feel anew the cock growing in her palm, so thick, hard, young virile and utterly ruthless and fulfilling, driving in to the yearning flesh of her vagina.

Each time of sexual gratification with a youth, any youth like Jay or Nathan, must, out of desire and necessity, be sufficient. Youth feeds on the new, the future. Young men will feed on your insatiable need for their cocks, she warned herself. And they will feed my demon with wondrously powerful orgasms, she replied, to herself.

"Lady," Jay said softly in her ear.

She looked into his eyes. Gently he manoeuvred her body to lie beside his. He smiled. "Look what I've got for you," he said, sounding like a small boy offering a gift. As, indeed, he was.

Lisa returned his sweet smile. And looked. He had one hand on his cock, holding his stiff hard on. "Is that *All* for me?" she asked, politely, the politeness concealing her desire for *All*.

"Hold it, Lady," he ordered her, roughly. Kissing her hard, her hand wrapping around the swollen warm sticky column of flesh. His lips moving over hers, tongue probing.

Jay withdrew his mouth. "I watched you after that first kiss in the kitchen. You looked so unhappy… almost lonely, so sad."

She kissed his cheek. "I did felt unhappy, and very, very sad, Jay,"

"Why, Lady? What over…?"

"I was thinking about you, Jay," she confessed. "Thinking about much pleasure your young naked body, how often your cock would lovingly extract orgasm after orgasm from my flesh. Thinking of your youthfulness, your endless stamina, your strength. The constant delicious sensations my pussy would sustain as you fucked me hard, again and again."

"But I don't understand why that made you look so desolate, Lady?" He said, sounding unsympathetic, aggrieved.

"It wasn't the thoughts of sexual excitement that caused my unhappiness, Jay. A feeling of sadness filled my mind when I realised you would leave, after you'd fucked me beautifully many times, with all the vibrant vigour that my flesh had never experienced before. You'd never understand this craving in my mind. Or the lust in my flesh to be ravished sexually by a youth of your age for the first time," she explained. The tone of her voice expressing her sorrow clearly.

"That I would have the pleasure only once, Jay for a few short hours. Then I'd spent the night alone, with only the memory of you and your young flesh after you'd left. That's what made me feel sad and appear unhappy." She concluded her somewhat deceitful confession. He wasn't the first, her first youth. Nathan had that honour. Lisa did have one tiny sliver of regret in her mind. Nothing serious. Just the thought of not sleeping in his arms naked. To kill the frustration and pain she'd felt in the previous couple of nights.

"I don't have to leave tonight." His tone a little resentful, yet tender.

"We've got this evening, well what's left of it, the night and in the morning." He grinned suggestively. "Bacon and scrambled eggs and some pancakes with syrup, Maybe."

"And it would be gratefully appreciated if it was served… *Naked*." he hinted, laughing.

Her spirits soared, he would stay the night. To Jay because of his youth, a night, a morning, is a life time. Lisa thought poignantly.

"I've still got your present, or have you forgotten it," he said, in a peeved tone. "Don't you *like* it?"

She made her eye's look at his erect cock. It pulsed invitingly against his brown tanned smooth belly. Conversation was no distraction, undiminished the eagerness of the youthful shaft, so obvious. Oh, to be young, she thought wistfully, and yet delighted at the same time. *If only I…* She banished the thought. If only? "Jay, you know I like *it*". she said, letting her passion show in her voice. "And I *Want* it. When am I going to *Get It?*"

"Now." Jay turned, straddled her, came on top. *"Now."* he repeated, hoarsely, pushing his hard throbbing shaft in one long steady sure thrust, sliding it smoothly through the lips of her pussy into her vagina.

He studied her face earnestly, watching, her facial reaction. Felt his cock surge gently as her eye's smiled, her mouth split wide in to a grimace, opening wide, her head twisted from side to side. Don't rush, take your time, control your wild urges. The more deliberate you fuck, the more she'll want to be fucked. He thought, attempting to empower his mind with self control, as the stretching sex-lips swallowed his weapon's swollen crown.

"You have a honey sweet pussy, Lady, do you know that?" he gasped in a whisper. "It's satin smooth; it feels and fits like tight warm glove.

"How could I know if you didn't tell me?" she murmured.

His fucking was patient, controlled, restrained, allowing her just the enlarged swollen head dividing the hot wet lips of her pussy. She could feel her vaginal muscles spasming, as it attempted unsuccessfully to suck his thick arrogant cock into the depths of her cunt. He teased her flesh with the incomplete stroke. It irritated the flesh chaffed earlier by the knots, magnifying her sensations, increasing her blossoming hunger until she beg him for more.

Then... and only then, still with deliberate slowness did he grant her fervent desire, rewarding her with complete penetration. Lisa came then, slowly... deeply, her warm semen exciting her beast within, the orgasm flowed, blending, mingling with the orgasm she failed to achieve before.

Jay didn't respond, She didn't want him to. Not yet. He increased his rhythm, speeding his stroke, displaying control and self-will, he kept it steady, true and deep. She felt her flesh warming and inside her vagina the weapon of flesh blossoming, her body seem alive with passion, her bones seeming dissolve in to the mattress.

"Jesus Christ, I've never had a hard on like this before, Lady," he told her, breathing deeply. "It's like a bloody rock I just might have to fuck you till dawn to get rid of it."

"Then fuck me till dawn," Lisa panted, surrendering her cunt to his *Cock* as before, he had surrendered his cock to her *Cunt*. He could dominate sexually, yet would submit to sexual domination, she thought lovingly, as he fucked deliciously through the final stages of her first orgasm and into the beginning of the next. Arching her thighs up to meet the next plunging thrust of the thick flesh. Focusing all her sensations, her craving lust on the heavy strong shaft, so real and young as it ploughed into her willing receptive vagina again. Lisa abandoned all thoughts and gave herself up to total lascivious sexual gratification of the body.

It appeared as though Jay really did *Intend* to fuck her till dawn. He started to experiment, going shallow, going deep, slow and fast, viciously hard, tenderly soft, fast then slow on one side of her vaginal love channel, fast then slow on the other. He lifted her legs, bending her backwards till she rested on her shoulders, before burying his cock so deep his balls rammed into her buttocks. With his instrument pegged in her pussy, he threw her legs over his sweating shoulders, pressing them so far backwards, her knees beside her ears to drive even deeper at a new angle of entry. Twisted and cramped as she was, Lisa moaned and gasped with exquisite carnal delight. He eased her back down to the bed, rammed several pillows under her ass, making it gorgeously different again.

Jay took greater pleasure, from her reactions then he did from his own sensations. His eyes ridged glued to her face, he grinned animal like, his cock rampaging more swiftly when he knowingly sensed her next orgasm. The pleasure turned to laughter when she begged him, in voice, unrecognisable as her own, to please fuck her over the top, shaft her body and mind into blackness with his cock.

Instead, teasingly, he slacked off, nearly coming out as she clutched after him, before finally satisfying her need.

She lost count after the fifth or sixth or seventh maybe it was even more she'd stopped counting after four. Her thighs were sore, numb with fatigue. The muscles in her legs quivering, as her toes curled, her heels beating a tattoo into the mattress in another agony of erotic sensation,

Jay raised his body off her sweating flesh. Lisa still writhing in orgasm, he sensed his weapon's urgency, suddenly he was coming, he drove his rod harder than ever, his come spurting like hot lava in her vagina. She groaned in anguished loss. The thick spurting cock was escaping her avid demanding flesh, and she couldn't bear it. In an instant, the hot huge swollen shaft was gone, thrusting upward it belched its remaining load of warm semen over her stomach and breasts. She gasped, as Jay's hands smeared the sticky mess of body cream, sweat and whitish coloured fluid in broad circles in to her skin.

Lisa quivering when his hands massaged the oily warm sticky wet mixture into her erected nipples. Fascinated by the sight of the shrinking shaft dripping tiny globules of semen on to her now matted black pubic hair. Each one, as it landed leaving a cobweb thin string of semen hanging from the purple coloured knob. And, with a sharp squeeze of her nipples, it was done.

Jay lifted his body from her collapsed flesh to sit, trembling, feet on the floor panting, head down, chin resting on his heaving chest on the side of the bed. Lisa lay spread-eagled, her loins parted to the extreme, tired aching and empty, yet sexually satiated in body and mind. Her breath sounded like ragged hoarse sobs. Maybe it was weeping; She was filled, gorged, sated, yet disconsolate, for she knew one day boys like Jay and Nathan, with all their vigorous power of body and flesh would only be a memory.

Jay, in simple fact, owned a potent capability, as all youth do, its power to great for Lisa Knott. She was, so vulnerable to youth, so addicted because she loved their ever hard instruments, so deeply her lust for them.

Fatigue overcame her tortured thoughts, a heavy weariness seem to cloak her mind. Jay lay beside her, dragged a blanket over her, kissed lovingly on her feverish brow, said ever so tenderly. "Sleep, Lady, you will never know how beautiful it felt or how much pleasure you gave me as I fucked you."

Chapter 12

It was after lunch next day. Lisa had kept her promise to Jay, only partly, she reminded herself, chuckling. The breakfast as he requested, with one small suggested requested omit. She did not serve it, *Naked*.

She had woke up completely refreshed, looked at the sleeping youth lying on his back next to her, arms akimbo, his face a picture of youthful contentment. Sliding out of bed, she cautiously lifted the blanket, admired his dormant slack cock, and it's still obvious thickness. Her nose wrinkled, the aroma that had greeted her nostrils as she gently raised the blanket. A heady overpowering smell of sweat, semen and body cream. A smell, Lisa adored, the aromatic evidence left after being beautifully and savagely fucked *Again*.

He hadn't said a word about her not giving him his breakfast naked. But his eyes had displayed the disappointed he felt, vividly, when he walked into kitchen. Shower, dressed, blonde curly still damp hanging in ringlets on the back of his brown neck. "Thank you, Lady, I'm bloody starving," he said sitting down unsmiling, eating without looking in her direction.

It was in the shower earlier, she decided, persuaded herself. This time you will not drive yourself crazy with longing or desire for the boy as you did with Nathan, forcefully drumming the idea in to her head. If he returns to fuck me another day. Fine. If he doesn't then I will find another young boy who will. Perhaps one even younger, less experienced, more susceptible and uncontrollably eager to discover and explore the pleasures of sex.

She *Envisaged*. A boy naked, innocent of sex. With a Virgin shaft. A Virgin Mind. His Virgin Body. It electrified her. The mind's pictured vision made her tremble, her hand's shook. Her vagina spasmed so violently it made her loins open as if it was going to receive the imagined virgin flesh.

It was that fantasy. And it was a fantasy. Or was it? Fantasy of mind? body? Or both? She turned off the shower, abruptly. Dried herself, dressing quickly into pair of black slacks, white blouse and no underwear.

Looking at her reflections in mirror while brushing her damp hair. Lisa could not expunge her mind's erotic image.

Fantasy is only thinking while we are awake. she concluded, in an attempt to explain the sexual tremor in the shower to her reflection.

Dreams are the fantasies of sleep. But dreams do come true sometimes, she reminded herself abstractly.

Her reflection, hair now neatly brushed, lips parted in a coy smile. Lisa jumped at the sound of her voice saying out loud. 'Yes they do don't they Lisa my Girl.'

'Live the dream. Experience life, blinking, she sounded like some advert she seen on TV or was it the other way round. Experience the Dream. Live the Life. No matter she decided, the grin on her face widened. We know what we are going to do about it, she told her reflection. *Don't We*!

Lisa watched him devour the last bite of his second plate of pancakes, with obvious enjoyment, lean back wiping his mouth with a luxurious pleasure in a napkin.

"Lady, he declared with a small grin, "You're cooking's nearly as nice as your fucking."

It was time. The right time, to ask.

"Jay can I expect you to call again?" she said invitingly.

"I might if I knew you let me stay the night," he replied, sounding unenthusiastic.

"Of course you can, Jay," she agreed quickly. A little to quickly she realised as his grin widened.

"And you'd be happy to indulged in few a different sexual practices I might invent, Lady, nothing nasty or vicious, a little dirty maybe, but nice like your cooking." An expectant look came over his face as he spoke, looking hard into her eyes.

Lisa didn't care for the idea. The memory of being tied fearful and helplessly flooded back.

"I promise I won't tie you up, or spank you, nothing like

that. Unless you want me to that is." The implied insinuation, not lose on Lisa. He would willingly inflict pain. At her request. "Come on, Lady, you'll really enjoy it, you know you will." his tone changing from one of disinterest, to subtle persuasion.

She was torn between agreeing or refusing. The weight of his thick shaft, or the loss of it, which she could still physically feel in her vagina. The thought of taking. *It All Again*. into her flesh made her want to say *Yes*.

Yet he had used deceit and clever cunning before she had enjoyed his instrument of flesh. Was this another deceitful ploy.

Lisa turned away from the table, rifled in cupboard draw searching for a cigarette, found a packet, opened it, placed one between her lips, bent her head lighting the white covered stick of tobacco in the flames from the hob.

The nicotine made her head spin. My God, she gasped silently. I haven't had a cigarette since Monday morning. Why the hell after being fucked do I always want to smoke. From one addiction straight to another. And I love them both, she gleefully acknowledged.

Exhaling the smoke, sitting down opposite Jay. Tentatively, calmly said. "I'm sorry, Jay, but to be perfectly honest I don't trust you, I would love to say yes and have you slide your nice big thick rod up my pussy. But I don't feel safe with you."

Jay looked around the sun lit kitchen, ignoring her. "I'm sorry you feel that way about me. I fucked up, treated you badly, frightened you. In return you gave me the finest screwing I've ever had," while he talked he shrank visibly, the vibrancy of youth evaporating, resigned to her refusal.

Lisa, looked in to the dull eyes, a defeated youth, a mere shell of the being, the youth who just a few hours ago had fuck more orgasms out of flesh with one erection she had ever dreamt possible.

"Let's meet each other half way, Jay. You want to screw me again. I told you would, didn't I?" She liked that. Having to remind him tactfully. "And I love being screwed by strong handsome young men." Pointing out explicitly what was obvious to both of them.

Jay's posture altered, his shoulders widened, a small

immature smile touched the corners of his mouth. "I promise you, Lady, I wouldn't do anything you don't want me to do. And I promise to do anything you ask me to do. *You.*" He paused. heavily emphasised You. "If you don't like the way I want to shaft you. Tell me and I'll stop... *Instantly!* he cried, grabbing her hands, squeezing hard as if by touch he could convince her of his sincerity that his promise contain no pretence. Or threat.

The look on his face. The ringing conviction in his voice transmitted a powerful feeling to her, convinced her that he would observe the rules he'd proposed.

Lisa putting the final touches, as she changed the wet semen stained sheets, replacing them with a pair of pristine pink satin she hadn't used before. Gathering the soiled reminder from the night before, thinking to herself. How much time she been spending washing bedclothes after being fucked. The heady scent from the dirty bed covers, so exciting to her senses. An aroma from the past, the aroma of the future.

The future was the return of Jay. Or Nathan. Happy now, the euphoria of body and mind she felt on Monday rekindled by the young erect flesh after extracted from her body so many delicious orgasms.

Before Jay had left the house. Swearing an oath he would not stray from his committed promise to respect her sexual inclinations.

She kissed gently him before opening the front door, his enthusiasm for her body evident in his every gesture. "I'll be here knocking on this door, Lady, at five o'clock sharp next Tuesday." he said, with a wolfish look of expectancy on his face.

"Just you make it better than last night, you sweet boy, perhaps I'll invent a few special dirty but nice ways of my own, I might even consider letting you enter me differently," she whispered coyly in his ear. Elated, as she closed the door gently behind him, by the look of confused lustful expectancy on his smiling face.

Jay, striding down the drive felt a new man. Enthralled, his very entity, his being as a man had been expanded, in the arms of the woman he lusted after for so long, chuckling, turning his head for a last look before he left the drive. Oh, you sweet hot horny lovely Lady. Will I hump your marvellous fluid moving body next time. Breaking into a cheerful whistle, shoulders squared, with a swagger, happily anticipating the pleasure's he enjoy in the very near future.

Lisa switch on the radio in the kitchen, twiddled with tuner for a few seconds, stopping at the blaring sound of some rock band singing. "I'm going to love you all night long." Most apt under the circumstances she gleefully told herself, stuffing the soiled bed clothes into the washing machine.

She spent the next hour or so doing the usual chores. Decide to have a ham salad for lunch with a little cottage cheese. Tripped, as she walked into the lounge, stumbling over her purchases from Monday. I must have thrown them on floor, she couldn't remember.

Stupid to chuck so thoughtlessly expensive clothes in a heap like that, scolding herself angrily, as she picked up bags, carrying rather carefully by the handles to the bedroom.

Relieved, delicately removing each garment. Thankful that they hadn't been ruined by the rough treatment, chuckling wickedly, stretching each of the new panties in front of her crutch over her slacks, studying each one in the mirror, assessing the effect it had on her and the person she'd give the pleasure to of viewing the bright flimsy slivers of material barely covered her sex lips. I'll wear the shiny dark green ones, next Tuesday for Jay, she decided, giggling childishly.

The panties covered little in front. The material in rear was a tiny dark green string. With another, even thinner string that would seat itself high over the hips holding the minuscule garment together. Abruptly, she ceased to giggle. Lisa shivered, a tremor of heat chilled her flesh. Her beast within stirred. Amplifying an atom of thought, that stopped the silly giggling. Would the sight of her almost explicitly naked bum cheeks stimulate and arouse Jay's youthful hunger to a passion he would fuck her in the *Ass!*

Placing the chosen panties, to one side, separating them from rest, opening the last bag. The lucid ramifications of what pleasure's Jay's instrument could and would evoke in her flesh as the girth of the thick shaft filled her rectum still filling her imagination.

Lisa slide out a very short yellow backless satin dress, with it's low cut neckline, held it up, eye level, arms outstretched in front her. Shook her head. That neckline is cut so low it's indecent. In fact it is bordering on obscene. Her observation, for some unexplainable reason. Exciting her.

"Oh My God, *Shona!*" she cried out, in a shocked alarmed voice, instinctively her hands flew to face, on the brink of dropping the yellow dress she grabbed it, threw it on the bed. Her mind distraught with guilt, running, heading for the phone in the kitchen. Lisa savagely unbraiding herself on the way. How the hell could you forget about Shona, her mind admonishing her? And don't blame the Vodka or the Temazepam, you gorged yourself into that condition because you never had those two young studs Gregg and Wayne nice big shafts screwing you simultaneously.

Lisa was close to tears, in wild panic to get to the phone she bumped into a kitchen chair, yelped, when her bare toes stubbed themselves against the wooden leg.

Clutched the end of the black topped table, scattering her carefully prepared lunch, cursing as her favourite cup shattered in to pieces on the hard wood floor. Grasping the black receiver she punched in the first five digits. Then paused, her middle finger poised to strike the sixth.

She stared at the phone. Placed it back on the hook in a slow thoughtful manner. Composing her mind, leaning against the wall, lighting another cigarette. I always think better with a smoke, wriggling her ache toes, praying they wouldn't blacken into bruise.

Lisa evoked the memories of her Monday adventures with the pretty diminutive blonde child-woman Shona. Did you really desire her? Was your behaviour, the desire for her body stimulated and inflamed by having two cocks at once? It probably did contribute in some small way, she agreed, ruefully.

But that happened before I had Jay. Jay with a lovely thick tool and stamina to match. Oh well, she decided boldly. At least I can phone and apologise. First time I've ever paid for sex, that damn dress cost me eight hundred dollars. A hell of a price to pay for one orgasm, I must been out of my tiny mind. Paying for sex, with a female, when men middle-aged men and lovely young boys are willing to ravish me over and over again for *Nothing*.

Lisa rang the Gym. Drawing on the cigarette slowly, waiting patiently, listening to the ringing tone on the other end. At least my lunch is still on the table that pleased her. The broken cup did not.

A pleasant helpful sounding voice in her ear interrupted her musing.

"Could I speak to Miss Shona Raul please," she requested in a matter of fact tone.

"Yes ma'am, and who shall I say is calling."

"Lisa, Mrs Lisa Knott." Instantly an excited child like voice gushed.

"Lisa, I've been calling you two or three times a day ever since you left that beautiful dress. I began to think you'd had second thoughts about Saturday night. You haven't have you Lisa?" Shona's question tinged with a degree of expected disappointment. Lisa felt a tiny stab of conscience.

"I'm awfully sorry, Shona. I feel terrible for letting you down. Please forgive me." You'd better think of a glib excuse, truth is a poor substitute for disappointment, she cautioned herself.

"Oh well, I suppose it's no good crying over split milk, Lisa. It's nothing more than I expected." The now subdued voice, unable to disguise her sadness and disappointment. Lisa suffered a sense of guilt as the unhappy sounding voice threaded its way into her head.

"Aunt Rena told me last night, this would happen. And she was right wasn't she, Lisa?" She didn't answer.

"Auntie said you were probably horny, lot of lonely divorced women like you, especially the wealthy kind, always take advantage of young girls or boys which ever happens take their fancy at the time."

"It wasn't like that, Shona, and you know it wasn't," she defiantly replied.

"Oh yes it was, Lisa. Have your fun and buy me a present. Salve for your conscience was it, Lisa, a little thank you present? Something in return for making you come while you were driving the car. Or maybe it was for having me naked on the front seat so you could experience what it tasted like having a woman come in your mouth instead of a man."

The sudden accusation, so convincingly spoken angered her. "Now you listen to me, Shona Raul." Lisa indignantly retorted. "I called you to apologise. I can understand your disappointment. I except that I am responsible for that. What happened between us that day we both wanted. You didn't have masturbate me, Shona. You wanted to. Perhaps you forgot to mention to your Aunt that you wanted me to make you come with my mouth. The dress was a mistake on my part. I'd have never bought the damn thing if I'd have known it would be construed as a payment for sex. It was simple a heart given present from me to you. And your Aunt Rena should leave you live your life your way. I'm sure she has the best intentions, Shona and you can tell her that, for me." Now is the time for that glib excuse, Lisa reminded herself. You have her undivided attention. Say it quickly, don't give her time to interrupt.

"I think a woman of my age being accompanied by someone as young and lovely as you, Shona, as much as I would like to. Is belittling you, your truly beautiful with a wonderful loving friendly nature. I'm truly sorry for what happened. I feel devastated by the fact that something I thought was a spontaneous act of affection could be made to sound so sordid and dirty. Goodbye, Shona." Replacing the phone, abruptly her sense of culpable guilt intensified.

Another slip in her moral standards. Blatantly lying her way out of a difficult situation. So what, she thought ruefully. *My Moral Standards*. I don't have any left. Lisa fumbled in her mind for a few minutes, while bending, collecting the scattered fragments of the cup. I spend forty years living within the confines of moral convention, never swore, never lied, never cheated on David. And what was my reward for living a life of principled respectability. Divorce, heartache, abject misery and forlorn loneliness.

Lisa, arose, consigned the debris of the cup to the garbage bin.

Admitted, frankly to herself, her unprincipled immoral

sexual life style, was infinitely more suitable and exciting.

She eaten lunch, removed the now clean smelling bedclothes from the washing machine, hung them out back to dry in the hot afternoon sun.

Angered by the sight of the unkempt lawn, the weed infested flower beds. The front lawn, she knew, looked even worse. Wrinkling her nose, disdainfully, making a mental note. If no one arrived tomorrow morning to sort out this bloody shambles, then Mr Jack Morse will by replaced.

Lisa, was gently, almost delicate, in hanging the yellow dress in the closet. The skimpy underwear already placed with the utmost care in the top drawer of her dressing table. If your going to enjoy wearing those panties, and that new nearly naked bikini, my Girl you better shave your pubic hair tonight, she decide closing the closet door.

She breezed through the rest of the chores. Sitting outside on the patio later, drinking coffee, relaxing in the hot summer, eyes closed, flavouring the taste of the cigarette in her mouth. Startled by the sudden shrill ringing of the front door bell. Inexplicably, instantly, Nathan. Oh boy, *Please!* let it be Nathan. She muttered excitedly.

Lisa, her mind already savouring the pleasures her flesh would receive and endure when she grafted her vagina to his massive tool.

Ignoring the ringing bell, heart pounding in anticipation, she ran round to the side gate. Approaching the corner of the house, she called out loudly.

"Hello, I'm over here, around back."

Chapter 13

Turning the corner, she ceased her head long dash. Walking gracefully towards her. Not the young lover she so wrongfully assumed ringing the doorbell. A red-headed elegant looking woman, wearing a very expensive pair of white Armani trousers with matching top.

"Good afternoon, Mrs Knott. I'm Mrs Rena Judd, I understand you're friendly with my niece Shona Raul." she said rather formally, smiling benevolently extending her hand. Lisa, recovering her composure, shook the offered fingers.

Shona's Aunt Rena. Mrs Judd certainly was a strikingly handsome woman, her eyes registered instantly. The natural looking dark complexion, and dark grey smiling eyes the generous wide thick red painted lips enclosed within the beautifully arranged ringlets of bright red hair. Broad square shoulders, large shapely voluptuous breasts filling her blouse. Lisa, shrewdly discerning, the breasts, as hers, bra-less. A narrow waist, surprising narrow for a woman of her build, with wide powerful looking hips, long straight legs, she could identify the heavy muscles of her upper thighs beneath the perfectly shaped cut of the trousers.

Lisa had the impression, sensed, the dark grey eyes assessing her with equal female inquisitiveness. The conscious awareness, the aura, of the appraisal containing a sexual periphery.

I wonder if Shona rang Auntie and told her about our rather unpleasant conversation earlier. The thought in mind, she said, warily, "I'm delighted to meet you, Mrs Judd. Shona told me quite a *Lot* about you." Lisa paused, her emphasis of the word Lot, much to her surprise, made Auntie chuckle.

"I'm sure she did, the little minx," she laughingly agreed. "I might add she told me *All about you. Including* the pleasures you both enjoyed." Her mocking insinuating tone aggravating in the extreme.

"Well we seem to know so much about each other I don't think we have anything to discuss, so goodbye, Mrs Judd, nice of you to call." Lisa said, looking defiantly into the dark grey eyes.

"I think you and I have, for some reason Mrs Knott, have started on the wrong foot. Relax, chill out, as Shona would say. I haven't called to behave like an aggrieved parent. I know Shona, believe you me. I love that tiny little girl more than you or any one will ever know. I just had to meet the woman that impressed my sweet Shona so sexually. If you're a friend of Shona's, then have become a friend of mine." The red headed woman so convincingly offered verbal olive branch. Lisa, touched by the sincerity, excepted, unconditionally.

"I think you and I should have a friendly heart to heart chat," Lisa invitingly suggested with a gently smile. "Over a drink perhaps?" she added laughing.

"Now that is a suggestion I totally agree with, Mrs Knott. If the offered drink happens to be Southern Comfort lead me to it, I certain could strangle a glass or two, my mouth is as dry as the inside of a Arab's jock strap."

Lisa tickled by the humorous description of thirst, collapsed, howling with laughter. "Let's go round back, we can sit on the patio in the shade, and chew the fat while we enjoy a few drinks," she panted, breathlessly as her laughter subsided.

"Wait just a moment," she replied, chuckling with amusement. "I had better tell my chauffeur Chet where I'm going, he'll only follow me. Fusses over me like an old woman. The most slavish obedient man I've ever meet, Mrs Knott. Utterly reliable, He will perform any instruction I give him to the letter. No questions asked." The look in the woman's eyes, her manner of speech gave Lisa impression their relationship went much deeper that employer and employee.

Shona had mentioned that very fact. But how deep. The thought intrigued her. To find out why, excited her.

Lisa concealed her thoughts. How in God's name did I miss seeing the gleaming white Rolls Royce parked in the drive, she wondered, studying Chet leaning against the bonnet, face obscured by the brimmed cap and large sunglasses. He appeared tense, stiff, making him appear like a coiled spring.

Auntie slipped an arm through Lisa's, just above the elbow, the soft warm fingers gently brushing the inside of her forearm, the touch fleeting, the result. A minute sexual quiver in her loins.

"It all right Chet, I'm going round back for a drink or two with Mrs Knott. If I need you I'll use the pager." The loudly shouted commands, Lisa thought sounded a little rehearsed.

Approaching the patio. Auntie leaned her head close to Lisa's ear. "Let's drop the Mrs. You can't have a really good chin wag unless it's on a first name basis, Lisa. You really must get your lawns and flower beds seen to, their a bloody disgrace, I've seen better tended garbage dumps," she snobbishly whispered.

"Your absolutely right, Rena," agreeing, ignoring the implied insult.

"Take a seat, Rena." Lisa offered, waving a hand in the direction of the white wrought iron patio table and chairs, wrinkling her nose at the sight of several flies perched on the rim of the half finished cup of forgotten coffee. "You take you liquor straight?" she asked, solicitously, picking up the offending cup and saucer.

"On the rocks, but easy on ice please. No pointing diluting a good drink before you swallow it, I always say, Lisa," Rena replied, wetting her lips with the tip of her pink tongue in anticipation.

Lisa, praying to hell she'd find some Southern Comfort somewhere in the drinks cabinet, kneeling down wildly pushing aside bottles of wine and vodka. Haven't seen a bottle since David's departure, she remember, the recollection saddening her somewhat. Elation dismissing the pained image in her mind. The very last bottle. Yippee! Southern Comfort. Two minutes later. Blinking when the bright sunlight attacked her eyes, she placed the drinks tray on the table, containing, One bottle of Vodka, one of Rena's preference, two tall glasses, and a full ice bucket.

Lisa sat drinking slowly. Rena silent, her features alive with pleasure taking big gulps of the light brown liquid, Adam's apple jerking with every swallow.

"Lisa, you have no idea what pleasure I get from stiff drink in the middle of the day," sounding a little sort of breathless, refilling her glass before adding two or three ice cubes. "From what Shona told me about you it appears we have a lot in common," she added, taking another mouthful. "I bet since the day of your divorce, Lisa," a knowingly expression, fleetingly invaded her eye's. Lisa detected as she spoke. "You've never spoken to a living soul about your pain and misery and I'd bet twice as much. You have never shared the secrets or methods you employed in learning how to build what can only be described a totally new life." She paused for a few seconds, allowing the words to sink in. "I know I never have, not even to sweet little Shona, my tiny saviour." Lisa silent, watching the red head tilt forward, neck bend, the chin almost resting on the chest, the shoulders seeming to shrink.

"Come on now, Rena". She understood her feeling. She'd live the same mental agonies. The hell only a woman can feel after years of loving devotion then to discover it meant nothing.

To have lived a life believing the affection so freely bestowed was out of love. Then, the realisation it had been nothing meant nothing, in the due process of time Lisa had developed a deep angry feeling inside. The mental anguished enmity of having had her soul raped, her needs and affections heartlessly used and abused. Oh yes, she remembered the pain.

"Well now, Rena," she said, quietly. "As two old divorced middle-aged women, having, as you put it. 'A good old chinwag' Why don't we get it off our chests?" she suggested, then added rather recklessly. "Warts and all, just tell each other, no fancy frills, call a spade a spade, hiding nothing." Finishing the remains of her glass. refilling it, she waited, impatiently for a reply.

Rena regarded her, thoughtfully. "Hell why not?" she enthusiastically replied, "You first, Lisa, seeing as it's your suggestion, and I'm your guest."

You first, Lisa thought. She remembered when, ten years old, she'd lifted her dress and pulled down her knickers for a classmate because she wanted so much to see what a boys private parts looked like. With vivid clarity, she remembered her excited conclusion. They're so much fancier and prominent than mine

This time also because she expressed her wishes, she was forced to go first once more.

"I'll have to think, she said thoughtfully. "I'll skip the agony part, Rena that's all behind me now. I'm over that, and so are you, if what Shona told is true. Besides I'd prefer to forget it anyway... *Okay!* To be perfectly honest I'm more interested in discussing the methods and manner in which I disposed of the heartache. How it changed me from a conventional middle-aged respectable divorced lady into sex hungry woman, which I will readily admit, Rena. I wish the hell it had happened twenty years ago." She paused, emptied her glasses, lit a cigarette, studied the face opposite for any sign of displeasure at her confession.

"Now that's what I wanted hear you say, Lisa. You love to *Fuck*. I love to *Fuck*. Just like you, I had to get divorced before I discovered what the hell I had been missing out on all my life." Rena openly confessed, chuckling, brushing aside all Lisa's timid doubts.

"It wasn't all down hill, Lisa, you must admit we've had the luck to keep our figures, haven't we. I suppose like me, you have suffered gallons of black coffee and endless salads. Putting vanity aside, you have to agree we look better, and sexually more attractive than most women half our age. I must confess Lisa, looking at you now, I wish to hell I had got my hands on you before little Shona."

Lisa was pleased. Yet, wistfully, replying a little timidly. "I think, having met you, I wouldn't disagree."

Rena grinned, chuckled. "Hey maybe I could spend an afternoon exploring your naked body." Her eyes flushed, narrowing.

She shivered inwardly. The lustful desire blatantly obvious. Her own desire, warmly responsive

"How many women have you made love with, Lisa?"

"Just Shona," she affirmed, then regretted the instant confession.

"Now I really feel jealous of Shona, the lucky little minx. Perhaps you'll allow me to become your the second female lover, Lisa?"

She never answered. Just shrugged her shoulders.

"I'm sorry Lisa," she said, recanting softly. "We'll leave that for another time. I shouldn't have changed the subject," she reassuringly apologised. "I've never trusted anyone enough to be able to talk about my sex life until today, Lisa, not even my Shona. Yet I feel I can trust you. Now tell me your story, in simple words. I promise not to interrupt."

Lisa, looked around the unkempt lawn. Then questionable stared into Rena's dark grey eyes. Curled a hand around the half-filled glass, lifted it, holding out, offering it as a toast. She would trust Rena with her secrets. Lisa could read the desire to share, to exchange, to unburden their innermost thoughts, to drive the final nail in to the coffin of their heartache, in the red haired woman's face. In a swallow, she drained the glass, the fiery liquid burned her throat, stomach churning for a few seconds making her shudder. Pausing for the effect to settle. Tell it straight and simple, she commanded herself.

"I'd been divorced about two years, Rena, I went out to dinner with an old friend from my college days, got hopelessly drunk, found myself in bed naked being fucked by a man. A total stranger. That was the first mans cock other than my husband's I had ever come on. Would believe that, Rena. Forty years old before sampling my second man. I loved it. It was three men later before I discovered the pleasure of having a man come in my mouth, I must admit, the idea of being fucked in the mouth never appealed to me. I'd never have done it if he hadn't slapped me around first."

The memory flooding back of that afternoon, the wondrous expansion of her mind to the new pleasures it had exposed to her flesh almost made her forget her own advice. So strong the desire within to relive the experience, *Again.* Being slapped into submission first. *Now* would give pleasure.

"Then he fucked me. I had an orgasm the like I have never experienced before. A couple more men followed. I dieted, did aerobics endlessly, went jogging. Had lovers to stay at week-ends, the more times I had their cocks, the more I wanted. It wasn't very long before the need change to want. When that happened the misery vanished. And my cravings for man's flesh became a source of happiness, I had a feeling of contentment. I felt reborn, alive again, my own person, a free spirit. A middle-aged woman with a sexual appetite of teenager. Having unearthed this new font of delicious physical sexual pleasure, my happiness. This elixir of lust laden delight made me addicted to being fucked. To having orgasms. The taste of a mans erect flesh in my mouth. For being reduced quivering, moaning, and writhing as my shuddering cunt coated the tongue inside me.

"The more flesh I had, so my cravings increased. My lovers changed more frequently. Eventually I had no conscience, no regrets, no hang-ups. I willingly confess, Rena, I have no morals whatsoever when it comes to sex. I will take any man, old, ugly, rich, poor, black, white, the younger they are, the more sweeter my enjoyment. I suppose I'm what you call and old slut. But I've never been happier in all my life." Lisa drained. Yet, uplifted mentally, her confession, sordid as it was had cleansed her very soul.

"There's a lot more to tell, Rena, perhaps one day we can discuss the matter in greater length. But that is it basically," Her story finished, the inside of her mouth feeling like rough sandpaper, throat dry, gagging with thirst putting the vodka bottle to her lips gulping down a large swig.

"Oh Boy." Rena regarded her with a species of awe. "You really do like being shafted don't you, Lisa. I wonder if size is important to you?"

"What the hell, exactly do you mean by *That*?" Lisa endeavouring to keep her tone light.

"Oh, you know." Rena brooded for a moment. "Do big large pricks turn you on?" I'll admit. Honestly. A real big one reduces me to jelly."

"No," Lisa lied quietly. "A cock is a cock. Its size, big or small will do the same job."

"I have an odd feeling, Lisa." Rena's tone suspicious. "You are being a little evasive, but we can leave it for now," she added, smiling broadly.

Lisa wasn't deceived by the smile. The red haired woman's perception of her sexual desire is too acute to be fooled by the lie.

"They say confession is good for the soul, Lisa," pausing, emptied her glass. Averted her gaze. Exhibiting to Lisa, a marked reluctance to continue.

She inexplicable sensed the turmoil in Rena's mind at that minute. Her own confession still alive in her head. "Just get it off your chest, Rena, you'll feel better. I know I do," she advised softly, reaching across the table taking Rena's long strong fingers into her palms caressing them slowly.

Her touch galvanised Rena. The touching flesh on flesh transmitting between them, an empirical bond that linked them through their experience of life. The sensation, a warming within, different to all others gently expanded in Lisa, of affectionate sympathy and friendship towards Rena. A bonding inspired by the inner knowledge of each other's experiences.

Is out of sympathy, a feeling of compassion, she asked herself. She didn't know. What I do know, she told herself, inwardly convinced. We are two of a kind. A pair of middle-aged wealthy divorced women. Adjusting to a new life, one which we were totally unprepared for. Our saviour and salvation, if what Shona told her was the truth, and she have no reason to doubt it wasn't the truth. Lisa obliquely observed. Was and *Is Men, Cock* and *Fucking* in that order.

"Your secrets will be safe with me, Rena. As mine are with you. Just think what new pleasures *'WE'.* can share *'TOGETHER'.* Lisa opened her legs slightly, the sexually implications of her statement bring a moistness into her sex lips. Instantaneously, without thought, Lisa leaned forward, lips apart, kissed Rena's full red painted mouth. The thick warm lips opened wide taking her offered mouth, enclosing it within, their tongues like wet snakes slithering from mouth to mouth. Lisa's nipples slowly hardening, her pussy oozed moistness. When, with lungs afire, their lips parted, gasping for breath she sat down.

Rena, her condition, Lisa noticed joyfully, in keeping with her own. I wonder if my eyes are mirroring the lust, I can see in hers, she pondered, excited by the thought.

"Do you kiss all your female guest's like that Lisa, or would I be right in thinking that sudden display of affection was prompted by a more deeper desire?" she inquiringly in a husky voice, topping up her empty glass with slow deliberation.

"I'd say your thinking was right on the money, Rena". Lisa laughing replied.

"That is beautiful, Lisa, now we have become friends we'll spent time together. But I want to be certain you understand what being good friends with me entails, Lisa." She paused allowing Lisa a few seconds to digest the implications of the unsubtle warning.

"You may not enjoy, in fact some of my more, I'll call them games, I like to indulge in might disgust you. You have no idea how! Oh to hell with it, Lisa… If I can't tell a friend, you are the only woman I've called friend in the last four years or so, Lisa, Shona apart. No body would or could ever understand what it's like to go through the hell you and I have suffered, Lisa. You have to live it first, and we've live it, it makes us kindred spirits, two middle-aged women, suddenly, through adversity, overcoming our heart break, and in doing so, we have released, within ourselves, something so powerful, so pleasurable. It dominates it us utterly. Speaking for myself, I have to admit, if there is any emotion, or happiness in this world, better than this. Nobody's found it yet. And we travel the same road, I'd lay odds, on the fact our experience in overcoming our misery is almost identical, Lisa, and that in itself must make us friends. If you can't tell a friend your troubles, honestly, who can you tell?" her anguish clearly apparent, defiantly, with a shake of her head emptied her glass with a quick gulp.

Lisa hotly excited, her curiosity in overdrive, agog mentally to hear Rena reveal her sexual soul. Affirmed her agreement with a big smile, touched Rena gently on her left cheek, smiled, saying impatiently, "Tell me all about it, Rena."

"Well here goes nothing, Lisa," pausing for a moment. "Oh to hell with the niceties, I need to get it off my chest, so here it is Lisa. I screw with men and women, sometimes three of four at time, in any combination, Lisa, I like to watch men fucking men, woman fucking women. I love others watching me being fucked, From time to time I like to be abused, whipped, and adore lashing a naked ass. I've explored so many different scenarios, Lisa. All of them give me a feeling I can't ever describe, no words can convey the pleasure I derive from sexual depravity, Lisa. Be warned my found new friend, I will try involve you in my games." She pointed a forefinger in Lisa's face continuously as she spoke, as if to emphasise the depth of her sexual degradation.

"Do I take it that was your story?" Lisa, said, hoping it sounded calm and unruffled.

"No, not entirely, I was going tell you about me and Shona, how Chet became to be involved. I meant to. Until you kissed me, Lisa. I'm sorry, but that's the way I am. I can't stop myself. Once the urge for sex takes me…" she left the rest unsaid.

"No need to apologise, Rena," cheerfully she replied. "Besides it sounded so much better than mine."

"Your not shocked then?" the incredulously startled stare made Lisa laugh.

"Shocked, Rena, not on your life my friend. Quite the opposite. I'm excited and very curious indeed. Do you know, Rena, the idea of being introduced to a world of erotic sexual games, is certainly appealing, very appealing indeed." Lisa was, she knew, making a fateful and irrevocable decision. All her life she had chosen safety, security, totally avoiding risky adventures of the flesh. Even with Nathan, Jay, the locker room escapade, Shona, had been a safety net. It was her choice, her decision.

She realised, in this moment of decision, she was burning her bridges, the foundations of her personal sexual choice's had already been weakened by her past sexual affairs. The thought of Lisa Knott being random used and abuse hadn't crossed her mind since the night she found herself naked, being fucked by a strange nameless man.

"Do you realise what you're saying, Lisa? You have no idea whatsoever, of the scope or depths of sexual depravity I indulge in". Rena was bewildered, speaking in a perplexed voice, baffled, she couldn't believe the unhesitating eagerness Lisa exhibited. Shona's perception, bless her heart, had been right on the money. She'd told her on the phone, she believed Lisa was a nymphomaniac, only didn't she realise it, well not yet. Rena felt satisfied nevertheless. This visit, the plan, with Chet's assistance, was working like a dream.

Lisa accepted, believed this was her time to be strong now. Follow her desire to achieve complete sexual satisfaction. Pay, with her flesh, her body and mind whatever the cost. For pleasure. Rena's voice gave her the impression she was unconvinced of her sincerity, her willingness. Lisa, with slow deliberation explained. "I have over the last few years, Rena, developed an insatiable hunger for sexual pleasure, it's become an addiction. A demon deep within me". Recklessly resolute, her bravado surprising herself, continued. "I had been deliciously fucked by five different men in…" pausing, mentally recalling how many days had past between Dean and Jay, aware of Rena gazing, mouth open, in to her face. "The last ten days, plus making love with Shona."

A chill iced her mind. She never realised her addiction for man-flesh and orgasm had become so demanding.

Under the thrall of her quietly spoken words, Rena allowed her to slip a hand inside her top, let her squeeze the nipple hard. Her shiver, as the nails bit into the soft flesh warming her already damp pussy.

"That's why I agreed, Rena". Lisa, offering, her justifiable reason. The iced chill in her mind became a freezing chard. It destroyed her last remaining grain of conscience. Forever.

"All that cock, having countless orgasm's, I have been fucked almost every other day, Rena, you'd think it would satisfy me. Quench my thirst for flesh. *It doesn't.*" she said, in a whispered voice. Lisa withdrew her hand, poured another drink. Leaned back, tilted her head, staring vacantly up at the cloudless blue sky.

"A problem shared becomes a problem halved, Lisa." Rena's gentle advice interrupted her dark thoughts. "Tell me what troubles you, then perhaps together, two old horny woman can solve your problem."

Horny seemed the right word. Just a word too many. To me it's becoming a disease, Lisa sadly reflected. The disease, no big deal. My problem lies in getting enough of the right type of medication to control it. *Sex.*

"Come now, Lisa," she urged. "You're not the type of woman that gives in that easy," she was genuinely curious for two different reasons. How deep was her need. And how to take advantage of it. *Now. **Today***.

I hope to hell Chet plays his part correctly, fingering the pager, in anticipation.

"I thought I have left my troubles behind me, Rena. Now telling you all my secrets about sex, and its pleasure. I suddenly realise, and isn't easy having to admit to one's self you've become a nymphomaniac."

"It's my fault, Lisa, I'm sorry, me and my big mouth. I should have listen to Shona, she said you were a nympho. I just didn't believe her. To be honest I treated it as one of her silly off-hand jokes." She said in bright manner. Yet her eye has held a guilty gleam. Or so it seemed to Lisa.

Rena laid a coaxing hand on her arm. "Lisa. There is no shame in being what you are. And we all have a God given right to enjoy the to limits all the pleasures we get from being ourselves, and how we achieve our satisfaction. Providing that is we don't hurt anyone but ourselves."

Lisa, still not convinced, haltingly replied. "Life just isn't that simple, Rena."

"But it is." She persisted firmly. "If you apply common logic. Think about it, Lisa."

"How the hell does one apply logic to explain how a middle-aged woman changes into a raving sex mad nymphomaniac, Rena," she snapped back belligerently.

"If you're looking for an explanation, Lisa. There isn't one. Logic is a process of applying every day experiences of life, to each situation as they arise. Then adjusting your mind to those changes that effect your own life. It's that simple, Lisa."

"Simple is right, Rena, what you've just said simple is useless *Crap*." Lisa totally confused, growled an angry response.

"Calm down, my new friend, chill out." Laughing softly before continuing. "You have been fucked by five different cocks. Did you cause them any hurt, mentally or physically? Did you enjoy them fucking you? Of course you did. And they enjoyed screwing you. That is an every day experience of your life, Lisa."

"Then an unexplained change occurs in mind and body, you

discover being shafted by five different men no longer satisfies your cravings. That change effects your life."

"Tell me, Lisa, if one packet of cigarettes a day will not satisfy you, what would you do?" Automatically she replied,

"Buy two."

Rena smiled, her features had look of expectancy. Lisa waited with a patience she did not feel. "No different to sex, is it? so were is the problem?" Then it hit her. The realisation. You've made yourself look damned stupid haven't you, she admonished herself severely.

Lisa's facial reaction betrayed her thoughts. Rena's pulse raced. Come on Chet, make quick, squeezing the pager. She's ripe now, ready to pluck. "You know the cure for your problem, don't you, Lisa?" Rena ecstatic in her success, assured, confident, leaning across the table, gently, yet firmly kissed Lisa passionately on the mouth, tasted the vodka on pliant lips, used the tip of her tongue to caress the soft warm flesh.

Lisa, elated, overwhelmed with a feeling of affection interlaced with gratitude surrendered her mouth. The kiss ignited her cravings, inflamed her flesh with stabs of desire, she chewed the red thick warm lips with her own, she rubbed her pussy hard against the edge of metal patio table separating them.

"Excuse me, Mrs Judd, I apologise for disturbing you but you did say you wanted to be home before six thirty because you had invited Miss Shona for dinner tonight at eight. I felt I should remind you it is almost five thirty."

The voluptuous kiss ended when the spoken words ceased. "Thank you Chet, this is Mrs Lisa Knott." Lisa breathless, her legs quivering, grasped the table's edge for support. "It's all right Lisa, Chet accepts *Everything* I do with out question. Don't you, Chet?"

"*Everything* Mrs Judd, and *Anything*..." He added agreeing obediently.

Lisa took a large sip from her glass. To steady her shaking legs and quell her the hunger. Chet, she noticed, was as Shona described. Short, average build, a thick mop of black curly hair, lovely clear blue eyes, a nice wide smile.

"While you're here, Chet show Mrs Knott your cock." The

crude outrageous command shocked Lisa. Rena chuckled softly, at her obvious discomfort. "That wouldn't be necessary, Chet." Lisa said quickly, to cover her shocked embarrassment.

"I think it is, Lisa, just to prove to myself, you really don't care what size of weapon you get screwed with." Smilingly dismissing Lisa's earlier assertion.

"To tell the truth, Rena, that would will not me bother at all. But taking in to account what we have discussed this afternoon, I think seeing a mans shaft will be hell for the rest of the day, and sleeping tonight will impossible."

The reason, honest as it was left Rena unconvinced. "What is your impression, as a man, Chet?" she asked suggestively. "Of Mrs Knott."

"She is extremely lovely lady, Mrs Judd," he replied, paused, slowly ran his gaze over her body, the flicker of passion in his eye's made her loins twitch, "With a body shape that would give any man a hard on. In a nutshell, Mrs Judd. My impression, as a man, she would make a great *Fuck*."

She her feminine pride inflated. Chet, a stranger, a man, correctly assessed her sexual capabilities, his valued appreciation of her looks and body left no doubt in her mind. His facial expression, the brief, yet graphic flicker of lechery in his eye's transmitted his intention. Chet's want's to fuck you Lisa, she told herself. And I won't refuse him, she silently concurred.

"Damn you, Chet, I've told more than once, not to use crude language, you apologise to Mrs Knott this instant." Lisa, taken aback, by the venomous tone in Rena's outburst. "And then get yourself back to the car." The volume of her voice increasing with every word, eyes blazing with anger, stepping in front the man. Ignoring Lisa, who was rooted to spot, stunned, yet unexplainably enthralled by the sudden undercurrent of violence. Rena, slapped Chet across the face so hard his peaked chauffeur's hat flew off his head, the mop of released curly hair falling over his eyes. The viciousness of the blow, delivered with such force, sounded like a gunshot in the still hot humid air.

"My apologies, Mrs Knott, forgive me for my crudeness," he said in a servile humbled voice. "But I make no apology for my description of your physical shape, or the physical effect I experienced. My apologies again, Mrs Knott, it's been a pleasure just to look at you." Chet's courteous polite, almost gallantly delivered apology. Inspired in Lisa a desire to reciprocate. To give in requital. A mutually expectable offering of thanks. Her lips parted in a warm secretive smile, he bent to retrieve the fallen cap. With her eyes, a widening smile, attempting to convey a silent message. *She... Would...* like him to fuck her.

"I will be with the car, Mrs Judd, remember now. Five thirty at the latest." he said calmly, appearing unaffected by Rena's sudden assault. He grinned broadly, looking defiant. Their eye's meet. The angry red welt on Chet's cheek causing him no apparent discomfort.

She sensed, the two heads, Chet's cap covered, bent slight backwards, Rena's the opposite, downwards, their gently smiling lips, had a tender appearance, their fixed gaze, totally out of character in the context of the hard ruthless slap. No anger, no regret, no shame, no remorse. The silence during the brief interlude, produced in Lisa, an eerie uncomfortable sensation. A moment, an oddly unreal pause in time. She shivered, in unpleasant tingling awareness. Rena and Chet's relationship, their bond, for some unexplainable reason held a deep dark sinister perverse aspect that gave both pleasure.

She perceived, in their features, reminding her of a scene from Gone with the Wind. Rena, laid a hand on Chet's shoulder. Nodded her head slightly, then motioned with her head. Their eye contact reverted to one of employer and employee. He touched his cap with his forefinger, saying in a servile tone. "As you wish, Mrs Judd, I'll be with the car."

"Sorry about that, Lisa, but there is nothing I find more aggravating than a man using the word fuck in the tone Chet used." Rena explained lightly as he turned and walked quickly away.

"Well even so, Rena, you didn't need to slap the poor man, and why so bloody hard? she asked, picking up her cigarettes. "After all you did ask him for his opinion".

"His opinion was fine, his wording of was not," she replied, in sharp shrill voice, her annoyance obvious.

"It seemed all right to me, Rena, in fact thinking about it.

I'm delighted to be told by a younger man, he finds my ageing body desirable," reaching for her lighter while talking. Rena shook her head with a flourish, a salubrious looking grin on her face.

"Would you have been so delighted if I said it, Lisa?" she asked slyly. Chet had been perfect, tonight she'd reward him, in the manner he real enjoyed. Punishment.

Lisa demurred with a smile, nodding her head, gently.

"Did Chet's polite apology impress you?"

Lisa repeated her previous wordless answer

"He wanted to fuck you, Lisa."

"I know he did."

"Would have let him, Lisa? Won't you? Go on admit it?' You'd let any man inside your panties, won't you? Especially if they are young. Won't you Lisa? interrogating her in a husky whispered tone.

"Oh Yes, Rena." For the second time today, irrevocable, boldly, she agreed.

"If our position's had been reversed, would you have wanted me to fuck you, Lisa?" The sexual innuendo, the implied implications, Rena's slyly yet so skilfully concealed physical intentions crystal clear.

"Would *You* want to screw *Me,* Rena?" Lisa, adroitly circumventing Rena's sexual cross examination. Congratulating herself for calling to mind the subterfuge she had used so successfully as a teenager. When an answer will reveal a secret intimate personal thought or desire. Answer that question with another question.

Chet, leaning on the Rolls, rubbing the sore cheek. Nice one Rena, he thought chuckling. Shona, you little treasure you've had unearthed a beauty. If only she knew everything had been planned. He massaged his crotch, grinned wolfishly. Oh Mrs Lisa Knott, if you knew what I do. The pleasures Rena and I will enjoy before we leave. You'd shit yourself.

Rena eased slowly round the patio table towards her. Her flushing cheeks, a lazy sensual smile, making the corners of her mouth harden, the slight narrowing eyes, the tip of her pink tongue gently wetting her thick lips. This was going to be something very special indeed.

Lisa's mouth, suddenly parched, her legs trembling, her heart's quickening rhythm. She knew Rena's answer. All their conversation about men, about sex, the nipples she caressed, Rena's talk of multiply coupling. The memory of Wayne and Gregg. Chet's verbal offer. The sudden act of physical violence, abhorrent to her until today. The wetness of her loins.

It incarnated, into a need. A conscious lascivious craving for an ***Orgasm.***

"Rena, I think you and I should continue this conversation in private," insinuatingly she whispered. Slipping a hand into Rena's.

"In private, Lisa, you and I will not be talking," she panted hotly, offering no resistance when Lisa took her hand guiding her through the patio doors.

Lisa, turned to close the patio door. It slid shut effortlessly. The bright shining sunlight reflecting off the empty glass's and near empty bottles caught her eye. Rena's hot breath touched her neck, her large breasts pushed against her back, through the material of her blouse, her two hard nipples felt like warm pebbles. Rena's pelvis rotated against her buttocks, her strong hands ran over her hips, before slowly travelling down over her stomach. She trembled, opening her thighs as they touched her clothed pubic hair before cupping her damp pussy.

Lisa, her desires rising, bent her head back, resting it on Rena's broad shoulder, closed her eye's surrendering her flesh to the red-haired woman enticing hands.

"Life hasn't treated you kindly has it, Lisa," Rena commented, while, with stiffened palms, prising her loins wider apart.

Lisa grimaced, as one finger slowly traced the line of division of her pussies wet sex-lips. "Oh it hasn't been all that bad really," she protested, trying not remember the desperate black day's went she had felt suicidal. "It had its compensations, she laughed flippantly.

Rena's hands slid delicately to her waist, one slipped inside her blouse, the other the waist band of her skirt.

Simultaneously, a breast, squeezed so viciously it made her

flesh cringe, two straight hard fingers slid through her damp pubic hair, curled, pushed swiftly into her vagina, Lisa winced, the fingers nails scoring the tender flesh within, groaning, pushing herself backwards, entombing the two glorious intruding digits of flesh in her cunt. "Poor, Lisa. You've had a bad time all in all, haven't you," Rena murmured again softly, massaging slowly the blossoming bud of the clitoris with her thumb, amazed by the pliable flexibility and plenitude of swollen wet flesh, sending sharp tremor's of passion up her spine.

Lisa eye's closed, relaxing, body succumbing, yielding to the hunger rising within her. Pleased that she'd decided not to put on any underwear after showering earlier. Snuggling her body back against her newly found friend, slipping a hand behind her, pushed it between their tightly infused bodies, cupping hand, with fingers stiff clasped Rena's pussy hard, enfolding with a squeezing grasp, felt the tremor of Rena's excitement.

"Is this your compensation, Lisa?" she whispered huskily. "You… you don't mind sharing it with me do you?"

Lisa shook her head. "No, Rena, I do not mind at all," she responded softly.

Lips softly touched her exposed throat, kissing the warm flesh. "You've got lovely firm breasts Lisa" she murmured as her fingers started slowly frigging Lisa's vagina. "I want to…"

"Oh yes? Want to do what, Rena?" she interrupted impatiently.

"I want to run my tongue over every inch of you, taste your flesh, anoint it lovingly," Rena gaspingly admitted.

Lisa, her breathing quickening, her vagina, its tiny pleasure membranes warming to the increasing friction of the ever moving fingers. If they didn't stop, she warned herself. Your going to… *Come!!!*.

Lisa, twisted and wriggled, desperate to forestall the impending orgasm, she torn the hands from her body. Spun round sharply, pushing a startled, much surprised Rena backward with a strength she never realised she possessed.

"You don't want me? Do you, Lisa?" she cried, so angry and frustrated by the suddenly turn of events. She gazed at the flushed agitated expression of on Rena's face, made it appear she was close to tears.

Lisa slowly unbuttoned her blouse, removed it even slower. Raised her arms above her head, dropped it. Her naked breasts, nipples still swollen, bouncing delightfully. Rena sigh with pleasure, bent her head forward, gently, ran the tip of her tongue over Lisa's throat, the hot smooth skin pulsing when she closed her mouth over a hard corded nipple.

The lips closed over the nipple, caressing it tenderly, she felt it hardening, enlarging ever further in response, heard Rena's quiet sigh of contented pleasure. Her stomach fluttered deliciously, her vagina warmed.

"Oh that is nice," Lisa breathed, "It feels so good." She leaned back, arched herself, pushing her breast up tighter to Rena's lips. Rena, with a shiver, suck the now rigid nipple into her mouth, encircling it with her warm soft tongue. Lisa sighed again, as the breast was slowly sucked deeper into the mouth, groaned loudly, when sharp teeth bit into the soft flesh, felt another powerful surge of Rena's rising passion transmitted by the bite.

Without removing the mouth, somehow. Lisa never knew how. Rena shed her top. Lisa her flesh inflamed, eyes shut reached out, searching, in her desire to feel naked flesh, her hands, fingers spread, curved in to talons, sinking them with all her strength deep into the soft flesh Rena's large firm breasts.

Why did she do it? What had enticed her to inflict pain. Was just a reflex action, a knee jerk to Rena's bite, was it retaliation, pain for pain, like for like. Or was it, she meditated ruefully, as Rena, pinching the nipple of her other breast with such venom, involuntarily her eyes flew open. Another dark sexual pleasurable desire her demon wanted her to *Satisfy,* thighs dampening like never before, her clitoris started to tingle with a pins and needles like sensation.

Rena's mouth disgorged the breast. Her dark grey eyes wide, with a shake of her red hair, clamped her lips on the Lisa's, fingers roughly, feverishly, her nails scraping skin, tore off her skirt. Rena was afire, mentally, physically, and above all, sexually. Aroused and inspired by her intuitive touch of genius, instinctively guessing, the naked woman trembling in her hands desire's match her own. Brutally she chewed her lips, before driving her tongue savagely between the partly opened lips.

In one swift movement, her hands, ripped off her Amini trousers. What a way to treat such beautiful clothes, Lisa thought, as Rena's hands closed over her buttocks, pulled her forward into her loins, rotating her hips wildly.

Lisa, her lungs draining of oxygen, digging her nails deeper in to abundant breasts, wrenching her lips away from avid mouth enclosing hers, heart beating furiously, gasping out loud as Rena's wet swelling clitoris intermeshed with hers.

"Well you'll never leave by five thirty, Mrs Judd, if you intend to finish what you both seemed by enjoying immensely." Chet, in a quite hot voice, his instrument hardening, standing inside the now open patio door watching the two naked women. Lisa gasped with undiluted shock and horror. Franticly she pulled back from Rena's sexual embrace, searching desperately for something to cover her nakedness.

Chapter 14

"Oh hello, Chet," Rena said calmly, unruffled by his surprised intrusion, unaffected by his somewhat familiar look.

Lisa, got the distinct impression it wasn't the first time they had witnessed this situation.

"I wasn't expecting you, Chet," she told him firmly.

"I can see that." Chet advanced in to the room, Lisa could see a lewd gleam his eyes. Despite her embarrassment, her nakedness, she couldn't help but see a funny side to it, what if her husband, David had arrived home early and found her standing naked in the lounge locked in a passionate embrace with another woman, while being watched by another man. The effect it would have had on him. She had become well aware during the past few years how men fantasised about this sort of scenario.

The thought heightened her desire, making her feel even more aroused. Chet or no Chet, she wanted Rena.

He stood in front of them, eyeing Lisa's naked body from head to toe, with stare of undisguised coveted lechery. She could well imagine the effect her nakedness was having on him. If his reaction matched her vagina's trembling flutter, his hot stare drove all thought's of hiding her naked body out of her mind.

Lisa no longer had to imagine his reaction, the swelling outline of his cock, already growing stiff, hardening through his dark grey trouser. His eyes flickered minutely, looking at Rena, observing instinctively, as another ripple of sexual longing spread swiftly through her flesh. *They were communicating*. In a flash, a split second in time, she realised, in that one brief look. *Everything,* Shona, Chet, Rena's confessed sexual malpractices. Chet's servile devotion. Shona telling her about Rena's sex life. She had been, not duped, up to this point, she was a very willing participant. Talking on the patio, Rena's type of love life, the promised pleasure and satisfaction held a hypnotic appeal. You make your decision. *Now* do you really want this, explicitly questioning herself. Lisa didn't have to think. The wetness of her vagina, the pulsing nipples, Rena's naked body, Chet's rising flesh, her own body's smouldering hunger for orgasm. Made the decision.

"Lisa and I were..." Rena started to explain.

"I could see what you were doing," Chet interrupted, His voice hard, sounding jealous.

"No need to stop on my account," he continued sullenly. He sounded, Lisa thought, like a child who missed his share of the goodies.

"Just forget I'm here." While he spoke, his hand adjusted the growing bulge in his trousers. Lisa's vagina fluttered again, at both the signs of his now obvious arousal, and the implications contained in the words.

She had felt no nervousness, no shame about what she and Rena had been doing. Could she continue with him watching? Yet, she didn't want to stop. Her hunger was growing stronger by the second, the need for orgasm, the lust for Rena's caress becoming ever more acute. Her mind burning for the feel Rena's warm flesh again. And to be perfectly honest, the sight of Chet's erecting cock, so obvious to both them was adding to her passion.

Rena placed a hand on her buttocks, squeezed the soft flesh softly. A touch Lisa felt, not out of passion, more as encouragement. She glanced quickly at Rena's face, then at Chet's. His instrument less prominent since being adjusted.

Lisa could not mistake the look in their hot eyes, the slight smile's that tugged at the corners of their lips. The same gaze she noticed after the slap. Rena's hand massaging her bum cheeks quickened. Was this one of games Rena like to indulge in? If it was, Chet must play a very active role in the proceedings, she decided reflectively.

It is no difference really, she ruminated. Then, she eased her buttocks gently back against Rena's warm palm as the memory of orgasming, for the first time in her life. *Being,* being fucked by two cocks simultaneously, flitted briefly across her mind.

Including the aftermath of not satisfying your lust she obliquely reminded herself with a small shudder. The present make-up may be different. The end result would be totally different. *This Time…*

Rena's lips touched Lisa's neck. Misinterpreting the twitching bum cheeks she slipped a finger between the round orbs of flesh, titillating pucker of flesh around Lisa's rectum.

"Something you require, Chet?" Rena questioned him brightly, just as if there was nothing unusual about the situation.

"Yes" he barked, stroking his bulging groin. "I require a fuck," delivering the words in blunt snarling tone.

Rena shook her head. "I'm sorry, but you're going to be disappointed, Chet. Mrs Knott isn't as accustomed to multiple sex as we are I'm afraid." she regretfully explained.

"Perhaps we could persuade her?" he suggested, grinning.

"Perhaps under the circumstances, *I…* could be?" Lisa admitted timidly. Stiffening with startled shock as Rena's insistent probing finger push roughly into her ass.

"Maybe my Chet has the means of persuasion you'd find every hard to resist, Lisa?" Rena whispered knowingly, and slyly in her ear.

The finger in her rectum, expertly exciting her inner flesh. The idea. If by refusing, she'd suffer more hellish days as she had earlier in the week. The fact she is more than happy to have Chet's shaft, made being fucked much more exciting sexually. Having Rena watching. Blew her mind, what was it the young called it. *What a rush.*

The rising tide of orgasm expanding deep in her stomach, feeling the sharp points of Rena's teeth on the base of her throat. A gentle pressure being applied to loose skin below her Adam's Apple.

"You want me just to show her, Mrs Judd? Or do you require me to strip naked first?" Chet asked politely.

"Oh yes, Chet, naked if you please." Lisa replied quickly. Rena in no position to instruct him, her avid mouth to preoccupied.

Lisa slipped her index finger in to Rena's vagina. She experienced a vicious stab of pain as the teeth on her throat bit hard in to the skin.

"Give me *another* one, Lisa" she mumbled incoherently, with out releasing her teeth.

Lisa obliged instantly. The cunt on her fingers felt as slippery wet as her own, the probing fingers swallowed completely by Rena's arched body.

She shuddered from head to toe Rena's strong finger's slithered over her clitoris, before frigging her pussy with a salacious erotic rhythm in unison with the one in her rectum.

This woman's lusts can be exploited. I wonder if she'd enjoy fucking a man as I whipped her. Rena speculated.

Lisa didn't want… *Not Yet…* she screamed, silently in her mind. Oh please not yet, begging her self-control to assert itself. The pleasure in her flesh too powerful, too servile to it's own pleasure's, body ensnared by Rena's clever expert manipulations. Head rolling from side to side she felt her inner flesh convolute, coil on itself, spasming helplessly, her orgasm gushed over the stabbing fingers. Moaning and writhing in ecstasy, at the moment of completion she scream in agnostic pleasure and excruciating pain as Rena's muscle stiff jaws drove her teeth savagely deep in to the flesh of her throat.

The rampant pain, the explicitly felt sensations within her vagina, the feeling of her warm glorious semen inside her vulva, all came together in canopy of lust that induced Lisa's flesh to expunge a second minute exquisite climax.

Lisa, the fire within subsiding gently, panting heavily. Was it sweat or blood she could feel lazily trickling down her chest on to her breasts, she wondered? Rena's wet pussy palpitated against her hand, her knees bent, forcing her hot cunt down hard on Lisa's fast stabbing fingers, felt the knuckles ram hard up against her sex lips, her teeth left the throat, sagging, with quivering flesh her come, coated Lisa's ridged thrusting fingers copiously.

Rena twitching spasmodically draped her arms around Lisa's neck, gasping hoarsely. Lisa, her legs jelly, a trembling weakness affecting her every bone, copied Rena's action, resting heads on each other's shoulders in mutual contentment. With passion's subsiding they clung to each other for physical support.

"I must say, Mrs Judd. It is a long time since I last seen you become so wildly erotic. When do I get *my* turn?" Chet asked questioningly, a wide grin on his face, hand stroking his hidden erection.

Rena winked mischievously at her, before turning towards Chet. "Seeing as you weren't actually invited. I think he should take a back seat, don't you, Lisa?"

Lisa smiled, agreeing. "I thought you would have stripped by now, Chet," she sounded rather annoyed to Lisa. "Get your clothes off. *Now*." Rena ordered him roughly.

Lisa watched, anticipation growing as first the dark grey jacket then matching neck tie, followed by his white shirt, deposited, she observed, carelessly in a untidy heap on the floor, disentangled herself from Rena's sweaty embrace, turning to study the disrobing Chet. God was he hairy, Shona's description been correct, she recalled excitedly. Thick black matted curly hair covered his chest, his short thick arms, the sunlight shining through the glass patio door behind him creating a shimmering effect on the bunched black hair sprouting on the shoulders.

His lusting hot expectant eyes never leaving her naked body as he stripped, sending a new ripple of lust crawling up her spine. His black shoes and grey socks joined the scattered pile, wetting her seeming dry lips, the gesture not missed by the nearly naked man. Her breathing became uneven, watching his fingers, with deliberate slowness unbuckling the black belt.

Something about him, his lust filled eyes, gazing ever more hungry at her flesh, the suggestive smile on his lips. Shona said he wasn't much to look. Dressed in a crowd he'd appear nondescript. Naked, short though he may be, his broad squatness made him look powerful. His lack of stature compensated by an explicit sexual presence.

Rena disturbed her scrutiny, offering her top to dry her thighs, in the precise and thoughtful appraisal of Chet, the wetness on her thighs she'd forgotten.

Lisa, smiled, gasped, blinked in shocked surprise, stared at Rena in stupefied shock. "God Almighty, Rena, your bush is as red as the hair on your head," she exclaimed in excited surprise voice.

"It has the same effect on every one," she laughingly responded, brushing it gently between her fingers, "I've had men masturbate themselves just to see their come splash over it," she added, still chuckling. "Pity you never noticed earlier, Lisa. If you had, maybe you would have made me come with your mouth instead of your exciting fingers." Lisa detected a note of disappointment in the voice.

"I'll rectify my error next time, Rena," Lisa whispered carnally, reach out stroking the gorgeously striking red down gently.

Rena started to reply, a look of happy delight lit up her face as Lisa said. *NEXT TIME*.

"This might also be available next time, Mrs Knott, providing, of course Mrs Judd will allow it." They turned together at the sound of Chet's voice.

He stood hands on hips. Black hair covered legs parted. Displaying his length of erect white flesh with unashamed pride. Lisa gasped, stared, mouth wide open. For the second time in less than a minute. Put her hands on her face. Thunderstruck, tongue dry as sandpaper, speechless, frozen to the spot. She stared back and fro at both of them in silence, realising the conceal advantages of Chet's passive servile nature. It confirmed her earlier suspicions. They'd done this sort of thing together before, feeling a stab of jealousy towards Rena. For having Chet first.

Rena stood in front of the naked Chet, hands on hips. Hiding the instrument from Lisa. "That's very good, Chet my boy, but it's not quite right you know, I think you should stand closer to Lisa and you behave yourself." The warning was delivered with a heavy emphasis of threatening reprisal for any disobedience. Lisa heard the hidden man say in a quiet totally compliant docile sounding tone. "I'll will oblige Mrs Knott with what ever she requires of me, Mrs Judd."

Lisa in a state of disbelieving wonder, listened to the words in astonishment. "Lisa, isn't Chet really something else?" Rena asked, proudly, she reached out her arm.

Lisa closed her eyes. Without looking she knew, the hand was caressing Chet's erect flesh. "I have no idea, Lisa, the size of the cocks you've been having, but my Chet's lovely rod is the biggest I've ever tasted." she bragged loudly. "Why don't you come here, and we can enjoy it, *Together*."

An offer Lisa could not, would not refuse, it wasn't her conclusion. It was her *Cunts*. Stepping forward, flesh tingling standing beside Rena watching her fingers manipulating the huge shaft. "Now tell me, do you still maintain the size of the instrument screwing you isn't important, tell me now, if you had to choose between an average sized one, or this monster, which one would it be, Lisa?" she asked in a serious inquisitive voice.

Lisa studied the thick long instrument intently, not wanting to blurt out her answer, after expressing her opinion earlier that size wasn't that important. Watching Rena's fingers slowly massaging Chet's erect flesh produced a warming heat in Lisa's vagina that made her shiver.

Rena's referring to the cock in her fingers as a... *Monster*... seemed an understatement. It's length exceeded Nathan's, the thickness far greater than Jay's. And joy of joys it was circumcised. Lisa sex lips flexed at the thought of the pleasure's to be experienced while being fucked by such a tool.

"Isn't it the most magnificent weapon you could imagine, Lisa? You wouldn't believe the feelings it elicits from my pussy when I come over it. Do you know: it's over 10 inches long and 6 inches in circumference, Lisa, and boy do I love it." Rena tone, a sense of personal pride, and undisguised awe.

Lisa stepped closed to the kneeling Rena. "Let me see it," she demanded.

Obediently Rena arose, releasing the entrapped shaft of flesh, the weapon standing naked, full exposed, "Oh My God," Lisa, whispered in stunned admiration.

Chet's cock, standing rigid, jerked insistently against the taut drum of his black hair covered belly. *Never,* had she seen a cock of such size, *Never had* a penis beating with a life of it's own so effected her.

So beautiful! Thick, massive in length, it was an instrument of bright white pulsing flesh. A shining shaft, she thought feverishly, eclipsing every shaft I have ever received, I want to feel it slicing deep into my aching pussy. No matter how high the price Rena demands in return. Its light coloured skin was taut, appearing to throb; she could count the pulse of gorged blood travelling through the bloated surface veins. The inflated bulbous head, reddened healthy, gleaming with a sheen of wetness. The ball sack almost hidden by the abundance of black hair, not dangling like many she'd seen, or handled; faintly rigid with wrinkles, fitted smoothly beneath the rigid shaft.

"Would you like to taste its flavour, Lisa? Go on take in your mouth, you may never have the opportunity again," Rena's suggested quietly, raising her eyebrows.

Lisa, her mouth moist with desire to cherish, to savour the young massive instrument, instinctively knew how sweet and tender it would taste.

A reckless desire flooded into her, in one swift movement, she leaned forward, lips apart, the corners of her mouth stretching painfully as the huge bulbous head slide in to her receptive mouth.

She sensed Rena stepping behind her, her hands massaging her buttocks, then slide up over her hips, down her belly, before cupping her hot wet pussy. Lisa slowly slipped her mouth up and down the moist warm pulsating delicious flesh between her gaping lips, shivering in ecstasy when Rena's two stiff fingers pushed deep in to her vagina.

"I'll let Chet fuck you, but in return, Lisa, you'd have to allow me to watch?" Rena whispered hoarsely. "I think you would find the experience a new exciting pleasure, which is both addictive and sexually gratifying."

Lisa's gave scant consideration to the suggestion. She needed the man flesh. The only thought in her mind, the only desire in her heart was **To have the massive cock inside her Cunt!** Slowly extracting her mouth from root, stood up, wrapping her fingers around the saliva wet organ, Rena's fingers remaining imbedded between her slippery wet loins.

Lisa looked into Chet's hot looking lust hooded eye's, smiled, gently masturbating the hot huge rigid shaft of pleasure giving flesh. "Just you let me have Chet fuck me, Rena. *Please!*" she begged. "You can watch, I don't care, honestly, you were right, size is important. Please don't refuse me now, Rena. Please, Rena," she begged imploringly.

"Fuck Mrs Knott, Chet, and you make sure you do it, hard

long and viciously. I want her satisfy her completely Chet." Rena bluntly commanded the naked man.

Lisa's cunt quivered in anticipation. At the same time she felt a little disturbed by the dictatorial tone in Rena's voice.

"Certainly, Mrs Judd, please instruct me, if you consider my performance in anyway inadequate," he replied subserviently. Lisa, her passion's afire, nevertheless jolted by the manner in which Chet meek acquiesced. She wondered how deeply they were immersed together. The depth of their sexual perverse desire's, collectively. Rena's, she knew. Her relationship with Shona, incestuous. With Chet? Chet and Shona? All three? maybe.

"Perhaps you could suggest somewhere more conducive, Mrs Knott standing up to fuck, enjoyable as it is from time to time, will not allow me to satisfy you in manner suggested Mrs Judd," he humbly advised in a croaky voice.

"You are absolutely right, Chet," Lisa interposed quickly. The hot flesh in her hand igniting sharp tinkling stabs of desire in her vagina. "I think the bedroom is the place for us, Chet, it would be a great shame if I did not receive it *All, Chet,"* caressing his tool faster as she spoke.

"Now follow me, you give me hard, Chet, until your beautiful instrument can fuck me no more." Kissing him on the mouth, as her words ceased she turned on her heel heading for the bedroom.

"Come on," she said over her shoulder in a shaky voice. Rena forgotten. *"Hurry!"*

Her need, the want, her feminine hunger for sex so strong at this moment to experience his massive young implement savagely romping in the yearning slippery wetness of her pussy.

Not pussy, inexplicable remembering she had exactly the same thought with Nathan. *Cunt… He's going to fuck it like a cunt,* she told herself rashly. The crudeness of sexual thought, this time seemed natural. The lust within, so powerful, overwhelming her.

Lisa, spun round, her calves against the mattress of the bed, leaned fiercely against Chet, delighting in the tremor her groin induced in his flesh as it rubbed against her bush. His shaft sprang eagerly into the grasp of her warm fingers, his exploring hands found her breasts, gripped the engorged swollen nipples so hard it hurt. His mouth closed over hers, she ravaged his tongue with her own, avidly, heard their rasping breathing in the sunlit room. It was loud, gasping, the sound, a sob of desire and carnal sensual need.

A blind reckless gripped her, in one quick movement, she laid down, opening her thighs wide, caressing her hot wet pussy with one hand, the other squeezing a nipple. She slipped her middle finger into her body, removed it slowly, traced a line with the wet finger up her flesh, over her mound, her stomach, between her breasts, over her Adam's apple, under her chin. Fixed her eye's on Chet's, smiled into his face closing her mouth over her wet, sticky salt tasting finger, sucked into her mouth slowly.

His cock trembled, her cunt pulsed, she lifted her legs. ***"Now, Chet! Give it to me Now!"*** she feverishly panted.

Chet grinned. His hand was busy in her pussy. "First things first, Mrs Knott. Now this is the first thing," he gleefully chuckled, wrapping his free hand around his enormous instrument, directing the shaft of flesh towards her vagina.

She had never made love with a man who made it so obviously transparent his sexual intentions. But it was too late now; the weight of his body pressed down heavily into her open thighs, his rigid cock had nailed itself hard, fast, and deep into her steamy wet vagina. His mouth was set in a grim line of determination as he fucked her with an incredible savage vigour. Lisa relaxed, let herself go limp, indulging her flesh in the luxuriant pleasures inflicted by the power of his rod so diametrically larger, in sensation and feeling, from the flesh she'd experienced before. So filling, so deliriously hurtful, so beautifully satisfying to body and flesh.

Her mind, distant from her body, warned her. Chet's shaft, its immensity had taken dominion over her avid willing, too willing flesh. He had acted upon Rena's commands. He'd applied his flesh to her mouth. Now he meant to reassert, in the most sexual primitive way know to man, his male rights.

Lisa, for a few minutes savoured the luxurious ripples of

pleasure the rod inside her vagina provoked in her burning flesh, she surrendered herself to the savage rampant thrust. Then Chet was grinning down at her, saying, "This is what you have to have, isn't it, Mrs Knott? You'll do anything for a big prick, won't you? Say it, Mrs Knott, admit it, You love being... *Fucked"*.

With an act of sheer will power, she arrested the response of her wild flesh. Gripping his buttocks hard with both hands, she stopped his body's driving thrust. "Yes, Chet... *I love it!*" she acknowledged with a smile.

"And the bigger the prick, the greater... *I*... fuck." Her voice, to her astonishment, calmly confessing. "I don't want a man inside me who romps around and ejaculates a few times, you know. I want a man – *a real man* – a man who satisfies me utterly, a man big enough in flesh to make me moan, to writhe in the agony of pain and orgasm, a man with the stamina and strength that makes me come over and over again."

Rena watched, vagina burning hotly. Let Chet have his fun, when he'd finished. She'll be mine, slipping a hand between her moist thighs, priming the passion, her inflammatory desire's festering, riled by naked bodies, coupling, their gyrations rousing delicious sensations within.

Lisa stared into his eyes, an expression of lust laden anticipation on his face.

"I'm the man you're looking for, Mrs Knott," he said, smiling with self-assured confidence. Slowly he withdrew his hard rod, she whimpered, as like Jay, he stopped when the thickest part of his cock rested just inside her vagina at it's narrowest.

"You could be, Chet, but saying you are, isn't enough. You have persuaded me your a real man." she replied, trying to sound sceptical.

"I'm sure Mrs Judd will not object to you trying prove you are the man you think you are," she continued in a devious sly voice.

She had come to realise Chet wouldn't respond unless Rena instructed him.

"If Lisa desires you to attempt screw her senseless, Chet,

you do it, and do it well, or you'll suffer painfully if you fail boy." the tone of Rena's words harsh, insinuating a harsh vicious reprisal for failure.

She couldn't see Rena, her eyes fixed on the sight of the profusely covered black haired body arched above her, squirming imperceptibly in an erotic frenzy she feasted her eyes on the spectacle of the long column of thick heavy looking white flesh bridging the gap between her pussy and the black hairy groin.

"Let me show you," he said, a broad smile on his face. He gripped her hips with both hands. "Mrs Knott you are about find out how much of a real man I really am."

Lisa twisted, whimpered softly, as he slowly pulled her bodily forward, sliding her cunt up his shaft of hard flesh, arching her spine, she clasped her thighs tightly around his hips, twisting wildly, shivering, intoxicated by the stabbing pain as the huge cock finally achieved complete penetration, welding it's self to the very core of her vagina.

"There. Right there. Oh Yes. *No!* I, ah, ah, *Yesss!* **There** again, easy, slow. Ah… yes, there Chet, again, keep it just *There*. Oh, oh, oh, shove harder now. *Ahhhh,* Mmmmm, again, ahh. **Harder!** Oh, oh, Ahhhhhh. Oh yes. I'm going to come, Chet".

"Yes," he said, gasping triumphantly. "Oh, God, yes."

She felt his weapon swelling, engorging towards ejaculation, her vagina warming, hungry to savour the spurting jets of jism exploding before coating her vagina walls.

"Don't you. *Dare* Come, Chet!!!" A shrill angry sounding command shattered the aura of the moment, her vagina shuddering as her orgasm bathed the instrument welded into her flesh. Cutting through the hazy of her whimpering groans of sexual pleasure, slaps like pistol shots. Rena was smacking his buttocks viciously.

"Hold it deep now, you keep it *There*. I want to watch you make her come again," she forcefully directed the panting Chet.

Rigid, he keep his rebellious body still, his colossal young cock true and deep in the depth of her pussy, Lisa rotated her hips, writhing herself into a second orgasm before he released himself into movement once more.

"All right, now you fuck me. *Again,* Chet." Lisa instructed.

Subdued, appearing confused, he stopped, His features twisted in a mask of pain staring down into her face.

"A real man would never be told how he should fuck a woman, Chet." She paused, letting the words sink in. "A real man would know how to shaft a naked woman. I'm a naked woman. Now you shaft me like a real man." Her voice was throaty, her tone invitingly insinuating.

His deep blue eyes shrank to tiny slits, his chest swelled, his mouth contorted, his pained features became cruel looking and angry.

Lisa, smiled sweetly, felt a stab of desire and lust deep in her soul. She relaxed. A sense of elation filled her very being. She'd humbled him, belittled his prowess as a man. Bruised his male ego. She'd implied it was Rena who controlled his manly desires.

"You shouldn't have suggested Chet wasn't a real man, Lisa, he is very sensitive to such criticism. His reaction to it is uncontrollable rage," Rena's voice warned her ominously.

The sinister advice filled Lisa not with fear. It only inflamed her voracious appetite for man-flesh. Chet, breathing heavily, thrust his rod viciously, her mouth gaped wide, her head rolled from side to side as the rampaging cock parted her inner flesh, his hands clasped her ankles, in one swift movement her legs were forced up and backwards towards her face.

The sinus and tendons in her groin and buttocks stretching agonisingly to their limits until her knees almost touched her ears.

The shock of the unexpected invasion, the tremors of pain subsiding into warm luxuriant sensations of pleasure, her senses swooned.

He lifted his body, she noticed obliquely, positioned above her, stretched out like an arrow. The only parts of him touching her flesh, his hands gripping her ankles, and his testicles wedged tight against her pussy.

Lisa pucker her lips, smiled sweetly in to his eyes. Glanced down her body viewing the wet looking cock slowly lengthening as it he extracted from her spasmodically fluttering vagina.

Quivering with expectancy, when the only the enlarged head remained concealed.

His shaft, a ten-inch bridge of rigid white flesh uniting his body to hers.

"Now, Chet, *Now!*" she whispered, slipping her arms inside his, sliding her hands through the matted black hair covering his muscle hard torso, over the stiffened stomach, down over the hips, then clasped the muscle hard roundness of his buttocks, one in each hand.

Momentarily he resisted. Then his shaft spiked her to the bed, his cock filled her vagina, with a frenzy of unbelievable power it see-sawed in and out of her wet sexual avenue, the friction. Incredible. The gratification to flesh, and body, indescribable.

Lisa accepted, with grateful abandon the barbarous ferocity that Chet's monstrous instrument delivered so savagely, as it scythed like a burning dagger deep in to the citadel of her being, deeper than any man flesh had ever been, it ravaged virgin flesh she never knew she possessed. It was more pleasurably fulfilling than any previous fucking had ever been, a revelation of the flesh, a mental revelation of the fact. Her sexual addiction for man-flesh, her craving for multiple orgasms reached new heights. Her clitoris warming as her vagina muscles began to respond to the ruthless plunging male organ, pulsing frenziedly against the thrust and withdrawal of the stiff prodigious cock.

"Release my legs, Chet," she demanded hoarsely, crying out in tortured anguish. His weapon of flesh nailing her to the bed, before he obediently lowered her legs.

The stiffness in her hips, the throbbing pained muscles of her buttocks mingling with the sensations of pleasure within her body infused her lust. Spreading her loins wide, transferring one hand to the nape of his sweaty neck, opening the other hand, fingers wide spread, gripping both flexing orbs of round flesh, her middle finger indenting the rectum orifice, she pulled his face to hers, lips parted gorging his mouth with hers, with slow deliberation she forced the finger into Chet's rectum.

Lisa freed of restraint, ached her body, raising her pussy to meet the vigorous stabbing instrument, rotating her loins wildly.

Chet ripped his mouth away. Lisa sucking in oxygen in wheezing gasps, heard herself moan loudly as he began to fuck with long quick deep thrusts. For a long minute, two minutes, three, they fucked silently, hard driving, the rhythmic wet slap of flesh bruising flesh, tortured panting breathing accompanying their groaning moans of pleasure filling the sun drenched bedroom

Abruptly, Chet paused. Wedge penetrating deep in her, he said in a throaty remorseless voice, "Not yet, Mrs Knott... *Not yet...!*" Nailed together by his huge cock pegged root-deep into her cunt, they glared into each other's eyes as though they were antagonists. Lisa read the twisted grim line of his mouth as the outward sign of cruel restraint. She had been on the very edge of orgasm; she ached hungrily for just one more savage thrust that would push her over the edge.

With strong arms, he turned her on her side. Grasped one leg, lifting it up and back at the same time, kneeling, he straddled the upper thigh of her other leg, his shoulder pushed into the calf of the upright leg, hands gripping the upper thigh, his organ somehow still graft deeply in her vagina. Lisa, marvelling at his athleticism and strength, lifted her torso, supporting her half raised body, elbow pushed into the mattress, watched, waiting in breathlessly expectation of the pleasures of being screwed in a new unexplored position.

She felt the slow almost total extraction of his shaft; then his loins rammed into her loins, making her gasp loudly. "Chet," she croaked harshly. "*Oh, Chhheeettt!*" He started slowly, full out then full in. With each thrust, he moved his hips gently from left to right, her hot eyes surveyed the massive circumcised shaft of flesh disappearing inch by inch. She moved her loins, stroking the hard column of flesh with the throbbing pulse within her vagina, while with her free hand she masturbated her swollen clitoris vigorously in circular motion.

Chet, root pulsing rock hard. Rena your some fuck. But the hungry woman on my dick now. Is even better. I'm going to be a good boy, Mrs Judd. Oh Yes. He decided instantly. Anything you want, Mrs Judd, *Anything*. To have more of this Lady.

"All right, Lady. Now you are going to get well and truly... *Fucked...!*"

Lisa lay passive, waiting breathlessly, moist pussy spasming. With bated breath, held in anticipation of the threatened new brutal sexual assault on her flesh. Her shoulders fell back on the pillows, his cock lanced into her pussy, filling it, instantly, she groaned wildly, his slicing shaft, withdrew, returned, she was being fucked savagely, so ruthlessly she could only take it.

Lisa gloried in being taken. Once more she exalted in being fucked as never before. Eyes closed, mouth opening and closing. Each thrust slammed her head into the headboard, each time he pulled her bodily back as his cock drove upwards, her stomach convexed, bulging roundly. The demon. Her Beast. Had awakened. Spreading its tentacles of desire uncontrollable in to her mind, through her flesh.

His cock pulsed. The first spurt of ejaculation was like the blow of a tiny fist. With enormous effort, for an interminable moment he held it.

Then came the flood as he submitted to imperative male orgasm, yet still fucking more rapidly than seemed possible. Inexplicable, her own orgasm spewed over the surging, pumping cock. Together they came, in a united orgasm, clenched-tight, moaning and irreversible.

It had to be over, she couldn't take any more, the muscles in her thighs were quivering from fatigue, her vagina fluttering with untamed tremors of passion, before fluttering gently from satiation. It was not over, Chet, still without disengaging though his sex device was becoming softer, laid her raised leg back on the bed, slide both his hairy arms under her shoulders, rolled on his back, turning her on top.

He grinned happily. "All right, Mrs Knott. Now you can fuck me."

She lay inert exhausted for a few moments. Then, excepting the challenge, because challenge it was, she realised. Slowly she forced her hips to move. Lisa had fucked in the superior position. Both Jay and Nathan would give testimony to her expertise, she called to mind. She liked it, immensely, when mounted on a huge rigid cock.

But this… this was different, much different. Chet had tilted his hips, his instrument rock-like in its hardness once more, penetrating deeper than any cock before. The sensations, her thirst for pleasure replenished Lisa, the passionate energy to propel her hips in a faster rhythm than she believed possible.

She reached the point of climax in an instant. But then Chet's cock, so demanding, and virile, began to thrust up into her, meeting her downward plunge, she began to come. Not a single orgasm this time, several, beginning small and hard-clenched then expanding into a spreading linked sequence of ever increasing ecstasy.

Chet lay under her, grinning broadly, he goaded her into greater effort, as his hips effortless yet relentlessly thrust the man-shaft into her plunging pussy. Lisa, head was swimming, her senses spinning, she did not believe she could feel, or experience so much pleasure, so much satisfaction. After Nathan, then the fucking with the two giants in the locker room, and Jay, did she imagine that she would, or could ever fuck, or be fucked with even greater satisfaction.

Lisa shuddered, gasped hoarsely, as another orgasm rippled over the deep plunging instrument. She couldn't stop coming, didn't want too.

Chet, body rigid with the desire to ejaculate, did not come. The grin had vanished, he strained mightily, but found no release.

"Let me get on top," he gasped in a strained agitated voice.

"Oh no," she said firmly…*"No!"* She was determined to make him come in the position he had demanded. Rising into a crouch, she redoubled her efforts. Until at last he did come, thin and meagre as it was. She sprawled, exhausted, lungs pounding on his wet sweating chest.

After a while, she felt tension remaining in Chet, still unfulfilled undrained his flesh in her remaining solid and heavy. She raised her head.

His eyes pleaded with her, as did his voice. "Give me head. *Please,* Mrs Knott. Use your mouth, Suck it. *Suck it Out*!"

Sliding down his sweating body. This is your moment of triumph, she proudly told herself, gazing for a brief second at the huge wet moisture coated cock. He is mine for the next few minutes. Not Rena's. That though in her mind. She took the wet slippery gleaming cock, tasted the semen when she went down on him. With her mouth full of swollen glands, the edges of her mouth aching again, she pulsed her lips, slide them up and down frantically, she couldn't breathe. It wasn't necessary to breathe, not yet, with stiffened rounded mouth she masturbated the throbbing flesh-rod with her lips until she sensed the beginning vibration of ejaculation. He put his hands on her head, she pushed them away, heard him groan, his cock swelled, juddered, the bulbous head expanded then his warm semen flowed, and she swallowed it as it flowed. And loved it… ***Loved it!***

Lisa sexually satisfied, her demon sedated once more with the sweetness of their bodies lovemaking juices, shrank gently in to peaceful repose, she collapsed exhausted beside the sweating gently quivering male body.

"Well now, Lisa, I believe my Chet as answered two questions for you, has he not, size is important, and you now know. To quote your own words.' He is a real man." She detected a note of pride in Rena's tone as she spoke.

Rolling on to her back, her breathing shallow, her vision a little hazy, looking up at the naked red-haired, well-built woman standing beside the bed. "I agree, Rena, your are right on both counts." she demurred.

"All right, Chet, you've had your fun, now go and clean yourself up. I'm sure Mrs Knott won't mind you using her bathroom. When your finished, go to the car and bring me my shoulder bag," she ordered him gruffly, yet smiling.

Lisa watched him rise, standing up he turned, smiling slavishly into Rena's face said. "Thank you, Mrs Knott that was a most enjoyable fuck." Nodding her head in reply, his penis she noticed, soft now was still longer and thicker than many of the erected shafts she had received in the past. What a great shame, she thought. In only having the pleasure of the massive organ. *Once.*

"Goodbye, Chet, and thank you, it was magnificent, my only regret is I may not have the pleasure again," she said sadly, sounding disconsolate.

Rena chuckling as Chet walked away, ran her warm finger

tips ever so gently, smoothing Lisa's hot sweating skin. "It need not be that way, Lisa, you know. I can think of circumstances by which I might allow my Chet to service you regularly," she said insidiously. "It would mean, of course, you have to be prepared to. How shall I put it… Enter in the spirit of such circumstances willing? I'm sure you understand what I mean, after all, I did mention earlier my interest. Passion for unusual games," she said quietly, the insinuation alluding to bizarre sexual practices was nothing compared to the insinuation within her flesh Rena's clever fingers were producing.

Lisa, her desire's rekindling within, considered thoughtfully. Sex in beginning, with different men had become a pleasure she'd learned to enjoy. As her enjoyment had amplified, so had the pleasure, so much so. Sex, men, and cock transmuted in to avid hunger. A need for more pleasure, more enjoyment, more man-flesh and then more orgasms. Out of want, she had seduced Nathan, a youth half her age. He satisfied her wanting, for a short while, less than a week. That satisfaction became a demon within. She subdued the demon with Nathan's youth, his vitality, his rampant manhood. With the two big weight lifter's she sated her flesh while being shafted simultaneously with two nicely erect instruments. Then Shona. Then Jay. Now Rena, a woman. She made love with her standing in lounge. Followed, by being screwed the first time by Chet, a man, witnessing everything. She had just been fucked, with the biggest male organ she had ever seen. Rena had watched ever movement, every panted moan.

She'd excepted it all, without conscience, without any feeling of shame, to be honest, she admitted readily. Those thoughts never entered her mind. The pleasure was all encompassing, if, to society, what she taken part in was, immoral, depraved, perverted, vile, or humiliating.

Her perception of it was. Straight forward, well to her it was. She wanted it. That want had become a need. As one need's breath to live. So she needed fucking, cock and orgasm's so she could live. Without mans flesh inside her body, and the pleasure it evoke within. She was just an empty breathing human shell.

Lisa knew, inexplicably her hungry need, as it had over the last few years, would lead her to sink ever deeper in to a dark morass of sexual degradation to satisfy the demands of her body and mind in her uncontrollable lust for male flesh.

The finger tips still exciting her skin, she looked into Rena's flushed looking face.

"You would find it most advantageous, Lisa, if you decided to except my offer. No more lonely nights having to use your own fingers, no more long agitated days waiting to feel a man's flesh," she paused, waiting patiently for a reply. "You realise in return, you have be prepared to willingly take part. Oh to hell with it, Lisa. It's no good beating about the bush, I'm too hot and horny. You'll find yourself getting shafted by three of four men at a time in every conceivable position, having sex with women, you'll have take part in sexual practices which will include, sadism, masochism, sodomy, lesbianism. With total strangers not only will they fuck you, they'll watch you. How much would you enjoy, Lisa, being shafted by two men, one underneath, one from behind, and woman with her pussy in your mouth, while at the same time feeling a lash whipping your naked back. That's what all it means, Lisa."

"I find your proposal most interesting, I must admit, Rena. Would you explain more fully please," she answered, in excited curiosity.

"If your so horny, you know, pussy all moist, aching for a cock, just call me, if Chet's available I'll sent him along to ease the pain, if he isn't, he has a few young well endowed friends who will very discreetly administer to *all* your sexual requirements. Two or three at time if you're desperate. And of course, Shona might want to spend a night with you, if you wanted that sort of pleasure, Lisa?" Rena held her breath. This was the crunch time.

Her pulse raced. Would she refused, she didn't think so. But you can never tell, still cautious unsure. "If your needs require a more diverse method of satisfaction, you just asked, Lisa, two young men supplement with a tender young girl like my Shona is an experience, once sampled, you'll lust for it over and over again. I know I do," she explained persuasively." Very persuading indeed Lisa thought. "If you feel, and think, it's not what you want. I'll understand, Lisa, and no hard feeling, we can still be friends. I'll not mention it ever again. Okay. But I'll never let Chet make love to you again, if you do refuse." If persuasion don't convince her, maybe a little blackmail will. Rena wilfully decided.

"Rena my friend you've convinced me. I'll admit, openly and honestly confess. My lust for men is endless. My hunger for orgasm is insatiable. My appetite for sex increase's constantly. In heat, a man can use me, any way he desires. When I am being fucked continuously in to orgasm. My morality is the flesh. The flesh inside me," she said, in a crystal clear precise voice.

"That is absolutely beautiful, Lisa," she cried, face beaming with excited pleasure. "I can't begin to tell how delightfully happy I am at this moment to hear you say that," smiling sweetly she bent over, then gently brushing her lips loving against Lisa's before gazing tenderly into her eyes. "I fervently believed I would never meet another woman who would ever understand how I feel about sexual pleasure. Not anymore, Lisa, we are kindred spirits, your lust and desires are mine. Mine are yours," as she spoke, moving her fingers, caressing the sodden hair of Lisa's mound.

"I don't suppose you have a Bud in the ice box, or a Coke? My mouth is as dry a desert after all this talking, and watching you shagging Chet," she said laughing, abruptly changing the subject.

"I've a few Coke but no Bud in afraid, Rena," she gaily apologised. "You go and freshen up while I get us the Coke's."

"Good idea, then we can cement our agreement with a cool drink before I leave," agreed in a light pleased sounding voice.

In the kitchen, pouring the Coke's into two tall glasses. The feeling of languid contentment in body and mind. Lisa reminded herself, it had first manifested itself with Nathan. Now it enveloped her completely every time she had sex.

Lisa, leaving the empty cans on top of the ice box, hurriedly cleansed her body, wiping away wet moistness of love-making. A soft white towel drying her pussy, still feeling the presence of the physical weight and length Chet's massive root inside her vagina.

Rena, looking thoughtfully at her reflection in the bathroom mirror, smiled at herself. It has worked out perfectly. Chet had followed her instructions to perfection. Her vagina warming at the memory of the number times, she had him rehearse, shafting her over and over again, learning every move, making sure Mrs Lisa Knott, became ensnared.

A little to damn perfectly, for my liking, she angrily told herself. I ordered him to fuck her. That's all. I didn't tell him to make her fuck him, or to come in her mouth. Well I suppose it's no good letting jealousy get in the way of hitting the jackpot, consoling herself, thinking of the many pleasure's to come.

Shona telling her on the phone all about what happened, what she had done, about a woman named Mrs Knott stripping her naked on front seat of her car, then using her mouth to make her come, in a parking lot, in broad daylight. Made you as horny as bitch on heat, didn't it, she scolded herself chuckling.

She just had to explore the possibilities, discover what a woman who do a thing like that had to offer, And she just *had to* find out, with Chet's expert assistance. Would this woman willing want to take part in her dark sexual games.

Congratulating herself for correctly, intuitively knowing. A woman like Lisa, once her eye's feasted on Chet's superb shaft, would submit to any humiliation, after she'd tasted the pleasures produced by such a gigantic weapon.

Stepping back, abstractly aware of the expensive luxury of the bathroom fitting. That bloody Chet, watching him fucking Lisa in to a frenzy had her turned on something awful. Lisa's writhing and moaning heightening her own desires.

I need an orgasm, a long moaning climax. Not later, *Now!* in a hoarse remorseless voice, out loud, she whispered at her own reflection.

Chapter 15

Rena was on the bed when Lisa returned with a glass of Coke clutched firmly in each hand. With her knees raised, hiding her breasts, arms wrapped around the knees, her red hair covered head resting on her arms. "I sure as hell need a drink," she said thirstily, reaching out and take the glass from Lisa's offered hand.

Lisa sat in front of her, kneeling, buttocks touching her heels, drinking slowly. She looks like child, sitting like that Rena thought. Which she certain was not. Not with those breasts and large brown nipples.

"You have a beautiful tanned skin, Lisa," she said softly, putting her now empty glass aside, then taking Lisa's offered glass, placing beside hers on the bedside cabinet.

Rena reached out and gently, very lightly, stroked Lisa's thigh. To her relief, Lisa didn't flinch. "So soft, so smooth."

"As yours is Rena."

For one brief second, She thought Lisa she was about to touch her warm flesh, but she merely brushed her hair back over her head. Unless she had misread the gesture, there seemed a hint of defiance, or was a challenge, or maybe a symbolic trace of expectancy. Whichever? Her loins becoming damp with desire. She had to make the first move, if she waited for Lisa, it would never happen. She rarely considered the other person feelings or desire's, man or woman but Lisa was so different. She wanted her flesh, her body, not just once, not just today. It would be a tragedy if she frightened her off. There seemed, judging by their escapade in the lounge little likelihood of that happening, but she wasn't prepared to take risk of being wrong.

"Let me touch your smooth soft skin," she whispered softly.

Lightly she laid her fingertips on Lisa's thigh again, ran her fingers down the warm smooth silky length of thigh. Lisa watched the hand, felt her flesh tingling under the gentle touch.

"Exquisite, delightfully exquisite," Rena murmured. Lisa gazed nervously into her face. Locking Lisa's eyes with her own, Rena lay down, raised both arms.

"Come and lie beside me," she whispered, in warm coaxing voice.

Obediently, yet hesitantly nervous, Lisa responded to the enticingly alluring request laying down on the bed, placed her head on the pillows, and crossed her arms over head, hiding her eye's. Rena stretched out beside her, resting on one hip, one hand propping up her head, to feast her eyes on the Lisa's beautifully shaped body. Rena could feel the increasingly abnormal irregular beat of her heart, her pulse raced with a combination of anticipation and nervous sexual expectancy, the latter being the most definable. She ran her fingers, over Lisa's face, then down ever so softly across her breast, pausing for an instant, squeezed the nipple, before running fingers over the soft smooth stomach to brush the mound of curly hair above her tight clasped thighs.

"Come now, Lisa, there's no need for shyness." Rena murmured softly. "Not with a beautiful body like yours. You shouldn't hide the beauty of the charms you possess."

"You have a far better body than I have, Rena," Lisa replied in quiet subdued voice. "Your breasts are gorgeous... so big and heavy.

"Touch my breasts," Rena panted, wetting her drying lips. "*Touch them!*

Timidly, Lisa lifted a hand, closed her fingers around the soft orb of flesh, gently rotated her hand, before moving her fingers to trace the outer circle of the nipple. It hardened instantly at her touch.

"God almighty, Rena, what lovely flesh, so soft," Lisa gushed, unable to disguise her feeling of pleasure and wonder she felt.

Any entirely new feeling of desire swept over her. An emotional sensation of tenderness, a soft soothing tranquillising tremor of desire in her flesh. She felt the same desires for sex. But not for the heated passion of the physical abusive strength of a man's cock. For an orgasm, with a gentleness, with slow and soft tenderness.

"It is no different than yours," Rena replied. "Relax and allow me to return the same pleasure to your flesh with my fingers, as yours are giving to mine," moving her strong hand to caress Lisa's smaller perfectly rounded firm breasts.

"It feels so nice, having my breasts fondled and stroked by a hand as soft and gentle my as own," she acknowledged.

"It feels amazingly good, doesn't it, Lisa? Of course the feeling will become more delicious, more exciting pleasurable when you're being caressed with soft skin all over your body, don't you think?"

"I'm sure it will, But. I've never done this with woman before."

"What about little Shona, and earlier in lounge?"

"It wasn't like this, Rena, I didn't feel the same. I did it out of need. It was just sex, my need of an orgasm overcame me. This is different." she mumbled.

"I know, Lisa," she said understandingly, increasing the motion of her fingers on the swelling nipple in her hand.

"I know," she said repeating herself.

"I've never had any real desire for a woman before. Not like I have now. I'm innocent to the ways of making love, in way woman do. I'm not sure what I'm supposed to do with a woman," Lisa stammered hesitantly.

Rena trembled at the words, for two reasons. In the bathroom she'd felt so horny, she decided to seduce Lisa, into making love with her, in ways only a woman understands. That was one. The other, she'd be Lisa's first real female lover.

"Just enjoy, Lisa. Trust me. I will make it very special, so wonderfully special, for both of us," Rena replied with amused satisfaction.

Lisa doubts, nervous fears, remained unspoken. Rena leaned over, and with a gentle feathery touch took the reddened swollen nipple between her lips, swallowed it slowly before sucking it softly. Lisa's gasp of pleasure, a gently tremble stimulated her desire, as much as the way her hands involuntarily went to Rena's shoulders before slipping down her back smoothing her skin. Rena wiggled closer, to bring her thighs to touch Lisa's. She move her mouth to the other nipple, closed a hand over the breast her mouth had just released, squeezed it once before taking the nipple between fore finger and thumb.

She was going to take Lisa ever so slowly, in spite of the fact she was in high state of arousal. If I have to I'll love her a second time, she decided, it will be all the more rewarding, for both of us. She lightly sucked each nipple, moving from one to the other quickly, pausing briefly, to sink her teeth occasionally into reddened hard crowns. It was becoming quite obvious to Rena that Lisa had surrendered to her mouth's seductive dispensed caresses. Rena began stroking the warm smooth belly, then the thighs, her fingers teasingly circling the hairy black mound.

Lisa's breathing quickening, when the hand, fingers closed, slipped through her mound. Lisa opened her loins, when Rena rolled her closed fingers against her clitoris. With a low moan of sexual arousal, Lisa raised her head, lips wide, panting, sought Rena's mouth.

So unexpected, so unashamedly offered; a feeling of intense joy and affection surged through Rena, as her lips meet Lisa's hungry mouth. She opened her soft willing lips, her tongue found Lisa's, her own mouth returned every touch of her pliable lips to her. They were both beyond reason, breathing heavy. Lisa broke the kiss. Rena slid her hand between Lisa's moist thighs, found her hidden zone. Ran her finger slowly along the curve of her pussy, inserted a finger. She could hardly breath. Lisa writhed, she heard a soft moan as she inserted a second finger, pleasure exploded through her very being. As Lisa squirmed, with long drawn out mewling groan into climaxed.

"Oh, Rena, that was unbelievable, it was so, so warmingly tender, so satisfying in its softness. Thank you for being so gentle," Lisa gasped, crumpling back against the soft pillows.

"Was it now?" she asked, intrigued by the affectionately spoken words.

"Yes, I knew this was going happen after meeting little Shona."

"Did you now?" she repeated probing, in a whispered tone.

"Oh yes, Shona with her clever fingers, and lovely shaped

dainty naked body unveiled a desire unknown to me," Lisa explained, her frank confession, the quick flash of memory of it, arousing her desire. *Again.*

"Well I will have to make sure your not disappointed... won't I?"

Rena was determined to make sure that she wasn't disappointed *either.*

She knew only to well the pleasure and satisfaction, that little minx Shona could elicit, and give. She pictured it, aroused by images in her mind but not shocked, annoyed possibly, *Jealous,* definitely.

She forgot all about Shona as Lisa bent over her, taking her smarting nipple into her mouth. Shivered as the wet tongue traced a circle around the stiff rosy teat, then sucked it gently. Every light deft touch had a soft pliant gentleness to it that was so deeply pleasing, her sexual arousal soared.

Lisa, intuitively, instinctively knew how to give pleasure, Rena realised, as all women did.

They kissed again, warm mouth to mouth, soft lips against soft lips, Rena shifted closer, smoothly, in a languid easy movement lying her body almost on top of Lisa. She breathed in gasping low sobs, on the brink of climax. Every gentle caress from Lisa inched her orgasm ever closer. Lisa's applied her arched hips to hers; their breasts in unison, nipple to nipple sending delicious shivers down Rena's spine. Lisa caressing hands so soft as they moved down her spine, so gentle on her bum cheeks, so lovingly persuasive when they had solicited Rena's smarting fully erect nipples with her warm fingers. The movements were slow yet ever touching, fluid, so volatile, and exciting. Rena had to suppress the urge to touch herself; her swelling clitoris craving for attention.

She felt Lisa's lips replacing the insistent hands, inflaming her higher. The lips warmer than the cool fluttering fingers. Rena trembled as Lisa's lips kissed her clitoris softly and her thighs parted involuntarily. Rena thought she could take no more, she couldn't stand the titillation no longer,

Lisa's lips traced the indentation separating her moist sex-lips making her groan out loud in ecstasy. Her need becoming unbearable, her lust immense.

She had to have release. Lisa's tongue flicking over her clitoris incessantly, drawing her tortuous creeping orgasm ever closer to discharge. Rena's thighs responding to every touch, intermittent jerking as her orgasm began. Her need, sheer desperation, she wanted to hold the sensations, but Lisa didn't relent. The tongue probed her pussy lips, the pointed tip deft parted the cleft, Lisa's hands reached up enclosing her breasts, pressing then squeezing continuously. Rena's vagina cleaved to invading tongue, as it made it's slow passage upwards, ever deeper. Her pleasure immeasurable. Rena's desire to prolong the pleasure, so powerful it overwhelmed her need.

Lisa's female mind and flesh interpreting Rena's every twisting thrust, her every sigh, every low tiny moan. She patently knew. Rena was on the verge of climax. Inexplicably their desire had become one. Their objective the same, but for with opposite designs. Lisa's goal; to prolong the pleasure of her giving. Rena's she realised, the pleasure of receiving.

Lisa probed relentlessly, fast and hard. Rena squirmed as seemly endless tremors of voluptuous sexual pleasure vociferously erupted within the canal of her vagina. Lisa's snake-like tongue so merciless, so remorseless, she felt her vagina clench powerfully, then pulse luxuriously, as orgasm seized her flesh. Her legs kicked out, heels drumming the bed's mattress frantically before her body grew limp.

Rena, her pleasure still a slow dying tremor in her pussy, lay eyes closed, flesh shivering erratically.

"Your handbag, Mrs Judd," said a distant interloping voice. She didn't open her eyes.

"Put it on the bed. And get out of here. *Now Chet!* And don't you come back again. If I think for one moment, you sneaked in here, to watch. I'll strip the flesh off your back to bone. Now get ***Out!***" she screamed viciously.

The venomous threat. Lisa heard, but didn't remove or stop her tongue's now gently pleasure giving intrusions.

Rena heard the bedroom door slam, opening her eyes, gazed down at Lisa. She could see from the swollen breasts, the hard erected nipples that Lisa was in very highly agitated state of sexual arousal.

Watching the kneeling Lisa. Rena feeling of elation inflated. Lisa undoubtedly exhibited all the hallmarks of a woman totally addicted to sexual gratification. In the last few hours. She'd stripped her naked, fingered her into orgasm while being watched by Chet. Lisa had taken great pleasure in having an audience watch while Chet had savagely fucked her. She had observed closely, very closely Lisa's reactions to his abusive sexual assault, and then, with very little encouragement, made love, real love, not a quick instinctive act like it had been with Shona, with her first woman lover. I bet that sneaky little bastard Chet watched our performance, Rena, thought angrily remembering. When she'd mention two or three men or women shafting her at the same time she didn't bat an eyelid.

She's now just made love to me, given me so much pleasure I cannot believe she's never had a woman before. Oh yes lovely Lisa, she said, silently in her head. I will take great pleasure in leading you into so many sexual pleasures are far beyond anything you ever thought imaginable.

"I have a little something in my bag, Lisa. Something very different and new. I know you'll enjoy it," she whispered suggestively, sitting up kissing Lisa's on the top the head.

"How will I tell if I'll find it enjoyable, if I don't know what it is?" Lisa replied, sounding curiously excited.

She reached over Lisa's shoulder to the hand bag laying beside her, opened it, slipped her hand inside, slowly taking out a large black latex Dildo, laughing quietly at the look of shocked surprise and undisguisable excited delight on Lisa's face

"Do you want it?" she asked, wrapping her hand round the bottom holding it upright, arm outstretched offering it to her.

"I *Want it*," Lisa purred in husky whispered voice.

Rena rubbed it over her own heavy breasts, pushed it gently into a nipple, noted Lisa's eye's hot gleam, the tip of her tongue caressing her lips.

She extended her arm, rubbed the tip of Dildo against Lisa's wet flesh, a pang of desire touched her flesh at Lisa's muted blissful whimpers of desire.

"But where do you wanted it, Lisa? This lovely instrument

gives pleasure in many areas, where do you want it the most desperate?" the question deliberately instructive, suggestive, yet cryptic.

It is a very large phallic device strangely attractive, it's potential sexual impact. Lisa thought, uneasily, enormous, the pleasure it would give her, unknown, unexplored, mysterious, made her feel nervously, apprehensive.

Rena detected the look of indecisive concern on Lisa's face. Precipitating her answer. Afraid Lisa would balk, refuse, in one swift movement gliding the tip down over the smooth flesh, through the pubic hair she eased the smooth black bulky tip amidst the wet labia. Lisa squirmed at its touch, she ran her hands greedily along its length, pushing on to the phallus, wanting more of it. Rena understood the feeling only to well; many times and hours had she enjoyed the pleasures of the Dildo's wide range of erotically compelling manoeuvres. She watched Lisa's face, pushing it deeper inside her vagina, the small beads of sweat glistening on her forehead, the sheen of wetness in the valley between her breasts.

The imitation cock, more rigid and less pliable than a man's; its hard solidness injecting tiny arrows of hurtful pain in to vagina, only increasing Lisa's appetite.

"It's delicious but don't I can't take it *All.*" she cried, grieving, "It's to hard, to rigid, and painful."

"You'll be astonished by what you can *take.* And how good it will feel, Lisa," she explained, coaxing the Dildo deeper.

With fascinated eye's Lisa watched the large Dildo, as Rena slowly withdrew it, the moist ring on the black latex showing the extent of its penetration. Lisa spread her loins to their limits, gasped in shocked bewilderment, the phallic rod appearing larger, longer, thicker. When it was first offered, Rena had held her hand around the base, the wrapped fingers hiding its true dimensions. It wasn't large, it was monstrous, more impressively massive than even Chet's huge shaft.

Rena, her lustful cravings unfurling within her flesh wanted to give Lisa the most devastating experience of sexual pleasure and pain she had ever known, a maelstrom of orgasms, of sensation, of pain, of wild physical writhing and uncontrollable verbal exclamations of sexual gratification.

Lisa shivered, her flesh warming desires unconcern now by the picture in mind of the Dildo's potency she gazed at the false cock. Smiling, in a low persuasive reassuring whispering voice, Rena said. "Relax now, enjoy my sexy toy, it wouldn't harm you." Twisting her wrist quickly, with a sucking sound, it began to elongate and retraced it's latex head in a remorseless rhythm, her free hand parted her own labia, the other held the pulsing head against her moist pussy.

"Oh yes, by the way, Lisa. I forgot to tell you. This magnificent sex toy has a small motor inside, it vibrates and flexes unaided and it can be used in two pussy's at the same time," she gasping muttered.

Rena wanted to give pleasure, for her, in giving she received *Pleasure.*

She inserted the head of her delicious Dildo, its first forward thrust producing a segued paroxysm of thrusting writhing, the frantic twisting of Lisa's hips, the feeling transmitted to herself.

Rena, with a shuddering gasp eased the other end inside herself, bent back as the waves of pleasure rippled through her body. With eye's closed she sought Lisa's wet sex-lips. Lisa needed more than that. She grabbed the phallus, arched herself upwards and sank back, writhing and groaning with pleasure as it filled her vagina completely.

With effort, she lifted her head to gaze down the length of her body. To her delight and horror, the gigantic shaft, over a foot long, at least, and enormous in girth was pegged in her vagina, except for a about four inches or so, almost hidden inside the red hair lips of Rena's pussy.

Rena's eyes sprang open. They both were masturbating themselves on the latex phallus, their labia majoras, the outer of lips their vaginas touched then parted, giving a feeling as if they were joined together. Rena could almost believe she had a cock of her own, a huge highly susceptible cock that was pounding hard into Lisa.

"See," Rena panted, moaning hoarsely. "You can take a lot more cock than thought.

"Don't talk," Lisa gasped. "Just you *give it to me."* Rena

groaned as she felt Lisa's index finger push inside her supplementing the Dildo, increasing the pulsing pleasure and she instantly returned the favour.

Lisa's cries of pleasure, her breasts wobbling furiously, the caress of her wet cunt as it rotated lavishly against Rena's equally moist cunt made her shiver and they cried out in unison. Their gyrations grew more frenzied, their gasping panting whimpering yelps of sexual rapture intensified as they both thrust against the Dildo, she squirmed in ecstasy when Lisa added a second finger, then a third, she returned the favour. Instantly. They both knew how to please each other.

Rena screamed as an orgasm shook her body, juddered at its pleasure giving vibrations. With a couple of driving thrusts Lisa shivering violently, shrieking wildly, also climaxed.

They collapsed sweating profusely, exhausted but satiate utterly, their arms wrapped around each other, entwined in an embrace of mutual satisfaction.

Lisa lay arms and body entwined around Rena's. Her body and mind trembling, her flesh heated inside and out. Small tremors of acutely felt sexual sensation's coursing within her vulva and softening nipples.

Rena, panting, her flesh warm and sweaty, the sexually satiety within her mind saturated with the pleasure's experienced. "Ain't it a bitch, Lisa. We both go through hell, a hell inflicted by two selfish bastards, before we discover each other, and our own real inner-selves. God I wish I could make my ex-husband's life a misery. Make the rotten shit go through the hell," she said, in angry voice full of hatred.

"To be honest, Rena, I've never really given much thought to getting my own back on David. I suppose the shock and suddenness of it all hit me so hard I just wanted to forget everything about him. Yet the turmoil and mental anguish has made me stronger, in body and mind so much so. Like you Rena, I love to pay the bastard back *In Spades*. Gut the son-of-a-bitch, put him through same tormented misery I suffered," she agreed with impulsive audacity.

"Well now, Lisa." smiling with delight, gazing fondly and kissing her briefly. "How do two, middle-aged over sex-sexed women. Highly over sexed, to the extreme, I should say, set about making the lives of two very rich powerful ex-husbands a living hell. I hope you can up with a few ideas, Lisa. The only one I've ever come up with is catching Roy screwing somebody, photographing him fucking her, then sending the photo's to his bimbo wife." Her offered suggestion, which she admitted to herself, sounded stupidly unimpressive.

"Sure, why not? Sounds good to me," Lisa demurred.

"Great, but how the hell do we set about getting it done Lisa? Because I haven't a bloody clue how or where to start," she asked in an exasperated tone.

"Set them up, Rena. We arrange some ploy. And catch them with their pants down." she laughingly proposed.

"Oh yeah, just like. I don't think so Lisa. For a start, how on earth do we set them up? How do we catch them to screwing? and who with?" she asked, looking at Lisa sounding confused and sceptical.

"No problem really, Rena. I'll seduce your ex-husband, you seduce mine. We've never met them have we? Wear a wig, a little carefully applied make up, the right clothes. We both know the places they frequent. A few meetings. A little sexual enticement. A arranged a motel room in advance. Chet hidden in the room with a video camera. Bingo, we'll have them trapped like a fish in a barrel," excited by her scheme, she burst out laughing.

Rena, smiled, like the idea, still she did not feel convinced it would be so easy.

Lisa sensing her scheme needed further explaining before Rena would understand and except her proposed scenario, continued slowly and thoughtfully. "We could, of course, use the same methods and destroy their wives lives at the same time. If Shona and Chet were willing to help us, Rena, Shona makes their acquaintance, introduces them to Chet. He fucks both of them. Hey, even get little Shona to have some fun with them as well. Film everything. It's quite simple really, Rena. If we use what we have learned over the last few years about men, sex and women. How can it fail?"

"So what you're saying, Lisa, is we try and screw them all

up. That's bit strong don't you think?" Rena deliberated for a few seconds, then laughed softly. "Why the hell not, just as well get hung for as sheep as a lamb, and Shona will really get a kick out of helping." she agreed, but in spite of her enthusiasm couldn't displace the deeply held feeling that it wasn't going to as simple an operation as Lisa suggested. "You realise, Lisa, that men with their position in society and in the financial world, will fight back to protect themselves. My ex-husband, Roy, will break the law, or hire others to do it for him. Yours will do exactly the same. Have you thought about that?" she said, all though the idea was much to her liking, but not the consequences if all went pear shaped.

Lisa rising knelt beside Rena, looking down at the now unsmiling face.

"We make sure they don't find out who's behind it all. Send everything addressed to them personally. Just enclosing our evidence and cryptic typed note saying things like: 'Have you told your wife?' or 'I wonder what the press would make of it?' 'Does the board know?' we sign nothing, we ask for nothing. Use the same method with all four. Imagine, Rena. Your ex-husband opening an envelope one morning and photo's of him naked, licking my pussy, or me with his dick in my mouth, or him fucking me in the ass. Falling out of the envelope on to his desk. A short note suggesting his adulterous affair was going to be exposed to his wife. He'd have a fit, I know David will. The beauty of it's they will have no idea whatsoever where it came from, or who sent it. Use the same approach quietly, over a period of time. Just think of the pleasure's we'd have if by some strange coincidence, Rena, we all got to fuck both their wives. Picture having you, Shona, and Chet and your ex-husband's wife naked and the three of you fucking her together, and me with my ex-husband's. I mean, Rena, they may not be willing, but it won't stop us all screwing them. We'll get Chet to force them into doing it. If you know what mean." The perception of making love to a woman against her will gave Lisa a feeling of odd sexual desire, it made her vagina moist and she kissed Rena roughly.

"Oh what the hell, nothing ventured, nothing gained. Let's

get the son-of-bitch's. Win or lose, Lisa, the satisfaction of trying to fuck with their lives, will be a pleasure in itself," she animatedly gushed, filled with exuberance at the thought, her worried doubts evaporating at envisaged sexual perversion to come, and the memories of past pleasures enjoyed, always materialised when living dangerously.

"That's settled then, Rena. We go for it We apply stealth and patience. And carry on living our normal lives, change nothing, continuing to seek sexual pleasure, as if nothing has changed," hesitating for a few seconds. If hurting David meant less sex, fewer young men, less Cock! She'd forget the whole damned idea.

"Don't worry about it, Lisa," Rena said, shaking her head extravagantly grinning. "Get the bastards we will." Then leaned her head to one side, smoothed Lisa breasts slowly and smiled into her eyes knowingly. "You and I, Lisa, will nevertheless still enjoy all the pleasure's of wild sexual orgy's, and delight's of the flesh while we do it. No way is getting even ever going to interfere with that," she said in firm reassuring voice.

"Rena, you and I are on the same wavelength." Lisa whispered thankfully, curling her fingers in the red pubic hair, brushing the bush gently.

"Shona will take to scheming, like a duck to water, the little minx. Chet will be a great help. He's a very clever cunning swine. He spent five years in the marines, most of it as a master sergeant with special operations, whatever that is. He'll organise the plan better than we ever will, Lisa," she disclosed softly, reaching a hand down, slowly sliding it underneath Lisa's parted thighs, her finger tips tingling at they touched the wet slippery swollen flesh of the warm sex-lips. "Next Wednesday is Shona's free day. Why don't you come to my house for lunch? Then the four of us can work out a strategy, map out a method of approach."

Lisa, nodded agreement, the finger's caressing her pussy's entrance doorway distracting her thoughts.

"Once it's done, we'll celebrate. Chet can invite a few old marine buddies, at my suggestion obviously. Then, Lisa, you can enjoy the pleasures of multiple sex, with male and female for the first time. What do you think, Lisa, heavenly, I hope," she crooned in a soft alluring voice, slipping two fingers inside the wet trembling pussy lips.

"Heavenly, indeed, Rena," she panted quietly, her desire swelling. "But I don't think I can wait that long, Rena."

"Don't fret, Lisa. I told you, phone me if the need for a man gets real bad. No reason to suffer for flesh. Not any more. I'll give you my number before I leave," she murmured, sensing only to well her finger's effect on Lisa, skilfully introducing two more into the gentle pulsing channel.

Lisa shivered with sexual indulgence, let her gaze creep slowly down over the Rena's powerful strong well defined body lying below her. The big solid breasts and large nipples, the flat stomach, the glorious red bush of hair that disappeared between her heavy thighs. She closed her eyes, a small groan escaping from deep in her throat as she push all her fingers in a single thrust deep inside the waiting vulva.

Rena gasped, thighs bucking into the stiff driven fingers. "Oh God, Lisa, kiss me, kiss my pussy. *Please!* she croaked, begging in a hoarse wild voice. .

Lisa's sexual arousal matched Rena's. She heard herself omitting bizarre mewling noises as she swooped down, mouth open wide, tongue extended to it's limit she drove to it's maximum into the shiny wet red-lipped fissure between Rena's spread-eagled loins.

Rena felt the convulsions rippling through her vagina, the rampant tongue ripping tiny trembles from her inner flesh. Groaning with ecstatic pleasure she gripped the soft hips above her, lifting the body. For a brief instant, affection for Lisa touched her mind. She'd understood instinctively her desires. Unaided Lisa, straddled her face, thighs parted, placing her twitching pussy over her waiting open mouth, stayed kneeling for a second, showing her totally exposed vagina and rectum, the pink soft shiny wet flesh appearing to quiver before her hot eyes, before it descended over her open lips.

The bright sun lit room became filled the wailing moaning reverberation sounds of unbridled animal like lust. The two writhing sweating bodies mouths attacked each other's flesh with the ferocity of crazed beast's.

"Lisa, lie with *Me!*" Rena gasped in an agonised cry.

Lisa was afire, mentally, bodily, and sexually as never before, orgasm building, she obeyed slavishly, turning, laying her burning flesh on top of Rena's. She felt Rena strong powerful arms dive around her back, hard fingers dug into her buttocks, forcing her throbbing vagina in to Rena's, she cried out as her clitoris rammed against Rena's swollen clitoris, her sex-lips married Rena's, she jerked continuously, hardened nipples bruising hardened nipples.

"Rena, *I'm coming*!" she screamed irrevocable.

"*Together*! Lisa, we are coming *Together*!" came a high pitched screeching retort.

They crumpled into a heaving tangle of sweating flesh, intoxicated with sexual gratification, drained of all energy, except for the fluttering throes within their flesh only experienced after completely and utterly surrendering their entire beings to gratuitous voracious sexual pleasure.

Lisa sat at the kitchen table, a cup of coffee in one hand, her second cigarette burning slowly in the other. Rena had left ten minutes ago, looking very happy but dishevelled wearing one of Lisa's tops, in place of the Amini she'd trashed in the lounge. Smiled, noticing the time. Rena had kissed her warmly on the lips, brushing her hands sexily over all her body, smiled at her displaying honest heart felt affection, apologising, regretfully for having to dash off in such a hurry. She didn't want to be too late picking up Shona.

Waved goodbye rather sweetly before climbing in to rear seat of the Rolls as Chet shut the door. Lisa smiled to herself, remembering Chet, his gesture in shutting the door. He turned, smiled, saluted her, two fingers touching the peak of his cap, called out in a warm suggestive voice. "Next time we meet, Mrs Knott, I sincerely hope the circumstances, and the result is as enjoyable for both of us as it was this time, only more prolonged."

Next time I'll make damn sure it will be, she promised herself chuckling gleefully, watching the big gleaming black car disappearing down the drive.

So Lisa, my girl, one hell of a day, she reminded herself happily of the somewhat tangled loving making she had the delicious pleasure of sharing.

Two more new avenues of sexual delight to explore, and enjoy. Lesbianism and Voyeurism, she'd loved *it*. How many is their left, she mused, drawing heavily on the cigarette. Not many, she concluded. I've sampled giving and receiving oral satisfaction, loved… *It*. Been Sodomised, loved *It*. Tasted a little Multiply sex, loved. *It*. Been fucked by two young men, half my age at least, loved… *It*.

A sudden dark thought appeared in her personal assessment. Sadism and Masochism, one you inflict on another, the other is inflicted upon you. Which was which, she honestly didn't know. Well if it happens, while I'm naked with man, or taking part in some wild orgy, recalling Rena's vivid descriptions of such goings on, added, with a small laugh, *three or four* if a whip or something like that lashes my flesh. If they keep making me come while it's being done. Aw, so What! she concluded, firmly asserting herself with strong conviction. If it induces me into orgasms by new and differently exciting methods, I will fall in love in with *It*. Besides, bolstering her conviction and decision with the thought. Every time she'd experienced a new sexual practice she loved *It*. So why the hell should physical pain, and inflicted cruelty, providing it leads me into sexual pleasure, and agonising orgasm's of course, be any different to all the others.

Lisa understood herself, her growing needs and ever expanding desires, her deep rooted love for erect… *cock*… Realised her growing need for sexual gratification. Understood her new pleasure for Lesbianism.

The clock on the wall, showed seven o'clock, she suddenly felt tired, a calm sense of well being filled her mind and body. I'll have an early night, a long slow soak in a nice warm bath first, then a nice fresh pot of coffee to take to bed, a few cigarettes. A goodnight's sleep. And tomorrow I'll phone Rena, and ask her to send me a couple of big strong well-endowed young men to fuck me, she decided happily, heading for the bathroom.

The envisaged early night she'd planned dissolved. After re-making the tangled bed, complaining to herself continuously about the number of times she had remade the bed with clean sheets in the last ten days, griping more strongly when remembering how long and how often she spent time washing dirty semen stained bed clothes. Made mental note to buy new one's, a lot of new ones. Telling herself, to have them laundered in future.

After soaking in warm bubble filled bath, smoking a number of cigarettes in the process. Drying her wet warm flesh, a hand full of soft towel smoothly rubbing her pubic hair, she remembered the tiny flimsy panties, and bikini, and she needed to shave off most of the hair in her hand before she could wear them.

It took nearly two hours of slow deliberate concentrated effort, standing in front of the mirrored bathroom. Applying a thick lather of soap, using a pair of sharp scissors, followed by a slow methodical use of a lady shaver, a finally some generous applications of hair remover, hoping, as she rubbed it into her skin it won't cause any sore irritation to her pussy.

Eventually studying her handy work in the mirrors, she shivered at the sight of her virtually bald mound. The now bare skin, starkly white surround by the deep brown sun tanned skin of the rest her stomach together with the tiny vee of black hair, so small, it made her pinky clitoris protruded visible. She considered if she'd done right in shaving the vee of hair so short, it was that closely shaven to her skin, she'd cropped it so short, in the mirror it look no more than stubble.

She turned one way then another, observing the dramatically altered area of her body from every angle. Shivered again, this time her reaction contained a sexual feeling. Smiling at her new redesign pussy covering, chuckling wickedly, tickled, when realising, what she could see, could never be described as a covering. Lisa like the new, the strange yet stark picture in the mirror. To her eyes and mind it gave the impression, and looked oddly perverse, giving it an aura of bizarre sexual attraction. She grinned at her reflection, glanced at the shaven pubis. Nodded, winking at her image, saying out loud. 'I love It'."

A fresh pot of coffee brewing. Shrugging her shoulders, unconcerned the kitchen clock how displayed past nine thirty.

Relishing the freedom of parading around her home naked, a pleasurable feeling of enjoyment in her mind.

Next time, definitely, she decided, laying a cup and a jug of cream on the table. When Jay or Nathan visits next time, she'd greet them naked.

Why not, corners of her lips lifting into a tiny grin. It's what they're calling for.

Lisa turned, going to the white note board on the wall beside the phone, lifting the marker for it's clip, stood, the end of marker in the corner of her mouth, arms crossed over her breast's. Considering thoughtfully for a minute or so. Time to become much more thoughtful and careful from now on, she meditated earnestly. Taking revenge on ex-husbands, specially the likes of David, and Rena's Roy was a dangerous game to play, very dangerous indeed.

She also realised, the wild sexual orgies, promised by Rena, had a risk factor which shouldn't be overlooked. Planning was everything, caution a must.

No time like the present to start being decisive, if you aren't you're going to fail. Squaring her shoulders, agreeing with her own advice, took marker in her hand began writing. Paused. Working out what day of the week it was, surprised when she realised that six days past since Nathan called.

Saturday. Phone Macy's, order ten pairs sheets, matching pillowcases. Satin. Underlining, Satin. Every time I get fucked on my bed, from today, Satin sheets, she decided, chuckling.

Vodka, Southern Comfort, Coke, Soda, Dozen packs cigarette's. Bud. Lambrusco white wine. Lawn's. The name Leroy Matts flitted through mind as she scribbled.

Phone Rena, two young big strong well endowed men to call in the evening. Grinned adding. Two *at least!*

Rena, information. Dildo, motorised, *big*, **Very Big!**

Sunday chill-out and sunbathe.

Monday. Seduce the delivery driver, if I like him.

Tuesday. Seduce the man trimming the lawns, if I like him. Jay in my bed if he call's.

Wednesday. Rena's. Check bank account. Phone accountant.

The bubbling coffee pot adjacent to her left hand clicked off as she replaced the marker. Taking it to the table, filling the cup, sitting down, thighs wide splayed, legs stretched each side over the edges of the chair seat, balls of her feet firmly planted on the crossed spars under chair. She began rubbing the hot shaven sex-lips of her pussy delicately on the cold wood surface beneath her loins.

Lisa sipping the hot liquid, rhythmically easing her thighs back and forth, twitching as tremors of pleasure gently irritated her inner flesh, staring intently at the note board.

She had never concerned herself with money. All her life, it had always been available, as a child, teenager, all through the years as a married couple during David's time in college money had never been a problem, their parent's had sufficient wealth to give them allowances far in excess of their needs. David's charm and undeniable abilities as a lawyer, plus his background as a son of banker had let to constant and ever increasing higher salary. He had been made a vice-president of the bank within five years with salary, plus share bonus, of half a million per annum. As president, it doubled.

She had never paid any household bills. Bought a car, rarely bought gas. Paid her credit cards. David paid a generous amount monthly in her account. Which, if my memory serves me right. I rarely spent more than half, she reflected, lighting a cigarette. Everything was paid by David through the bank.

Lisa, blowing smoke rings, stroking her pussy a little faster against the now moist surface, the increased friction gently warming the slack flesh around the cleft of her vagina. *Money* is vital *now,* she impressed into her mind with categorical certainty.

She refilled her cup. Realising she had no idea whatsoever how much wealth she really possessed, ruminating while adding a little cream, putting in order when and how she'd amassed the money she believed she could be worth. She'd inherited three hundred thousand dollars from her parents. David invested it in long term, high interest bonds, ten years ago. She'd never touched the investment. Her alimony settlement, two hundred thousand dollar's for the first year, a hundred thousand per annum there after. Four years divorced, equals five hundred thousand dollars, she reckoned, calculating quickly in her head.

"Holy Shit, Jesus H Christ, she yelled loudly in a wild excited outburst of elated delight. "I'm worth over a *Million* dollars. Intoxicated by the realisation, unknowing she was very rich, so animated in the knowledge, hand's shaking so violently the cup in her hand spilt coffee over the table.

Lisa squeezed her hands stiffly around the cup, breathing heavy to bring her frenzied mind under control. The value of house and car was over a hundred and fifty thousand. Interest on her inheritance, at possibly, ten per cent, over ten years would have doubled the original sum invested.

Interest on her alimony interest, plus whatever her bank account contained, even after taxes, most leave more than a million.

She was so overwhelmed, the mouth-watering prospect of what such a large amount of money could provide made her tremble. With shaking hands, setting the cup down, scrabbling wildly at the cigarette packet, grimacing in annoyance finding them soggy wet with the spilt coffee, in blind hasty scattering the white sticks over table until she found a dry one. Lighting it, her lips and hands shaking so badly it took several attempts before she could inhale a loud deep swallow of the calming smoke laden nicotine.

Lisa, the smoke in her lungs reducing the state of her excited mind, felt the warm wet wood caressing her pussy burning her bare flesh. I'll leave it, till tomorrow, she informed herself. Astutely aware she needed time to adjust her mind to the true implications of her now realised new financial position. And the fact, the excitement in her mind, was arousing her sexual desire at the same time. Damn, I wish I had the use of Rena's big Dildo now, surprised by how deep her feeling of disappointment she experienced at the thought. Equally surprised, to think. That after having spent so long fucking with Chet and Rena, her desire for an orgasm had returned so quickly.

Surprised I might me, resist it, *never* dispelling money from her mind, sliding a hand under her loins, rubbing the moist flesh of her pussy luxuriously before easing two fingers into her vagina. Moving the fingers in wriggling motion against the slippery smooth walls of her vulva. Lisa surveyed her kitchen, the wet mess on the table, the dark brown coffee soaking in to scattered cigarettes. The pleasurably lust filled desires rising in her flesh and mind, dismissing the mess, smiling broadly she climbed off the chair, looking thoughtfully at the icebox, paused, the smile on her face widening dramatically. *'Oh... Yeah...'* she breathed, under her breath, stepping forward, opening the door. Gazed at contents, stroked herself between the legs, bent forward, reached inside, shivered, slowly extracting a long thin cucumber. 'Oh...yes!' she whispered in low husky accent. 'You'll do nicely', shutting door, placing the cold green vegetable in her mouth. It's cold skin, the tiny ridges and lumps, the minute pimples in the skin gently scratching the soft flesh of her tongue.

Lisa absorbing the curious sensations in her mouth, speculatively imagined the effect the same sensations would have inside her. Her anticipation exploded. Slamming the door shut, spun round and headed to the bedroom at a run.

She needed to orgasm, had to, her passion drove her body, panting, partly because of her headlong dash to the bedroom, but mainly from desire. Lying on her back, loins spread to the limit, knee's bent, feet planted firmly into mattress, moaning softly she inserted the cold crown of the cucumber into her pussy, rocking her thighs while pushing it deeper and deeper. Come on, baby, she crooned happily, aloud... Fill my. Stopped, she had intended to say pussy. The unusual electrifying thrills within her flesh caused by the abnormal intruder, made the word pussy obsolete, to soft, to insufficient, to match her dark desire's it was igniting within **Cunt!** Fill my *Cunt!* she whimpered, the expletive more in keeping with her festering need.

She manipulated the cold shaft faster, arching her buttocks high off the surface of the bed, thrusting the cold shaft savagely into her vagina. Holding it deep, flexing her bowed thighs in short sharp rhythmic strokes, propelling her vagina along the column, impaling herself on it unceasingly until twisting her bridged body from side to side, moaning with sexual pleasure while coming deliciously.

Lisa, subside gently into repose, the climax, the artificial makeshift cock retain within her flesh, warm now, slippery smooth. Reclining contentedly, marvelling at the ability of her body to extract and enjoy the beauty of orgasming so often, shivering with bliss in the knowledge that whatever method, whatever implement, immaterial of size, her body accepted, the pleasure's and sensation's in her flesh they always remained constant and progressively broadening.

Sitting up, placing all the pillows behind her back, bum cheeks solid on the bed, looking down her body, half the green rod protruding from her loins. Placing both hands over the rounded end, holding her breath, watching, eased the remainder of the object inside her vulva. Holding it imprisoned, flexing her inner vagina muscles harshly she gripped it tightly within her body. Wriggled a couple of times, shook her head, pushed two fingers inside her pussy, found the rounded end, closing her eyes drove the shaft upward, stopping only when it stabbed painfully into the core of her love canal.

Lisa, delighted now, cupped her pussy hard in her palm, lifted her buttocks slightly, slid a finger tip just inside her rectum. Felt a little disappointed in feeling the finger was to short to infiltrate beyond the first joint, to compensate for the loss of her pleasure, manipulating her wrist, after a little difficulty, secured her thumb firmly against the swollen nub of the swelling clitoris. Drawing short huffs of breath, carefully she closed her legs, trapping fingers, hand, and the deep seated artifice securely between her thighs.

She trembled, gasped, the caressing thumb rubbing her clitoris hard, the finger in her rear hooked, scratching the inner flesh, the two fingers in her vagina plying the rod inside strongly, the rough skin of the cucumber constant sharp chafing of the wet inner wall's, aggravated the soft flesh beautifully, yet painful.

Lisa, moaned softly, using her free hand to smooth the warm soft flesh her stomach in circular movements, she whispered lovingly. "Now my beast. You be nice to Lisa. Let me enjoy my pleasure. *Very Slowly*. Then

Lisa, will be nice to you and introduce to you a new gratification." Persuading the imagined mythical creature as if it was a child. Which, to her... *It was.* She had given birth to the beast, in her sexual desires and lust's, her pleasures in body for flesh and orgasm had spawned it in her mind.

No rush, she entreated to herself, be slow, make the enjoyment last, prolong the pleasure, make it special... *Exceptional... Bizarre...* and shamelessly **...Perverse!**

Lisa, shivering with a dark lustful yearning to exploit her own sexual thought's, shoved her fingers hard against the object inside her vulva, writhed as it rammed unbending into her inner flesh, grasped the underside of a breast, digging her nails into the soft plaint flesh pushed it hard upward. Held it, with neck stiff, head bent forward, mouth wide, swallowed the orb of flesh as deep as the mouth could accommodate it, sinking her teeth in flesh, holding tight, paused, laid the nail on her thumb on the pulsing clitoris. Now Lisa, find out if Pain *given Pain received* is to your *Liking.* In unison, she sank her teeth viciously into the breast, and drove the hard sharp thumb nail savagely into the tender flesh of the clitoris.

She could not believe the ferocity or the enormity of the blinding excruciating consequences of her behaviour. Agonising excruciating pain, of a level and intensity she ever thought possible, ripped and torn through her mind and flesh in maelstrom pain, so powerful and destructive her body bucked and contorted with uncontrolled convulsions.

Lisa, her desire to scream, blocked by the flesh in her mouth, heard strange inhuman guttural sounds spewing from her wide flared nostrils.

The violent charge's of pain ripping through every sinew and nerve in her body afflicted her reason. She wanted it to stop, but her flesh was ridged, her mind fragmented by pain. The terror within her abused senses prevented her resisting, fearing that moving would heighten the agony.

The rippling waves of torment twisted and convulsed her body in wild frenzied contortions. The thumb in her rectum, attacked the flesh. Her writhing body had welded the two fingers and imitation cock to it's extreme into her vulva. She was worrying the breast in her mouth like mad dog, shaking her head wildly. The gripping teeth drawing blood. Her free hand now, finger's embedded in the nipple of the other breast stretching the teat unmercifully.

She couldn't take any more pain. Then, inexplicably, the

spasms of electrifying suffering within changed, not in its intensity. It's shape altered, convoluting, from many arrows of destructive agony, into a burning heat within her flesh, she felt her body quivering, hundreds of little tiny fingers of shimmering warmth began slithering through every nerve in her flesh, she felt a pins and needles type tinkling in her bones.

Slowly at first, then with a sudden surge. The pain, the agony, the burning sensation, the pins and needles, the hurt in her behind, the pain laden pangs in her vagina, the torment in her breast's, began, like small calm meandering streams seemed to rippled through her entire being before joining, one by one, into an ocean of sexual related sensation's within her flesh.

Lisa juddered, relaxed, wallowing in the most glorious magnificent sensations of pleasure in her mind, body, and flesh, she had ever endured or experienced in all her sexual life.

Her mental, physical, and sexual sensibilities, the searing pain, the paralysis of her will and mind, the sexual want in her flesh, merged, intertwining, harmonising. She felt her fleshes sensitivity in its abused state maturing, interweaving every emotion of her mind and body into a breathtaking spectacularly lurid awareness, it's very essence saturated all reality.

Lisa, moaning as she released the sadistically brutalised breast, her mind imbued with a burning craving, a desire to exploit the most lucid sensations her body ever. The uncontrollable twitching attacking of her flesh, the furore within her vagina, pain no long agonising, became an erotic feathery flowing carnal excitement. She opened her eyes, the wetness of her cheeks surprising. Everybody cries when they're in pain, she explained to herself, reassuringly. The observation brought her entity back to reality, from the moment the sharp teeth bit the soft flesh of her breast. Reality had been a limbo of sensations. A plateau for blinding pain. An alien world of unimaginable suffering.

Smiling, stimulated, thrilled, sexual aroused, the excitement within her fermenting, sucking in her stomach shrinking her buttock's, easing her loins off her fingers gently, held the breath, lips stiffened releasing it slowly, returning her wetted thighs into the fingers.

Lisa, laid her head back languidly on the propping soft pillow's, serenely sliding her vulva and rectum back and fore, every feeling within, now one deliciously warm caressing erotically fused gratifying sensation.

Calmly, free hand smoothing the slippery wet flesh of her stomach. Contented, she gazed around the bedroom, studying the decor, the closet, the shades. Not the style of bedroom one would expect to find in the home of a rich woman, she decided, remembering her wealth. Increasing the pace of her self masturbation. It lacked character, it had none. It was a bedroom. A room she slept in. Nothing more.

Lisa shivered with pleasure at leisurely growing desire in her vagina. Nothing more, she mused, chuckling, was the most inappropriate phase she could ever apply, considering the how *much* enjoyment and time she spent *fucking* in the room.

I'll put it on the board in the morning. Bedroom, redecoration, mirrored wall's, four poster bed, with lace. mirrored above. So I watch ***Everything!*** she concluded unhesitating decisive.

Lisa sensed her lusts passion for a more aggressive assault, her orgasm building, opening her tingling thighs, spreading her legs wide, whimpering, withdrawing her fingers and the precious artificial shaft.

She looked down, watching the object slowly lengthening as it slid easily out of her vagina. Gasped softly at the sight of the shiny wet skin, the green now superficially discolour with a whitish substance, the tip displaying tiny red pinky traces of blood. Lisa, to her astonishment, experienced volatile gratification, not repugnance.

She excitedly replaced it in her flesh, agitated when the wet device, so slippery now she could not control it's manipulation to her satisfaction she had to employ both hands. In an attempt to curb her growing hunger for climax, her loins riding the shaft fluently, lifting her legs perpendicular into the air thrusting the implement faster into throbbing vagina.

It didn't overcome the dissatisfaction in her flesh or her fiery lustful need, her two hands preventing her vulva obtaining the total length. With groan of desperation, whining softly rising, kneeling over her hand's, the end of the shaft anchored into the bed, mouth trembling loosely, with deliberate care she slid her pulsing inner flesh down until she'd swallowed the rod entirely.

Lisa, shaking, the swelling orgasm within, lapping like waves gently washing over a sand beach, rippling lucid in her belly, so rhythmically intense, so pure in sensation, tears of sheer bliss running down her sweating face, a flood, a ruptured dam of molten hot semen, a burning flowing river of come rained down her inside's. Head rolling, eye's wide, shaking and quivering, body and mind a burning pyre of animal like sexual sensations. "Here my beautiful beast, *Take It!*" Uttering her husky whispered plead while caressing her sweating stomach with fast yet soft rotating strokes.

She grunted, a vicious hammer like blow seemed to smash her insides in to smithereens. A snarling evil sound invaded her ears, swooning as her insides, somewhere deep in her gut expunged another, more powerful prolong river of hot come gusting into then over the deeply submerged prong in her vagina. The vortex of unbelievable pleasure reached it's apex, the fire of her avid lust exploding she realised the ugly heinous depraved sound's in her ear's, were being composed, of their own volition in her own throat.

Every sexual sensation, every thought, every man's cock that had tasted and enjoyed her flesh, every orgasm, Shona, Rena, now incarnate in her mind and flesh, encapsulated into a single sensation didn't compare with the voracious insatiable lascivious sexual depraved pleasure she was experiencing. It lifted her whole sexual psychic far beyond the realms of normality. A new domain, one which she desired and would take residence in at every given opportunity.

Lisa felt her mind slip in to a strangely odd limbo, a trance like void, a grey soft misty like languid place, conscious, feeling everything, her being a suspended lifeless mass of nothing, except carnal pleasure, and deep sensuous satisfaction.

She felt the pleasure's within fading ever so slowly. Nathan, Jay and Chet, all fucked me senseless. A brief spark of desire touched her flesh, at the recollections. They were superb. Yet, she had no words to describe to her mind or flesh the pleasure's or degenerate corrupt desire's she now had irreversible implanted within her.

Lisa lay for a long time, unmoving, savouring the sensation's declining within her flesh. Two times, without moving a muscle, semen oozed delightfully gentle into her trembling pussy. 'Well you know now, don't you Lisa Knott? she thought happily. Confirming, to herself, That Sadism and Masochism... *was*... much to her... *liking*... I will undoubtedly enjoy it even better, when I get a *couple* of men's hard cocks inside me to supplement the pain.

Eventually, sore, but extremely happy in body and mind, rising, groaning softly when the abuse she inflicted on her body achingly reminded her, she rolled the soggy badly stained duvet with cucumber, rather misshaped and somewhat crumbled inside, walking a little unsteadily, stumbling one or twice she headed for the bathroom.

Throwing the soiled bed cover haphazardly in a corner. She took a quick shower. Dried, naked, in the kitchen, deciding to ignore the mess on the table till the morning, cigarettes in one hand, a large mug of coffee in the other, switching off the light she went to bed.

The effect of tumultuous physical abusive excesses inflicted on both body and mind. Wonderful, and enjoyable, reminded by the sore irritation of savagely bitten breast, she concluded, feeling the tense reaction of her body loosening.

She had a feeling of rebirth, a further mental commit, to herself. As if, the sadistic induced sexual frenzy, had been, and was. A symbolic gesture. A physical destruction of herself, and of her past life.

Her barbaric debasement, by her own hand. The act of her defilement went far beyond the boundaries of the natural human behaviour. Her life had been built, she lived within those boundary since birth. In ripping aside those boundaries of normality, she had also stripped away the veneer of her own truth. In its place, was a deep conviction of herself, of her desires, of the personal pleasure's so long denied. The very act in her mind. Had been the complete and utter destruction every belief, every thought of what had been normal, no longer existed.

She had saluted her new sexually liberated mind and body.

Lisa felt reborn, no bondage of mind or conscience to inhibit her newly unearthed sexual desires or freedom. Her licence to; for the rest of her life, to fuck, to be fucked by man or woman, to give and take every diverse, perverted act of sexual pleasure she desired. Free to let her pursuit of gratification of the flesh flow with out commitment or conscience.

She lit a cigarette, letting the smoke drift aimless out of her lungs. The pleasure of life, the reason's for her very existence, clear, now written in stone, in her heart.

The events, since Dean left, Nathan, Jay, Shona, Gregg and Wayne, Rena, Chet, everything, so many beautiful orgasms, so much man flesh, it had all happened so fast, through it all her avidness for carnal pleasure had remained a constant relentless growing need, inexplicably she understood, shivered sensuously at the thought in her mind. Her first sexual orgy, would surpass every pleasure, every physical sensation she'd experienced.

Lisa stubbed out the cigarette, drank the last remains of the coffee, lay down, wrapped the bedclothes comfortably around her naked body.

She smiled with contentment. Her future now held the most wonderful adventures. Man flesh, *Cock* being *Fucked*, as a problem, irradiated forever. Her proposed retribution on David, a *must*. Her money, the means to protect her new life-style, in years to come, once her body fails to attract men, to use as bait to lured young fuck-boys. Two or three at a time.

Lisa slipped into slumber, imagining the fun and enjoyment to come, with Rena, the pleasures, the sexual satisfaction, her personal delight, and escapades to be experienced in future she surrendered herself happily to sleep.

END OF BOOK 1

Follow Lisa's further
adventures and thrills in

Book 2

'Lisa's and Rena's Retribution'